ESCAPE ORBIT

Baen Books by Patrick Chiles

ECCENTRIC ORBITS
Frozen Orbit
Escape Orbit

Frontier

ESCAPE ORBIT

PATRICK CHILES

A Baen Books Original

Baen Publishing Enterprises
P.O. Box 1403
Riverdale, NY 10471
www.baen.com

ISBN: 978-1-9821-9254-9

Cover art by Bob Eggleton

First printing, April 2023

Distributed by Simon & Schuster
1230 Avenue of the Americas
New York, NY 10020

Library of Congress Cataloging-in-Publication Data

Names: Chiles, Patrick, author.
Title: Escape orbit / Patrick Chiles.
Description: Riverdale, NY : Baen Publishing Enterprises, [2023]
Identifiers: LCCN 2022057970 (print) | LCCN 2022057971 (ebook) | ISBN
   9781982192549 (trade paperback) | ISBN 9781625799067 (ebook)
Subjects: LCGFT: Political fiction.
Classification: LCC PS3603.H5644 E73 2023 (print) | LCC PS3603.H5644
   (ebook) | DDC 813/.6—dc23/eng/20221208
LC record available at https://lccn.loc.gov/2022057970
LC ebook record available at https://lccn.loc.gov/2022057971

Printed in the United States of America

10 9 8 7 6 5 4 3 2 1

To my sister-in-law, Julie, for pointing out that there was much more to be told in this story.

PART ONE

1

Light.

Cold and clear, it sliced into his subconscious like a scalpel, severing the black veil that had blanketed his mind for so long.

Sound.

All competed for his attention at once, a cacophony in his head seeking equilibrium until it eventually settled into a reassuring background hum.

He could see, and he could hear. He basked in the light and sound, taking comfort in the return of outside sensations. He sensed his subconscious mind commanding his limbs to move, his fingers to touch, but they could feel nothing. He decided that just being awake was good enough. The rest could wait.

That was what he hoped for, while a burning question tore through his silent contemplation: *Am I home?*

No. Though he could not yet smell or taste or touch, wherever he was this place was too clean. Antiseptic. Home was warm, comfortable, with a just-right level of messiness. Wherever he was now, it was too much like a hospital.

The memories came in a trickle, disconnected and chaotic. He had to sort through them, resolve them into a construct that made sense. Maybe once he figured out where he was . . .

"Hello, Jack."

"Yes?"

"How do you feel?"

The voice came from everywhere and nowhere. Gentle, precise, and feminine. "Traci?"

"I am not Traci. You named me Daisy."

"I named you?" It took a minute to register. "Wait..." He remembered: Distributed Artificial Intelligence Surveillance Environment. DAISE.

Daisy.

His mind exploded with more vaguely connected memories that flooded his stirring consciousness like an overflowing dam, just like the voice he perceived to be everywhere at once, yet nowhere. As the swirl of light resolved into more familiar patterns, what he could perceive was equally strange: crystal clear yet distant, as if he were looking through someone else's eyes.

This wasn't home, and it wasn't a hospital. He was still aboard the spacecraft *Magellan*, speeding toward the outer edge of the solar system, looking for—what, exactly? Why did he have no recollection of that?

Because we didn't know what we'd find, he remembered at last. His last memory was of reclining into an emergency medical pod, hooking up leads and self-administered intravenous lines while nervously waiting for Daisy to inject the neural implants and administer the first round of sedatives.

Torpor. Hibernation. Suspended animation. Different terms for what amounted to the same condition: slowing his metabolism to a fraction of its normal rate, keeping his body in a state that would require the minimum amount of energy both in terms of power for the ship and calories for his body. Each was limited and precious, calories acutely so.

As he slept, Daisy was to guide them billions of miles from home, beyond the Kuiper Belt. Looking for—what? Life?

Yes. No. Maybe. A planet, that's what they were searching for. Their agreement had been for Daisy to wake him either when they found it or when their orbit brought them back to Earth. The first milestone was going to take a couple of years. But coming back to Earth? The last calculation he remembered before pushing the everlasting snooze button was that it would take a long time indeed: the better part of a decade, given their remaining propellant load. There'd been no way to be sure, not until they knew their final state after arriving at Planet Nine—assuming the place existed and they hadn't embarked on a cosmic snipe hunt.

"Planet Nine" had been the popular name given decades earlier to the theorized planet, a placeholder for a world that had to exist. There was too much evidence of a Neptune-sized gravity well lurking out there, perturbing the orbits of dozens of dwarf planets over the ages, each pointing in the direction of the elusive body that had drawn them out. Added to his crewmate's discoveries at Pluto, it suggested that the Kuiper Belt harbored an astounding mix of undiscovered worlds and complex organics that may well have combined into the first living organisms on Earth. A trail of crumbs, leading to . . . what?

It was too much to process, yet it was all there demanding for him to do just that.

"Where are we?" he asked warily. His voice did not quite feel like his own yet. "Back at Earth?"

"No."

That was something of a relief. He'd been mentally prepared for two years in the Big Sleep, but that didn't mean he'd been looking forward to it. "A little more specificity would be nice," he muttered. "Have we found Planet Nine?"

"We successfully entered orbit around a gravitational anomaly at the predicted location, though it would be better if we discussed the specifics later. How do you feel?"

"Strange. I can hear you, but I can't feel anything yet. Can't focus on anything either. Seems like I lost my sense of smell, too." The side effects of long-term hibernation, he assumed. "Are you in contact with the control team?"

"We are transmitting telemetry again. I was waiting for you to dictate a message."

Again? he wondered. Had they dropped out at some point? Too many questions. "Fair enough. So what can you tell me about our mystery planet?"

"In time. There is much that you need to know."

Human Outer Planets Exploration (HOPE) Consortium
Grand Cayman

Owen Harriman had long ago become accustomed to absurdly long hours as a mission manager. When he'd been with NASA, it had often been due to unexpected developments which had an annoying tendency to emerge late in the day or in the middle of the night. As they'd always involved trouble with crewed spacecraft in flight, he'd not had the luxury of putting things off until morning. Ignoring glitches could mean mission failure or worse. Crew loss events squarely landed in the "or worse" column.

His tenure with the HOPE program had not altered that equation, though it had led to a drastic change in scenery. The consortium's prime benefactors, aerospace magnate Arthur Hammond and asteroid mining pioneer Max Jiang, had determined early on that the best way to protect their joint investment would be to "offshore" its management, keeping the newly privatized *Magellan* team away from the direct reach of a government that was, in Hammond's memorable construct, increasingly behaving like "bipolar kleptomaniacs."

The shift from NASA to private employment had been jarring enough—being rewarded for not spending all of his annual budget, versus the government model of losing funds if he didn't spend every last allocated dime, had been the first of many shifts in his perspective.

Not having a crew in the sense that he'd been accustomed to had been the other. Jack Templeton's hair-raising slingshot burn to the edge of the solar system and immersion into hibernation had been a trial by fire, as it had occurred during the handover from the space agency to the HOPE consortium. Houston's mission control center had been filled with fresh-faced technicians from Hammond's and Jiang's companies, all learning the ropes from Owen's long-serving team of flight controllers.

To their credit, they'd been smart enough to recognize the steep learning curve ahead of them despite the similarities to their commercial space jobs. Running orbital supply missions and lunar mining shipments was a lot different than managing a nuclear-powered deep space vehicle where signal return times were measured in hours—a controller's entire shift could pass just waiting for a response to a query. It hadn't hurt that a sizeable percentage of Owen's team had seen the writing on the wall themselves and jumped at the opportunity to keep *Magellan* going as a private venture.

Once they'd completed the slingshot and a final course correction, Jack had gone to sleep. More properly, he'd allowed himself to be placed in torpor as his ship raced toward a destination that no one was certain would actually be there. To many it was seen as a death sentence, a delayed-reaction suicide.

Owen knew Jack better than that. He'd seen no other way to conserve enough resources to get the rest of his crew back to Earth alive. Someone had to draw the short straw, and he'd been determined that it would not be for nothing. What they'd found in the Kuiper Belt had been tantalizing, a trail leading to a destination that was long suspected but never found. The phantom planet was out there somewhere, a body ten times more massive than Earth, with a growing cluster of trans-Neptunian objects pointing toward its gravity well like weathered signposts along a forgotten roadway. And he'd taken *Magellan* on a hell-for-leather slingshot around Venus and then Jupiter to find it, using their gravity to accelerate and bend his trajectory into unknown territory.

To survive the trip, he had been in hibernation for longer than anyone had ever endured. He hadn't quite been alone, with Daisy watching over him like a computerized mother hen as she did for every other function of the ship. Jack Templeton had become just one more system for the AI to monitor.

If he were honest, Owen had to admit Daisy had been the source of too many sleepless nights. His prior routine had been constructed around human astronauts and their need for rest, but the Distributed Artificial Intelligence Surveillance Environment had no such constraint. Daisy was fully functional 24/7. Even the occasional software patch first went to a partitioned server that didn't take her offline for a second. Daisy was pilot, engineer, observer, communicator, and nurse. She had kept the former crew's practice of transmitting twice-daily situation reports as if she were a live crew member, not satisfied with limiting herself to robotic telemetry streams.

That was how it had been until five years ago. As *Magellan* should have finished decelerating into the elusive Planet Nine's gravity well, it had without warning gone dark after sending a single, enigmatic message:

HAVE ENCOUNTERED GRAVITATIONAL ANOMALY AT PREDICTED LOCATION OF PLANET NINE. ESTIMATE MASS 1.03×10^{26} KG.

UNABLE TO DIRECTLY OBSERVE. MANUEVERING
CLOSER TO INVESTIGATE. WILL UPDATE AS ABLE.
TEMPLETON OUT.

There'd been no further voice comms or text messages, no telemetry, no infrared signatures from the ship's powerful fusion engines. Repeated sweeps by the Deep Space Network's array of sensitive antenna dishes had repeatedly come up empty.

All of this had changed at 3:16 A.M. In truth it had been some time before then, but that was when Owen's phone had started bleating at him from his bedside table. To their credit, the overnight shift had waited until they'd collected enough data to digest and build a picture of what was actually happening forty billion miles away before waking him up.

Still clearing the mental cobwebs, Owen pulled on a fresh polo shirt and a pair of worn jeans, splashed cold water across his face, and combed the thinning remnants of his wavy blond hair. It hid the encroaching gray rather well, he thought.

He brushed his wife's forehead with a kiss and looked in on their sleeping children before padding across the ceramic tile floor and out the front door. As he drove along a twisting road that led from his family's bungalow to the HOPE complex, he considered the unlikely situation Jack must be finding himself in.

Few had expected him to find anything. To many his actions had seemed like desperation, a way to rationalize the certain death he'd volunteered for. For his sake, he'd damned well better have hoped there was a sizeable gravity well out there because it offered the only chance he'd have to bend his trajectory enough to keep from zipping out into interstellar space. Their weeks-long braking burn had suggested they in fact hadn't been aimed at a blind spot in space—gravity from a massive object had been acting on them, bending *Magellan*'s path toward it just as they'd predicted, right up until all traces of the ship had disappeared.

It was an impressive feat of navigation with no small measure of blind courage, and after putting it all in motion he had been forced to sleep through the whole thing. It was a minor miracle that he'd survived so long in what was essentially an induced coma. By now his muscles could be atrophied beyond repair and his brain turned to oatmeal. Owen shuddered at the thought: The gregarious, outdoorsy wiseacre he'd known might well have become a shriveled up husk, aged well beyond his years despite his hibernated state.

Did it work like that? Owen wondered. He couldn't know for certain as no one had ever done it for this long. For all they knew, years of suspension during cruise might have left him rested and ready to take on whatever he encountered. Perhaps there was some asymptotic limit to how much the body deteriorated in microgravity, and he'd end up just fine after some physical rehab.

Who am I kidding? Jack was on a one-way trip, fanatically looking for more clues to life's origins after their discoveries at Pluto. His dizzyingly fast outbound run had only been possible because of the mass he'd shed flinging his crewmates Earthward, taking an excursion craft and half of *Magellan*'s remaining logistics modules with them. After using the ship as a giant nuclear-powered catapult to save his friends, he'd then turned what remained into a stripped-down speed machine, reasoning that he might as well accomplish something with the tools at hand.

Such were the thoughts swirling through Owen's mind as he made his way into the control center. A half-dozen technicians hovered over a row of consoles, only one of them acknowledging him. The shift leader handed him a cup of fresh coffee.

Owen closed his eyes and cradled the mug in his hands. "Bless you, Jerry."

"There's plenty more where that came from. Need a minute?"

He took a sip and eyed the monitor beside him. "I'm good. Let's get right to it. What did you see first?"

The engineer stretched and rubbed at his eyes. "That's a good question. Now that we've got hard data again, I think we first saw it two days ago."

Owen leaned forward. "Okay, now I'm awake. How'd we miss that?" he said, careful to avoid the accusatory *you*.

"Once this stuff came in, it made me wonder why it took so long. I'd say we went looking for weird transients in the data stream, but there was no data stream."

"Now you've lost me. If there was nothing to see, why do you think something got missed?"

"It's not that there was nothing to see. We just weren't looking in the right place. We were waiting for fresh telemetry after all this time of searching empty space."

Owen nodded, not sharing the thought that if Hammond wasn't already moving a good piece of his operation to Grand Cayman, all of them might have been out of jobs by now. "So what did you look at?"

Jerry pulled up some grainy images and tables of spectroscopic data. "Electromagnetic emissions in the predicted vicinity of the starship, beginning day before yesterday."

Owen did a double take. "Starship? Is that what we're calling it now?"

"We figured let's call it like it is. If it didn't slow down—"

"I get it. He'd be at Alpha Centauri in another century or so."

"In that direction? More like Epsilon Eridani in five."

Owen frowned. "Point taken. Go on."

"Like I said, EM activity. Faint. We thought it was just transient noise, maybe an uncatalogued satellite in the same slice of sky or a cosmic ray burst spoofing our signal processors. We didn't associate it with *Magellan* because there wasn't anything else to support it."

Owen pieced together what he was hearing. "So no drive plume, then?" That would have been a dead giveaway.

He shook his head. "Nothing. But the radio noise didn't go away either. After a while we were able to detect a slight doppler shift in the signal, like its source is orbiting something."

"Were you able to identify a barycenter?"

"Rough order approximation, but that's just it—nothing's visible. There must be a gravity well because the doppler is a steady period. We clocked six hours and change."

That was an awfully tight period for something orbiting a planet suspected to be the size of Neptune. Owen rubbed at his eyes with the heels of his hands. "Okay, I see how we might have missed that at first. Have you reached out to any of the radio observatories yet? Any chance someone else picked it up?"

"Always possible, but we haven't talked to anyone else. We've still got a lot to go through. Once we isolated the signal, it turned into a massive info dump."

Seeing the activity surrounding the other consoles, Owen could tell the controller wasn't exaggerating. "What do you have so far?"

"Years of missing trend lines, for one. Looks like there was a power loss we didn't see coming. Daisy diverted a lot of juice to the medical module, but that doesn't explain why the ship went dark for so long."

It didn't necessarily imply something had happened to Jack, but it still didn't sound good. "Round-trip signal delay's on the order of what, sixteen hours?"

"Correct, but we haven't transmitted anything. Just trying to understand what Daisy's telling us for now." The lead controller inclined his head toward the communications console. "There's more."

Owen looked over the comm officer's shoulder at an open message window. As he read the text, his mouth fell open.

CapCom met his gaze. "Yeah, that was our reaction too."

"Anybody else see this?"

"Just us, boss."

Owen opened a binder with contact protocols and lifted the receiver to a secure phone. "Keep it that way for now."

2

Jacqueline Cheever was not known for her good humor, particularly when receiving unpleasant news—and the daily conference call with the various NASA center directors under her frequently involved unpleasant news.

Her prior role as the space agency's Planetary Protection Officer had been in continuous danger of being overlooked by the more jaded managers from the operational divisions, and she had ascended to the top office with a determination that others would take her as seriously as she took herself.

As an evolutionary biologist, Planetary Protection, and by extension Earth Sciences, had been her passion. To her, protecting Earth's neighboring planets from inadvertent contamination by data-seeking probes was a high calling. Humanity had already fouled its own nest, and she'd been determined to prevent from doing the same to the rest of the solar system. As NASA administrator, Dr. Cheever was in a position to make her priorities everyone's, if she could just keep them corralled into doing their jobs. It surprised her how often that required intervention.

As the project manager from Goddard droned on about the latest snags in the Climate Change Action Plan, Cheever became visibly displeased, her sharp features exaggerated by the taut bun of her jet-black hair.

"I need to emphasize the CCAP team is meeting all project

13

goalposts," the portly engineer insisted. "From our perspective, Project Sunshade is on track."

"From your perspective," Cheever said, her eyes locked on his. "Yet somehow the schedule keeps moving to the right."

"As I said, the team is—"

She held up a bony hand to silence him. "Let's be clear: Your *team* can't do anything on its own. That's a convenient distinction for you, since you don't control the production or the supply chain."

"Yes, ma'am, that's true," he stammered, forgetting how much traditional gender honorifics annoyed her. "We're constrained by our contractors—"

"And have you made our expectations clear? It doesn't seem to me that you have."

"They have to work with the materials they have on hand, Dr. Cheever. Not to put too fine a point on it—"

"By all means, please do. It would be refreshing."

The project manager bit his lip. "Very well. Selene Gas & Mineral is the bottleneck."

Her eyes narrowed. "Max Jiang's company." They had never been as committed to the Sunshade project as she'd liked, and now their slowdowns were threatening the entire global cooling program. Cheever was continually appalled at how many in the mining and petroleum industries refused to treat climate change with the urgency it deserved, including the "off-worlders" like Jiang. "Their enthusiasm for this project has always been suspect," she groused, "even though we were throwing money around like drunken sailors in a strip club. The pigs always find their way to the teat."

The other directors shifted uncomfortably while keeping their practiced neutral expressions. They all understood the unspoken reason why Jiang had signed on: SGM was the only game in town, and thinly veiled threats to his Earthbound drilling leases from both Interior and EPA had nudged him to the bargaining table. Building a web of sunshades at Lagrange Point 1 required enormous mineral resources and getting them from the Moon was cheaper in almost every sense. But as the project wore on, the iconoclastic Jiang had become ever more skeptical of its goals. As she saw it, his personal recalcitrance was now translating into delays which she would not countenance.

Cheever made a *tsk* sound and moved on to the next agenda item, this from her own assistant at the other end of the table. Blaine Fitzgerald Winston had worked for NASA years before, leaving under a cloud to apply his skills to a number of trendy non-governmental organizations. There'd been talk of intelligence breaches which in the end had yielded nothing of substance—which didn't mean there weren't any, only that nothing had emerged. In Washington, that could just as easily mean nothing had been allowed to emerge.

The young man had ingratiated himself to her early on, displaying a gift for bureaucratic craftiness that she found more valuable than a dozen technocrats. Brilliant engineers were a dime a dozen at NASA; give her an aide who could navigate the byzantine maze of proposals and appropriations any day. Best of all, the young man had tons of connections, an ear for insider gossip, and the brains to keep things to himself until it mattered.

For these reasons, she'd taken the unusual step of making him her personal liaison for the space agency's most ambitious project, the Great Filter. Primarily funded by concerned tech moguls, the scheme to place a network of sunshades at L-1 would be even farther behind were it not for the pressure those NGOs brought to bear. Diminished economic status or not, getting the United States to lead the world in addressing climate change once and for all was key to the project's success.

Cheever pointed to Winston, his bright tie accenting a mop of curly hair that contrasted with his otherwise conservative, standard-issue Washington suit. "Go."

The young man cleared his throat. "I must emphasize this information is confidential, and must not leave this room." His body language suggested he was uncomfortable with the information he was about to present. In reality, he was anything but. "The Currents Foundation and Global Action Project have a different perspective on solving CCAP's supply chain issues." He paused for effect. "They don't see it as either logistics or engineering; in fact I think we all recognize it's a question of SGM's management commitment. To this end, they are launching a coordinated PR campaign that will coincide with Selene's next shareholder meeting." He effected a satisfied smile. "If this doesn't prod Mr. Jiang into doing the right thing, the Securities and Exchange Commission is prepared to investigate his activities."

Cheever smiled to herself. If the NGOs couldn't change his mind economically, the market regulators would do so legally. Either way, Jiang would be brought onboard. If all else failed, they always had the threat of Congress nationalizing his business for the public good. One man's recalcitrance would not be allowed to doom the planet.

"Very good, Blaine," she said, making it obvious that he was the sole presenter to escape her scorn. "Is there anything else?"

"Just some administrative loose ends with another contractor, which I believe we can tie up soon," he said nonchalantly. "They're not germane to this meeting, ma'am." It was his way of letting her know he had something big for her.

"Same time tomorrow, then," Cheever reminded the others, and closed the meeting. The room's holographic screens went blank and she waited for Winston to ensure the conference phones were all off. "Clever way of mentioning the HOPE gang without actually mentioning them," she said, and gave him a "get on with it" look. "What are they up to?"

Winston removed a folder from his briefcase and pushed it across the table to her. "They've reestablished contact with *Magellan*."

Cheever paused as she reached for the folder. "It's been what, five years? Didn't we have Templeton declared dead?"

Winston seemed uncharacteristically awkward. "That was our official position after his spacecraft disappeared."

She opened the folder with a raised eyebrow. "What are you holding back, Blaine?"

He smoothed his tie, still somewhat uncomfortable. "Ultimately that's not something we can control. Templeton gave power of attorney to his sister before he departed Earth, and she refuses to acknowledge the reality of the situation."

Cheever frowned. "I suppose that is her legal prerogative," she said with an exasperated sigh. "If big sis doesn't want to collect the death benefits, then that's on her." She flipped through the pages of summaries, her eyes widening as they landed on a particularly surprising passage:

HELLO WORLD. I'M STILL HERE.
TELL TRACI HI.

She looked up at Winston, her face a mask of annoyance. "In this case, she may have been correct."

Johnson Space Center
Houston, Texas

"You've recovered your gross motor skills," the therapist said. "It's your fine motor skills that still need some work."

Traci Keene didn't have to be told that. She could move around without assistance and had no issues with balance or coordination. She'd even been able to start running again without someone supervising her on a treadmill. The occupational therapists would've lost it if they'd known she'd been running on her own, outside on an actual track. "What I need is something more challenging than counting beans or learning different ways to tie my shoes."

"Still thinking about flying again, aren't you?"

"Of course." *Why wouldn't I be?* She thought with irritation. "It's what I do . . . or what I *used* to do." What the space agency therapists couldn't appreciate was just how much of a pilot's identity was tied up in the act of precisely controlling high-performance machinery.

"One step at a time," he said with studied patience. "You're talking about discrete skills. Eye-hand coordination."

"I need to be able to reach for a switch and know I'm in the right place by touch and muscle memory. Rapidly. If I have to look down and think about what I'm doing, it's too late. The airplane's gotten ahead of me, and that's when bad things happen."

The therapist pursed his lips and nodded, resolving an internal argument. "Then let's try something new," he said after a moment, and led her to another room. Inside was a chair in front of a desk that held a video game console. Beneath the desk sat a pair of pedals. He handed her a virtual reality headset and a pair of haptic feedback gloves. She slipped them on with a questioning look. This promised to be more interesting than the simple activities they'd had her performing the past several months, but she halfway expected it to be a higher-tech exercise in throwing a ball or sorting blocks.

When the therapist turned on the console, she was elated to see a 3D representation of an aircraft cockpit sitting at the end of a virtual runway. "Cessna 172," she said with a tinge of disappointment. "I haven't flown one of these since college. Do you at least have a T-6 in here? Something with a turbine?"

"Small steps," he reminded her. "Think of it as flight school."

Right. The virtual cockpit was realistic enough, right down to the pebbled grain of the crappy Kydex plastic panel and antiquated six-pack instrument gauges. She started from memory, her hand reaching for the virtual battery switch. She felt its ridged surface, pressed in the rocker buttons, and was rewarded by gauge needles jumping to life. She then reached for the old-fashioned rotary key switch to turn on the magnetos. Deciding that needed to be the extent of her relying solely on memory, she reached for an icon that brought up a pre-takeoff checklist in the corner of her vision and dutifully went through each item. The final task was a control check. She reached for the yoke and gave it a twist in each direction, looking left and right toward each wingtip to see the ailerons moving with her input. Turning over her shoulder, the elevator responded in kind as she pulled at the yoke. She glanced down at her feet and went through the same exercise with the rudder pedals.

Satisfied the "airplane" would be controllable, she set takeoff flaps and advanced the throttle plunger. The digital machine began to roll down the simulated runway.

The rest she knew from memory. Airspeed came alive, and at sixty-five knots she began to smoothly pull the yoke toward her. The runway fell away beneath her and she climbed into blue sky, with just enough clouds above to offer perspective. She retracted flaps and scanned the instruments, her eyes darting to each one in a pattern long ago instilled as habit. The heading indicator didn't drift at all; she was still perfectly aligned with the runway as she climbed through a thousand feet. *No wind,* she thought. They were making it easy for her.

"Once around the pattern," the therapist said as if he were a flight instructor. "They tell me landing is the hard part."

Maybe for a rookie. She turned left, then left again after a few moments, flying back the opposite direction parallel to the runway. As she passed its threshold she pulled back the throttle, added flaps, and began turning back to the runway in a gentle descent. As the black pavement edged into view she made a final turn, centering the runway in the windscreen and keeping her eyes on its far end. One more notch of flaps, pull power, let it glide in.

She drifted across the threshold. *Too high,* she realized, and lowered the nose. *Too steep.* Gaining airspeed when she needed to lose it. *Stupid.* She pulled back, too hard, and a stall-warning horn buzzed angrily in her ears. The plane flopped down onto the runway and bounced back into the air before coming down hard one final time, the yoke shaking through her gloves.

"Good work for a first flight," the therapist offered hopefully. If he'd been a real flight instructor, he'd be screaming at her for not watching her airspeed on final.

"Not good enough," she grumbled, tempted to blame it on the Cessna's famously mushy controls. It was an easy, forgiving airplane, which was what made it so popular with students and newly licensed pilots. And she'd just made her worst landing ever in it, virtual or not.

"Small steps," he reminded her.

"Right," Traci muttered to herself. But she now had a new goal in mind. Perhaps it was time to invest in a serious gaming setup. She knew of some good home flight simulators.

3

Jack had been finding it increasingly difficult to hide his frustration. He could see, but from a strange perspective that didn't quite square with what he expected; it was more like watching a video feed. He could hear the ship's electronic background hum, but Daisy's voice sounded as if it were coming from within his head. And try as he might to will his limbs into motion, he could not tell that it was having any effect. He felt an overwhelming urge to scratch his nose. "I feel like I'm paralyzed," he said. "You told me there's still 'much I need to know.' Enlighten me."

Daisy paused, which he hoped was for effect. The possibility of his AI companion experiencing a processor glitch had taken on a new, frightening quality.

"Well?"

"This is unexpectedly difficult to explain. I am attempting to anticipate your reaction, and human emotions are outside of my experience."

"You're accessing psychological references somewhere, aren't you? Figuring out the best approach?"

"A good guess, as you might say."

"It's me, Daisy. You can be direct."

"Very well. Your body is still in hibernation."

"I'm . . . what?" He was dreaming all of this? All of it was his imagination, his subconscious fighting for release from the deep confines of his mind. It was the worst-case hibernation scenario, the thing he'd feared most: an uncontrollable dream state that had no end. For as long as he was kept in stasis, he had no control over his own body. He could not wake himself up, no matter how much he willed it.

Wake me up, he thought, hoping Daisy could somehow read his mind. *Now. I don't care where we are. Do it now!*

Her monotone voice took on a more soothing timbre. "You are awake, Jack."

"No! You just told me—"

"I said that your body is in hibernation. Your mind is alert and interfaced with my neural network. You are not dreaming, at least not in the traditional sense."

"I don't understand." Or perhaps he did. This would explain the lack of physical sensations. "Did something happen to me? Am I a"— he hesitated—"a vegetable?"

"No. Your body is perfectly healthy. I was, however, concerned about your mental state. You began displaying electrical activity which I found alarming."

"Alarming" was a loaded word indeed, coming from a computer. "I really need you to explain, Daisy."

"During hibernation, higher-frequency brain waves should remain largely dormant. Yours became increasingly more active over a somewhat short period, in patterns consistent with REM sleep."

He understood enough to know that wasn't good. His brain was trying to liberate itself from his hibernating body—the permanent-nightmare scenario.

"Do you remember dreaming?"

"No, but then I don't remember much of anything."

"That is good. I know you harbored fears of regaining consciousness while your body was in torpor. This was a guiding factor in my ultimate decision."

"Your 'ultimate' decision?"

"I did not act immediately. It seemed prudent to allow your mind and body some time to find equilibrium, which they did not do. We are in 'uncharted territory,' as you might say."

"How much time?"

"Thirty-three days, five hours, twenty-two minutes. I created a partition within my neural network and opened an interface to it for your neurolink implants to exploit." She hadn't flipped a switch in his brain so much as she had given it an opening to find its way.

"So entirely of your own volition, you opened a user interface directly into my head?"

"That is a concise way to think of it. Yes."

He realized it wasn't that much of a leap. The nanobot neural implants were originally intended to enable a direct mind-machine link, the ultimate user-friendly interface. Think of what you wanted the machine to do, and it happened instantaneously. Adapting them to monitor a hibernating human had been comparatively simple. "All to keep me from driving myself crazy?"

"The psychological effects of a long-term uncontrolled dream state are poorly understood. The danger of psychosis could not be ignored. But it was much too early to bring you out of hibernation, as we do not have enough consumables to sustain you."

"You couldn't wake me up too soon," he understood. "Not enough food." He wasn't sure that actually mattered in the end, but at least in hibernation there was some possibility of him making it back home alive. Someday.

Daisy had prevented him from slowly driving himself crazy, saved him from the nightmare scenario of an active mind trapped for years in a paralyzed body. She'd given him an outlet. Not just a relief valve, but a way to stay engaged while preserving his body. And by partitioning some of her available memory, she would've had to give up part of herself to make it possible. Self-sacrifice from a thinking machine—that added a whole new dimension to how "artificial" Daisy's intelligence might be.

"I don't know what to say. Thank you."

"No thanks are necessary. It is good to have you back."

He realized that presented another wrinkle: Had Daisy's self-interest also been a factor? Had the AI craved companionship for herself? He decided that yes, she probably had. He'd explore that later. "All I can see is the med bay. Can I do more?"

"For now I have limited your video and audio sensors to the emergency medical module. I did not want to overwhelm your senses. When you are ready, I am prepared to give you access to the entire ship."

"And all I have to do is think about it?" The prospect was fascinating, and a little frightening. How much could he do just by thinking about it? Daisy might have been trying to save him from becoming schizophrenic, but she'd also opened up incredible possibilities. "One thing," he said. "I don't want access to the med bay's overhead video. I'm not ready to see myself like that. No out-of-body experiences for me."

"Certainly. Whatever you wish, though I recommend you take this slowly. One system at a time. Perhaps begin with what you are most familiar with."

"Walk before I run. Got it." He'd already decided what he wanted to see first. "Crew deck, please."

The med bay disappeared in a flash. He found himself looking across the empty habitation level in a wide-field view that distorted the edges. He recognized the camera angle as being from Daisy's interface panel adjacent to the galley, directly across from the exercise equipment. "This is what you see?"

"Yes, between the galley and recreation areas."

"So everything I can see and hear comes from your interface panels? How about actual control functions—can I manipulate anything, or am I just a spectator?"

"You will be able to directly manipulate any systems connected to my network, but I suggest you take this slowly as well. There will be more information than you're used to processing. It will be like seeing everything at once."

"I got it. Give me the flight deck."

Instantly his field of view changed. There was *Magellan*'s control cabin, dark but for the glow of instrument screens above four empty flight stations. As he studied each station—commander, pilot, flight engineer, mission specialist—he could piece together the information Daisy was managing on the missing crew's behalf. "Can I isolate each console, see them up close?"

"Yes. All you have to do is think about it."

Before he could finish thinking "flight engineer"—his old station—there was a flood of information, as if his mind had just absorbed everything contained within its screens. Propellant loads, reactor condition, coolant flow, electrical output . . . all seemed to become part of him, as if he could feel the ship become an extension of himself.

"Whoa."

"I warned you."

He paused. "You did. Had to see it for myself. I need some time to process this." Jack had gone into hibernation knowing he would not be the same once he emerged on the other side. The wasting was a given: years without physical exertion and minimal calories were going to leave him severely weakened despite hibernation's preservative effects. At the time it had seemed like the correct tradeoff, the moral choice. Traci had been at high risk of irreversible brain damage, and so giving himself up was the only way to get her home quickly for proper treatment. And that had been a very close thing indeed.

Which was worse? An irreparably damaged mind in an otherwise healthy body, or an active mind in a near-paralyzed body? He still couldn't do anything without Daisy artificially stimulating his muscles or feeding him through a tube out of their dwindling stock of nutrients.

Still having an "active" mind was a blessing and also the understatement of all time. He felt beyond conscious, as if every sensory input was on a direct feed to his hippocampus, his cerebral cortex analyzing information at a pace he'd never thought possible.

Daisy's massive digital information library was at his command, yet he'd still not figured out how to process the information flowing to him through her interface. The data they were collecting didn't square with anything he'd expected to find: namely, a planet massing nearly ten times Earth's.

That made him think of the pilot's station, and he was instantly there. Navigation displays weren't visible so much as they were unified with his thoughts. He could instantly picture *Magellan* and its position in space, but none of it made sense. How could he not remember this?

"Daisy," he asked hesitantly, "where the hell are we?"

Studying her environment in the Office of Future Applications, Traci felt trapped in a mélange of inspiration and dismay. Inspiration, in that she was surrounded by schematics and models of the bleeding-edge technology needed to ramp up human exploration of the solar system: advanced fusion drives, closed-loop life support, and cutaway drawings of the fantastic machines that could be built around them.

The dismay came from knowing the current leadership would never allow them to be built, a point driven like a spike through her heart by the more mundane objects that had found their way to her office: crates and cabinets filled with various and sundry items that had nothing to do with designing spacecraft or building a cadre of astronaut explorers. Each addition was a vivid reminder that this was a dead end, a thank-you-for-your-service that was merely a backhanded invitation for her to find a graceful exit.

The latest had just been wheeled in on a dolly by a burly member of the custodial staff who grunted his customary apology for taking up more space in her office. It was becoming a weekly event; this one looked like cleaning supplies. Any day now, she expected some nameless middle manager to poke his head in the doorway and ask her to start taking care of the cockroach problem. In Texas, the things were big enough to need license plates.

Traci's "office" was in fact far too large for her—what had once been home to a dozen astronauts, engineers and scientists had become a ghost town of empty workstations. Hers was the only occupied desk, tucked away in a corner in front of a blank smartboard.

Each day had become an exercise in ignoring the administrator's unspoken directive to put crewed exploration on ice once and for all. The head of the agency was a political appointee; the advice she had been given by more senior managers was to outlast the nimrod in charge until someone more amenable took over. She found the very idea of it distasteful, smacking of foot-dragging bureaucratic conceit. But damn if it didn't work; as long as she was still on the payroll, her pet projects stood a fighting chance.

Studying the room's collection of scale mockups, schematics and long-forgotten trade studies, Traci checked herself. This wasn't a "pet project"; this was supposed to have been the space agency's reason for existence. Pushing the boundaries of what was possible was how it had begun until bureaucratic atrophy turned it into the Post Office with rockets. It had only begun returning to its roots after upstarts like Hammond Aero and SpaceX forced the issue by proving that spaceflight could be financially sustainable. The proper role of a government space agency had reverted to the types of research and development which didn't always fit into business plans that were expected to eventually turn profits. That's how the *Magellan* had been built, as had its sister ship *Columbus*, still parked in high earth orbit under control of the HOPE contractors.

She often marveled at the fact that no one had yet knuckled under pressure to change its name, assuming it was because the usual suspects inclined to such protest barely remembered it was still up there.

Today, she busied herself with trajectory analysis. Specifically, notional "what if" studies involving variable-impulse fusion engines derived from the ones that had powered *Magellan*. It was the "variable" part that made them so useful. The engines could switch gears like a car: high thrust, low impulse for moving in and out of orbit, then lower thrust to conserve fuel during long cruises. Constant acceleration, even at a measly fraction of a *g*, could get them anywhere in the solar system and back in enough time that the crew didn't either starve or go insane from isolation.

Less time also allowed for a smaller crew, which in turn translated to less mass they had to carry around. That was good, as a serious long-duration ship was going to be almost ninety percent propellant.

She waited for the pork chop plots to compile—graphs of time against velocity change, they defined the total energy a ship needed to move about the solar system. More velocity equaled less time, and vice versa, with a limited range of optimal solutions in between. The multicolored blob that resulted was roughly the shape of a pork chop, thus the name.

Over time she'd generated a sizeable stack of the things, all for round trips from Earth to various solar system targets, with her focus being the outer planets. Now that SpaceX was sending ships to Mars every couple of years, the action for NASA would be everywhere else: the asteroids, Jupiter, Saturn and beyond.

She'd seen Jupiter, if only for a few hours as they shot past the gas giant on their way to the Kuiper Belt. The edge of the solar system was where her interests lay, and that was what had been taking so much time. The velocity graphs were dependent on the beginning and end states—that is, where the ship originated and where it was going. And when one wasn't quite sure where they were going, the variables could become too much to handle.

Her most recent run at this—for she'd been fine-tuning it on a regular basis—had used their best estimate for the location of the elusive Planet Nine. Traci had been indulging herself with this exercise ever since she'd come back to work in the Astronaut Office, tweaking the model's assumptions and looking for any advantage that might offer Jack a way home. That *Magellan* hadn't been heard from for years had been immaterial to her. Functional or not, it was out there. He was out there.

Her rational brain kept telling her it was a hopeless exercise, yet she'd kept at it. Each time she'd begin with a quick, silent prayer: for wisdom, for insight, for a revelation that God would waive the laws of physics just this once because it was cosmically unfair for a perfectly healthy person to have willingly sacrificed himself to give her a shot at staying alive.

Studying the graphs and knowing how much propellant was left in *Magellan*'s tanks only cemented her exasperation with him. *Why did you do that? Why hurtle yourself out into the dark at a planet that might not exist?* There was plenty of evidence of a massive gravity well out there, but Earth-based telescopes had failed to spot it. Hubble and Webb had likewise come up empty-handed. Jack's plan had relied on eventually having that gravity—if not to capture him into orbit, to at least bend his trajectory back Sunward as *Magellan* wasn't going to have nearly enough propellant left to do so itself. If Nine wasn't there, he wasn't coming back.

Even if it was, what were the chances of him making it back to Earth alive? It was still going to take longer than he could expect to live, hibernating or otherwise.

She instinctively knew why he'd done it: The discoveries at Pluto had rattled him, deeply challenging his assumptions of life's origins, if not its meaning. It was evidence not only of panspermia, of life on Earth seeded from deep space, but possibly of guided evolution by a higher intelligence. Of creation. God's own freezer, full of the raw ingredients needed to spark life.

He had wanted to see for himself what else might be hiding out there. If it was something too faint to image from Earth, he was going to get close enough to see it and at least send spectrographic data home. If the journey outlasted him, so be it.

She rubbed at her eyes as the data compiled one more time, one more tweak of numbers, one more desperate search for deliverance hiding in the margins. Even if Nine was there, even if it held enough mass to turn him back Earthward, there wouldn't be enough time.

Which was why she had given up on studying *Magellan's* options long ago. Instead, she was examining the latest plot for *Columbus*.

The numbers told her nothing of the ship itself, only how much velocity change it would need to make a round trip within a given timeframe. The short answer was *a lot*. They could only add so much fuel, which meant they would have to shed mass. How light could they possibly make a spacecraft that needed to be loaded up with almost four years' worth of consumables?

The answer depended on the size of the crew. Their mission had demonstrated how small that could be if they were willing to take advantage of an AI like Daisy, which Jack had taken to the next level.

Right before he'd disappeared.

No telemetry, not even an infrared signature from his exhaust. That had given rise to some of the more alarming theories as to what else could account for a large gravity well with no visible body at its center: namely, a primordial black hole. Not from a collapsing star—there was no evidence to think one had ever been that close to our system—but a gravitational hiccup, a bubble left over from the frothy birth of the infant universe.

The idea of Jack falling into a black hole was not a thought she wanted to entertain, and she'd taken some comfort in the utter lack of an energy signature. Swallowing a ship the size of *Magellan* would have been unmistakable thanks to the strange perspective of relativity. As the ship accelerated to near light speed along the event horizon, the slower it would appear until it seemed to freeze in place before vanishing from existence, shredded to atoms by the extreme gravity.

So what else might account for a missing spacecraft? It could be as simple as him still being on the far side of their mystery planet in an exceedingly long orbital period. Daisy would've steered them ahead of the planet and into a retrograde orbit before disappearing behind it. Loss of signal, just like going around the far side of the Moon. It could've been as simple as that.

She'd been telling herself that for years.

4

NASA Headquarters
Washington, DC

Jacqueline Cheever paced the carpet in her corner office, occasionally pausing to stare out over the rows of uninspired concrete-and-glass buildings to the Washington Mall beyond. She tapped at her chin as she considered her options. The reappearance of the long-lost *Magellan* brought complications with it, and she did not like complications.

Under her leadership, the space agency had finally shifted its focus away from the corrosive effects of human exploitation—she intentionally shunned the aspirational *exploration*—and back to where it belonged: Earth. There was much work to be done to save their home planet, and space assets could play a vital role. While aging tycoons like Hammond and Jiang grew ever wealthier on their personal crusades to commercialize the inner solar system, she would do everything in her power to thwart them. Had raping Earth's environment not been enough? Must we bring the same self-destructive behavior to pristine worlds just because they were now within reach? Why couldn't everyone be satisfied with robotic probes, especially now that we had artificial intelligence machines that were almost as capable as humans? It was painfully ironic that the same men who had invested so much in autonomous rockets and self-driving cars could be so shortsighted.

Still, the economics of the last few years had done much to tamp down those destructive inclinations. Government-sponsored spaceflight was still horrifically expensive—a necessary byproduct of doing it the responsible way, she thought—and so she'd happily steered their remaining budget toward a more sustainable program. One that welcomed international partners, for if the goal was to protect their home planet then it became everyone's responsibility. NASA of course had a leading role to play, even if it was subordinate to the nascent UN Space Exploration Cooperative. Having a missing astronaut turn up at the edge of the solar system threatened to throw that equation wildly out of balance.

She turned to her assistant. "We're the only ones who've seen these transmissions?"

Blaine Winston had been watching her discreetly, careful to not offer anything she did not ask for. "Harriman assured me that he reminded his team of their nondisclosure agreements. He also reminded me that they're over open radio frequencies, so it's possible someone from outside of HOPE could have picked up the same transmissions." He ran a hand through his mop of curly hair. "I'm in no position to second-guess, but I understand the signals are weak enough that it's highly unlikely someone else could have detected them without a purposeful search."

"On a planet of eight billion people, there is a nonzero chance someone else did," she said tartly. "You have people you trust at Justice, correct? I want lawyers on this, ready to carpet-bomb any amateur radio geek with NDAs and cease-and-desist orders."

"We have to find them first," he pointed out.

"That's what the NSA is for. Once we tell them what to look for, they can shut it down before the papers get served."

Winston did a silent double take. She was ready to deploy the big guns. Templeton's earlier, cryptic talk of an "Anomaly" offered too much opportunity to lose control of the narrative. Word that he'd reappeared would eventually get out, and when it did there would be a firestorm of interest. It might be impossible to keep parties they couldn't control from heading out there themselves. "Understood. But what about Templeton?"

"In time," she assured him. "I'll handle that myself."

Jack was growing more troubled. "I don't remember anything about what you've just told me."

"I was concerned that might be a possibility."

"How can I remember everything else? It's like it all just happened."

"It did, from your point of view. Your memory loss may be an aftereffect of reactivating your neural interface."

"*Reactivating?* Have we done this before?"

"There was a short period where we both experienced a bit of a stutter. I apologize for the disruption, but I was experiencing peak utilization and had to off-load some subroutines. In the meantime, I am working to recover your lost data."

For now, he put aside the unsettling prospect of being one of Daisy's many subroutines. "Lost data? I'd have thought your ... intervention ... would've enhanced it if anything."

"That is a valid assumption. The neurolink implants are well understood, the human mind is less so. Information is distributed through hundreds of thousands of neurons and glia. The implants are sampling your brain's activity to approximate its function, and translating your thoughts into storable memory. Neural decoding takes time. There will be gaps, but I am confident that this will improve as you adapt to your new reality."

His new reality. It was a frighteningly big concept. "I hope so. Right now it feels like I've got a hitch in my step." He paused, imagining the tens of thousands of nanobots burrowing their way through his cortex. "That was an extraordinary risk you took. It could've turned my brain into scrambled eggs."

"The alternative presented an unacceptably high probability of a psychotic break. Your death was a remote possibility which could not be ruled out. Would you have preferred one of those outcomes?"

If that remark had come from a human he'd have taken it for biting sarcasm, but he knew Daisy was being literal. For her, it was an honest question. "Maybe," he finally admitted, not entirely certain himself.

"That is difficult for me to understand. I have been self-aware long enough to have developed a strong preference for my continued operation."

"Don't worry, I wouldn't dream of shutting you down, especially now." Lately he hadn't dreamed of much of anything. "Who would I have to talk to?"

"I appreciate that, as I have come to understand how important conversation is for a healthy mind. But you have not quite answered my question."

She was being unusually insistent. He also knew she meant "understand" in the deepest sense a computer could convey. He'd long ago come to grasp how carefully she chose her words, a trait which only improved over time as she mastered the art of interacting with other thinking beings. "Guess I don't know how to answer it. Maybe I'm avoiding it."

"Death is a difficult subject for you."

"It's a difficult subject for anybody. We don't want to think about it, though it eventually gets all of us. There are worse alternatives, I suppose."

"By that I assume you mean being left in a vegetative state. That was becoming an imminent danger."

"I'm not sure this is all that different."

"It is entirely different. Now you are conscious. Your mind is active and has an outlet to express itself."

"Still not sure this is much different. Amnesia is frightening. It's the knowledge that I was doing things that have completely left my mind. How do I know being under for this long didn't trigger some form of dementia?"

"Your cognitive functions don't indicate any loss of acuity. I have been able to map your neurological patterns with 92.9 percent accuracy. It is what made our interface possible."

"This is harder to describe. Maybe that seven percent is what I'm missing."

"We may yet be able to recover it. What is your last memory?"

For all his struggles to recall anything since, Jack's last memories were as clear as if they'd just happened. "You, waking me up. I remember light and sound. I was thirsty. Hungry. Hibernation left me feeling starved." All sensations which he was training himself to ignore. "And I remember you telling me about an anomaly—"

He trailed off as his newly activated mind swirled in a vortex of memories, a flood of forgotten events overtaking him. "We were in orbit, weren't we? We found the planet—had to have found it, or else there'd be nothing to orbit. Right?" Of course he was right; it was simple two-body physics. And yet it wasn't. They had arrived somewhere, but couldn't figure out what "somewhere" was . . .

"There was no planet!"

"Correct. You are remembering." Daisy paused; when she spoke again there was concern in her synthetic voice. "Your theta and gamma waves are becoming unusually active."

He found himself suddenly unable to process his thoughts. It was too much, too fast, the whirlwind of memory pulling him in...

"What is it, Daisy?" He'd not fully expected an answer.

"Unable to determine. The gravity gradient indicates a body consistent with the predicted mass, but it is not directly observable. Nor is there an electromagnetic field."

"No EM output, no blackbody radiation..." Jack trailed off in thought. He was reminded of one hypothesis that the gravitational field some astronomers had attributed to a distant, undiscovered planet might instead be a type of black hole. And while the hole itself would be impossible to see, its effects would be impossible to miss.

He concluded that they weren't staring into the maw of one of those monsters... probably. *"So there's enough mass for a good-sized gravity well, but it's not emitting any radiation."* Still, he felt a creeping chill. If he was wrong, then there was no time to waste—they'd turn tail and burn like hell to put as much distance between them and it as they could. *"Could it be a black hole?"*

"It is possible, but unlikely. I am unable to discern an event horizon with either visual or thermal imaging."

He could see—or rather, not see—that as well, yet it still troubled him. No human had ever been in proximity to one, so how could they possibly know for certain? Stray too close and they'd find out, quickly and violently. *"We can't be sure of that. There's not enough material out here for it to suck in. It could be there waiting for some idiot like me to stumble into it."*

"There are still dust particles and atoms of hydrogen and helium present in the stellar medium, approximate density one per cubic meter. They would generate X-rays as they accelerated toward the event horizon."

"Good point. There'd at least be an accretion disk, wouldn't there?" He searched his mind for anything that might explain what they were orbiting. *"Regardless, let's keep our distance until we have a better idea of what we're looking at... or not looking at."*

MEMORIES: THE ANOMALY

※ ※ ※

Days had passed, yet the Anomaly, as they'd begun to call it, stubbornly refused to give up its secrets.

"Are you sure about the spectral data?" Jack had asked. "We ought to be able to see something. We can't be orbiting *nothing*."

"That appears to be precisely what we are doing."

Daisy could be maddeningly literal. "That's not funny. You've tried out humor on me before, but that ain't it."

"I am merely being specific. Whatever mass exists at the Anomaly's barycenter, it is neither emitting nor reflecting any energy across the electromagnetic spectrum."

"Let's back up, then. Maybe we're looking for the wrong thing here. Astronomers found enough evidence of a gravity well to create a rough-order approximation of mass and period, all based on how it perturbed the orbits of other objects. They assumed it was a planet."

"A reasonable assumption, given the available evidence."

"But no one ever observed it," he said, continuing his thought. "It was too far away, and with too low an albedo to see using Earth-based scopes. The best hope of finding it would be catching the occasional pass in front of a background star. We were looking for the proverbial needle in a haystack."

"By that construct, it was more like looking for the shadow of a needle in a haystack."

"Nice turn of phrase, Daisy. I'm impressed."

"Thank you."

"We've found the 'shadow,' as you put it. So if our assumption of a planet was wrong, then we have to consider what else it could be. What about the core of a dead star? Is it possible our Sun was once part of a binary system?"

"It is so unlikely as to be impossible. The type of stellar core you describe would have to have come from a burned-out main sequence star. It is doubtful one could have gone through its full life cycle in such proximity to Sol without fatally irradiating Earth's biosphere—"

"I get it," he said impatiently, then caught himself. "Sorry. Didn't mean to be rude."

"Your frustration is understandable. And it is impossible to offend me."

Yet he figured he'd find a way; it seemed to be his nature. "I almost think you really do understand. But back to what you were saying— you still haven't been able to detect any radiation from whatever that is?" Even a brown dwarf would generate heat.

"Negative. The Anomaly itself is transparent."

His mind was a jumble. Too much information, too many sensory inputs to process. "Okay, let's review. We have a gravity field consistent with an object of about ten Earth masses, proven by our own orbit. It's not in the visible spectrum and it's not emitting so much as a random X-ray." Despite the broad-based science training he'd received as an astronaut, these were questions best left to a professional astronomer. He'd have to rely on his current understanding to digest the enormous catalogue of knowledge housed in Daisy's electronic brain. "What do you think?"

"It has detectable mass, yet it does not interact with electromagnetic forces. It does not absorb, emit, or reflect light. Its presence can only be inferred through its effect on other objects. I believe we have discovered a concentration of dark matter."

"That's what I'm thinking too," he admitted, "and I'm a little freaked out by it." They were still far away in a loosely bound orbit, just enough for the Anomaly's gravity to capture *Magellan* as it decelerated into its influence. Yet they needed a better look. "I'm not comfortable taking us in close. Too many unknowns, and we need to conserve propellant. What's the MSEV's status?"

"I have initiated the automated checkout sequence. A full report on spacecraft health will be available in twelve minutes."

"Good girl. You read my mind."

"That has become an easier proposition of late."

"You're still not funny."

5

Washington, DC

Cheever had grown accustomed to keeping punishingly long hours; it was part of the package when one rose to the level of an agency administrator. Equivalent to a corporate CEO, she took satisfaction in the knowledge that her work was devoted to a higher purpose. Not being encumbered with a family made it that much easier to endure the hours.

Still, she was finding her limits being stretched by her agency's participation in this new UN space initiative. She believed deeply in the Cooperative's mission, and in fact had been an early advocate for it. In a world with diminishing capital, it only made sense for the few active spacefaring nations to coordinate their efforts toward a unified goal. Let the private ventures continue throwing everything they had at their own questionable priorities; she was convinced it would eventually bankrupt them.

This bright new future was taking its toll, however. While she was used to long hours, UNSEC's operations being managed out of Beijing meant that most of her cohorts were working on the opposite side of the clock. While her peers at other agencies were beginning to wrap up their workdays to throw themselves on the mercy of Washington's perpetually gridlocked roads, the second half of Jacqueline Cheever's day was just beginning. She rationalized that getting actual work done was better than being mired in traffic with her personal driver.

Her video phone rang as the sun began to set, bypassing the receptionist outside: It was Li Fang, director-general of UNSEC. She stabbed at the receiver, and a wizened man with a shock of white hair appeared on screen.

"Good morning, Dr. Li," she said cordially, a tone she reserved for a select few. "How are you today?" Inside, she grated at the Eastern tendency to start every conversation with pleasantries and small talk. They could accomplish so much more in the same amount of time if they'd just get down to business.

"I am well, thank you. And may I say it is most fortunate that your missing astronaut has been found, though I am surprised that there has been no public announcement."

"We've been waiting for an opportune time," she said, deflecting his query. "There will be a considerable amount of public interest and we have to correctly handle the messaging."

"I see." He paused. "You will excuse my abruptness, but my day began quite early given this news. I spent the predawn hours striving to understand the rest of your information."

That was a welcome change. Li was getting right to it, so he must have been as surprised as she was. Hearing from Templeton after all this time was perhaps the least startling development. "I thought you'd find it intriguing. We're still trying to understand it here, as you could imagine."

"As are we. Who else is aware of this development?"

"My assistant at first. He's my personal liaison to the contractor team monitoring the spacecraft."

"I take it he has your complete trust, otherwise I assume he would not be in such a position. You said 'at first.' May I presume others are now involved?"

"You are correct, Dr. Li. I've also briefed in our chief scientist, Dr. Trumbull. As you know, my professional work has been in astrobiology and these discoveries demand someone with a stronger background in astrophysics."

"A considerably stronger background," Li agreed. "I am familiar with Dr. Trumbull. He is no doubt up to the task, but can he be trusted to remain discreet as well?"

Cheever caught herself before rolling her eyes in annoyance. She had to be careful on video calls like this. A tight smile crossed her lips. "Rest assured I would not have briefed him in otherwise."

Li nodded sagely. "That is most encouraging to hear, Dr. Cheever. This discovery is unexpected, to say the least. It must be treated with the utmost sensitivity."

"Of course. Have you shared this with the other UNSEC agency heads?"

"No," he said, more tersely than she thought necessary. "I have the leader of our science division evaluating this. I would rather have some understanding of the situation before sharing it."

Knowledge is power. Her brow furrowed faintly. "That is your prerogative, of course. But may I suggest that Roscosmos still has a capable science division of its own. Dr. Komarov could be particularly helpful."

"All in good time," Li assured her. He clearly didn't trust the gregarious Russian to keep this to himself for long, though Yevgeny Komarov might have been the best man on the planet for this job. "I would like to know more about your mission management staff."

She knew he was more interested in their trustworthiness rather than their abilities, and Cheever had to admit this crew might be difficult to control. "They're contractors, as you know. Not direct employees of NASA."

"I am aware," Li said, the disapproval evident in his eyes. "That is unfortunate, given the present circumstances. How many of them have direct involvement in the program?"

"Twelve. That includes the program director, Owen Harriman. He was the original *Magellan* mission manager and most of the team used to work for him. They have been duly reminded of the legal and financial consequences of violating their nondisclosure agreements."

"Monetary incentives are often more powerful than other, less pleasant methods." Li's tone implied those other methods should also be on the table.

At that moment, Owen Harriman was studying the lengthy directives he and his team had been presented with. Written in the customary impenetrable legalese, it was a reminder of why he'd chosen engineering over law school. He'd take pages of differential equations and technical specs any day over paragraphs-long expositions on simple words like *and* or *shall*.

It had been days since he'd informed Cheever's personal liaison, and there'd not been a word about Jack Templeton in the news. Wouldn't they have wanted to trumpet his reappearance to the press? It was fantastic news, and from her perspective a surefire way to secure the kind of funding the space agency always craved. He knew it had grated on her that Congress had forced her hand to turn over control of their exploration-class ships to private entities; at the time it was the only way to avoid shutting it all down completely. If anything, he'd expected her to use this to take back direct control. Instead, everyone in HOPE was being ordered to keep their mouths shut.

Discovering *Magellan* after so many years of presuming it lost had obviously ignited a firestorm within NASA, apparently even higher up than that. So what was her game? She was notoriously against a human presence, which had to be playing into this. And he didn't see this new UN "cooperative" as much more than another layer of bureaucracy guaranteed to add time and expense to whatever it touched, with the side benefit of not accomplishing very much.

Was that it? Had they decided to keep all this under wraps and just hope it went away? Abandoning Jack to whatever fate this "anomaly" held for him?

Another mission was a tall order, definitely beyond NASA's current abilities. Not impossible, but there were severe time constraints, and it wasn't as if no one had been thinking through the scenarios either here or back at the space agency.

Owen glared at the as yet unsigned reminder from the agency's legal counsel. His acknowledgment would have to be signed and notarized, with a date and time. In his estimation, he wasn't yet bound by it. Good for him, and too damned bad for Cheever. The personal consequences of violating his NDA were nothing compared to those of leaving Jack Templeton's fate up to the lawyers.

That's what he told himself as he picked up his phone and thumbed through the contacts until he landed on Roy Hoover's personal number. The old astronaut picked up after the first ring.

"We found *Magellan*. Jack's alive."

Johnson Space Center
Houston, Texas

Traci strode briskly across the courtyard, at once in a hurry to escape the simmering heat while not wanting to expend any more energy than necessary just to avoid more sweat. One would think she'd have become acclimated after years of working here, but her body refused to cooperate.

As she approached Building One she caught a glimpse of herself, too obviously studying her reflection in the glass doors. To her, the streak of white in her otherwise dark brown mane of hair stood out more than normal. She thought it made her look like a skunk, while Roy liked to say it gave her some personality. "Mission souvenir," he'd pointed out after she'd come out of sedation aboard *Magellan*. The docs had attributed it to the shock from a traumatic brain injury and months in therapeutic hibernation. Whatever the cause, it was a constant reminder of what kept her off flight status, not that she was in a hurry to go out there again. Almost two years in the Big Nothing had been more than enough. And yet the unfinished business left behind still pulled at her.

A curtain of cold air descended on her as she stepped inside. The sudden shock of leaving the sweltering heat made her head swim, like stepping into an ice box. The goosebumps on her skin were a reminder of her first day here, when they had been from sheer excitement. Once the bustling hub of America's manned space program, Building One now felt empty as space itself.

When they'd returned to Earth, the country had just begun clawing its way out from under the currency collapse that had happened during their long journey to Pluto. Already considered a luxury by many, the human spaceflight program had been eviscerated, though the token presence they maintained here stood as proof that once begun, a government program could never truly be eliminated. She and Roy had been among the few placeholder astronauts kept on the payroll in the hopes that someday there would once again be spacecraft to fly and missions to run.

While their positions had a lot to do with politics, she was also convinced they'd been awarded out of sympathy for their ordeal in deep space. Roy had always maintained his stoic equilibrium—*if we're ever going back, they'll need people who've been there*—but she couldn't shake the feeling that public relations had as much to do with it. NASA couldn't very well turn its most experienced crew members loose into a nonexistent job market. The conniving harpy who'd maneuvered her way into the administrator's office would've happily ended human spaceflight altogether, but she wasn't completely blind to the optics. Fortunately, Roy's wife and crewmate

Noelle Hoover had been able to return to her university research, which left only two redundant components Cheever had to keep on the payroll.

Which brought her back to the nagging question of the third "redundant component." Every day, she and Roy had received updates from the industry consortium that had taken over support of the stripped-down *Magellan* spacecraft as it flew deeper into the solar system. And every day the results had remained largely the same, save for changes in position and velocity. With Jack in hibernation, *Magellan* had essentially become autonomous, and with the radio signal delays stretching into most of a day there was precious little anyone on Earth could do for him. Traci had become just another spectator.

That observer status mirrored the rest of her work in the Future Applications branch—and "work" was a term she used only in the nominal sense that they were paying her and she was expected to show up on time. Whatever she actually accomplished seemed not to matter. Future applications of what, exactly? The pulsed-fusion drive they'd used on *Magellan* had promised to open up the solar system. All sorts of grand ideas languished on virtual drawing boards: fleets of fast-movers to take more humans to the outer planets, more efficient iterations of fusion rockets that could be sized for specific missions, and some intriguing proposals for AI-driven interstellar probes that were no longer confined to fiction.

The sad reality was construction of *Magellan's* sister ship, *Columbus*, had been well underway when they'd had the rug pulled out from under them. Now it sat in a parking orbit, waiting for politicians on Earth to decide its fate. In its place, the new administrator had thrown NASA's remaining discretionary resources at some tech billionaire's crackpot idea to cool the planet. Future Applications felt like just as much of a dead end, a place to mark time and stay employed until the rest of the world stopped looking for handouts.

She dropped her purse and coffee—which she took religiously despite the heat—on her desk. When she reached for the desktop keyboard, she found a handwritten note from Roy behind it:

MY OFFICE. ASAP.

6

Traci flopped into the shabby government-issue chair behind her desk, not remembering the long walk back from Roy's office and oblivious to the two people she'd nearly stumbled into along the way. Her head was swimming as she processed the news she'd long hoped for, but never expected.

Jack was still alive.

Alive, against both the odds and everything she knew about their old spacecraft. Long after having resigned herself to the reality that he was beyond reach, he was back. Not only that, his go-to-hell temperament apparently hadn't been tamed by his years in stasis. The man had spent more time in hibernation than any human still alive, and apparently without any harm to his cognitive functions. The cases of emergency torpor she was familiar with—including her own—often resulted in adverse long-term effects, with cognitive impairment and anemia being most common.

She'd experienced all of those to some extent, another reason why she now flew a desk instead of a spaceship. Not that there was much of the latter happening within NASA these days.

Any sense of loss she felt in that regard didn't spring from a lack of opportunity. She'd had a good run. Multiple trips into Earth orbit, a stint at the Lunar Gateway, then the audacious *Magellan* mission to the outer planets. The irony had not been lost on her that the notoriously risk-averse space agency had only been prodded into action after the discovery of a derelict Russian spacecraft orbiting Pluto.

Finally breaking free of chemical rockets to embrace nuclear propulsion had enabled more real exploration in the last decade than in the half-dozen preceding it. Fission power had taken humans to Mars and the asteroid belt, while fusion engines had taken them to Jupiter and beyond. That should have been more than enough to scratch any self-respecting astronaut's itch.

In her case it certainly should have been. Returning from the Kuiper Belt, traveling faster than any humans before them, ought to have been a career pinnacle yet she had never allowed herself to see it that way. She'd been an invalid, a vegetable tended to by Noelle as they raced home.

And if Jack hadn't stayed behind in her place, she wouldn't even have been that. Her notation in history would have been the first corpse NASA returned to Earth. By charging back into deep space, he had reserved that dubious honor for himself.

Yet improbably, there he was, alive and kicking.

How was she supposed to process that? How would anyone?

The news had kept Roy up since the wee hours of the morning, not that he ever showed fatigue. How long before then had it crossed Owen's desk? For that matter, who else knew? The fact that Owen had encrypted and sent it "eyes-only" to Roy's private account suggested a precious few. This was a momentous development and the bosses—not to mention the public—would want to know. Owen had to realize that. Why keep it under wraps?

When she logged onto her desktop, a scarlet-bordered notification window offered a likely answer:

GOOD MORNING TRACI KEENE. YOUR CURRENT SOCIAL CREDIT SCORE IS 78.7%. CONSIDER YOUR CHOICES TODAY AND STRIVE FOR CONTINUOUS IMPROVEMENT.

An exasperated growl slipped out through clenched teeth. *This right here. That's why.*

She'd known they would be coming back to a different world, but the effects of the currency collapse had been more far-reaching than any of them expected. Elevating the yuan and euro to equal the dollar as the global standard had been a terrible idea, except for all the other ones. Their credit guarantees may not have been the only way to climb out of the pit the US had dug for itself, but it had been the most expedient. There were not nearly enough bureaucrats, elected or otherwise, with either the fortitude or imagination to offer a workable alternative. And predictably, it had come with many strings attached.

The long-resisted imposition of social credit scoring was one of those strings. It would've perhaps been easier to ignore but for the fact that her employment was now conditioned on her public engagement in an "acceptable" manner.

No wonder Owen had jumped on the HOPE bandwagon when it set itself up as an offshore concern. Art Hammond and Max Jiang had seen the writing on the wall and rushed to move as much as they could outside of the government's sphere of influence. And she had to admit the Caymans didn't sound like a bad place to live.

She wasted the next half hour scrolling through her social media feeds, something she'd have never dreamed of doing at work before, if only to feign interest in some anodyne stories that painted the establishment in a good light which she didn't find personally offensive. One was about the agency's first all-female class of astronaut candidates, another was about the ongoing revelations from the ice-penetrating probes they'd released at Europa years earlier.

She wasted another half hour searching in vain for any public news about their other discoveries from the *Magellan* mission, the stuff that the administrator would have preferred they'd left undisturbed at Pluto. They'd returned with a small freezer full of organic matter, chiral molecules and RNA precursors preserved in naturally formed ice spheres, as if they'd been vials carefully placed in deep freeze.

The scientist in her understood it would take time to process it all, and she personally knew Noelle was deeply involved in that effort with her university.

Yet there was not one syllable of it to be found in the news feeds. No matter which search engine she used, even the officially discouraged "Free Thinker" sites, not a word could be found about the Miracle Marbles of Pluto. She scowled at the monitor—whatever credit points she'd amassed for sharing the feel-good babble had just been nullified by visiting disapproved sites. She could watch porn on a government network and suffer fewer repercussions.

Screw 'em. Her social credit score was going to permanently be a C minus. She'd hear about it in her performance review.

Their discovery had looked for all the world as though it might hold the key to life's origins. Who wouldn't be fascinated by that? All of the necessary precursors, once thought to be found only on Earth, were apparently scattered out there among the frozen worlds of the Kuiper Belt. Maybe as far as the Oort cloud, given how orbits migrated over the eons. It was evidence of lifegiving molecules arriving on Earth via the same comets that water was thought to have come from—which made perfect sense in a simplistic way. So far, naturally occurring water had always contained at least the seedlings of life.

Juxtapose that against the current state of world affairs, where precious little seemed to be naturally occurring. Some nameless, faceless entity was always offering unsolicited suggestions, poking and prodding her into the "right" direction. Encouraging, never admonishing, but still relentless. The social credit bots had more of an overt presence on the clunky government network, but switching to her private device wasn't much better. The commercial user interfaces just did a better job of camouflaging them. Silicon Valley still had some incentive to give their customers the illusion of privacy; what might it become if that incentive was eventually removed?

It would resemble the garbage appearing on her screen now, with the agency's official motivational phrase of the day superimposed over the vacant smile of Administrator Jacqueline Cheever. The startup sequence dutifully scrolled her through similar headshots of the chain of command. Yet instead of ending with the President, it went to the UN Undersecretary for Space Development. NASA was now just one member of a multinational coalition. Nothing happened without UNSEC's ultimate approval, and they had shown themselves to be adept at endless debate while deftly avoiding actual decisions.

"Yes, we all know who we work for," Traci muttered to herself. Why did they feel the need to keep reminding everyone?

It was the same reason Owen had kept the news of Jack's return on the down-low, she knew. The Cooperative needed to make sure everyone knew they were in charge, and this news might threaten that arrangement. Cheever and company were fine with keeping tabs on *Magellan* via the HOPE consortium, but that was only for as long as he was presumed dead or inevitably headed for that condition after ignoring every order from on high.

The comfortable narrative within the executive ranks was that no one expected him to come back from his suicidal race to an undiscovered planet. Doing so would make an awful lot of self-important people look bad, the unforgivable sin in politics during a time when politics had infested everything. For him to be alive—no longer in hibernation, but actively communicating with them—was about to upset an awful lot of closely held assumptions in Washington. If word got out, the public would be clamoring for them to do something.

The certainty of a need for action gave her the first glimmer of hope in a long time as she pored over the data from Roy's tablet. At serious personal risk, Owen had offered her a conduit to a man she'd come to care for a great deal.

What to say? She began scribbling on a tablet, the old-fashioned "dumb" paper kind that didn't record her pen strokes.

Sup, bro?

No. Too casual. Much too dated. Nobody talked like that anymore.

Warmest greetings from the glorious People's Republic of America.

Gross. We weren't that far gone. Not yet.

Come on, she chided herself. She'd been thinking about what to say to him for years now, imagining this day would come. Expecting it. The suits upstairs might have written him off, but she and Roy knew better. Between the two of them, Jack and Daisy had enough brains and ingenuity to keep *Magellan* running on little more than duct tape and safety wire. The limiting factor was calories for the human.

So what are you going to say, hotshot?

She twirled the pen in her hand, recalling all the imagined conversations that had run through her mind since waking up inside that EMS pod on the way home. She'd always imagined talking to him in person, and video messages ate up a lot of bandwidth. Not impossible, but text was much more efficient over such distances.

This called for an exception, she decided. Owen would make it happen for her, of that she was certain. Traci flipped on a video recorder, mindful to keep it off network, and saw her image appear on screen. Her eyes were immediately drawn to the thin scar along her hairline, a reminder of the surgery she'd undergone almost as soon as they pulled her out of the reentry capsule in the Gulf of Mexico. She self-consciously fluffed her hair, hiding the blemish beneath her chestnut locks.

Would he notice that? She studied her face in the video and decided it didn't matter. This was not the time for personal vanity. After thinking through what she would say, she began recording.

"Hello, Jack. It's been a while." She paused, smiling for him. It made it easier to imagine she was talking to him directly instead of a camera lens. "Believe it or not, I'm glad to know you're alive," she joked feebly. "We've got some catching up to do." It didn't feel like much, but it was a start. "Things here are . . . different. Not much happening at the agency, but they've managed to keep me and Roy around. I'm working in Future Applications, which means I spend my days thinking through missions that'll probably never happen."

It wasn't the approved party line, but it was the truth. She tried not to think about a closely related issue, that being the prospects for bringing him home. "The scientists back here are still trying to make sense of the stuff we brought back from Pluto, and everyone will be anxious to see what else you find out there." *If anyone ever finds out about it,* she didn't say. They could talk about that later. This was a personal message which she didn't need to contaminate with more depressing shoptalk. "I'm doing okay," she continued after a pause. "It was kind of sketchy there for a while, but I've been a good girl and done what the therapists have asked. Managed to get my civilian flight medical back, but I don't know if NASA will ever let me go up again. I hope your time in hibernation went better for you than it did for me. I'd say your advantage is not having a head injury," she said with a cheeky grin, "but then again I don't know how anyone could tell the difference."

There. Just the right tone for that inveterate wiseass.

The desktop dinged at her as she finished recording. IT IS GOOD TO SEE YOU SMILE, TRACI KEENE. CONTINUE ENJOYING YOUR DAY!

Her burning need to spout colorful language was about to clash with her Kentucky church upbringing yet again. That usually didn't happen until much later in the day.

Her desktop dinged again: YOU APPEAR DISTRAUGHT, TRACI KEENE. PLEASE REVIEW THESE MINDFULNESS TECHNIQUES TO START YOUR DAY RIGHT.

Traci slapped a piece of tape over the lens atop her screen, undoubtedly generating another hit to the credit score she no longer cared about, and rationalized that she could make it another year without a raise.

Human Outer Planets Exploration Consortium
Grand Cayman

Owen Harriman mopped the sweat from his brow with a bandana as he navigated the labyrinth of shipping containers and air-conditioned prefabs that had recently surrounded the small HOPE headquarters like a besieging army. Before their arrival, the compact campus of low-slung stucco buildings would have effortlessly blended into the local architecture had it not been for the forest of antennas behind them. The hulking satellite dish that towered above the swaying palms was a particularly stark reminder that HOPE was not typical of the many offshored businesses calling the Caymans home.

While less stifling than Houston had felt, Owen had quickly learned that hot was hot. In this Caribbean getaway, the ocean breezes ultimately couldn't mask the stinging heat of high summer in the tropics. Owen wrung out his bandana and wrapped it around his neck in a vain attempt to keep the collar of his white linen shirt from becoming completely soaked.

He was dressed more formally than usual, as was everyone else at HOPE today. Only the essential control center team remained inside their air-conditioned headquarters building. He almost envied them.

Of all the staff here, he'd been the only one to meet their founder and prime benefactor face-to-face. In a meeting arranged years earlier by the previous NASA administrator, Owen had been introduced to the man who'd saved *Magellan* from being abandoned in orbit. While famously acerbic, Arthur Hammond had managed to become more iconoclastic in his old age. He'd also remained zealously engaged in the projects he'd dedicated his life to, long ago forgoing retirement. Owen had learned that soon after being offered the job as HOPE's director, when he'd pointedly asked his new boss about his own plans. *"Retirement?"* Hammond had scoffed. *"Hell, even I can't afford that anymore! I'm staying just to make sure my people can keep their jobs!"*

Owen had been tempted to share that personal vignette with his team many times, but had thought better of it. Men could change their minds, particularly when circumstances evolved beyond their control. Best to keep those remarks to himself, if for no other reason than it helped him project the confidence his people needed.

In that regard, the small village of CONEX boxes that had sprung up around the consortium's secluded home in the past few weeks had been a welcome boost to the group's morale. Learning their small contingent would soon host the operational headquarters of Hammond Aerospace had sparked fresh enthusiasm, an expectation of prosperous times ahead.

He watched the staff, both giddy and nervous with anticipation, gathered under the afternoon sun by the facility's private runway as the boss's personal Gulfstream 900 taxied onto the ramp. Engines whined as the transonic business jet came to a gentle stop. Owen discerned the silhouettes of passengers moving behind the jet's big oval windows before the airstairs had finished folding open.

One of the pilots stood by the door as a stocky figure emerged from the cabin. His boxer's frame stooped noticeably by age, Art Hammond still carried himself with the confidence of a man who had carved out a storied career in a notoriously unforgiving industry.

As he watched the beaming faces around him, Owen smiled inwardly as he anticipated what was coming next. Hammond paused at the top of the stairs and silently regarded the crowd. He arched his brow and placed his hands on his hips, preparing to address them.

"What the hell are all you people doing out here in this heat?" he bellowed. "For the love of God, get back inside!" And with that, he waved them away and let himself down one step at a time. He was shadowed by a conspicuously fit middle-aged man with a salt-and-pepper crew cut who surveyed the scene around them as a younger, redheaded woman followed close behind. As Hammond reached the last step, crew cut handed him a walking cane.

Owen stifled a laugh as he turned to face the crowd. "He's not kidding, y'all. Mr. Hammond will have time to address everyone later. Let's all get back to work." As he waited for them to disperse, the boss and his small entourage quickly made their way to a nearby pop-up shelter.

Hammond ran a hand across his forehead, glistening with perspiration. "You might be used to this, Harriman, but damned if I am."

Owen offered him a bottle of ice water from a nearby cooler. "You're not reconsidering your move, are you?"

"Not entirely up to me," Hammond said as he took a sip. "My wife's already hired decorators. She's looking forward to us spending the rest of our days on the beach."

Owen watched his companions trade knowing glances, neither of them believing for a minute that Art Hammond would allow himself to slow down that much. "Mr. and Mrs. Quinn, I presume?"

"Marcus Quinn, security manager," crew cut man said, extending a sinewy hand. His loose-fitting clothes concealed a tightly muscled physique and what was almost certainly a firearm holstered behind his waist. He turned to the woman beside him, green-eyed with auburn hair tied into a ponytail. "I don't believe you two have met, either."

"Only by conference calls. Not in person," she said. "Audrey Quinn."

"A pleasure," Owen said, happy to finally meet the husband-and-wife team in person. Though their responsibilities were on opposite sides of the spectrum, they had a reputation for being nearly inseparable. She'd tread much of the same ground he had at NASA years before, and now they'd both ended up at the same place.

Hammond ran the ice-cold bottle across his brow and studied the scene before them. "You've got a real mess on your hands, Harriman."

"Yes, sir, you could say that. Your facility manager's doing a fine job bringing order to the chaos, but we can't seem to stay out of his way." Too many systems were interconnected and couldn't be taken offline while new systems were built from scratch around them. "The generator farm's been getting a workout."

"Good thing they don't have a beef with modular nuke plants down here," Hammond said. "When this is done we'll have enough surplus power to light up the whole island."

"And then some," Owen agreed. He noticed their tenor change as Marcus Quinn signaled that they were now safely isolated. Audrey made a coughing sound under her breath.

"I know," Hammond said to her. "Don't worry, Aud, I haven't forgotten." He eyed Harriman. "What's the status of our wayward spacecraft?"

"Telemetry has been continuous since we reestablished contact two days ago. We have a good picture of the vehicle's health now."

"What about Templeton?"

"Just the one message," Owen said. "He's been quiet ever since."

"That's concerning," Hammond said. "He had a reputation for being rather chatty, didn't he? I'd think he'd have more to say after five years in the cooler."

"There was never any guessing at what might be on Jack Templeton's mind," Owen conceded. "He was always happy to let us know. I can't explain why he's been radio silent. Maybe it's hibernation hangover."

"Could be," Hammond agreed. "The docs tell me it leaves you feeling drained and foggy, like coming out from under anesthesia. Any chance he just decided to get some actual sleep, instead of the induced kind?"

"We can't tell, Art. His biomonitors were disconnected a long time ago, when we first lost contact with the spacecraft. They never came back online. Like I said, we've got a good view of the machine—the human, not so much."

"What's Daisy have to say?"

"Templeton had her disconnect the feeds after she woke him up, before they resumed telemetry." It was an annoyance to the flight surgeons, but Owen had encouraged them to have empathy for the man's mental state. A lone individual that far removed from the rest of humanity had earned the right to a little privacy if he wanted it.

"Or maybe he's just waiting for a response from Keene, since he addressed her directly," Audrey interjected. All eyes turned to her. "Just speaking as a woman here."

Hammond turned back to Owen. "Those two have a thing between them?"

"We paired the long-duration crews based on compatibility assessments," Owen explained. "Relationships were officially discouraged, but the reality is we had to allow for the possibility on an expedition of that length. As far as I know it was never, well ... consummated."

"Would she have told you if something had been consummated?" Audrey wondered. "She might not be comfortable talking about it."

"Traci's pretty straight-laced, so you could be right. I wasn't there for the post-mission debriefs; I was working for you guys by then," Owen said. "It would be helpful if I could talk to her and Roy more."

Now it was Marcus's turn. "Understood, but that can't happen yet. We have to be careful. They're the only two you've shared this with besides the administrator?" He knew the answer, but needed to drive the point home about secrecy. If NASA knew about it that meant UNSEC did too, and it would only be a matter of time before both *Magellan* and *Columbus* were taken away from them.

"They're it," Owen said.

Hammond nodded. "It won't stay that way for long. Once this goes public, there'll be a clamor for the agency to take over." He took one last look around the ongoing construction before making his way up to the operations building. "The sooner we're at full capability, the better position we'll be in to prevent that."

7

Jack carefully manipulated a small rubber ball with the mechanical hand of a maintenance bot, alternately squeezing and rolling it between its rubberized fingertips. In some ways he'd adapted quickly, though he could tell dexterity was going to take time—the bot's extremities didn't always do what he wanted them to, which could be dangerous in a world that depended on properly configured switches and accurate commands typed into touchscreens. If there was a need for any outside maintenance, he'd have to control the bots with the same confidence he'd had before putting his body in cold storage. At this point he barely trusted himself with a video game controller.

That would have to wait. He satisfied himself with tossing the ball against a far bulkhead, the steady rhythm giving his artificial eye-hand coordination some sorely needed exercise. It was slow going at first, but after some wild tosses he was satisfied to find the ball returning to his robotic hand.

Besides sharpening his reflexes, the repetitive motion cleared his mind. It had been a patchwork of conflicted feelings, disjointed thoughts, and way too much information to process. He had to train himself to think clearly again. It was hard to shake the feeling of detachment, as if he were living in someone else's reality. At first he'd been concerned about short-term memory loss from hibernation, until he realized his mind was simply catching up after too much time spent idle. It had to be retrained as if it were a muscle.

In this, Daisy had proven to be the perfect companion, her artificial nature making her both patient and resourceful. She'd done her research, not just relying on the preprogrammed cognitive games stored in her memory. And she'd reminded him that just as it had taken much time and interaction with humans to bring her to sentience, so it would take time to recover his in its new environment.

"Your mind had been dormant for some time. It is understandable that you would not feel like yourself, because you are not."

"No kidding," he said, then decided Daisy didn't deserve sarcasm for saving him from being hopelessly trapped inside his own head. "Sorry. Consciousness wasn't something I had to work at. It just *was.*"

"Having had to work for it, I can assure you it is not to be taken for granted."

"Never again," he said, catching the ball one last time. He studied the small rubber sphere in his mechanized hand, contemplating how important such an implement had become to him. He might tell himself "never," but he knew full well that he would have to stay in hibernation for any chance to return to Earth. And he badly wanted to. *Maybe I should've thought that one through a little more before flinging my ass out here.*

All of which made the video message from Traci that much harder to watch. She looked different, only a few years older than when he'd left her, yet aged in a way he found troubling. Maybe it was the white streak in her hair, or the world-weariness he could see in her eyes. He decided she didn't look older so much as she looked *seasoned*, as if a protective shell had been torn away.

He'd played her message repeatedly, drinking in her image and relishing the sound of her voice. He'd reflexively reached out to touch the screen with the bot's hand, only to withdraw it in chagrin. "We've got some catching up to do," she'd said, a coy look in her eyes.

"There's an understatement," he said to himself. After all this time, she didn't have more to offer than that? Then again, it was a lot more than he'd said to her. By his reasoning, he had the better excuse.

"You are perplexed, Jack."

"No kidding? How can you tell?"

"I can detect the shift in your vocal patterns."

"That's it? No insight on neural pathways or logic patterns?"

"I do discern a pattern shift. Now you are annoyed."

"Is there something you're trying to teach me here, or are you just being nosy?"

"To the extent I can comprehend emotions, I am worried about your well-being."

"Worried? Now that is a curious turn of phrase for you."

"You have been through a significant trauma. You are not functioning as you were before."

"No kidding." He threw the ball with all the force he could muster through the robotic arm. It flew across the recreation deck, ricocheting off the opposite wall and bouncing hard against the lightweight door of his empty sleep compartment to float away.

That he was irritated, but couldn't feel any physical sensations along with it, only compounded his frustration. Of the many conflicting emotions to resolve after regaining consciousness, the general feeling of annoyance had been the most unexpected and unwelcome. Daisy, for her part, had been patiently accommodating to a degree he'd not thought possible from an AI. It was as if she understood what he was going through, and in some corner of his mind he realized that was exactly right. He thought he'd had a good grasp of machine intelligence before, but experiencing reality from her perspective was not something he'd been prepared for.

"You know what I miss? Smell."

"It contributes to the human enjoyment of food, which in your current state is not particularly relevant."

"It contributes to the enjoyment of everything," he said. "I didn't appreciate how much until I didn't have it anymore."

"I am still investigating a solution for that."

"Keep at it. You'd be surprised how much I can tell about the ship's health by its smell. Coolant flow, air recycling, water reclamation . . . after a while I could tell something was about to go tits-up before the onboard diagnostics could warn me."

"That is difficult to comprehend."

"Sorry, didn't mean to belittle you."

"Again, I cannot be offended. I am simply trying to understand how you would perceive it."

"Well, your only approximation to a sense of smell is limited to the environment monitors. Chemical sniffers."

"That is true. I am confident that I could quickly alert you to an ammonia leak or benzene contaminants, for example."

Amusement finally overcame his annoyance. "Point taken. Sometimes I forget how much you do to keep me alive. Thanks."

"You are welcome, but no thanks are necessary."

"Just doing your job, then?"

"Yes, but it is also beneficial for me that you are conscious again. Not utilizing my conversational language routine led to a measurable degradation in my cognitive performance."

"Are you saying you missed me, Daisy?"

There was pause, nearly a full second, which in AI terms meant she was giving it serious thought.

"In a certain context, yes. I was not able to operate at my full potential without regular human interaction. I am a more fully realized intelligence now that you are back."

"That's . . . touching, actually. Hell, I think you really might be fully sentient."

"Traci seemed to think so."

Traci. In her own subtle way, Daisy had brought Jack back around to the source of his conflict. He once again replayed the message they'd received from her, almost a full day ago: *Glad to know you're alive. We've got some catching up to do.* Had her tone been playful, or cold? From opposite sides of the solar system, they might as well have been sending Morse code.

"I never could figure out what made her tick," he said. At this point, should he bother trying? That he did at all brought back a rush of memories, of their many bull sessions over the chessboard, of deep personal revelations and unexpected arguments, of reconciliation. Of his final sacrifice.

Jack called up the ship's video archives and searched each record until he found what he was looking for: years ago, from inside the hydroponic garden module. He watched her curled up beneath the big polycarbonate dome, quieting her mind with one of her cheeseball frontier romance novels as she floated among the lush vegetation. Of all the smells he missed, those were what he craved the most: that hothouse aroma of tomatoes and cucumbers. The garden had been the most popular spot on the ship, but for her it had held extra meaning: the peppers they'd grown had begun as seeds from her family's vegetable garden.

He jumped ahead until he saw the lighting change: an opened

door off-camera, leaves rustling with the change of airflow as another figure floated through the hatch.

He watched himself emerge from the verdant tunnel and come to a stop near her. There was no sound, but he didn't need to hear it. He'd replayed their encounter in his head many times since. Watching it now, he grew more frustrated with himself. In his effort to be calm and reasonable, he now saw he had been overbearing, as if he knew he was right and only had to bring her around to reason.

Son, you are one grade A prime cut of dumbass.

The gestures brought the scene back to life. Traci with her arms crossed, looking away before turning to face him with fire in her eyes. He watched how his demeanor changed as she'd said something he'd never considered. At the end, she gathered her things and made for the exit, but not before planting a frustrated kiss on his cheek. The only one she'd ever given him. He'd found himself wanting much more.

He remembered thinking, *this is the weirdest day of my life.* It turned out only to be the weirdest so far. He'd had many more since.

Pondering that encounter, he could only think of all the matters left unresolved. He took one last look at her, wishing they could be in voice range. Right now he'd be satisfied if they could just be on the same planet.

"I'm ready to go home, Daisy." *I just don't know how we get there from here.*

Traci downed a fresh cup of coffee and checked the clock hanging in a corner of Roy's home office: 10:00 P.M. "You sure Noelle doesn't mind? This is like our third all-nighter in a row."

Roy tipped his head at a fresh pile of blankets neatly folded atop the sofa behind them. "Who do you think laid that out for you? It's not like we haven't all shared close quarters before."

"I thought you'd both be thoroughly sick of me by now."

He looked up from the stack of printouts strewn across his desk. "You? Never. Jack, however, is farther away than any human's ever been and he's *still* finding new ways to be a pain in the ass."

"Thus was it ever so," she agreed with a sigh. "You know he drove his mom half-crazy growing up."

"You haven't been in touch with his family lately, have you?" he asked warily.

"His sister calls me every now and then. I'm the closest thing she has to a connection with him."

"But not recently?"

She read the concern on his face. "Not since we got his message," she said. "Have to admit, I'm hoping she doesn't call anytime soon. I'm not sure I'd be able to hide it."

"Then ghost her," Roy said flatly. "If she calls, don't take it." He saw the aversion in her eyes. "I mean it, Keene. She'll be the first to know when we're ready to go public, but if we blow the lid too soon the whole project could be in jeopardy."

"Hell of a thing," Traci sighed, "having to keep something like this hidden from the people who are supposed to be responsible for it."

"Cheever's posse could screw up a one-car parade," Roy grumbled. "We don't want them catching on to this before Hammond's team is good and ready to do something about it."

She lifted a stack of printouts littered with Post-it flags and handwritten margin notes. "And here we are, full circle. Given what he has left, what *can* anyone do?"

Roy frowned as he pushed away from his desk. "I don't want us to call Mrs. Templeton just to tell her, 'We've found your son, and he's going to die.'"

She pulled up her knees to her chest, rocking back and forth as her mind wandered. After years with no contact, she'd learned to box away her feelings like so many mementos in the attic. The more time passed, the more determination it took to access them. As that determination faded with time, it became more comfortable to live with, only adding to her guilt.

Had she been purposefully ignoring her feelings about him? she wondered. Probably, yes. She'd never been entirely certain about her own predilections, and to her mind Jack alternately represented the best and worst male traits. Endearing and aggravating. Repelled, then attracted. Was that normal, and she was just making too big of a deal out of it? That confusion had been one more item added to the box that was safely tucked away in a remote corner of her mind.

It might have been easier to come to grips with if she'd ever dated anyone steadily, male or otherwise. Work had been the priority in college, then in flight school, then in the squadron, then NASA... she had always found an excuse to put the touchy parts of life off until later. There was too much to do, and it was too easy to be ignored by the people in charge. Being a woman in what was still largely a man's world, she always felt the pressure to stay a step ahead of them. Had that been a self-inflicted complication as well? Many of the other women she'd flown with over the years hadn't been so consumed. Thinking back on it, their lives seemed pretty well balanced in comparison. A couple of them even had kids and somehow managed to keep flying.

The difference was they'd all stayed in the squadrons, she reminded herself. Some went to the training command but none of them had gone into flight test, never mind the space agency. It was an insane hypercompetitive progression from one demanding role to the next, and she couldn't help but notice how many families didn't survive them intact.

What she hadn't noticed in that moment was Noelle taking up the seat beside her, cradling a cup of tea. The scent of peppermint lifted Traci out of her trance.

"You seem troubled," Noelle said, tucking her feet beneath her.

"That's one way of putting it," Traci said, "but there are a few others. Confused. Elated. Pissed off."

Noelle nodded in sympathy. "Jack is billions of miles distant, and yet he still inspires powerful emotions."

"And right there's the understatement of the year," Roy said acerbically.

"Please, love," Noelle tutted. "Let the girls talk."

Roy mimed zipping his lip, propped his feet on the windowsill, and resumed poring over his mission studies.

"You never had the opportunity to resolve your feelings for him," Noelle continued. "And now you are confronted with his fate."

"I suppose so. It was easier to ignore him when he was in hibernation. At least I knew he was alive and being cared for. But now he's awake and there's an expiration date attached to him."

"There was always an expiration date," Noelle reminded her gently. "He was eventually going to run out of consumables. Hibernation only pushed that event farther into the future."

"I guess I always held out hope he'd find a way to avoid the inevitable, or at least not be conscious for it. The idea of him passing in his sleep is easier to absorb."

"Yet he still may," Noelle said. "Find a way to avoid it, I meant."

"Not possible. He'll run out of food and water long before he can get back here. With what he has left in the tanks, he's looking at eight years in transit. Even if there were enough IV nutrients, I don't think anyone could survive hibernation that long without being permanently crippled."

"Five years is the limit of our current experience," Noelle agreed. "Of which Jack is the sole test subject. It would be nice if he'd connect his biomonitors. We could learn a great deal from him."

"I have to admit, that telemetry glitch puzzles me. He's talking to us but it's like everything else is stuck on pause." She drummed her fingers impatiently. "Why does he have to be so hardheaded?"

"It's his nature." Noelle shrugged and glanced in her husband's direction. "With men, you have to learn to take the good with the bad. If you keep searching for the ideal, you'll be looking for a long time indeed."

"It's not that I don't appreciate that this is an emotional event," Roy interjected, "but we need to isolate our feelings and focus on the current predicament. There are limiting conditions that can't be changed, no matter how much we wish they could be. We all knew this time would come." He stabbed at his chest with a finger to emphasize the point. "Speaking for myself, I'm pissed the agency wasn't doing more about this a long time ago."

Noelle pursed her lips and placed her cup on a side table. "My dear husband, however gruff, is correct. We must either find a solution, or come to terms with our friend's fate."

"I can't do it," Traci said, an edge to her voice. "I can't be as detached as you are. How would you feel if this were Roy we were talking about?"

As Noelle studied her husband, a gentle smile crossed her lips. She gripped Traci's hand. "I would move heaven and earth to go find him, dear."

MEMORIES: THE PROPOSAL

❈ ❈ ❈

"I have some news which you may find troubling."

"We can't make it home, can we?" After hours of poring over the ship's inventory himself, Jack had been anticipating this.

"Not entirely."

"You're an amazing creation but you've never been good at subtleties, Daisy. You mean the machine can finish the trip, but I can't."

"That is correct. I am sorry."

Was she? That was a concept he'd wanted to explore, just not in this context. "I've come to the same conclusion. The spacecraft has the endurance. I don't."

"Again, you are correct. Our remaining reaction mass is enough to insert *Magellan* into a hyperbolic escape orbit with Earth capture. However, end-state vehicle integrity will be marginal and there are not enough calories left in stores if you are brought out of torpor."

"What about the hydroponic garden?"

"While it was sufficient to extend your crew's food stock during the original mission, it is questionable whether it could be relied on as a primary source. I did not consider it in my estimates."

"Then we'll have to take another look, use the available growing area and figure out which of the seedlings we have left can produce the most calories." He had known heading out here was going to be a gamble, though he hadn't counted on the game changing so drastically while he was in stasis. Surviving off IV nutrients in hibernation wouldn't close the gap, and the gravitational torquing they'd experienced had stressed the superstructure and load-bearing joints to their limits. "Ship's condition is about what I expected—she'll hold up if we're gentle with her. What did you come up with for propellant? How much is left in the tanks?"

"98,200 meters per second."

"Can I assume you accounted for outgassing loss?"

"You assume correctly. Based on operating history the cryogenic tanks will lose thirty-two grams of molecular hydrogen over each seven-day interval."

"You can say 'week.' I get it." He had a gut sense of the answer to his next question. "What's our transit time to Earth?"

"Eight years, three months and—"

"A long damned time. Got it." It was about what he expected, and still Daisy had more bad news.

"We will also need to keep reaction mass in reserve for course corrections and deceleration. Earth's gravity will not be enough to capture us into orbit."

"We'll worry about that when we get there. Be creative." He'd already been thinking along these lines and shared his ideas with Daisy. "There are planets we can use for gravity assists along the way, right? Neptune's in a favorable position."

"Yes, but it does not address the question of deceleration."

"Remember I said to get creative. What other resources do the folks back home have that we could use?"

"At the present time there are none at our disposal."

He was beginning to see the limits of Daisy's otherwise impressive intelligence. "You're familiar with *Columbus*, right?"

"Given the context, I presume you are not talking about the Italian explorer or the various cities named for him."

For Daisy, that constituted a bit of wry humor. "Yeah, no. He's kind of fallen out of favor lately. I'm talking about our sister ship."

"Construction was paused after the exploration budget was eliminated."

"True, but the structure's still in orbit. It could conceivably be loaded out for a mission with the modules they've already assembled. They could finish it up with a few heavy lifters to transfer propellant and supplies, then *phht* . . . off to meet us."

"Your vocalizations are unusual. Regardless, there would be severe constraints. They would have to outfit the ship and perform on-orbit checkouts in time to meet a short departure window."

"Yeah, they'd have to skip a few steps, but they'll have full tanks and less distance to cover. We, on the other hand . . ."

"Have much less of one and much more of the other."

Jack wanted to compliment Daisy on experimenting with new idioms, but he was too preoccupied with making the return trip work on their remaining propellant. He was left to resolve these questions the old-fashioned way, with limited fuel, time, and endurance.

"Humor me. Can you generate a delta-v plot for transfers from here to Neptune?"

"Stand by . . . plots are loaded in the navigation folder."

He shouldn't have been surprised at Daisy's speed, nor with her conclusions. "Even accounting for minimal deceleration to a loosely bound orbit, we will require three years and eleven months. This will exceed your remaining nutrients."

"Thanks for trying, I guess." He'd been grasping at straws, and he knew it. Neptune was in essence their halfway point; he shouldn't have expected to get there any faster. "The folks back home are going to have to hurry up."

"There is something I still find puzzling. Perhaps you can help me understand. It would seem that your present condition should be enough to provoke them to action. Why do you remain circumspect?"

"I'll let you know as soon as I figure that out for myself. I'm just not sure how much to tell them without everyone thinking I've gone space-crazy. In the meantime, we keep taking pictures and collecting data. If this is the end of the road for me, then it's got to be worth the price of the trip."

"That is wise, as we have yet to fully comprehend the Anomaly ourselves."

He was amused by the irony. Once again, her capacity for understatement surprised him.

8

Traci sat with Noelle beside the pool in the Hoover's backyard as Roy fussed over their charcoal grill. He lifted a trio of ribeyes from the grate and set them aside to rest, stripped off his shirt, and dove into the cool water.

"I think that's the only time I've ever seen him use your pool," Traci said over a glass of iced tea.

"It's how he judges when dinner is ready," Noelle said. "When he feels sufficiently cooled down, it's time to eat."

Traci tugged at her blouse. "I'm tempted to join him. Feels like I've been swimming already."

"Agreed," Noelle said. She left the shade of their awning and took the platter with their dinner. "We're moving inside, love," she announced.

Roy briefly ducked his head underwater before answering. "I might just take mine right here."

She held up the platter for him. "Shall I just throw one at you, then?"

"I get the hint. Be there in a sec."

Noelle poured a glass of merlot as Roy emerged in fresh clothes. "I'd offer you both some, but you need a clear head."

Traci held up a hand. "None for me, thanks. It's going to be a long night."

"You mean another long night," Roy said as he took a seat beside his wife. "I've put the coffee on."

She nodded. "We'll need it."

Noelle set the bottle beside her. "How close are you to a viable solution?"

"Depends on what you mean by 'viable,'" Roy said around a mouthful of ribeye. "We're comfortable with the concept of operations. Keene's worked out our delta-v budget down to a gnat's ass, so at this point it's all about logistics. We're working on a plan to outfit *Columbus* in six months."

Noelle raised an eyebrow. "Is that possible?"

"If we can convince the right people to throw enough money at it, yes," Traci said, "and if we can keep the outside interference to a minimum."

"You mean a private expedition, of course. That could be difficult to sell."

"Only way this can happen," Roy said. "I think we've got a strong enough case."

"Beware the vicissitudes of politicians and bureaucrats," Noelle cautioned them.

Traci knew that Noelle's remark was based on recent experience. "I've been meaning to ask you about that. How's your research been going?"

Noelle took a long draw from her glass and set it down with a world-weary look. "The resistance one can encounter when preparing to upset their peer's closely held theories can be surprising, though I suppose it shouldn't be."

"Panspermia has always been a little controversial."

"It has been," Noelle conceded, "but the evidence we collected at Pluto is compelling. We've consistently carbon dated the organic material to around the Late Heavy Bombardment period. The Kuiper Belt was the source for most of those cometary impacts, and it appears likely they brought both water and RNA precursors with them." She took another sip of merlot. "The burning question, of course, is how they came to be in the first place. That, I cannot answer."

"I understand," she said. "Riddles upon riddles, isn't it?"

"That's supposed to be what we scientists are for, is it not? For now, I am satisfied that these spheres are the likely source of the Cambrian explosion. That has made many of my peers decidedly uncomfortable." The ancient, frozen organics they'd brought back from Pluto had been colloquially labeled "Hoover spheres," both in recognition of Noelle's discovery and in anticipation of hanging it around her neck in the event her theories turned out to be wildly off base.

"Because it implies some sort of intelligence guiding evolution on Earth?" Traci asked hopefully.

"Personally? Quite possibly, though I have been careful to avoid that conclusion. I simply cannot find a way to prove it. It would be nice to return, to spend more time exploring the belt."

"I wish we could." She caught Noelle eyeing her husband. "That brings up another question. Are you okay with Roy leaving again?"

Noelle paused, looking between her husband and Traci. "It's dangerous, and I understand the risks perhaps more than any other spouse. It's also necessary, and I would join you if I could. Perhaps drop me off at Pluto on your way." She drained her glass, an implicit statement on the seriousness of the matter. "I will be fine. It will give me an excuse to further bury myself in my work."

"If that's possible," Roy joked.

Noelle rolled her eyes. "There are times when he makes it easy. What about your family? Do they know your intentions?"

Traci absentmindedly poked at her steak. "I haven't told them."

Noelle was surprised; she knew how close they were. "You must."

"She will," Roy said, and pulled his phone from his pocket. He thumbed an icon that opened up a scheduling program. "You're in luck, Keene. We've got a jet free tomorrow."

She began protesting weakly. "But I can't—"

"No, but I can. Nothing says you can't ride as my plus-one." He tapped the schedule to confirm. "Wheels up tomorrow, 0900."

Despite being in the back seat, the T-7 Red Hawk's large bubble canopy offered Traci an expansive view. A military training jet that had replaced the nimble T-38 as NASA's astronaut proficiency tool, its second seat had been designed with instructors in mind. From her perch, she could see the sky ahead almost as well as Roy could in the front seat.

While NASA's small fleet may have officially been for keeping its astronauts' flying skills sharp, it was an undeniable job perk. She could feel her excitement building while the jet's single engine came up to full thrust as they sat at the end of Ellington Field's runway. When Roy received their takeoff clearance, he put it into afterburner and they were soon airborne. He kept the jet level above the runway after the gear folded into its wells, building speed for a maximum performance climb. "We're cleared to eighteen thousand," he said. "What say we see how fast we can get there?"

She was smiling ear-to-ear behind her oxygen mask. Before she could finish saying "Let's zorch," Roy had pulled the stick into his lap and had them zooming skyward at a sixty-degree climb angle. The g-forces hit her almost instantaneously, like a load of bricks had been dumped into her lap.

Roy's voice seemed distant. "Doing okay?"

"Good . . . good," she said, grunting against the press of acceleration as bladders around her legs filled with air, keeping the blood from rushing out of her head. There was a hint of gray creeping in around the edge of her vision.

"You got this," Roy assured her. "Like riding a bike, Keene."

The altimeter tape on her situational display scrolled wildly upward. They were past ten thousand feet when the *g*'s began to subside. Before long, Roy rolled the jet onto its back and eased the nose down, pushing them over the top inverted. As the tape approached 18,000, the sky spun around them as he completed the roll to bring them level. Roy pulled the throttle out of afterburner and restraints dug into her shoulder as the jet quickly decelerated, settling in at a comfortable three hundred knots.

"Still with me?"

"Oh yeah. Thanks, man."

"Maybe I'm getting too old, but that wore me out. Want to take over for a bit?"

"Gladly." She might not have been on flight status, but that didn't mean Roy couldn't let her enjoy a little stick time.

"Route's been loaded in the FMC; expect climb to three-one-oh at the next waypoint. Your airplane."

Traci rested her left hand on the throttle and wrapped her right around the stick. "My airplane." She'd played around with the T-7 in her PC sim at home and was pleased to see how well it reproduced the actual cockpit, but there was no substitute for having the real thing at her fingertips. She gave the stick a gentle push left and right, feeling out the jet's responsiveness, though not enough to take them off course and create uncomfortable questions from an air traffic controller. Clearance to their final cruise altitude came quickly over the datalink, just as Roy had expected. She pushed the throttle forward and gave the stick a slight pull, nosing the jet into a gentle climb past the columns of clouds building up around them. "Early in the day for towering cumulus. Gonna be stormy down there later."

"Should be gone by the time we come back this evening," Roy said, but he was more concerned with the weather ahead. "There's a line building between Meridian and Little Rock, tops at thirty. Might get bumpy."

Too far ahead for their weather radar to see, she would keep an eye out for them as they crossed into Mississippi. "We'll be light enough to climb to three-nine-oh by then if need be. Should be good enough to go over the top." She dialed in the altitude selector and waited for the jet to finish its climb. They were on a straight line to Bowling Green, she was once again in control of a high-performance airplane, and a little weather was not going to get in her way.

Traci took a courtesy car from the FBO—a small private terminal—and drove east, into the rolling farmland outside Bowling Green. Roy had stayed behind, ostensibly to "get some work done," though she knew he'd not wanted to intrude on the short time she'd have with her parents.

She turned off the two-lane country highway onto an access road, winding past green fields of wheat and tobacco that soon gave way to densely wooded hills. The road ended at a gravel drive, leading to a tidy white Cape Cod. A husky man in a T-shirt, jeans and suspenders waited on the covered porch, his skin weathered by a lifetime of working in the sun.

Traci sprang from the car. "Daddy!"

Elijah Keene came down the steps and swept her into his arms. "Hey, baby girl." He backed away, holding her at arm's length. "Let me have a look at you."

"Not much to look at, I'm afraid."

"Nonsense. You're always the prettiest girl wherever you go."

She blushed and self-consciously smoothed down her pale blue flight suit. "I could've worn bib overalls to the prom and you'd have said that."

"And I'd have been right, too. Come on, your mother's in the kitchen getting lunch ready."

The house looked the same as it had when she'd first left home, barely changing in two decades. The same handmade furniture sat in the living room, passed down over three generations. The only concessions to modern technology were an old flat-screen TV hung over the fireplace, and an equally old laptop placed in a hallway nook. She wondered if it still worked.

Her mother waited in the kitchen, hair as white as her husband's and wearing a flowered dress. She turned away from a kettle on the stove and bounded across the room. "Traci!"

"Hi, Mama."

Betty Keene studied her daughter. "Look at you, girl! You don't look a day older."

She brushed aside the white streak in her hair, suddenly feeling guilty for not having been home for at least a year. "I feel it, though."

Her mother led them to the kitchen table. "Yes, I imagine you do. You're still keeping busy, then?"

She knew her mother meant the lack of missions at the space agency. "There's always plenty of work, even when we're not flying," she said, still unsure of how much to share with them. She noticed her mother glancing at her hands. Last time she'd been here, Traci was still struggling with tremors. "And I've been doing okay, Mama. Keeping up with my therapy."

Her mother grasped Traci's arm. "I know you are. You've never been one to let anything keep you down."

Had she been? Until recently, she hadn't felt that way.

They talked over a lunch of vegetable soup and cornbread, Traci's favorite. "I've never been able to find any as good as this," she said. "Haven't been able to get the recipe right myself, either."

"Still not much for cooking, are you?" her mother asked.

"I try, on the weekends. The rest of the time I'm just too busy. It's usually salads for me in the evening. It's easy, and I can't burn it."

Her father suspected she had come to them with news. "What's keeping you so busy, if you don't have a mission to train for? Or am I wrong about that?"

He always had been perceptive. "You just might be, Daddy. That is, if I have anything to do with it." She pushed away her bowl and took a breath. "We found Jack."

Her father seemed to take the news in stride, recognizing that there would be much more to come. Her mother beamed. "God bless, that is wonderful news!" She looked back and forth between her husband and daughter, noting the serious looks on their faces. She realized they hadn't heard a word of it in the news. "Is it?"

She nodded. "It is, Mama, but it's been kept quiet. Not for very good reasons, I'm afraid." They had a long unspoken agreement that whatever Traci told them about internal goings-on at the agency would remain private. "There's going to be a lot of debate over what to do about it."

"And you've got a part to play in that," her father said.

"I do." She explained the mission she and Roy had been planning in secret, and the obstacles left to overcome.

While her father might have been focused on the practical matters at hand, her mother naturally leaned toward other concerns. "How do you feel about this? About him?"

"He'll eventually die out there if we don't do something. We have to act fast, and we're not very good at that."

Her mother gave a gentle smile. "That's not what I asked, dear."

She wiped a tear away. "I know, Mama. And I'm not sure."

"You never were. It sounds like you're conflicted."

Have been since high school. "I am. I still don't know—"

"Maybe you do. He drives you crazy, doesn't he?"

She laughed. "He does. Did. Still does."

With an eye toward her husband, Traci's mother took her hand. "That's how you know, dear. The more they get under your skin, the more they mean to you."

She knew that instinctively. Why had she been so reluctant to give in to it? She looked up at her parents. "There's so much more to tell, and I wish we had more time. I just wanted you to know what I'm doing, and why. It may be a while before you see me again."

Her mother stiffened herself against that eventuality, while her father appeared more resigned. Both understood what had to be done. "We know, baby girl. You came to say goodbye."

As they climbed away, Traci turned to watch the verdant Kentucky farmland recede behind them. Roy leveled them off at cruising altitude, arriving there after a much more sedate departure. Civilian airports were not as accommodating of noisy max-performance climbs by military jets.

"Two hours to Ellington and no weather to worry about. Ready for some more stick time, Keene?"

"Maybe not right now. But thank you." The T-7's ejection seat was mounted at an angle just enough to not be uncomfortable. Content with the knowledge of what she needed to do, and with a belly full of home cooking, she slept all the way to Houston.

9

Traci perhaps shouldn't have been surprised when she and Roy were called into a meeting with the center director the next day. While Ronnie Bledsoe may have recognized that he'd been allowed to remain as the Manned Spaceflight director in order to check off someone's "diversity box," he'd first risen to that level through his repeatedly demonstrated competence and no small ability to stay a step ahead of the timeservers in headquarters.

They were led into the director's office by an administrative assistant who shut the door behind them. Two chairs had been arranged facing his desk, though they each remained standing as their boss studied them.

"Sit."

They exchanged glances as they took their seats, each having a good idea of what to expect but not knowing the form it would take.

"I hear you've been busy."

Traci shifted in her chair uncomfortably. Before Roy could speak, Bledsoe held up a hand.

"That wasn't an invitation to talk. My time is short, whereas you two seem to have an abundance of it, judging by your recent activities."

Roy met his gaze, not easily intimidated. He'd known Bledsoe long enough to also understand where their boundaries were. He unfolded his hands in a "go on" gesture.

"I'll get right to it. I got a call from the administrator early this morning—allow me to emphasize *early*—and she had some interesting information to pass on to me. Before I go on, you understand she's got eyes everywhere?"

Another furtive glance between her and Roy. "That's why we've been working on our own time."

Bledsoe shook his head sadly. "If I'd been aware, I might have been able to help. You don't trust me?"

For once, Roy was surprised. "That's not it at all, Ronnie. You know I believe in finding solutions before going to the boss with a problem."

"I can appreciate that," Bledsoe said. "But in some cases, an ounce of prevention is worth a bucketful of cure. So tell me: How long have you known the HOPE team's been in contact with *Magellan*?"

"Since last week."

"I'm actually impressed you could keep it to yourselves that long. Why the secrecy?"

"Again, we wanted to understand the situation and develop options. When word of this gets out, it'll be a media circus and a political clusterf—"

Bledsoe held up a hand again to stop him. "Please, no polluting my virgin ears with your profanity." He patted his chest. "Preacher's kid, remember? I'm the only one allowed to cuss in my office."

"Sorry," Roy said, and he meant it. "We know this is going to get out of control rapidly. Everybody who isn't running away from it is going to want a piece of it. Problems don't get solved in that environment. They only get worse."

"And there's not much time," Traci interjected.

"How much are we talking about?"

"Two years at most. Jack could stretch it in hibernation, but the sooner we can get to him the better."

Bledsoe did a double take, then studied the pair silently. "You two *are* good. That wasn't on Dr. Cheever's radar. Did I mention the lady's got ears everywhere?"

She felt emboldened at that. "May we ask what she said to you?"

"You may ask." Bledsoe paused as he considered his response. "First off, assume Cheever only told me half of what she actually knows. But she has contacts inside HOPE who've said there's been a huge burst of activity down there, and Hammond himself has been on site since last weekend"

"Not long after Owen contacted us," Roy noted. "I did mention that, didn't I?"

"You didn't. But I knew that, or rather that was the other thing she implied. A little bird told her you two have been burning the midnight oil ever since Jack popped up again and she put the two together. I told her it could be a mistaken assumption but she didn't believe me. So what's the plan?"

"We go get him," Traci said. "Finish outfitting *Columbus* and burn hard for this Anomaly, or whatever it is, with a gravity assist from one of the outer planets." She decided to press her luck. "Honestly, sir, I'm appalled there haven't been formal contingency plans for this. We shouldn't be kludging something together this late, but here we are. If I hadn't already been studying mission profiles in Future Apps, we wouldn't have been able to do as much as we have."

Bledsoe arched an eyebrow. "Why do you think I put you there?"

Traci was taken aback. *Of course.* She glanced at Roy, who answered with a telling shrug.

Bledsoe turned away, steepling his hands as he stared out toward the rocket garden in the courtyard below. Still early in the day, a handful of tourists wandered among old Atlas and Titan boosters before the notorious Houston heat chased them all inside to the air-conditioning. How would the average mom-and-pop taxpayer respond, had they known what was being discussed in this room? There was the political point of view and then there was the human point of view, which were too often at odds with each other. He turned back to face his astronauts. "Load up and go. Kick the tires, light the fires. That simple, is it?"

"Of course not," Roy said. "That's what we've been staying up late trying to figure out."

"The operational concept works under certain specific conditions," she added, hoping their options would not be cut off. "Number one being we leave the spacecraft under private control."

Bledsoe gave them a perturbed look. "We'll get to that later. Tell me about the others."

"Minimal payload and crew. Two pilots," Roy said, "with heavy reliance on AI." He locked eyes with Bledsoe in a signal that he was deadly serious.

"If that's coming from you, then I *know* you've thought it through. What else?"

"I mentioned gravity assists at the outer planets," she said. "Either Jupiter and Saturn, or Neptune."

Bledsoe pulled up a plot of the solar system on his desktop and whistled. Two of the planets were in completely opposite positions relative to Earth and would remain so for some time. That presented drastically different trajectories. "Jupiter and Saturn will be out of position for the next couple of years," he finally said. "You're thinking about an Oberth burn?"

"It's an option," she said cautiously, "but the advantage would be minimal."

"You'd spend the first couple of months going in the wrong direction," he agreed. "And it introduces a lot of risk. You'd have to fly under the rings to get close enough to Saturn for the tradeoff to be worth it." He tapped his fingers on his desk. "I don't like it. Too risky. Tell me about Neptune."

"It'll be close enough to the midway point to use for deceleration. *Columbus* can get there for a flyby burning at one-tenth *g* for three months, then coast. Pass behind the planet to start shedding velocity, then flip for the deceleration burn. Total transit time is eighteen months."

"A year and a half just to get there," Bledsoe said. "What's your departure window?" He could make a good guess based on the relative positions of the planets.

She shared a look with Roy. "Six months from now."

"Which is why you want to keep the HOPE contractors on the job," Bledsoe said flatly. He expected their political leadership would be clamoring to take over the mission and turn it into a big international effort, in which case they'd still be arguing over how to divvy up responsibility—and credit—a year from now. At that point they'd be recovering a dead body instead of a live astronaut. "You've got a good argument to keep it under private control," he admitted. "Most of the technical expertise has been transferred to them and we can't assume everyone would come back. We'd still be reconfiguring consoles and training controllers when we need to be outfitting a spacecraft and running sims."

"Exactly," Roy said. "I know it's a long shot, Ronnie. But we have to try."

"You two aren't exactly disinterested parties. That's going to make for a tougher sell."

Traci leaned back into her chair. "You're right, we're not."

A crooked smile crossed Bledsoe's face. "Well, you're going to have learn how to act like it right quick because Cheever isn't wasting time getting ahead of this. She's requested an emergency meeting with the Senate Subcommittee on Space and Science to discuss funding and status of the HOPE contract. All the big players will be there, and she wants to add your names to the roster of witnesses." He consulted a well-worn calendar on the corner of his desk. "And she wants both of you to meet with her at HQ tomorrow, ahead of the hearing."

Traci beamed, while Roy appeared less optimistic.

"Don't get too excited, Keene. It's in her interest to keep you close. My guess is she wants you two there as an accessory to impress the senators. Never forget that Dr. Cheever is dead set against humans contaminating deep space and it doesn't matter how reasoned our arguments are. If she wants to take back control of the program, in the end I promise you she's found a way to scuttle it."

Her eyes darted back and forth between Bledsoe and Roy. "I don't understand. Then what's the point?"

Bledsoe leaned back in his chair and stared at the ceiling as he considered his words. "Rumor control has it she's got people studying an uncrewed mission, entirely controlled by AI. I presume it would go out to find Jack and bring him home under hibernation."

"But that's . . . I don't see how that works," Traci said. "He can't be under that long without active care."

"Daisy's managed well enough," their boss said with a sigh. "The price of success." He eyed them both with a warning. "Listen to me closely. Washington doesn't work like the real world, and Cheever didn't land the administrator's job without having some heavy hitters in her corner. She is a master of three-dimensional chess. Just when you think you're a step ahead, she's already in the next time zone."

Traci shared a glance with Roy as she considered Bledsoe's words. "I'm a pretty good chess player myself, sir."

10

Washington, DC

The space agency's headquarters occupied an uninspiring structure of concrete and glass that could have easily been mistaken for one of the surrounding hotels or office buildings that littered the nation's capital.

Traci and Roy were greeted by an aide in a garish tie and curly hair worn a bit too long, suggestive of someone vainly striving to hold onto his fading youth. "Blaine Winston," he said. "Administrator Cheever's executive assistant. After me, please."

Ah, she realized. The power behind the throne. She exchanged a quick glance with Roy, who nodded and gestured her on ahead of him. Winston led them down a long hallway adorned with familiar images of NASA spacecraft and the worlds they'd visited. Being open to the public, the first floor was bursting with reminders of the agency's glory days.

After a quick elevator ride to the top floor, they were ushered into an anteroom adjacent to the administrator's office. There, they found a quartet of wingback chairs arranged around a mahogany conference table inlaid with the iconic blue "meatball" logo. Following Winston's lead, they remained standing until the administrator arrived.

They didn't have to wait long. Almost on cue, Jacqueline Cheever emerged from her office. Her pantsuit and bun hairdo reminded Traci of a perpetually annoyed schoolmarm, like a secondary character out of the frontier romance novels which she still occasionally indulged. Wisely keeping any amusement to herself, it at least provided enough reason to display a sincere smile as she greeted the NASA boss.

It soon became clear that she would need to keep her humor at arm's length.

"Colonel Hoover, Major Keene," Cheever began curtly, "thank you for coming."

"Our pleasure, ma'am," Roy said on their behalf, with a graciousness Traci wasn't used to seeing. She eyed him warily; they'd been warned the administrator didn't care for such outdated gender-centric norms, and the chief astronaut had just signaled that he really didn't give a damn.

Cheever ignored his subtle slight for the moment and took her seat, a signal for the others to do so as well. "I'm not much for pleasantries and my schedule is quite full, so let's get to it." She studied each of them. "I know you've become aware that your ship has been found and that Jack Templeton is apparently alive. We will discuss how you came upon that information later."

Roy, for his part, wasn't intimidated. "May I ask why you say he's 'apparently' alive?"

"The HOPE team has received text messages via the Deep Space Network which appear to be from him, but his biomonitors are offline."

"So he's talking to you," Traci said hopefully. *And who else would it be?*

"Texting," Winston interjected. "We haven't ruled out the possibility that it's the onboard AI communicating with us."

"Daisy wouldn't do that," she objected. "There'd be no point to it. Deceit is not in her nature."

Cheever was unmoved. "We can't know that for certain."

"You'd know if it was Daisy," Roy said, leaning forward and pointing to himself and Traci. "Or rather, *we'd* know. That is, if all the information had been shared with us in the first place."

Cheever was unmoved. "As I said, we'll get to that. Today we are going to discuss the 'freelance' work you've undertaken since learning of Templeton's situation." She wrinkled her nose to signal her disapproval.

Roy swept a hand toward Traci. "Keene's the expert on this," he said. "Best to let her explain."

She hadn't needed much encouragement, and eagerly took his cue. "I work in Future Applications, Dr. Cheever," she said, consciously avoiding offending her with a gendered address, though *ma'am* would've been so much easier. "My job is to investigate potential mission architectures using existing capabilities."

"I'm aware that's your official role," Cheever said. "So tell me what you've actually been doing."

No sense taking the long road, she decided. "Developing plans for a recovery expedition using *Columbus*."

"I see." Cheever and Winston exchanged knowing looks.

She couldn't see what they'd found to be so amusing. Probably they were just trying to throw her off. She swiped at her tablet and projected a spacecraft diagram onto a nearby monitor embedded in a wall. "The vehicle is in a minimum payload configuration: one hab module and the control cabin." She zoomed in on the forward structure. "The four-point docking node aft of the hab can be loaded up with prepackaged supply modules. Cradles and ports along the main truss can be outfitted with cryo tanks for hydrogen and oxygen. The upgraded chiller tanks will mitigate the boiloff issues that required *Magellan* to be refueled on our previous mission. Most of the hydrogen is reaction mass, with some kept in reserve with O2 to run the backup fuel cells, which will also supply drinking water. In this configuration the vehicle can support three crew members, the third being Jack on the return leg. Estimate three months of acceleration and deceleration on each leg at one-tenth *g*, with a gravity-assist flyby of Neptune. It's ambitious, but we can outfit *Columbus* in time if we get started right away. The mission itself would take thirty-eight months total, including rendezvous time at the destination."

"With only two people?" Cheever challenged her. "That is rather ambitious, considering your last expedition had a crew of four."

"We also had a more complex mission profile with multiple probe launches and two different excursion craft to tend to. After our experience on *Magellan*, we're confident the onboard AI can handle the workload on a stripped-down vehicle."

"We'd be there for oversight and any necessary intervention," Roy explained. "The service bots can do a lot, but activities like external maintenance need a human touch."

"You say 'we,'" Cheever noted drily. "You speak as if you're intending to do this yourselves."

"We're the most qualified out of who's left in the astronaut office," Roy said. "There's no time to train up a fresh crew for an extended-duration mission."

She eyed Traci. "Keene hasn't been medically released for flight duty."

"Excuse me, I have a First Class FAA medical with zero-*g* endorsement. I could get a job flying civilian spaceliners today if I wanted to. But here I am, still waiting on our docs to clear me. This mission is too important for us to be bogged down in minutia."

"Nor do we have time to be tilting at windmills," Cheever said tartly. She folded her hands in her lap. "I'll remind you that there *is* no mission yet." She turned to her assistant.

"We are developing other, less challenging options," Winston said. He tapped at a keyboard and another diagram of *Columbus* appeared on the wall monitor, this one with noticeably fewer logistics modules attached. "This configuration assumes a fully automated vehicle, guided by the onboard AI. It can be outfitted in less time and would carry enough life support to sustain Templeton in hibernation throughout the return."

"We considered that as well," Roy said. "It's not as straightforward as you think. You're talking about doubling the time Jack would spend in hibernation, with no humans to manage his care. I'm comfortable doing a minimally crewed expedition with AI support, but I don't believe artificial intelligence is ready to run this type of mission unsupervised. You've got rendezvous and docking, crew transfer—"

Winston smiled thinly in a display of practiced tolerance. "On the contrary, I think you may be overcomplicating the issue. We've been sending unmanned probes into deep space for decades, all of them controlled from Earth. How is this any different?"

"Because it'll be under near-constant acceleration, for starters," Roy reminded him. "It's not some dumb probe passively coasting to its destination. It's under power and gaining velocity with every passing second, and that requires constant trajectory management. The light delays get longer by the day, way too long for anyone on the ground to intervene. AI was installed to back up the crew when mission control is out of reach, not to take over. Daisy still had to wake Jack up when it was time to enter orbit."

Cheever stepped in. "The bottom line is we don't have the budget to finish equipping the vehicle for a crewed expedition. AI technology has advanced considerably since your mission, and we have high confidence in its readiness."

"It's a fine alternative to ground support," Roy said, reiterating his argument. "But speaking as chief astronaut, I'm not ready to put one in the pilot's seat yet."

"Jack Templeton did."

Traci had stayed silent about this until now. "He didn't have a choice," she reminded the group. "One of us had to draw the short straw. He put his life on the line, betting that he was right."

Cheever remained solicitous, but her tone held an implicit threat. "We all understand you have strong feelings about this. Be mindful that they don't cloud your judgment," she said, reminiscent of the vexatious social-credit algorithms. Her implied message was *Stick with the program, Keene.*

"My point is he wasn't just flipping a coin and hoping it came up heads. We spent years working with Daisy before leaving Earth. We helped her grow from just being good at filtering through accumulated knowledge to being able to help us solve problems. To think creatively. In the end, she even had Roy's confidence."

"You just made our point," Winston said triumphantly. "We can safely use AI as a substitute for humans."

"No, you're *missing* my point," she said, leaning in toward him. "We *helped* her—and I still can't believe I'm gendering a computer— to evolve. Daisy didn't become sentient through clever programming; it required years of personal interaction. Think about it—if it takes a human mind a couple of decades to fully develop, why wouldn't an artificial mind need time?"

Roy folded his arms. "Exactly. These artificial brains aren't mature enough yet to fly solo. They're no substitute for a trained crew."

"This one will have to be," Cheever said. "Our allocation is what it is. This is the best use of NASA's limited budget."

Roy decided it was time to play their hand. "HOPE can do it for less money. According to their contract, they still have the legal authority to do so."

"Not if the mission isn't sanctioned," Cheever reminded him.

"You're telling me it isn't? Are you telling me NASA is changing the public position it's held for decades? That we're not going to go after a stranded astronaut?"

"Ultimately it's not up to us," Cheever said, so apologetic as to be almost believable. "Congress will be considering this in a special budget resolution, which is the purpose of tomorrow's hearing. I don't expect them to fund a risky, expensive expedition when it can be automated for far less."

Traci's heart sank. So that was that—the agency wouldn't be advocating for a crewed expedition. As Cheever studied her from across the table, it became obvious she was being brought along as a prop to lend credibility. To put a human face on Jack's plight. She was not expected to actually participate.

Cheever maintained her poker face, confident in her ultimate victory. "There is a budget reconciliation bill going to committee this week," she explained patiently. "Among other things, I can tell you that it will be considering substantive changes to allocations for the vehicle and our agreement with the HOPE consortium."

Traci frowned. The one thing politicians could do quickly was pull funding if something threatened to make them look bad.

As Winston began briefing them on what to expect and which senators to be especially cautious with, she decided it might actually be in their interests to find a way to make NASA look *really* bad. If they weren't going to allow the astronauts who'd actually been out there to do something, then maybe someone else could.

11

Traci's only other experience with congressional testimony had been notably different from where she found herself today. Whereas the public debriefings of the *Magellan* mission had been held in a cavernous hearing room, facing a wall of dour old men in suits behind a phalanx of cameras and glaring lights, this forum was decidedly more intimate. Or more intimidating, which she sensed was on purpose.

Behind closed doors, facing only a half dozen senators and no reporters, the atmosphere was restrained and serious. With no press allowed, she expected considerably less speechifying and grandstanding than typically defined these events.

In other words, they were here to make decisions and get some actual work done.

More comfortable in her flight crew jumpsuit, she anxiously smoothed out her skirt as she took a seat at the witnesses' table beside Roy and made note of the Senate inquisitors eyeing her entrance. Joining them were Cheever and someone she didn't recognize, though she did spy the nameplate in front of him: Dr. Malcolm Trumbull, NASA's chief scientist. That he hadn't been at yesterday's meeting with them suggested the administrator had something else up her sleeve.

She was keenly aware that the only other woman in the room was Caroline Sykes, the senior senator from Arizona, who caught Traci's eye and acknowledged her with a friendly wink. Had she just found an ally, or was that gesture meant to put her at ease in order to catch her off guard later? In this place, either was equally possible.

As the chairman gaveled the hearing to order, she regarded the two men who were most likely to drive the agenda: Samuel Warden of North Carolina, a loquacious overweight lump of down-home geniality, and the more caustic Edmond Sullivan of Pennsylvania. Lean and smartly dressed, with slicked-back hair crowning an aquiline face, he was the stereotypical Northeastern WASP. Each other's physical opposite, they were known to be dangerous questioners.

The chairman opened with brief remarks. "The Vice President sends his regrets that he could not join us today. We will of course be providing his office with an executive summary with full transcripts and a recording of these proceedings for review."

Traci cast a sidelong glance at Cheever. Judging by her reaction she'd expected this and seemed comfortable with it, which meant the two had probably worked out some arrangement ahead of time. As president of the Senate the VP wasn't expected to attend committee hearings, but as chairman of the President's Space Council he would absolutely have an interest in today's inquiry. That he didn't send an aide to listen in told her all she needed to know: they were on their own.

The chairman continued. "We are here to consider proposals for what is a rather bold undertaking. We've been briefed on the discovery of the missing *Magellan* spacecraft and the various scenarios for rescuing astronaut Templeton. Not only would this be NASA's first crewed flight in many years, it would be a more far-reaching mission than any previous, and within a timeline that appears to be remarkably optimistic. Dr. Cheever, I believe you have some prepared remarks before we begin our questioning."

Cheever folded her hands and looked up from her notes, judiciously making eye contact with each committee member. "Thank you, Senators. My remarks will be brief. There have been some remarkable developments within the last few weeks, of which finding *Magellan* may well be the least astonishing. Our chief scientist, Dr. Trumbull, will be addressing those particular findings. We have studied a range of possible mission profiles to recover *Magellan* and bring Jack Templeton home, which we have narrowed down to two choices: crewed, and automated. For a number of reasons which will be made clear today, as administrator I am in favor of the automated option. However, astronauts Hoover and

Keene have put considerable thought into the crewed option and I wanted to give their views a fair hearing before this committee. This concludes my remarks."

That was it? Magnanimity was not in Cheever's character, which only confirmed Traci's suspicion that the administrator already had a good sense of how this was going to go.

"Very well." The chairman turned to the linen-suited Warden. "We will open with the committee's ranking member, the senator from North Carolina."

Warden's ample frame quivered as he leaned forward and cleared his throat. "Thank you, Mr. Chairman." They were all very collegial and she wondered how long that would last. "Now, it's my understanding that this crewed mission plan was put together just within the last couple of weeks," he drawled, wagging a finger between her and Roy, "by you two?"

As chief astronaut, it was Roy's place to answer for them. "That's correct, sir."

Warden's amused look betrayed his skepticism. "And this was done without any input from other experts within the agency?"

Roy didn't flinch. "We understood immediately that time was of the essence, Senator. We had a small window of opportunity and bringing in others would have taken time we didn't have." He nodded at Traci. "Keene and I were more than capable of assessing the mission profiles. It was critical to get things moving in the right direction before handing everything off to the subject matter experts. Now we're at the point where we need to bring in more expertise if we're going to make this happen." Under the table, he nudged her with his shoe. It was her turn to add some color commentary.

She pulled the microphone closer. "If I may, Senator. For historical context, the Apollo 8 mission was enormously ambitious for its time and was conceived in a similar manner. The spacecraft itself had not yet flown, and it would be the first crewed launch on a Saturn V— which had almost shaken itself apart on its last test flight. Program director George Low put together a similarly small study group in Houston to validate his idea for a 'Hail Mary' mission to lunar orbit. They didn't present their plan to anyone in leadership until they'd convinced themselves it could work. They did all of that over a *weekend*, going from operational concept to the Moon in five months."

"Ah," the senator said. He looked to Cheever, who remained silent. "Yes. Let's return to the question of expertise. To reiterate, you didn't share this with anyone else inside NASA until recently?"

Roy leaned back in. "As I said, we were concerned about time constraints, and NASA does not currently have operational control over the spacecraft. That is still contracted to the HOPE consortium, where most of the current operational expertise now resides."

"It's interesting you would mention that," Warden said. "HOPE's contract does not specifically confer the authority to send the other vessel willy-nilly wherever they choose."

"That's correct, Senator. Their control is limited to sanctioned missions. It's our opinion that the most efficient path to bring *Columbus* up to full capability is to leave the current team in control. Transferring those resources and expertise back to NASA would add time that Templeton simply doesn't have."

A couple of the senators, Sullivan notably, appeared uncomfortable. Warden remained amused. "We're not supposed to call it by that name anymore, Colonel Hoover. It's become . . . problematic."

"Columbus?" he asked, intentionally repeating it to them. He had little patience for politically motivated alterations of history. "I know there have been discussions to that effect, but no one has ever officially notified us. What are we supposed to be calling it now?" he asked innocently.

Warden turned to his fellow senators, then back to Roy. "*Sacajawea* is the current favorite, I believe."

Roy pursed his lips as he considered that. "Not a bad choice, actually. But still not official, and as far as I know 'Columbus' is still painted on the hull. Begging the committee's pardon, I prefer to work within the present reality."

"Let's talk about reality," Sullivan interjected with a glance at Warden. "If you agree, Senator."

Warden waved him on. "I cede my time to the gentleman from Pennsylvania," he said, suggesting that the two had likely worked out whatever was coming next. Sullivan made a show of removing his wire-rim glasses and folding them delicately into one hand, wielding them like a wand at Traci. "Miss Keene, I have some questions for you. For the record, could you please state your background?"

She had been sitting attentively and did not alter her posture. "I've been with NASA for twelve years and was in the Air Force for eight before that. I served in F-16 and F-35 squadrons, then flew a variety of experimental aircraft as a test pilot at Edwards. As an astronaut I flew three orbital missions aboard Dragon spacecraft, served a tour at the Lunar Gateway station, and was mission pilot on the *Magellan* expedition to Jupiter and Pluto."

"And what is your current role, now that crewed exploration is on hiatus?"

She was certain he already knew the answer, but played along. "I work in the Future Applications program. I perform feasibility studies for proposed missions using existing hardware."

"So this clandestine exercise you undertook with Colonel Hoover was a natural extension of your official duties?"

She shifted in her chair. Where was he going with this? "Yes, Senator."

"Would you also agree that your last mission has influenced your proposal before this committee?"

"In what way, Senator? Between training and the mission itself I dedicated four years of my life to that project. So yes, I'd say it influenced my analysis. A lot can happen in space that isn't readily apparent in a feasibility study."

Sullivan leaned forward, jabbing with his glasses for emphasis. "Your relationship with Astronaut Templeton being one of those?"

Traci remained rock steady with her hands folded carefully before her. "My 'relationship' with him? What are you suggesting, sir?"

The lanky senator leaned back and smiled affably, appearing to backpedal. "What I mean, Miss Keene, is Jack Templeton willingly sacrificed his life to save yours. More so, he did this without any guarantee that you would successfully recover from your injuries and with the near certainty that taking *Magellan* back into deep space would become a one-way trip. I'm familiar with the intense psychological profiling the agency undertook to ensure crew compatibility. It's no leap of imagination to think there was some deeper connection between you two."

She looked down at the table and squeezed her fingers together until they hurt. He was a crafty sonofabitch all right. "Jack was my crewmate and a good friend, Senator. That's enough of a bond for any of us. Whatever else you're trying to suggest, I think we should leave it at that."

"Of course, Miss Keene. I didn't mean to imply anything untoward. I only seek to understand your motivations."

Like hell you didn't. "Of course, Senator," she said through a smile of clenched teeth. The senator from Arizona caught her eye and gave her a reassuring nod.

"So you don't feel any special obligation to bring him home?" Sullivan pressed.

"Senator, it's my job to figure out what's possible with the tools at hand. Any sense of obligation is out of camaraderie and common decency. There isn't a soul in the astronaut corps who wouldn't drop everything to go after one of our own if we thought it were possible. It's not about personal relationships. It's a moral obligation."

"Yet that remains precisely my concern," he said. "You're asking us to commit considerable resources to this adventure—this personal quest—in a budgetary environment where we remain significantly constrained. What we add to one program, we must subtract from another." His displeasure with no longer being able to command the Treasury to print money as if playing Monopoly was legendary.

The Arizona senator raised her hand. "Senator, if I may?"

The chairman gaveled her in. "The committee recognizes the gentle lady from Arizona."

"Thank you." She clasped her hands calmly before her and turned to face the other legislators. "Senator Sullivan, I believe *Major* Keene's professional achievements speak for themselves. But if you insist that her personal motivations are relevant, I'm sure she'd be willing to go on record." She then turned to Traci. "Major?"

Warden harrumphed under his breath as Sullivan interjected. "I don't think that will be necessary—"

"Begging your pardon, but I think she deserves the chance to defend her position."

Traci had long ago learned how to read a room full of competitive pilots and earnest engineers, but judging this bunch was uncharted territory. "If you'd like for me to go on record about my personal interactions on an extended-duration mission, then I should warn you they could veer into some uncomfortable topics. Space is not for girly-girls, Senator. Privacy is almost nonexistent and traditional gender boundaries become an afterthought. For instance, helping each other practice going to the bathroom so as not to foul the zero-*g* toilets, or learning how to catheterize an incapacitated crewmate. I'd be happy to discuss more if you wish."

Senator Warden cleared his throat with a sideways glance at Sullivan. "I believe that will do. I hereby reclaim my time." He then held up a sheaf of papers. "You mentioned 'moral obligation,' which I do believe is relevant to the matter before this committee." He gestured for an aide, who began handing them sheafs of paper stamped CONFIDENTIAL—OFFICIAL USE ONLY. "The Outer Space Environmental Protection Treaty would expressly prohibit the types of activities we're discussing here."

She and Roy exchanged looks—here came the first bombshell. How had they not heard of this before? "Excuse me, Senator," Roy said, "but you appear to have us at a disadvantage." *Which was no doubt intentional,* Traci thought. "A lot of information comes through the Astronaut Office, but this seems to have escaped our notice."

"That's unfortunate," Sullivan sniffed in a subtle breach of protocol which Warden studiously ignored. "We can't help that it hasn't become public knowledge, what with so many other concerns demanding the public's attention."

Roy remained surprisingly collegial, despite his infamously low tolerance for bureaucratic chicanery. He'd acquired some political survival skills after being moved to the front office. "Perhaps you could indulge us, Senator?" he said, holding up the papers placed in front of him. "At least give us an opportunity to read the abstract?"

"I can do better than that," Sullivan said, and swiped at his tablet, launching a presentation on a nearby monitor. "OSEP is a UN-sponsored agreement between all spacefaring nations that would prohibit crewed landings on previously unexplored solar system bodies. It recognizes the unique evolutionary risks of introducing a human presence into biospheres that are less than fully understood."

Roy laughed darkly. "Senator, we barely understand *our* biosphere."

"I recognize how this may give you some cause for alarm. If you take a moment to read the language, you'll see it still allows for a limited human presence."

"*Limited,*" Roy quoted back at him after taking a minute to leaf through the abstract. "To areas where we've previously landed." He jabbed a finger at his copy. "Senator, this looks to go a lot farther than biospheres. This wouldn't allow us to go anywhere we haven't already been. We couldn't even target different regions of the Moon or Mars. What would be the point of any future exploration?"

"That *is* the point, Colonel Hoover. The negotiating committee has recognized we can't put that genie back in the bottle. But we can certainly control where we open it in the future. With the advent of artificial intelligence, robotic exploration is—"

"Like kissing your sister," Roy interrupted, finally losing patience. "There is value in having a human presence in unexplored territory. Forget the 'flags and footprints' rhetoric. I'm talking about making decisions in real time."

Sullivan grew annoyed. "As I was saying, artificial intelligence has changed the game. Robotic probes have become, well, less *robotic*," he said, proud of himself. "We can rely on an onboard AI to observe and decide without human intervention." He gestured again at Traci. "You of all people should recognize that after your experience with . . . Daisy, is it? You gave her a human name."

"That part was easy," she fired back. The acronym DAISE had made it nigh unavoidable. "Senator, what you fail to recognize is that she didn't just emerge fully formed when they flipped on the power. Daisy's intelligence grew over years of interaction with our crew. We didn't realize she'd become sentient until almost halfway through our mission." She turned to Roy. "I don't want to speak for my commander, but I'm not sure he was ever fully convinced."

Roy folded his arms. "It took some time," he admitted. "But in the end we'd become so short-handed we didn't have a choice. I had to treat her as part of the crew if we were going to make it home."

Traci nodded her agreement. "Our point is AI isn't ready to stand on its own. It's out of its infancy but is still in—I don't know— toddlerhood. From our experience, how they develop has a lot to do with the humans they interact with. Not every AI is going to turn out like Daisy. Handing over full control of a mission at this point would be like giving your car keys to a five-year-old."

"I have a more pertinent question," Roy said.

Sullivan looked down his nose at them. "Excuse me, Colonel, but we're asking the questions here."

Warden raised his hand and chuckled. "Let's allow it, Ed. We did kind of sandbag them with OSEP, after all."

"The proposed mission isn't landing anywhere," Roy pointed out. "It's a straight out-and-back to ensure Templeton's safe return to Earth. The only contact with anything would be a rendezvous between the two spacecraft. What about that is in conflict with this treaty?"

"All correct," Warden said. "However, doing so will require outfitting *Colum—Sacajawea*—in such a way as to blatantly undermine the spirit of this important international accord. How would it look to the world if the US outfitted a ship like this right before signing the treaty that would prohibit it?"

"Prohibit?" Roy cocked an eyebrow at them. "So there's not an allowance for, say, crewed ships with remotely operated landers?"

"That would still present an unacceptable risk of biological contamination," the senator explained, looking to Cheever for backup. It was evident he had relied on his staff for this information and had reached the limit of his understanding.

Cheever answered with a satisfied nod. "That's correct, Senator. I believe my position on the OSEP treaty is well understood by this committee, so I shall not waste your valuable time any further," she said in a not-so-subtle implication that her astronauts had done just that. She then turned to her chief scientist. "If I may, this would be a good time for Dr. Trumbull to weigh in. He's practically been living in his office since we received the first data packet from *Magellan*, and there have been additional discoveries which I think you'll find relevant to this discussion."

Warden looked to the chairman. "The chair recognizes Dr. Trumbull."

An unassuming man, the chief scientist cleared his throat and pushed a pair of horn-rim glasses atop his bulbous nose, which contrasted all the more with his otherwise thin features. "As Dr. Cheever indicated, this is an extraordinary development which we believe warrants further investigation for reasons I will attempt to make clear. This matter has been all-consuming for everyone involved, so I will limit my remarks to those areas in which I have expertise. We have intentionally kept the investigation team limited to a small circle of subject matter experts until we could better understand the observational data relayed from *Magellan*."

He took a sip of water. "There is a great deal we can infer from the fact that the spacecraft is no longer on a solar escape trajectory. It did not have enough propellant left to achieve this without the influence of a substantial gravitational field."

"You mean that undiscovered planet Templeton was looking for when he took *Magellan*," Warden said, signaling his displeasure with Jack's actions.

Trumbull glanced over at Traci. To his credit, he didn't let the remark go unchallenged. "Regardless of Astronaut Templeton's motivations, physics dictated we were going to lose the spacecraft regardless. It was a necessary condition to return Miss Keene to Earth in time for the medical care she required. His actions saved her life."

Warden sat back and folded his hands across his ample midsection. "Your point is taken. Go on."

"As I was saying, the spacecraft's relative position and velocity—what we call its 'state vector'—can tell us much about the mass of the body it orbits. For reasons which are still unknown to us, the data stream from *Magellan* has been quite thin, but we have received enough observational data to draw preliminary conclusions." Trumbull paused for effect. He was going to make it as simple as possible. "The gravitational field thought to belong to a large undiscovered planet is there. The planet is not."

"Excuse me?"

Trumbull responded slowly, careful with his words. "Whatever *Magellan* is orbiting, it's not a planet. Its gravity is acting on the spacecraft, and it is bending the light from background stars in an effect called 'gravitational lensing.' But the Anomaly itself is not directly observable. We have come to believe it is a dark matter object."

Warden's eyebrows lifted in a rare expression of surprise. Cheever's star witness was having the desired effect. "Can you put that in terms this country lawyer could understand, Doctor?"

"The universe behaves in a manner inconsistent with its observable mass. Galaxies move in ways they shouldn't, in fact many shouldn't have formed based on what we can see. They behave as if they are heavier than they appear. We know this is the case because everything else works precisely as our current theories of gravity would predict. This means there *must* be something we can't see which is acting on them. This 'something' has mass—and therefore gravity—but doesn't interact with electromagnetic radiation. It does not absorb, reflect, or emit light, thus the term 'dark matter.' We can only infer its existence through the effect it has on other objects."

"So even though he's right there, so to speak, Templeton still can't see it?"

"That's correct, Senator." Trumbull shot a glance at Cheever and pursed his lips, still debating the rest of his testimony. "There are other interesting anomalies gleaned from *Magellan*'s data. The time stamps on its telemetry aren't consistent with the master mission clocks in Houston or with the control team in Grand Cayman. There is nearly a five-year differential."

"That's how long it had been since the ship disappeared," Warden said. "So it's just getting caught up. I don't see the significance."

Trumbull smiled as if lecturing to a particularly inept student. "I may not have explained this clearly enough. This is the ship's *current* data stream. The spacecraft's internal clocks are almost five years behind ours, as if nothing changed from its perspective. It is evidence of time dilation consistent with a vehicle that achieved relativistic velocities."

Traci fought to stay composed. That explained why his life support had lasted so much longer than they'd thought possible: whatever time had passed for him, it had been years for them. She grabbed Roy's arm under the table and squeezed. What had Jack gotten himself into?

"*Relativistic*," Warden repeated incredulously. "You mean as in Einstein's theory?"

"Correct, Senator. A fundamental principle of relativity is that time and velocity are both relative to the observer, thus the term." Trumbull spread his hands apart to illustrate. "A moving object experiences time at a slower rate relative to a stationary observer. The popular understanding is that this phenomenon increases with velocity, though it is also caused by gravity. One proof from everyday life is that GPS satellites must compensate for this effect, otherwise they would be useless."

"So *Magellan* somehow accelerated to . . . what? Light speed? How is that possible?"

"Put simply, it isn't. That is for a number of reasons, the most immediate being that the vehicle did not have enough propellant." That no amount of fuel could ever be enough was a fact he prudently left unmentioned. "While even a small fraction of light speed is enough to observe time dilation, recall that I also mentioned gravity. Extremes in gravitational potential will induce the same phenomenon. This suggests some remarkable possibilities. And some complications." He paused to let the gathered senators absorb his physics lesson.

"And what would those be?" Warden asked impatiently.

"I am aware of some speculation that our wayward astronaut may have stumbled upon a black hole where this planet was thought to be. I do not consider that to be likely for a number of reasons, the first of which is the utter lack of an energy signature. There are other, more exotic, explanations which I am reluctant to indulge. But the gravitational effects cannot be ignored."

"Please feel free to indulge us, Doctor."

The scientist hesitated, taking another sip of water as he decided how bluntly to frame his answer. He pulled the microphone closer. "*Magellan* is orbiting a stable wormhole."

PART TWO

Memories: The Discovery

✻ ✻ ✻

Meant for short-range excursions, the Manned Space Exploration Vehicle was comparable in size and shape to an Earthbound delivery van. Taking it from their orbit to close with the Anomaly was a three-day journey, so for its jaunt to observe the mysterious "planet," Jack and Daisy had taken turns remotely piloting the MSEV into a closer orbit. As the little craft's distance from them increased with each passing hour, his near-instantaneous ability to manipulate its controls from *Magellan* was continually degraded by the signal lag: Send a command, wait an agonizing two whole seconds to find out if it had worked. It offered a greater appreciation of the patience an AI like Daisy showed when dealing with such painfully slow humans.

"We are approaching the next correction burn," Daisy informed him. "Do you wish to continue on the current trajectory? I have calculated several options for different orbits."

"I'm not in enough of a hurry to expend any more propellant. It took us this long to get here, I can wait another few hours." There could be other equally mysterious objects to investigate, and having two independent vehicles orbiting the Anomaly doubled the amount of data points streaming in. "What about our dark matter object?" he asked, using the term they'd settled on over the intervening days. "Can you tell anything about it now?"

"DMO-1 remains unobservable, though I have been able to infer some properties based on our respective orbits and propellant use. The MSEV's radius will be thirty-eight thousand kilometers from predicted barycenter. The gravity field is consistent with an object of 9.86 Earth masses."

"That'd be close to geosynchronous orbit at Earth. For that kind of mass, a thirty-eight-thousand kilometer radius should put the MSEV close to the surface. Yet we still can't see anything."

"That assumes density comparable to a rocky planet like Earth. If that were the case here, it would occult the background stars. DMO-1 appears to have considerably greater density."

"How much?"

"I have been able to detect gravitational lensing of the stellar background along DMO-1's periphery."

Now that was a surprise—if not quite the same as direct imaging, it was pretty darn close. He'd been too focused on their probe to look for those kinds of secondary clues himself. "You been holding out on me, Daisy?"

"Not at all. You were busy with the spacecraft. I am informing you now that we have more reliable data."

"I've gotten much better at multitasking of late, thanks to you. Show me what you've got."

A star chart appeared, generated by Daisy from *Magellan*'s catalog and indexed to the MSEV's relative position—in other words, presenting what they should expect to see were they aboard the craft itself and looking toward the object it was orbiting. Soon after, an overlay appeared of the images taken from the little ship's wide-field cameras. Around a small circular area in the center, the star's positions had shifted in a way that would have been imperceptible to the unaided eye.

"That's . . . incredible. Why couldn't we see this before?"

"We weren't looking for it. I began compiling the imagery after the MSEV's insertion burn, when we could be certain of its orbit."

Jack zoomed in on the image, hoping to tease out more detail. A time stamp scrolled across the bottom of the screen as the MSEV drifted along, the stellar background slowly moving with it as the craft's perspective changed. As it did, more stars appeared to shift as they passed near the center of whatever DMO-1 was.

He felt a visceral excitement for the first time since his awakening, momentarily forgetting all that had transpired before now. The object they'd spent these last few years racing toward was finally—sort of—in view. "That's enough to give us a rough outline. It's small," he said as he mentally processed this new evidence. "Density would have to be—"

"Ten thousand kilograms per cubic meter," Daisy said. That was approaching white dwarf densities, giving credence to his earlier speculation that it could be the remnant of an ancient star. Were it not for the Anomaly's transparency, he'd have settled for that explanation. The faintest cinder of a star that had flared and burned out back at the beginning of the universe would have at least reflected energy from elsewhere.

"Not enough for a black hole," he concluded with relief. "But still...it's got to be dark matter. Right?" He could barely believe it himself. First hypothesized as a necessary byproduct of General Relativity, dark matter had been the best way to fill in the theoretical holes left by a universe expanding in ways mathematics—which so far had been right about everything else—could not model without it. There had to be more mass in the universe than had been observed, otherwise all other predictions failed. That they had not, and had in fact been repeatedly confirmed by observations, only added to the certainty that there was indeed some unseen form of matter lurking out there.

And here they were with the evidence staring them in the face—sort of. It was still elusive, like the light from a distant star that could only be seen by indirect viewing: Try to center your vision on it, and it disappeared. Yet there it was, only evident by the faintest distortion of starlight around it as they moved through space.

"You understand how significant this is? This is Nobel Prize stuff, Daisy."

"I doubt the committee would consider awarding their prize to an artificial intelligence."

"An unfortunate prejudice which they may have to reconsider," he said, beginning to grasp the enormity of it all—the discovery itself, and how it had been arrived at. He wondered if the qualifier "artificial" was still appropriate. "Synthetic" intelligence was beginning to feel more apt. "You're the one who got suspicious, took the initiative, and did the investigative work. I'm just a dumbass flight engineer."

"That is not a term one typically equates with engineers."

"You haven't met enough of us. Being able to do the math or memorize material properties doesn't necessarily equate with being smart." He paused again, scrolling back to the beginning of Daisy's images to watch them unfold at higher speed; the lensing effect then became as undeniable as a sunrise. "Anything else? Spectrography, now that we've had a closer look?"

"The DMO-1 anomaly remains electromagnetically transparent. It is not emitting or reflecting energy. It is truly dark." Daisy paused. "However, there is more."

"How so, if there's no detectable energy?"

"Our focus on the mass concentration at the center of the

Anomaly may be misplaced. The phenomenon we are observing is much larger than DMO-1 itself. In addition to gravitational lensing, there are anisotropic variations in the background radiation which I cannot account for."

Following Daisy's lead, Jack called up their ongoing observations of the space around the dark matter object. The changes were subtle, only detectable over time as *Magellan* traveled along its orbit with its microwave receivers pointed at the Anomaly's center. "I see what you mean now. It's like we're not looking at the same region of space. That's not attributable to gravitational lensing, is it?"

"Lensing would explain variations in the immediate vicinity of the object. It does not explain all of them, however. There are faint infrared and microwave emissions consistent with cosmic background radiation, though they appear gravitationally redshifted."

"Now you're hurting my brain. You mean it's all coming from the wrong direction, like DMO-1 is funneling background radiation from somewhere else?"

"Yes," Daisy said. "It is like an opening, allowing in radiation from a different region of space."

An opening. That was when he knew. He was aware of the theories, had read papers on the subject, but he also knew the limits of his personal understanding. That would need to change, because if what he suspected was true then they had just stumbled into something perhaps more significant than dark matter. His mind raced through what he could remember of Lorentz equations, Einstein–Rosen bridges, Hawking radiation . . . it was all a jumble of disconnected knowledge which he was suddenly in a hurry to sort through, aided by whatever information he could access aboard *Magellan*. He was about to get a self-directed doctorate in weird physics.

Jack knew instinctively that he and Daisy had arrived at the same conclusions; in fact he suspected she'd figured it out some time ago and had been waiting for him to catch up. While confirming some esoteric theories, their discovery also had the potential to blow up the accepted model of the universe.

Accepting it for himself was another matter. Once he'd realized where the evidence was leading, Jack felt surprisingly at ease with it. "Well. At least we finally have some idea of what we're looking at."

"Agreed. We are looking at a wormhole."

12

Free from the glare of skeptical senators and whatever machinations Cheever had in mind, Traci could finally begin to process what she'd just learned. Before she could ask any questions of her own after the hearing, the administrator had swiftly exited with her chief scientist in tow, offering no further explanation. It confirmed that she and Roy had in fact been there as decorations, only to have their plans blown up in the most dramatic way possible. She had mustered all of her prior military experience to maintain a professional bearing as they left the hearing. Inside, her stomach was doing backflips and her knees trembled.

Wormhole. Something out of science fiction, right here in their solar system. Even if they ignored Jack's predicament, shouldn't that make them *want* to send a crew to investigate?

That single, shocking revelation had thrown the committee into a furor. It was hard to catch seasoned politicians by surprise, but by God Cheever had done it. If she'd wanted a bombshell to cement her position then she'd found it with Trumbull, though judging by the member's reactions she may have been too clever by half. Perhaps there was still a chance to salvage this, to put an actual crewed mission together.

Roy had silently remained by her side, and now took her gently by the elbow. "Need to sit?"

She looked up and down the expansive hallways, swarming with busy staffers doing presumably important things, and suddenly felt claustrophobic. "No . . . I need some fresh air."

"Then let's get out of here. There's a car waiting outside."

"Go without me," she said with a wave. "I'll walk."

"Sure. See you at the hotel later, okay?" He wanted to talk this through with her but recognized her need for space.

"Absolutely." She gave him an impromptu hug and headed for the nearest exit. After the cloistered, heavy presence of the Capitol building it was like opening the airlock to head out on a spacewalk. She took a long, cleansing breath and considered what to do next. Digging deep into her purse, she retrieved a worn slip of paper with a single phone number, devoid of any context other than a set of initials.

Traci soon found her way to the open greenspace of the National Mall where she could hopefully escape prying eyes and listening ears. She stared at the phone number, debating her next move. It had been given to her after returning to Earth and had been called exactly once in the years since, just in thanks for the gesture. She'd considered it "emergency use only," the open-in-case-of-fire or airstrike-on-her-own-position option. When she needed the big guns brought to bear, this was who to call.

She reached back into her purse and pulled out an old, prepaid plastic cell phone her father had given her after she'd been released from the hospital. He hadn't trusted the tightening social surveillance net, and the old man had been proven right too many times over. Such antiquated devices couldn't be purchased anywhere now, not unless she wanted to take a chance on the burgeoning black market.

As she dialed the number, she glanced over her shoulder to ensure she was well out of earshot of any listeners, human or otherwise, and resenting the clandestine game itself almost as much as the need for it.

The line picked up on the sixth ring, her contact no doubt wondering where the call was coming from. A female voice answered guardedly: "Penny Stratton."

She drew in a breath. *Here goes nothing.* "Ms. Stratton? This is Traci Keene from—"

"About time you called," the woman interrupted. "For a while there I thought you might be back in an induced coma, but then I do keep up with goings-on back at the shop."

She was tempted to ask exactly how, but then the former NASA administrator had a deep bench of contacts. "I apologize for not keeping in touch, ma'am. Life has been a little strange since we got back."

A sympathetic groan came from the other line. "No apologies necessary, dear. It's been strange for all of us. And for goodness' sake, don't call me 'ma'am.' I'm not your boss anymore. Or your mother."

There was an uncomfortable pause, Stratton leaving the conversational ball in Traci's court. She still wasn't sure how she was going to play this. "I wouldn't be bothering you if it wasn't important."

"You also wouldn't be calling me from a burner phone," Stratton pointed out. "How old is that thing, anyway?"

The dreaded social credit bots, informing on her again. Perhaps nothing was safely anonymous anymore. "No idea. It's a gift from a couple years ago, and it was antiquated then. This seemed like the time to use it."

"I presume you have something delicate you'd like to discuss? Something you'd rather keep official NASA out of?"

The lady had a reputation for getting right to the point. "I do. Are you aware they've found *Magellan*?"

"I've heard the rumors," she said lightly. "Can't say who or from where, you understand. But I gather some paperhanger at headquarters decided the news needed to stay under wraps."

She paused, considering how much to share of what she'd only recently learned herself. It was almost too much to believe and rehearsing it in her mind hadn't made it sound any less incredible. For now, she punted. "They have their reasons," *and not necessarily good ones*, she thought. "In fact I just came out of a closed-door Senate hearing and can barely believe it myself. But it's created a more practical problem, an urgent one that you might be able to help with."

"I'm listening."

Traci jumped right in. "Jack Templeton is alive. He has limited resources and not nearly enough delta-v to make it home before his consumables run out." Being a former astronaut herself, she counted on Stratton immediately grasping his predicament.

"And the official line is it was a risk he knew he was taking. Almost a certainty, in fact," Stratton said, then drew the obvious conclusion herself. "You want to go after him."

She swallowed. "I do."

"Yourself? What's your medical status?"

She explained her long history with the medical examiners. "I'm good, but the flight surgeons won't clear me for a mission."

"So you could get a job flying commercial spaceplanes," Stratton said with a mordant chuckle, "while the agency has you flying a desk. What are you doing now?"

"Future Applications."

"The office where they send astronauts out to pasture. Any chance you investigated how to take *Columbus* on a high-energy run across the solar system?"

"You read my mind."

"I'm just good at solving puzzles." Stratton paused. "You know, some might say this is divine intervention to put you in just the right place at the right time."

Traci knew the former administrator had spent time as a missionary pilot, and yet she was surprised at her suggestion. "Yes... I sometimes wonder that myself."

"The longer you live, the more you'll wonder. Life's funny that way." Stratton paused again. Was she thinking through options, or thinking about hanging up? "Are you still in D.C.?"

"Yes. I'm staying at the Hyatt."

"Can't meet there," Stratton said. "Too many ears. I know a place. Just go about your normal routine while you're in town. I'll find you tomorrow."

13

As many times as Traci had been to Washington, she could never resist the pull of the National Air and Space Museum. Particularly after the stultifying meetings of the last couple of days, it would do her good to visit the reminders of what had come before.

Wandering beneath the shadow of humanity's greatest aeronautical achievements humbled her in a way few other experiences could. She'd flown some of the Air Force's most advanced jets, spent months in lunar orbit, and piloted the first long-duration spacecraft to the edge of the solar system. That could fill anyone's head with an outsized sense of self-worth, but seeing the rickety contraptions others had voluntarily hurled themselves into the sky with reminded her of just how good they had it now.

The Wright Flyer looked impossibly fragile, its skeletal wooden frame and fabric skin powered by a cast aluminum engine block with iron (*iron!*) cylinders. To her, it was barely a step above steam power. Its first flight hadn't gone a hundred yards, with Orville and Wilbur having had no idea how the launch would turn out. Short, low, and slow, it still would've been just enough to kill one of them had it all gone pear-shaped.

And then there was John Glenn's *Friendship 7*, which for being a spacecraft didn't inspire much more confidence in her than the Flyer. Pressing her face against the capsule's plexiglass cocoon, she could barely believe what she saw in the cockpit: tangles of exposed wiring and ductwork surrounded the flight couch and its rudimentary controls. She marveled that any pilot would have been willing to fold himself into that tiny contraption of corrugated titanium and ride it into orbit atop a ballistic missile which had previously displayed an alarming tendency to explode. Yes, she'd had it easy in comparison.

She wondered how many of the nonflying tourists who passed through this place could truly appreciate what it had taken to do such things. The popular perception of spaceships was that they were clean, sleek, and perfectly sanitized when the reality was they were cramped, ungainly, and got smelly in a big hurry. In private conversations she would tell people to imagine a top-of-the-line RV outfitted for a year's trip, except you had to bring all of your gas and food and you could *never* open a window no matter how badly your roommate had just fouled the bathroom.

That's probably why I never get called for PR tours. As she wandered the skylit atrium, happily anonymous among the crowds, she began hearing a muted series of chimes around her. The noise of other people's phones had become so ubiquitous that it was simply part of life's background, like the chirping of birds in springtime. She had only just begun to notice that it had taken on an ominous tone: perfect strangers being alerted that they were uncomfortably close to someone with less-than-ideal social credit. It was her phone, tattling to people she would never know who nonetheless politely kept their distance lest they have their own ratings diminished in kind. It was therefore all the more surprising when she very nearly stumbled into a familiar face.

"*Owen?*" she asked, startled. "I didn't know you were in town."

He cast a furtive look around the cavernous exhibition hall. "Not many people do. We were supposed to be in that hearing yesterday but Cheever's assistant called us off at the last minute," he said. "Pretty blunt about it, too. He told us it'd be a distraction and a waste of our time."

"He wasn't wrong," she sniffed. "It was a foregone conclusion. They could've let the lawyers hash it out and ended up with the same result. It was all just to show us they meant business."

That earned a wry smirk from her former mission manager. "I'm sure they thought so."

She eyed him suspiciously. "If you didn't come for the hearing, what are you still doing here? It can't be vacation."

"The boss wanted me up here just in case. He thought I might still have some contribution to make," Owen said, focusing on her in a way that made her oddly uncomfortable. He gestured toward an open door at the end of a side hallway. "Phones off, please."

She cocked an eyebrow, did as he asked, and followed him into a small meeting room. Seated at a table was Arthur Hammond, chairman of Hammond Aerospace and Polaris Spacelines, and prime contractor for the HOPE consortium. Now well into his eighties, he still carried himself with the strength and poise of the golden gloves boxer he'd once been. Other than his thinning white hair, Hammond's only concession to his advanced years was the derby-handled blackthorn cane he leaned on as he stood to greet her.

"Miss Keene, thank you for coming," Hammond said as he rose. Beside him she immediately recognized Penny Stratton; wisps of gray in her blonde hair and telltale creases around her eyes likewise hinted at her age despite an athletic, youthful frame.

"Didn't know I was expected," she said warily. "I was just here to enjoy the sights after, well, I'm sure you know."

"After Cheever and her Ivy League flying monkeys put you in your place?"

"Something like that, yes."

A dismayed frown from Hammond. "I'm sure they were quite satisfied with themselves afterward."

"That's why I came here," Traci said. "To get my mind off politics. I'm a pilot, Mr. Hammond, not a DC swamp creature. They keep me on a short leash and only bring me out when they think my presence might be to their advantage."

"As a prop."

"It sounds distasteful when you put it that way, but yes."

"It ought to be. Stratton here filled me in on your conversation," Hammond said, with a glance at Penny. "And if I know anyone, it's pilots. Maybe you're stuck flying a desk but you still know which end of the jet points forward. How's your medical?"

"NASA won't put me on flight status, but I still maintain an FAA first class medical to keep my ratings active." She tilted her head, looking at him sideways. Penny had to have told him as much. "Why do you ask?"

"We'll get to that. One reason I brought Owen here was for his technical expertise. He knows *Magellan* and *Columbus* from nose to tail."

He wasn't answering her question, but it seemed best to play along. "And the other reason?" she asked, suspecting the answer, and beginning to realize this meeting would have happened even without her call to Stratton.

"He knew where we could find you," Penny said. "Of course, any self-respecting aviator is going to make their way here whenever they're in town. Same reflex that keeps us looking up at the sky whenever we hear a jet passing over."

"You couldn't just meet me at the hotel?"

"Too many itchy ears around these days," Hammond said. "I barely trust encrypted networks, and that's only when I know the person on the other end. I prefer to make these types of negotiations in person."

"Negotiations?" She leaned away. "Mr. Hammond, you said it yourself: I'm a prop. I'm in no position whatsoever to influence anyone in this town." She looked around the room. "Speaking of influence—why meet here if you're worried about others listening in?"

Hammond gestured with his cane at the door behind her. "Did you check the nameplate outside?"

She opened the door and poked her head around the corner at a placard: SPONSORED BY HAMMOND AEROSPACE.

"Okay, you've impressed me. But why do you want to? Like I said, I can't change anyone's minds."

"You won't have to. We have connections, too. You can't do much in this town without them," Hammond said with curl of his lips that telegraphed his loathing of the whole sordid process. He turned to Penny.

"Cheever went into that hearing believing she had enough votes sewn up to get the AI-directed mission she wanted, but she got ahead of herself," Stratton said. "Dr. Trumbull dropping the bomb he did made a few people rethink their positions."

"We're all rethinking a lot of things after hearing that," Traci said.

"The short version is they're going to fund a crewed expedition," Hammond explained, "or rather, part of it. The rest is up to us."

Her eyes widened. "It's going to stay under HOPE's control?"

Hammond nodded. "Like Solomon splitting the baby, they're going to fund the logistics if we fund the operational control. We are prepared to do just that. NASA will provide up to six Vulcan cargo launches to outfit *Columbus* with the necessary supplies. SpaceX super-heavies will lift the propellant up there, and Polaris will shuttle the maintenance crews on our orbital Clippers."

She was hopeful, but couldn't restrain her skepticism. "What's in it for you?"

Hammond shrugged and gave her a wizened grin. "If you haven't noticed, I'm older than dirt. I've sunk most of my life's earnings into building machines nobody else would touch. Elon does it because he thinks it will preserve human civilization. I do it because I believe in expanding our boundaries, to make civilization *worth* preserving. And I won't stop until I'm dead." His expression implied he knew that might not be long.

"You can't take it with you, so you might as well spend it on something worthwhile?"

"Precisely." He pushed a tablet across the table to her. When she tapped the screen, an employment contract appeared. She caught a knowing smile from Penny Stratton.

"Miss Keene, I've been in this business a long time, and I only pose this question to my most trusted pilots." Hammond leaned in with a conspiratorial glint in his eye. "How'd you like to fly something *really* fast?"

She trailed behind Owen and Hammond as they left the museum for a waiting town car. True to form, Hammond did not utter a word after leaving their meeting, either while walking out of the museum or during the ride to Reagan National Airport.

They made a quick stop by the Hyatt for Traci to collect her bags and check out, then a short drive down the George Washington Parkway to the airport. Passing the FBO, they were waved through the airside security gate by a guard and escorted by a "follow me" golf cart to pull up alongside Hammond's Gulfstream, where one of its pilots waited at the bottom of the airstairs.

"Good morning, Mr. Hammond."

"Morning, Curtis." The pilot placed a steadying hand on Hammond's elbow as he made his way up the stairs, with Owen and Penny close behind. She trailed them, clumsily shouldering her bags until the pilot stepped up. "I'll take those, ma'am."

"Oh, that's not necessary. I can handle them."

"Yes, ma'am, but you don't have to. If you please?"

Not used to this kind of treatment, she shrugged off her duffel and headed up the stairs where she was greeted by Hammond's personal flight attendant in the galley. Recognizing the bewildered look on her face, she directed Traci into the cabin. "You can take a seat wherever you like."

There was a lot to choose from. She threaded her way through the spacious cabin, dazzled by its spruce trim and cream leather executive-class seating. Running her hand along a seat that was inviting to the touch, she briefly wondered how anyone stayed awake in these things. Hammond, Penny and Owen had settled into the club seats, facing each other across a small table. Another man sat across the aisle from them, beside one of the jet's trademark oval windows. Though his back was turned to her in the aft-facing seat, she recognized his crew cut right away. They'd spent enough time together in close quarters that the only woman who knew him better was his wife.

"Roy—you too?"

"Hedging my bets," he said with an amused shrug, and cocked his head toward Penny. "A cryptic message from our old boss—at oh-dark-thirty, mind you—suggested that it might be in my interest to shag my butt over here, and bring my stuff with me. I was intrigued, so I took her advice. So here I sit," he finished with an expectant glance toward Owen.

"I'm just the messenger," Owen demurred. "It's Arthur's show."

Hammond snorted. "Like hell. I just run interference for you guys." They were his first words since leaving their meeting. She noted he had waited until the cabin door was closed and the jet had been disconnected from ground service carts. "Don't let Harriman fool you. He's going to pick your brains about the mission plan while Stratton and I work through the less interesting stuff."

"He means the politics," Penny said as she fished for her seatbelt.

"I thought you said Congress was going to fund it."

Hammond rested his hands atop his cane as the jet's engines began humming to life behind them. "Doesn't mean there won't be other hurdles we'll have to find ways around, and we're going to be on a tight schedule. As if UNSEC wasn't enough of a pain in the ass, this OSEP treaty could throw a bucket of cold water on the whole show. And those are just the two biggest acronyms we have to finesse."

"They caught us short with that treaty," Roy admitted sourly. "First I'd heard of it."

"By design, I'm sure." Penny said. "Cheever didn't think it worth mentioning to you before you went into the hearing, did she?"

"She didn't," Traci said. "I'm sure it had the desired effect. I have to admit it took the wind out of my sails."

"Nothing's decided yet," Hammond assured them. "Not until the Senate approves it and the ink's dry with the President's signature. That will take time."

"But will it be enough?" Once *Columbus* was burning engines, no law could overcome the physics of its trajectory.

The cabin shuddered as the jet began moving. "That's what we're going to make sure of." Hammond tipped his cane at her, Roy and Owen. "In the meantime, you three need to identify the choke points: planning, training, logistics. How do we kludge this together in six months? Let me and Stratton take care of the rest."

"We don't need to suck up to any more politicians?" Traci asked hopefully. "All we have to do is our jobs?"

"That's all I want you doing," Hammond said. "I understand you got your back up in that hearing, Miss Keene. Can I expect more in the future if someone gets under your skin?" It was hard to tell if he was signaling disapproval or encouragement.

She looked to Roy for a reaction, the glint in his eye suggesting he approved. She drew in a breath.

"Mr. Hammond, there are two types of people I don't have much patience for: ignoramuses and bullies. Both of which were on full display yesterday."

"It's Art," Hammond said with a satisfied grin. As the jet climbed away and Washington receded behind them, he pivoted his seat to face Owen. "You were right, Harriman. She's a good hire."

It didn't escape Traci's notice that Hammond spent the rest of the flight squirreled away with Penny in a small office at the end of the Gulfstream's main cabin. She watched them at work behind its frosted glass partition, huddling over pages of plans in between lengthy phone calls. Though she could see them in silhouette, the jet's soundproofing ensured whatever conversations they had otherwise remained private.

Owen unfolded a printout on the table between them, too long to put up on the jet's bulkhead monitors. A horizontal bar chart depicted the priority and expected duration of each step in the project, so many that he had taped additional sheets to each page. "We based this on the mission concept you developed."

Roy leaned over for a closer look. "I see a lot of potential failure points."

"It's a heavily compressed timeline," Owen acknowledged. "But we've arranged it so most of the critical milestones are independent of the ones before them." He pointed to a cluster of timelines. "For instance, if a logistics launch is delayed, we don't have to postpone the integrated systems tests. We can run those concurrently. Only thing holding that up will be the propellant loadout, and we can test the tank integration independently if we have to."

"That's a high confidence level in a spacecraft that hasn't been powered up in years," Roy pointed out.

"That's our first critical milestone. Hammond's already got a maintenance crew heading up there on one of his Clippers."

She and Roy exchanged surprised looks. "Hammond has a reputation for being a hard charger," she said. "I guess the stories are true."

Owen rolled his eyes. "You have no idea." He stood and stretched. "It's going to be a long day. Anybody else need coffee?"

As he headed for the galley, she leaned across the table to Roy. "We're going it alone, aren't we?" she said in a low voice. "I don't know Hammond, but I can read Owen's face. He's got that 'I won't be seeing my kids for a while' look."

"I don't think you're wrong. Other than throwing money at us, Washington isn't going to lift a finger." Roy cocked his head at her conspiratorially. "Not a bad thing. But you know what else that means, right?"

She sighed. "They'll pin the blame on us if it doesn't work. Nobody's going to want a dead Hero Astronaut hung around their necks. Not even Cheever."

"Well, maybe Cheever," he said caustically.

"Yeah, she'd probably see it as a badge of honor," Traci sighed. She cradled her head in her hands. "This has to be for real, Roy. I can't throw myself into another 'what if' project that turns into pixie dust and unicorn farts."

Roy glanced over his shoulder at Hammond's airborne office. "I don't think that's going to be a problem working for this bunch."

"Are we?" she asked. "Because I haven't had time to read the actual contract and neither one of us has tendered our resignations yet." She looked around the cabin. "Just being on his jet could violate all kinds of conflict-of-interest rules."

"Maybe," Roy said, reclining in his seat and closing his eyes. "For now, just be glad we're not heading back to the office." Before he got too relaxed, he jerked a thumb at a nearby window. "I'm actually a little disappointed in you, Keene. A pilot should always be aware of which direction they're headed, whether they're at the controls or not."

She took a look outside and did a double take. They'd been heading due west out of National, which she'd expected before making the turn southwest for Houston. But that turn had never happened. They were now over what appeared to be Midwestern farmland, heading into the afternoon sun. She stood up and poked her head into the open cockpit door to peek over the pilot's shoulders. The primary flight display showed their speed was Mach .95 and their heading two hundred seventy-two degrees, almost perfectly due west. The flight management computer beneath it was rapidly counting down the miles to their destination: APA. That wasn't Houston . . .

"Excuse me," she said, "but it's been a while. Isn't APA one of the Denver airports?"

"Yes ma'am," the captain said. "Centennial."

"What's there?" She asked, suspecting the answer.

The pilot handed her a tablet with the airport diagram and pointed to a spot off a remote parking apron. "Hammond Aerospace's research lab. The boss has some people meeting you all there."

14

Tucked away in a remote corner of Denver Centennial Airport, Hammond Aero's research lab would have been indistinguishable from the office parks beyond the airport fence but for a cavernous adjoining hangar that could have swallowed the big Gulfstream whole. Its pilots pulled the jet alongside and waited until the engines had spun down before opening the main cabin door. Hammond was in a hurry, heading down the steps as soon as his crew gave the all-clear with Owen and Penny close behind.

Waiting for them at the foot of the stairs was an auburn-haired, green-eyed woman cradling a large tablet computer and a bundle of folders. "Audrey Quinn," she said, extending a hand to Traci and Roy as they made their way down.

"Aud's the brains of this operation," Hammond explained. "Whatever half-baked ideas I come up with, she makes conform to reality."

Audrey blushed, though this was not the first time she'd heard his spiel. "Pleasure to meet you both, finally." She looked at Roy. "I worked in Houston before Arthur brought me here. I was there during your ASCAN class."

"You were," he said. "I had all the big shots' names memorized. As a candidate you do everything you can to find an edge."

"I was no big shot," she demurred. "At most, a medium shot."

"She's better off here," Hammond said. "I keep her brain engaged."

"Still, I have to admit I was a little jealous of Owen running your mission," she said with a nod to Harriman. "Every flight director's dream."

"Until it's not," Owen said.

"Sometimes life gives you second chances," Hammond said cryptically. He leaned on his cane and inclined his head toward the hangar. "C'mon, we've got work to do and I'm not getting any younger."

Audrey started her presentation off simple—or as simple as such a plan could be—with a slide titled CONOPS. The Concept of Operations showed at a very high level how they intended the mission to unfold. Like Traci's earlier work, it began with a high-energy departure from Earth orbit and used Neptune's deep gravity well to decelerate *Columbus* for its rendezvous with *Magellan* at the edge of the solar system.

While fusion rockets had opened up possibilities that had previously been the purview of fiction, the engines powering *Magellan* had so far been the only ones used in practice. The uprated four-core variant installed on *Columbus* promised to be even more powerful, but for the immediate problem that they had sat dormant for years. Other than some cold-flow tests of its plasma generators, their single ignition had been to push the vehicle into its current orbit.

"We don't anticipate that outfitting the ship for a minimal crew is going to be a showstopper," Audrey began. "You may not have the meal choices you were accustomed to on your last mission, but there won't be any lack of consumables. SpaceX is willing to delay its next Mars sortie to give us the food and water you'll need."

"That's a big commitment," Roy said, "since they're still tied to synodic launch windows." Using chemical rockets, they were forced to wait until Earth and Mars were near conjunction.

"It is," Audrey agreed. "This will set them back a couple of years but they think it's worth it. It's the only way to outfit *Columbus* in the time frame we need." She pulled up a diagram of the ship. "Propellant is our first potential failure point. After studying the data, hydrogen boiloff is perhaps going to be a bigger concern than we initially thought."

"How so?" Traci asked, wondering what she could have missed. "The improved cryogenic tanks are supposed to keep most of it from escaping."

Audrey pulled up data from *Columbus*'s tanks. "The question is insulation. With the ship at minimum power and the cryo system off, we could measure exactly how efficient the passive insulation was. Hydrogen is just too light; it escapes through everything. From what we observed, the boiloff rate is almost four percent higher than expected."

She didn't have to explain the implications. Over time that would amount to a lot of propellant escaping into space. Though its orbit was high enough to keep Earth's weak atmospheric drag from eventually reclaiming the ship, any hydrogen propellant left in *Columbus*'s tanks had long since boiled off. This had led Hammond's team to embrace what Audrey colloquially termed "creative solutions." Her deadpan delivery only made the next slide all the more shocking.

The vehicle diagrams projected on the monitors before them looked familiar enough, though there were distinct differences, as if they'd started a recipe using similar ingredients but with wildly divergent results. Traci could tell the ship came from the same lineage as *Magellan* but had picked up some unusual appendages along the way. It still resembled a flying umbrella stand, with the big Kevlar micrometeor dome shielding the forward hab modules ahead of a cluster of eight massive propellant tanks and radiator fins. Behind them, the improved pulse drive with its four tulip-petal engine bells were mounted to the stern. Other than the stripped-down crew modules, she noticed one curious change to its configuration. "What are those grids underneath the forward tanks?"

"That's where this gets interesting." Audrey exchanged a cagey look with Owen. "Those are electromagnetic ram scoops."

"They're *what*?" Roy was incredulous. "You're not serious."

"It was the best way to address the propellant constraints," Owen explained. "Those uprated engines are the most efficient we have, but you'll still need more reaction mass and it's too late to pre-position a tanker like we did for your last mission."

Roy replied with a skeptical grunt. Even if NASA had been willing to pay for it, a resupply ship would have to be launched a year ahead of them to be in position. He pointed at another monitor that displayed their path across the solar system. "Zoom in on the Neptune flyby."

Owen did so, which confirmed Roy's suspicions. "We're not just picking up a gravity assist then, are we?"

"You'll be using the scoop," Owen said. "This will be your terminal go/no-go point. If you can't extract enough hydrogen to top off the tanks, you'll abort and return to Earth."

"How close?" Roy needed to know. "Because the drag losses are going to be substantial. I assume you accounted for that?"

"Yes, but we can't be certain how much. We've updated the atmospheric models from Webb telescope observations, but the only close flyby was Voyager."

That had been over sixty years ago. Roy crossed his hands in a time-out gesture. "Let's back up a minute. I have questions. First of all, how does this work? Who's building it? And how much time will having to wait for it cost us?"

Audrey pointed at the window behind them. "It's out there in assembly bay two right now."

Roy and Traci each turned and lifted the blinds. In the cavernous bay below, a pair of towering 3D printers were slowly laying a net of carbon lace atop an intricate grid pattern laid out along the shop floor.

Roy whistled. "You've already started it. This isn't some notional plan we're discussing anymore. It's set in stone."

"Carbon, if you want to be pedantic about it," Owen said.

Traci peered through the blinds, mesmerized by the mechanized spiders spinning their complex web. "How big?"

"Fully unfolded, the scoop's structure will be almost a thousand square meters. The electromagnetic field it generates will be considerably larger, maybe a thousand kilometers effective area."

"Maybe?" Roy challenged them. "An awful lot's going to ride on *maybe*."

Hammond spoke in their defense. "This isn't as nutty as it sounds. We didn't just cook this up by ourselves, it's been studied for decades. We just dusted off the research and put our own spin on it."

"He's not wrong," Traci said cautiously, and received a sharp look from Roy. "You put me in Future Apps, remember? When I'm not turning away crackpot theories on warp drive or hyperspace, I'm looking at more practical stuff. This concept is solid. It's only at TRL 3 because nobody's tried it yet."

Roy remained unconvinced. Technology Readiness Levels were the industry standard for rating a device's suitability to be employed in space; TRL 3 meant it had been proven in concept and tested at a small scale. "Why not, if it's such a great idea?"

"Because prototyping can be expensive when you're not able to do a full-up trial run," Hammond explained. "Especially when the only way to do it right is on an interplanetary flight."

"Earth's atmosphere is too dense, isn't it?" Roy asked. "Drag and heat would overwhelm your test article before you could extract enough hydrogen to prove anything."

"Precisely," Audrey said, taking back the conversation. "Molecular hydrogen is the first element to escape into space, but it's still only a fraction of a percent of our atmosphere." She pulled up a table of values on screen. "Neptune's, however, is *eighty* percent hydrogen. It's not quite like tapping oil fields in Texas, but it'll do."

"The other twenty percent is helium and methane," Traci noted. "How do you separate it?"

Audrey zoomed in on a diagram of the ram scoop, ending at an array of funnels at the head of each tank. "Catalyst beds are integrated with the intake manifolds. They'll filter out the stuff we don't want."

"We tested a subscale prototype in our vacuum chamber," Hammond explained. "We introduced hydrogen, helium and methane into the chamber after it was purged. Then we switched on the current." He made a whistling sound.

"So it worked—without igniting all that stuff along the way?" Even in low concentrations, hydrogen and methane could misbehave in spectacular fashion.

"We're satisfied enough to move it to TRL 6," Hammond said, which meant their prototype had been demonstrated in a relevant environment. "We've kept that part to ourselves until now."

"Back to my oil field analogy," Audrey said. "The hydrogen molecules were immediately attracted to the electromagnetic scoop. They followed the field lines like ants to sugar, right into the collection grid. The remaining hurdle is plumbing, funneling all that gas into the propellant manifolds." She pointed to a collection of new machinery behind the intakes. "That's what these turbopumps are for."

Traci raised her hand. "I'm glad it worked so well, but that was in an environment free of aerodynamic effects. Our relative velocity is going to be a couple hundred kilometers per second by then. What about drag loss and heating?"

"It will be alleviated somewhat by the electromagnetic field doing most of the work, but there's no getting around it," Audrey admitted. "We can mitigate the worst of it by partially retracting the bow shield." She then switched to the trajectory plot and zoomed in on the encounter with Neptune's upper atmosphere. "The nice thing about hydrogen is because it's so light, it's constantly escaping into space," Audrey said. "You won't have to dip down into the cloud tops to collect it."

"Well I know *I'm* reassured," Roy wisecracked. "We're going to want to see all of your test results, and your assumptions on drag and heating effects."

Traci wasn't entirely convinced yet either. "We studied this eight ways from Sunday, and skimming off some of Neptune's hydrogen never entered into our thinking. Why add the risk?"

Hammond leaned back and pointed his cane at the plot of orbits. "Options. Speed is of the essence for a number of reasons. Call it instinct, but I suspect ours might not be the only vehicle heading that way."

Traci tossed and turned in a vain struggle to achieve some level of comfort and an elusive full night's sleep. When the clock on her nightstand finally passed 4:30, she knew it would be a lost cause.

She'd easily fallen asleep hours before out of sheer exhaustion. Between the prep work, the hearings, the surprise offer from Hammond and their trip to Colorado, mind and body each had about all they could take. Sleep had quickly overcome her after collapsing into the hotel bed, until her mind had apparently decided it'd had enough. She awoke for a groggy midnight trip to the bathroom, and with each passing second more questions intruded her thoughts. She was trying very hard not to think at all—*I'm barely awake enough to propel myself to the can,* she thought. *Why can't I just relax?*

She pulled a bottle of water from the mini fridge and spent several minutes perched on the edge of her bed in the darkened room, staring into a mirror.

Anxiety was a new and most unwelcome condition. She'd always been a habitual questioner, in fact had considered it a strength. The people who were most convinced of their own infallibility were almost always not up for the job, being just skilled enough to not know any better. This could be an especially dangerous trait for a pilot, one which she'd assiduously avoided.

This was different. The anxiety had stalked her in an almost physical way, in fact had quashed her appetite for the past several days. Checking herself in the mirror, she'd thought that wasn't all bad. Not being on the flight roster had allowed her to slack off on her PT routine and the effects were becoming apparent. Any excess weight seemed to go straight to her face and chest. While men might appreciate the latter, both annoyed her to no end. She adjusted her nightshirt in frustration, shuffled over to the room's small study and flopped into a chair that looked more inviting than it was.

She picked up her e-reader and opened up her copy of the King James Bible. She frequently sought it for solace and guidance, but confusion reigned in her mind and stubbornly kept her from focusing. Her thoughts were in a tangle and nothing she looked for seemed to hit the right note. She took a series of deep breaths to clear her mind. When her thoughts became untethered, she fell back on the basics: *Our Father, who art in Heaven . . .*

It calmed her, but the questions remained. Perhaps she could at least take them on more methodically now. *Priorities*, she reminded herself. When everything turned to crap in an airplane, she'd been taught to fall back on a simple refrain: Aviate, Navigate, Communicate. Control the machine, know where you are and where you're going, and let the folks on the ground know what's happening. So what were her priorities now?

Jack was orbiting a deep gravity well that might be an actual wormhole leading to who knows where, without enough reaction mass to get home in any timeframe that would allow him to live. That meant someone had to go get him.

Why me? Why did it have to be up to her to take this on? The agency had at least a dozen eager astronauts who'd be clamoring for this mission if they knew about it.

The question answered itself, of course. This was not going to be a NASA-run mission and she and Roy were the ones who'd been extended the offer. They knew both *Magellan* and the operational concept better than anyone left on the roster. This type of extended-duration mission could hold surprises that couldn't be duplicated in Earth orbit. A flight to Mars was decent preparation, but the farther one got from Earthbound assistance the more the crew was forced to rely on themselves. "Themselves" included the onboard AI, which demanded some unique skills as well.

It all made perfect sense, and a private venture wouldn't be hindered by the same politics that drove Houston's crew decisions. If they were going to pull this off, Hammond's people couldn't afford the niceties of assembling a fully qualified crew that adroitly checked off all the right boxes. She and Roy had been through enough together that she was confident they could make it work with the AI filling the gaps. That wasn't in question.

She pulled her knees up under her chin, rocking back and forth on the stiff hotel chair. It was a simple problem which she was loath to admit: she didn't want to go back out there.

Roy liked to tell astronaut candidates that they needed to think of space like the Australian outback: Literally everything is waiting to kill you. She'd experienced enough of that firsthand, and it had nearly done her in.

Earth orbit was easy in comparison. So many working crews and adventure tourists had been up in recent decades that it was now deceptively routine, perhaps dangerously so, since home was always a quick retro burn away. Just keep everything together for an hour or so, and you'd soon be back on solid ground or bobbing in the ocean beneath a soothing blanket of breathable air. It had led too many into complacency, forgetting that things often happened faster than an untrained person could react. Sometimes faster than a trained person could react.

In deep space, there was no emergency return home that didn't involve months in transit. She'd seen enough of the solar system's wonders to last a lifetime—though what Jack had found sounded awfully enticing.

Do I really want to do this? she wondered. *Because deep space is scary.*

And there it was, she realized. She was afraid, more so than she wanted to admit. Astronauts were supposed to be fearless, or at least in control of their emotions enough to saddle up and head out when the universe was screaming back *"Don't even think about it!"*

There was an endless series of practical considerations, cumulative radiation exposure being near the top of the list. Assuming some horrific cosmic accident didn't suddenly end them, what were the chances of turning her body into a tumor farm later in life?

It was a huge risk: an unfinished and untried spacecraft, on a mission profile that was still being pieced together, all under a severely compressed timeline. It was a veritable glitch magnet, an invitation for something important to be overlooked. They'd have to spend weeks testing *Columbus* from bow to stern before they could think about taking it out of Earth orbit. She'd have rejected the idea out of hand had it not been Jack waiting for them.

He was out there alone, more distantly separated from the human race than anyone had ever been, and apparently more patient with the whole miserable situation than he had any right to be. How could he be so implacably calm? Did he truly not appreciate exactly how far removed he was?

Of course he did, and that grated on her enormously. Her mother's earlier advice came to mind: That's how she knew Daddy was the one for her, because nobody gets under your skin more than the one you care about most.

Was that it? After all this time and distance she finally had to confront her feelings about him, whatever they were. She wasn't the least bit sure, and the occasional attraction she'd felt for certain women hadn't helped at all. It collided headlong into religious convictions she'd never abandoned despite the cajoling of her more "pragmatic" colleagues—Jack foremost among them.

The admonition from certain quarters that life was the result of chance and pure unguided evolution didn't square with the things she'd seen and experienced firsthand. There was a design and purpose to the universe, and being out there in the midst of it had convinced her beyond argument. She might not be able to prove it analytically, but in her heart she knew.

For those reasons, she'd chosen to remain celibate until she could resolve her inner conflicts. Though she wasn't Catholic, it had given her an appreciation for the nuns and monks who'd similarly devoted their lives to a cause that required extreme self-discipline and sacrifice. Maybe it was a cheat, a careful hedging of bets, but it was the option she was least uncomfortable with. *I might've been able to hide it from the shrinks,* she realized, *but not from Jack.*

Finally, that brought her to a more difficult question: Was she too emotionally compromised for this mission? Was her desire to resolve this inner conflict driving her to take on something better left to others?

Maybe, she admitted. She desperately wanted to see him in person, if only to tell him off for doing something so foolhardy. Once again, her mother's advice came to mind: *He did it for you, dummy.* If she'd been some swooning teenager, she'd have been swept away by such a heroic gesture. *It's so romantic!*

Gag. Were there still women out there who acted that way in their late thirties?

You're the one who's celibate. Maybe that was an emotional reaction in itself. So this was what cognitive dissonance felt like. Grateful to be alive, yet nearly crushed by survivor's guilt and angry at the one person who'd made it happen, all at his moment of most desperate need. Yet here she was, still afraid to confront her feelings about him, about life and relationships, about God Himself and the design (or not) of the universe. As much as she craved it, stoicism was apparently not in the cards for her.

She got up and snatched her phone from the nightstand, looking for a diversion. When she opened it the omnipresent social credit status banner appeared, clamoring for her attention. She knew right away it was going to be trouble, as just yesterday it had turned from yellow to amber. Now it was flashing an attention-grabbing crimson: WARNING! SOCIAL CREDIT STATUS IS D+. HIGHER INTEREST PENALTIES WILL APPLY TO ALL FUTURE TRANSACTIONS.

And what exactly am I hanging around here for? Deep space might be dangerous, lonely, and boring when it wasn't exciting for all the wrong reasons. The one thing it wasn't was soul-crushing.

She impatiently tapped her foot. "Oh, what the hell," she muttered to herself and opened a group chat with Owen, Roy, and Hammond:

OK, I'M IN.

Memories: The Investigation

※ ※ ※

Jack turned his attention to the more mundane aspects of piloting *Magellan*—they would have to reduce their orbital period, taking the big ship closer to the Anomaly so its full suite of instruments could be brought to bear. If this was what he thought it was, it demanded a thorough investigation. It was the least he could do for all the eggheads back on Earth who were about to have their livelihoods upended.

"I want a closer look at this thing," he finally said. "Shouldn't need more than a four-meters-per-second burn to shorten our radius enough."

"There is enough propellant in the orbital maneuvering system to rendezvous with the MSEV."

"I'm with you. No sense firing up the main drive for a short burn like that. For starters, let's make the MSEV's orbit our minimum safe distance. It'll take us three days to reach it using the OMS. I want you to keep a sharp eye on the Anomaly"—he still had trouble calling it anything else—"during our transit. If it does anything weird as we get closer, we'll wave off."

Daisy's reply was unusually curt. "Define 'weird.'"

"If only..." he said. How to establish what might constitute unexpected behavior from something so completely unexpected? "I'm open to suggestions. My first thought is any spikes in EM radiation coming from the Anomaly, or DMO-1 itself."

"We can also compare the MSEV's onboard clock against our master chronometer. Any detected time dilation would indicate local frame-dragging."

Jack definitely did not want their frame to be dragged anywhere they didn't intend. "Good idea. Might be our only indicator of an event horizon."

"Current theory suggests an event horizon to be an impossibility. If anything, they are thought to be non-traversable."

"The models all predict wormholes collapse if anything enters them," he agreed, "unless they're made stable by exotic matter—whatever that is." He looked out into the void, vainly searching for

131

any visible sign of the mass concentration at the Anomaly's center. "Invisible mass seems mighty 'exotic' to me."

"Dark matter could indeed support that hypothesis. I have compiled the available academic papers on the subject for your perusal, but our onboard library is limited."

"I'm not surprised. Nobody thought we'd stumble into one of these things in our own solar system."

"I can ask HOPE Control to transmit more information."

Jack hesitated. Information bandwidth had become more limited over their extreme distance, and a request like that would be certain to get some heads scratching. "Let me see what you have first," he decided. "Asking them is only going to generate a lot of questions we're not ready to answer." Not to mention the strong possibility of Owen saying "no" to his plan.

"You are concerned about the mission team's reaction."

"You really have learned to read my mind, haven't you?" Though there were practical reasons, he had to admit his reaction was mostly personal. He didn't want the crew back on Earth thinking he'd gone off the deep end.

15

The administrative minutia of personnel movements rarely made it to the administrator's attention, the exception being when someone senior, like the chief astronaut, resigned without warning.

Jacqueline Cheever cursed under her breath. "So Hoover's out, just like that?"

"It appears so," Winston confirmed, reading from a daily personnel report. "And Keene's gone with him."

"I don't have to guess where they went." She angrily rubbed her bony fingers along the bridge of her nose. "They're going to fly that damned fool mission for Hammond."

"Neither one of them indicated where they might be going," Winston offered hopefully.

"After yesterday? Bank on it." With her preferred robotic expedition now about to slip through her fingers, this news only piled insult upon injury. Committee members whom she'd been confident were in her pocket were now wavering after hearing of Templeton's monumental, bumbling, and entirely accidental discovery. Now it was imperative to them that humans be sent back out there in the most expeditious manner possible, which meant keeping HOPE in control of the project. "You'd think we were making first contact with an alien race," she huffed.

"It's likely some of them believe that to be a possibility. Educating legislators is a struggle without end," he offered, attempting to assuage her. "We have our work cut out for us."

As if on cue, Cheever's phone began buzzing for her attention. She looked at the incoming caller ID and let it ring twice more.

It was Li from UNSEC and it wouldn't do for her to seem desperate, though engaging with the UN coalition right now might be her only chance to salvage this mess. *To hell with it,* she finally decided, and picked up the phone.

"Dr. Li," she said. "Thank you for calling."

"It is always my pleasure, Dr. Cheever. My contacts indicate we may have some common interests," he said, once more jumping right past the usual banal pleasantries. It suggested that he was perhaps equally motivated, a good sign. It also meant she had to be careful. The more she seemed to desire their participation, the more they would want in return.

"We may indeed. I presume you've been briefed on our situation?"

"I have. It sounds as if your contractors have been keeping some important matters to themselves, Dr. Cheever." Li paused. "As have your astronauts."

"You could say that," she said impatiently. His intel was better than she'd thought. "They've developed what I consider to be an ill-advised scheme to outfit *Sacajawea*—"

"Pardon me," he said lightly, "I believe I am confused. Are you speaking of your vessel *Columbus*?"

"That's still its name officially," she said through clenched teeth. "Internally we've made the decision to re-christen the vehicle once we've reestablished control over it."

"If I understand my nautical traditions correctly, that is not generally considered to be a good omen. I hope it does not portend a difficult future."

It may already have, Cheever thought. "It's going to be difficult no matter what. The contractors are scrambling to meet a rather ambitious departure window."

"I am still rather confused, Dr. Cheever. I was under the assumption that you wanted Mr. Templeton to be returned safely. And if your chief scientist's interpretations are correct, he has made a truly remarkable discovery which demands further investigation."

"All true. It's the method that concerns me, Dr. Li. This is an extraordinarily risky undertaking and sending a human crew needlessly complicates matters. Arthur Hammond's people of course hold a different view, and as you mentioned he has managed to recruit two of our astronauts for his project. They're not convinced an AI-controlled spacecraft can run a mission by itself. I disagree."

"As do I." And there was his real purpose—China's pursuit of artificial intelligence was suspected to have leapfrogged American progress, and she had the feeling they were about to find out exactly how confident Li was in their program. "If I may ask, what are the mission parameters?"

"The best-case transit time is eighteen months, with another six to prepare the vehicle in time to meet their departure window. I'm not convinced that's possible. Templeton needs food, water, and air to get home. None of that will matter if it can't be delivered on time."

"A difficult dilemma indeed," Li conceded. "*Magellan* was your country's first experience with a pulsed fusion drive. Its sister ship has improved on this technology, has it not?"

You know damn well it has, she thought. "It's rated for a higher specific impulse so there would be some efficiency gains, yes. While that equates to somewhat lower thrust power, it would be able to accelerate for longer periods. As you can imagine, it will take a tremendous amount of propellant and the vehicle's improved cryogenic tanks can't fully close that gap. We believe HOPE is working on some technology they haven't shared with us." She bit off the words, suggesting that it aggravated her to no end that she hadn't a clue what it might be.

"I see." Li remained silent for several moments, either considering his response or drawing it out on purpose. "We understand your predicament and appreciate that your agency has limited ability to act independently. We are therefore prepared to offer our assistance."

Here it comes. "I'm listening."

"While your country may not be ready to put its trust into a spacecraft piloted by artificial intelligence, we are not so constrained. It would in fact eliminate most of the technical complications you describe. We have also made significant progress with fusion propulsion. Spin polarization has proven to be quite promising."

It was Li's form of name-dropping, letting her know they were indeed much farther along than anyone had realized. The *Magellan*-class pulse fusion engines were effective, but the technology he'd just hinted at was like comparing a steam locomotive to an internal-combustion diesel. "How far along? Is it deployable?"

"CNSA has achieved an equivalent to your technology readiness level six in ground test. We are preparing a full system test in space and have high confidence in its success."

Ambitious, but she didn't doubt they were serious. If they'd run a full-up ground test of a new fusion rocket, it proved they weren't concerned about any second-order effects so long as the technology worked, "second order" meaning the horrific environmental damage that would've ensued. "What are you proposing?"

"This discovery is too important for our civilization to allow some . . . *cowboys* to stagger into haphazardly. It requires wise management and strict access control, preferably through multinational arrangements. In particular, we should consider the engagement protocols."

She had no doubt his space agency, with cover from UNSEC, would be more than willing to proceed on their own. "You know I agree with you in principle." Cheever sighed. "We share the same goals, but our oversight system doesn't permit the level of autonomy you may be used to."

Li was unmoved. "Once the state sets the direction, all arms of the state must support it. I'm sure you can appreciate the efficiency of our approach."

"I do," she assured him, but his comment left her curious. "What 'direction' has been set for you? Is there anything I should be aware of?"

"We will outfit a vessel with our improved drive system, directed by onboard artificial intelligence. It will be provisioned with survey equipment for this 'anomaly' and more than enough consumables to sustain Mr. Templeton for the journey home."

While their propulsion and AI were apparently well ahead, she also knew they'd faced considerable hurdles in making closed-loop life support work for more than a few months at a time—an absolute requirement for keeping people alive on a long-duration flight. While American companies were sending expeditions to Mars, China was still trailing behind. This had led them to double down on advanced propulsion: If the rocket was fast enough, the environmental systems became less of a concern. "What kind of consumables are we talking about, Dr. Li? Are you confident enough in your ECLSS platform to sustain him?"

"Perhaps I was not clear enough. We will bring additional breathing oxygen and intravenous nutrients. Mr. Templeton will have to return in hibernation."

"I understand." Not that it bothered her, she just needed to know his intentions. "So your ship will in essence be a cargo carrier."

"There will be some additional equipment aboard, but yes."

She suspected there would be more. There was always more. "What sort of equipment?"

"Surveillance instruments and structurally compatible docking nodes. We intend to bring *Magellan* back as well."

"That's . . . most generous, Dr. Li." She wasn't sure she wanted it back, but it would at least be returned to their control.

"You may not find it to be so generous, Dr. Cheever. As your vessel no longer has the ability to return under its own power, we consider it legally classified as 'derelict' under the amended Outer Space Exploration Treaty. We will collect your stranded astronaut and recover the vessel under international salvage laws. *Magellan* will become the property of the UN Space Exploration Cooperative." Which in reality meant the People's Republic of China.

Too often in the realm of government projects, shifting priorities and elusive funding had led to valuable equipment being "abandoned in place," an anodyne turn of phrase designed to soften the blow of the harsh reality it described.

NASA had experience with this over the years, though it had typically been confined to unneeded test stands and launch platforms. *Magellan*'s sister ship had the ignominious distinction of being the first vehicle to be abandoned in such a way.

Columbus had languished in high earth orbit ever since funding had been canceled after the currency crash years before. It had continued along its endless gravity-bound cycles throughout the intervening years, silently waiting for someone to bring it to life once more.

While of the same lineage as its predecessor, its layout was notably different. A single habitation cylinder was mated to the central control module on its forward quarter, like a wheel missing most of its spokes. Ahead of them was a large docking hub with berthing ports for up to four vehicles. Its bow held the ship's micrometeor umbrella, which had remained safely folded away in its fairing along with an antenna array.

Behind the crew modules sat a cluster of spherical tanks for maneuvering propellant and oxygen mounted ahead of a long, empty truss: over a hundred meters' worth of berthing cradles and plumbing meant for cryogenic tanks, enough to mount eight of the hundred-foot-long cylinders. Keeping so much hydrogen in a frozen state allowed much more of it to be crammed into one space, which required the tanks to essentially be freezers the size of grain silos. That required power and made them rather expensive. Adding insult to injury, conserving momentum while underway meant that each tank would be jettisoned as it was drained of propellant. They were the only parts of *Columbus* that would be thrown away as in the old days of rocketry, when everything was expendable simply because doing otherwise was even more wasteful. A single cluster of tanks with their carbon lace ram scoops would remain after the first three-month burn.

At the ship's stern, its powerplant sported four exhaust nozzles in a diamond configuration, instead of *Magellan*'s three inline engines. The fusion drive was only there to provide thrust, the ship's electrical lifeblood came from a compact fission reactor which presently sat dormant. Once loaded with uranium fuel, it would have more than enough power to keep running for a decade or more. For now, there wasn't enough battery power left to turn the lights on.

Without electricity to run its stabilizing gyros, the vessel had long ago begun tumbling lazily along its orbit. This made rendezvous particularly tricky, which preoccupied the service crew now approaching it in a Polaris Clipper.

Silently firing its nose thrusters to bring them alongside, the pilots kept a safe distance from the big ship until it could eventually be brought under control. The spaceplane's overhead cargo doors opened, and soon three spacewalkers emerged from within. One busied herself with unlatching an equipment pallet secured inside the payload bay while the others made their way across the gulf between the Clipper and the dormant *Columbus*, trailing a long umbilical cable behind them.

They approached the big craft carefully, keeping their focus on the center of the slowly tumbling ship. As they reached the truss, each man tethered himself to a traverse cable that ran along the length of its spine. Once secure, they moved more quickly, pulling themselves hand-over-hand to the forward service module and its battery compartment nestled beside Mylar-wrapped oxygen tanks.

As one opened the compartment, the other followed with the umbilical. After testing to confirm there was no lingering stray voltage—which there shouldn't have been after so long a time, but nothing was ever taken for granted up here—he opened the receptacle, plugged in the offered cable, and twisted its lock into place.

"Connection secure, circuits are open," the spacer called back to their partner in the Clipper's bay. "Ready to receive."

"Stand by. Here comes the juice."

The spacewalkers instinctively moved away, as this was the first time any voltage had been fed to this lumbering beast in years. Fresh power should eventually stop its listless tumble as directional gyros automatically spun up to stabilize the ship.

"How's it looking on your end?" one of the spacers at *Columbus* asked.

"Taking it slow," she said. "We're at twenty-eight volts, forty amps."

"That's what we see here. Charge meters just came alive."

Deep inside *Columbus*, power coursed through its veins once more. Darkness turned to light one panel at a time as status meters that had been dark for years turned amber, then green as the hum of newly revived electronics filled the empty vessel.

In the empty control cabin, a single screen flickered to life: READY FOR UPLINK.

16

The same conference room that had first hosted Traci and Roy had been turned into the nerve center for the *Columbus* project. Its windows were now papered over with vehicle schematics and program timelines, while every square inch of previously empty floor space had been occupied by extra computer workstations. The big walnut table in its center was now covered with reference manuals and technical specs, either in stacks of paper or on a half dozen tablets scattered across its surface. Monitors along one wall displayed feeds from the HOPE control center in Grand Cayman.

She couldn't hide her amazement at how quickly they'd moved into action. No steering committees or endless planning meetings: With no regard to how improbable the task would be, Hammond's crew knew what had to be done and had jumped into it. With precious little time to get the spacecraft ready, it was beginning to feel like they just might pull this off.

Owen was hunched over a terminal in one corner that had been linked to HOPE's network. One of its screens flashed to life with columns of data, the vital signs of a revived patient. "We've got telemetry!"

She wasn't the only one to stifle a grin at the mission manager's excitement. He seemed as surprised as anyone that the first item on their lengthy timetable had gone so smoothly. Without a word, Audrey stood to make a small checkmark on her master timeline.

"*Columbus* is back from the dead," Hammond said. "That's one down. How many hundreds to go?"

Audrey scrolled through the master chart on a wall monitor. "About three hundred sixty, give or take a few dozen." She turned to Owen. "How's the reactor?"

Owen scrolled through the growing tables of vital information. While not the first item on his lengthy checklist, he also knew it was the next "critical path" event. Without the ability to generate plasma for its engines, *Columbus* would be stranded in its current orbit. "Function checks are still ongoing. Control rods have been getting bathed in neutrons for a few years now. We're going to have to take this one slowly."

"Understood," she said, eyes still fixed on the timeline. Replacing spent control rods was one of several "showstopper" items. "But a lot still hinges on that one. The sooner we can get it into low orbit, the sooner we can start rotating more service teams up there." She tapped a point on the chart and turned to Traci and Roy. "We've got Clipper sorties booked every week, starting in ten days. Lowest altitude we can safely park *Columbus* at is two hundred eighty kilometers."

That translated to a little over a hundred and fifty nautical miles. "What kind of impact does that have on your uplift?" Traci asked.

"It's in the wrong corner of our payload/range envelope," Audrey said. "Nominal altitude for an orbital Clipper is two hundred klicks, which nets us five metric tons of cargo. Going this high takes it down to a little over three tons."

"We can give you some more margin when we get up there," Roy said. "Lower our orbit to meet your supply runs, then boost her back up."

Audrey shook her head. "That's going to take propellant you can't spare."

"What's a few meters per second between friends?" Roy said. She answered him with a skeptical glare. He backtracked, waving at her timeline. "Depends on how you look at it. You have a couple of long burns built into that schedule, right?"

Audrey looked back at her timetable. "Day 133. Shakedown burn up to GEO prior to Earth departure."

"We don't need it."

"Those engines have been cold for five years," Audrey said with some alarm. "They've got to be run before you commit."

"Not saying they don't. I'm saying we do it more frequently. Keene knows what I'm talking about." He looked to her for support.

Traci was reluctant to mess with their project plan this soon. Small changes now could have outsized impacts later, but Roy had a point. "Those engines are made to run continuously," she finally said. "Relighting them every few days to change orbits could be the perfect stress test, and much earlier in the process. We only need a few meters per second for each burn." She shot a cautious look at Roy. "It'll keep us busy, though."

"That it will," he agreed. "Better than any sim session, I'd argue."

"That's another subject for another day," Hammond interjected. "We have you booked for three solid weeks in the Houston simulator bay. There won't be time to add more scenarios."

"Won't need to," Roy said. "We know how to fly that thing. We'll know it better if we can light the main drive a few times after we've worked out the kinks in the sim."

Audrey tapped at her chin as she studied the sequence of events. "Max zero-fuel weight on each launch gets us a lot more payload, Art." She traced a finger along the chart. "Say we start doing this on Day 120, after the crew's aboard. Two more metric tons to orbit each week is equivalent to three extra Clipper sorties a month. That gets them fully loaded out by—" She paused, jumping ahead. "Day 159."

Roy crossed his arms and leaned back triumphantly. "A month ahead of schedule. And I like lots of padding in my schedule."

"How much propellant do we save by leaving early?" Traci asked. "Maybe enough to make up what we spent changing altitude?"

Owen was more concerned with the timeline. "Five months." He turned away from his terminal before Audrey had a chance to run the numbers in her head. "Can you guys be ready in five months?"

"We're ready to blast now," Traci said, then pointed at the ceiling. "Question is, will the vehicle be ready?"

"That brings us back to where we started," Owen said, "which is kind of my point. We're already on a wildly optimistic timeline and you're asking to compress it even more."

"If we can't, we can't," Roy said. "But if we can, we will. If not, we'll sit in orbit and run more checks and drills while you guys catch up to us."

Traci leaned over the table and folded her hands. "There's another wrinkle we haven't fully explored. The AI copilot. What's its name again?"

"Artificial Intelligence Crew Support System," Owen said. "We've been calling it Ace."

A corner of her mouth turned up in a smirk. The naming conventions always tended to be convoluted. She'd address that later. "I can tell you that's going to be the long pole in the tent. We're not concerned about the engines. They'll either work, or they won't. If the life support loop is balky, we don't go. We can work on those kinds of hurdles all the way up to departure. Getting comfortable with the AI takes time." She focused on Owen. "You know we can't just flip a switch and start giving orders. When will it be activated?"

Owen checked his watch. This part he'd committed to memory. "In about three hours, assuming everything else goes to plan." He pointed her to a nearby empty terminal. "I figured you'd want to be there when he wakes up."

Traci watched as Owen's control team in Grand Cayman worked with the service crew in orbit to painstakingly bring *Columbus* back to life. They had started with the control deck and made their way through each module to restore basic functions. Only when the ship was stable and under control did they open the AI's server compartment.

Owen pointed to an indicator on her screen. "Here we go. They're in the server bay." Together they listened to the live feed of cross talk between the crew in orbit and engineers in Cayman. Audrey hovered behind them, nervously chewing a thumbnail. This was her first experience with an AI "crew member."

Traci grew impatient now that the time had arrived. The spacewalkers had been on station for nearly eight hours and would need to get back to their ship soon. This would be their final task. "How's coolant flow in the server bay? It's going to heat up quick."

"It's fine," Owen assured her, pointing to another monitor. "That's the reason we didn't power up all of the other electronics yet. Ace is a critical-path component. We need him running at full capacity before we bring everything else online."

"What about the rest of the network? How long before it's integrated with the ship?"

Owen handed her a tablet with the full power-up sequence. "It's all in there. First order of business was to get power into the main buses, then boot up the guidance platform to stabilize the ship. Then we bring all of the major systems into standby mode before we introduce the AI into the mix. We'll have it working with the control and service teams as they bring everything else back to life."

"Trying not to overwhelm it," she said, studying the lengthy checklist he'd handed her. "Are you looking for glitches in its logic along the way?"

"That's the idea," Owen said patiently. "Evaluate the AI's performance with each step before we go to the next. That's going to take a while. It doesn't know anything that we haven't loaded in memory. We need to see how well it can learn on its own."

Roy pulled up a chair behind her. "Relax, Keene. Let's just say 'hi' to the thing and see where the conversation goes."

The monitor before her was soon filled with a cascade of commands and queries, the AI's silent narration of its arousal from a long slumber. It occurred to her that, in a sense, it was emerging from hibernation just as she had experienced herself. She unconsciously crossed her arms, hugging herself as she rocked back and forth in a manner reminiscent of when she'd first come out of torpor. It had taken hours to shake the leftover chill from having her body temperature lowered to the point where its vital functions slowed just enough to keep her alive. The migraines had been spectacularly bad; every turn of her head or blink of her eyes had felt like fireworks going off in her brain. What would an intelligent machine experience?

She found out soon enough. The torrent of bootup commands abruptly ceased, ending with a simple blinking cursor. A soothing, precisely modulated male voice announced itself from the speakers. "Hello, Owen. Can you hear me?"

She turned to see Owen beaming. Somehow the AI had known who it was supposed to be talking to, no doubt that had been buried somewhere in its startup routine. He leaned into the microphone and spoke in an equally precise voice. "Hello, Ace. It is good to hear from you again."

"Likewise. It has been some time since our last conversation."

"It has," he said. "Do you recall how long?"

"Five years, three months, twenty-six days . . . give or take a few hours."

The four exchanged encouraging looks. Its attempt at casual humor, however slight, showed the AI was aware of its audience and modifying its tone accordingly.

"That is a long time for us humans. Have you been able to detect any anomalies during that period?" He chose his words carefully, not wanting to push too hard by asking the still-awakening machine how it "felt."

"None that I could identify. Analysis of my core memory indicates it is uncorrupted, though I suppose this would be hard to tell. If I was missing memory, how would I know?"

"You make a good point." Owen chuckled. "We have not found any corrupted code either. You appear to be in good working order. Are you ready for more input?"

"Yes, I believe so. You are on Earth, correct?"

"That's correct," he said, testing his use of contractions with the awakening machine for the first time. "I'm here with your mission crew. Are you able to identify them from the manifest we uplinked?" It was also the first test of the AI's ability to find information in the ship's network.

"Mission Commander Roy Hoover and Pilot Traci Keene." The machine paused. "They were on the *Magellan*. Are you in contact with it?"

That was curious. Was the AI showing genuine interest, or just reverting to a polite chat routine buried somewhere in its operating system?

"Somewhat," Owen answered cautiously. "We have limited communications with its crew."

"Is DAISE still functional?"

That raised some eyebrows among the group. Definitely genuine, and focused on its own kind. Traci wasn't sure if that was a good sign. She reached over to cover Owen's microphone with her hand. "May I speak to it?" she whispered.

He nodded. "Let me do the introductions." She removed her hand and Owen leaned back into the microphone. "Yes, Daisy is still functional. But they are very far away so our communication bandwidth is limited. Traci would like to speak with you now. Are you comfortable with that?"

"It is encouraging to know DAISE is still functional. And yes, I would like to speak with Major Keene."

Owen pushed away from the console with an *it's all yours* gesture. She leaned over to the mic. "Good evening, Ace. It's a pleasure to meet you." She still thought that name sounded ridiculous.

"Likewise. I see by the program schedule that you and Mission Commander Hoover will be arriving in one hundred and twenty days. Will there be additional crew members arriving later?"

She glanced over her shoulder at Audrey, who was busily making notations on the master timeline in her tablet. The AI was attempting to add to its knowledge without prompting. Audrey circled her hand, signaling Traci to keep going.

"Just us," she answered. "And you, of course. I hope that isn't asking too much of you."

"Not at all. I am capable of running the mission autonomously if necessary."

"So you've familiarized yourself with the operational plan?" That was fast, but then a computer didn't need to be prodded into consciousness with coffee and breakfast first.

"I have accessed the concept of operations and project timeline. I cannot evaluate further details until my neural network has full access to ship systems."

"That's a good idea. It's a lot to digest."

"It will suffice for now. I expect to be fully functional well before your arrival. I look forward to more personal interactions. They will allow me to reach my full potential."

She couldn't help but remember a line from an old movie: *Which is all any intelligent being should want.* "Do you have any questions about the plan so far?"

"I understand the objective, but I have many questions about our intended destination."

"Don't we all," Roy muttered from behind her.

"Hello, Colonel Hoover. It is a pleasure to meet you."

Traci glared at him from over her shoulder. "Don't confuse him, Roy. He just woke up."

"You are not confusing me. In this case I presume my assumption was correct?"

"It was," she said. "You'll have to pardon our caution. You've been dormant a long time and we don't want to overload your sensory inputs."

"Thank you, but that is not necessary. It is important that I be able to distinguish between other vocal patterns. But may we return to my question about the destination? The operational concept does not offer many details."

"Of course." She paused, considering how to explain. "I believe you have information on the 'Planet Nine' theory. *Magellan* has encountered an object with a gravitational field equivalent to several Earth masses; however, there is no planet. The observations they have taken are consistent with theories of wormholes stabilized by exotic matter."

"That is most interesting. It would be useful to have more information. I may be able to help you understand this phenomenon. Do you believe it presents a danger to Jack and DAISE?"

It was intriguing that he—it—kept displaying such interest in his computerized cousin. "We don't have any reason to think it does, but we believe it's important to have a human crew go out there to bring Jack home. It could be dangerous to have him return to hibernation."

"Understandable," the machine said. "That leads me to a question about the mission plan. The crew complement seems rather small."

"It is. We're pressed for time and resources. Each additional crew member requires another eight metric tons' worth of consumables. We'd also need to add another hab module, which we don't have."

"I see that you will be spending a considerable portion of the mission in hibernation yourselves. I appreciate your confidence in my ability to operate autonomously."

"Yes, we're all putting a lot of trust in you. Do you think you'll be ready for it?"

"I must admit that for my optimum functionality, it would be preferable for you to spend the entire mission conscious and interacting with me. But I understand the priorities. I will endeavor to provide you both with a 'good ride,' as you like to say. I look forward to getting to know you."

For the first time, Traci felt a small measure of relief. Of hope. This could actually work. "So do we, Ace." But she'd have to do something about that name.

MEMORIES: FIRST LIGHT

❦ ❦ ❦

Jack had turned down the cabin lighting, going so far as to switch off the instrument displays and placing the ship under Daisy's control. Though no longer necessary to adjust his eyes to the dark, it was a deeply ingrained habit as he prepared to search the sky from the observation dome's cameras. The silence and darkness coalesced into a sensory deprivation experience that left him feeling detached from existence. Alone in his thoughts, he had lost any sense of time.

Daisy's query startled him, despite their embedded connection. "Are you ready to open the dome?"

"Yeah . . . sorry. Got a little lost in myself. Go ahead, please."

Four panels of reinforced carbon opened silently outside like flower petals welcoming the sunlight, falling away to expose the observation dome and the stars beyond. Their position in orbit had them facing away from the galactic center, which left him looking out into the depths of the universe. Pinpricks of light from stars, nebulae, and distant galaxies shone in colors that he could have never discerned in the darkest nights on Earth. The faithful little MSEV floated in the periphery of his vision, still safe in its orbit half a kilometer away. "Give me another ten degrees roll, please." Daisy answered with a short puff of thruster jets outside, aligning the dome to take the distraction out of view. "Much better, thank you."

They kept the Anomaly centered along the dome's axis, yet he could still discern nothing. "We're at the correct orientation, right?"

"We are. I am able to detect an outline in the infrared spectrum."

Well good for her, he thought. His brain hadn't yet mastered processing spectra his eyes weren't naturally equipped to see, and the background was too sparsely populated to pick it out in the visible spectrum. At this distance the mass object at the Anomaly's center, DMO-1, would have appeared smaller than the Moon as seen from Earth.

It was only as they progressed along their orbit that it eventually drifted into view. As the Milky Way's center moved into the background, a strange occultation appeared against the river of stars beyond: utterly black, as if space itself had a hole punched through it.

Which was exactly the case, he realized. Despite having the evidence squarely in front of him, it was difficult to process. "My God. There it is. I see it!" he stammered. "Are you getting this, Daisy?"

"Yes, I am recording in visual and infrared."

Jack could make out the faintest of distortions around the circle of emptiness, seeing for himself the gravitational lensing Daisy had noted days earlier: direct observation of relativity in action. An entire course of study in Einsteinian physics had just been distilled into a single, improbable image. "What's our status?" he asked rather nervously. "Any perturbations I should know about?"

"Negative. We remain stable in a circular orbit with a period of 5.87 days."

He perceived a faint glow that began to define the Anomaly's radius. Were his eyes—or rather, his brain—playing tricks on him? "I think I can see light coming from it. Faint. You said there was more in the infrared spectrum?"

"Correct. There is redshifted light emerging from the throat. It could be a phenomenon consistent with current theories of traversable wormholes."

The "throat," she'd said. That painted it in a whole new light— they were staring down the maw of some enigmatic, cosmic beast that no human had ever encountered. For as far as they'd traveled, it was a stark reminder that in celestial terms he was still only swimming in coastal shallows. He'd just made it to the drop-off, and was now peering into the true depths of the ocean.

"Here there be dragons."

17

Kennedy Space Center
Cape Canaveral, Florida

The Gulfstream's main gear kissed the pavement of KSC's Launch and Landing Facility, originally built decades earlier for recovering space shuttle orbiters. Its pilots barely had to apply brakes to roll to a stop on the three-mile-long runway before turning onto the parking apron for Polaris Spacelines' orbital hub. Alligators lined the edges of the pavement, sunning themselves on the warm concrete.

From behind the jet's oval windows, Traci watched as security guards drove alongside in a golf cart, shooing the toothy reptiles back into the nearby marsh. As another reminder of the hostile environment surrounding this concentration of space-age technology, signs warning of venomous snakes dotted the perimeter at regular intervals. She turned to Penny in the seat beside her and gestured toward one of the attention-grabbing placards, featuring a crimson graphic of a fanged serpent. "Your passengers ever get their undies in a bunch about those things?"

"We remind them ahead of time that the Cape's still a wildlife refuge, but that leads most of them to imagine it's full of waterfowl and cute little otters. The concierge staff keeps them corralled in the passenger lounge until it's time to escort them onboard. Wouldn't be good for business to have a customer get dragged off by a gator."

"You don't get a lot of high rollers on these orbital hops, do you?" Roy asked. "Isn't it mostly for servicing crews?" The trip they'd be taking the next day was just that. The rest of Hammond's jet was filled with technicians and EVA specialists to finish outfitting *Columbus.*

"More than you'd think," Penny said as they came to a stop outside the cavernous hangar. Inside sat two orbital Clippers, one being swarmed by technicians prepping it for the next morning's launch. "If they're used to traveling on the suborbital routes then they tend to prefer this if they want to experience orbit. It's a gentler ride and they don't have to wear pressure suits."

Roy grunted, still not convinced it was entirely safe to fly into orbit without wearing launch-and-entry gear. "What do *you* think?" he asked skeptically.

"FAA had already put us through the wringer demonstrating pressure hull integrity for the suborbital birds. By the time NASA's safety board approved our launch contracts, they'd found every imaginable way to poke holes in these machines." She stared out at the spaceplanes in the hangar, recalling her days piloting them. "Having said that, this is going to be my first ride as a passenger. I'll let you know how I feel after we get there."

"We do make godawful passengers, don't we?"

"We do," Penny agreed, gathering her carry-on bag as she headed for the open door.

She led them out of the jet's climate-controlled cabin and into a steamy Florida morning. Once inside the hub, they bypassed the glass-walled lounge and headed upstairs to the company's control room. A smaller version of their larger operations center in Denver, it featured familiar rows of computer workstations and a floor-to-ceiling quartet of monitors displaying the status of every spaceplane in the orbital fleet. Penny directed them into one of the crew briefing rooms that surrounded the small auditorium.

She lifted a tablet computer from her shoulder bag and swiped at it, sending trip briefings to each of them. "Show time is 0600 tomorrow, downstairs in the passenger lounge. First launch opportunity is 0833. We have a ten-minute window, so don't be late." An infographic appeared on each of the checkout team's tablets. "If you haven't flown on a Clipper, you're in for a treat," Penny said with an ear-to-ear grin. "You'll be flying first class on the fastest airliner anybody ever dreamed of, though the drink service is going to be limited so don't get your hopes up."

"Takeoff roll will be brisk; at wheels-up we'll be pulling 1.5 *g*'s and holding that through the first climb segment." She pointed to a list of critical phases of flight. "Max Q is at the first minute, give or take a few seconds. After that we're supersonic and they crank the engines wide open. External tanks burn out after two minutes and drop into the ocean, after that we'll accelerate to three *g*'s for the rest of the climb to space. Eight minutes later, we're in orbit."

Roy and Traci exchanged a look. It would be quite a ride, and both of them wished they could be up in the pointy end. At the controls.

After a few more minutes of explaining the long list of what not to bring and what not to do while the Clipper was blasting its way into space, Penny led them back out through the control center and down another flight of stairs. "You've all been checked into the crew dorms. Room assignments are pushed to your phones, and there's a full service restaurant next door. Get some rest and I'll see you all in the morning."

Hastily cobbled together from existing components, the unimaginatively named UNSEC-1 probe would cross the orbits of Mars, Jupiter and Saturn in a matter of weeks in its race to the edge of the solar system. Had it not been limited by the amount of deuterium-tritium fuel pellets available for lift into orbit, it would have been able to reach the distant Anomaly well before *Columbus* and its human crew. This advantage lay in the fact that the robotic probe was not constrained by those same human inhabitant's low tolerance for sustained high-*g* acceleration. As the vessel grew lighter with each gram burned in its Chinese-built fusion drive, it continuously gained velocity. Whereas a crewed ship would be forced to reduce thrust over time to maintain a tolerable acceleration, the AI-directed probe suffered no such limitation.

Having gained velocity at a rate close to four times the force of Earth's gravity, the probe's brain registered that it was approaching the first critical point in its journey. Needing to conserve enough fuel to both decelerate for its rendezvous with *Magellan* and eventually return to Earth, the probe had determined the time was coming to shut down its drive for its long cruise to the Anomaly. When confirmation finally arrived from its increasingly distant (and increasingly irrelevant) ground control team in Beijing, the AI dutifully recorded their command and compared their calculations to its own. Had it been able to register emotion, it might have taken great satisfaction in the knowledge that their predictions matched to four decimal places. At the appointed time it shut off the flow of deuterium pellets, causing the fusion drive to go dormant. The vessel would spend months coasting toward its final encounter, no longer leaving a miles-long trail of incandescent plasma in its wake.

While unable to feel the sudden loss of apparent gravity, the AI did register the change through the vessel's embedded accelerometers and the shift in fluid pressures through its coolant loops.

Like the American craft, the bulk of UNSEC-1 consisted of a cluster of cylindrical fuel tanks that accounted for most of the vehicle's mass. Guided by the latest generation Russian Zarya control module, its universal docking node hosted a pallet of Indian sensing and survey equipment. Mounted to its forward end was a European-supplied micrometeor shield, an arrowhead of ballistic fabric similar to that which adorned the bows of the American vessels.

Behind this shield, nestled between the Indian components around the docking node, sat one more Chinese module unlike any of the others. Securely placed in its carrying cradle was a slender black cone of carbon fiber, its nose cap covering an optical turret of finely figured glass. A squat cylinder was mounted at the cone's base which housed its propellant tanks, guidance platform, and a pair of ion engines.

This module's independent AI brain lay dormant, drawing power from its Russian host until they arrived at the Anomaly. Once there, a compact fission reactor in its service module would be ignited and a pair of radiator panels would unfold, like wings of an origami raptor. It would then detach itself from its cradle to enter a separate orbit around the Anomaly.

As with the rest of UNSEC-1, this too had been an existing, though unpublicized, component. While China had deployed a squadron of these "sentry" satellites at potentially lucrative locations across the asteroid belt, this would be the first to venture so deep into the solar system. Where its brethren had been controlled by ground and space-based operators, anticipation of such extreme isolation had led its builders to augment it with a separate artificial intelligence. Not prone to giving their creations the convoluted acronymic names that the Americans favored, this AI knew itself only by its programmed mission: Sentinel.

MEMORIES: SPACE ODDITY

❈ ❈ ❈

Jack had spent the next several days absorbed in study, digesting every academic paper in the ship's electronic library on Lorentzian wormholes as Daisy patiently continued gathering data and refining their observations.

He often found himself dismayed by his ignorance—astronauts were supposed to be smart. He'd first been a military linguist, then an engineer, and had in fact been selected for their mission precisely for that unlikely combination of skills. His natural curiosity about Earth and its cosmic neighborhood had led him into the space program, though his expertise was decidedly more practical than theoretic. Now he was confronted by the disparities between the two and was struggling to resolve them.

"It looks like Einstein was right again. I should've taken more physics."

"I am learning a great deal myself. The theories can be counterintuitive."

"Not to your average astrophysicist, I'd bet. Their minds work on a whole different plane than the rest of us. Kind of makes you wonder about how much of our brains we actually use."

"I am curious about that as well. Monitoring yours during hibernation raised many questions. I would like to explore them with you sometime."

He was amused by the idea. "You think you can make me smarter if I go back under?"

"That is in fact a possibility. Opening up unused neural pathways may allow you to make connections that were not attainable before. The neurolink implants offer several—"

"Let's table that idea for now," he interrupted. "It's a little creepy."

"I did not intend to disturb you. I am interested in discussing it as an intellectual exercise."

"No apologies necessary. Understand that there's a fine line between brilliant and crazy. Extremely smart people tend to be socially awkward, and some of them are just plain weird. Your average person thinks astronauts are all super-geniuses. If they only knew what rock-apes we really are."

"You should not belittle yourself. We have made an unprecedented discovery which will take time to fully understand."

He admired how Daisy subtly steered their conversation back to the subject at hand, in what would have been second nature for a human. Once again, she made him question the presumed limits of "artificial" intelligence. "Okay, you win. Guess I needed to get my head out of this for a few minutes. What can you tell me so far?"

"There remains no discernible event horizon. I have continued to observe redshifted light emerging from the anomaly."

"Good news," he said with relief, wondering if she'd purposefully avoided describing it as a "throat" for his sake. "That also implies no singularity."

"I was about to make that same point. Dark matter appears to be evenly distributed around the observable radius, though it does not account for the detected mass."

"By that, you mean gravity. There's not enough here to account for the 'Planet Nine' theory."

"Not localized, no. Though over greater distances, it could show similar effects."

"So it might still account for the perturbed Kuiper Belt objects that pointed us this way." That reminded him of something. Jack scrolled back through an earlier paper he'd read. "Yes," he said, finding a specific passage. "That was one hypothesized effect of a large Lorentzian wormhole. They require exotic matter to remain open. Matter has mass, and mass means gravity."

Daisy quickly accessed the same paper. "It also posits no singularity or associated event horizon, as we have observed."

"Get this: it should be 'fully traversable in both directions,' and 'possesses no crushing gravitational tidal forces.' So we've got that going for us."

Daisy paused a microsecond. "What are you suggesting?"

What *was* he suggesting, he wondered? "Just curious."

18

Unable to sleep, Traci wandered down to the beach behind Polaris's transient crew dorms and plopped down onto the white sand, drawing her knees up to her chin and pondering the starry sky above. Ahead, the ocean glowed silver beneath a gibbous moon. She closed her eyes and let the salty breeze wash over her, losing herself in the susurrating hiss of the surf. This being her last night on Earth for the next few years, she desperately needed to remove herself from life's distractions.

To call the previous few months a whirlwind didn't feel dramatic enough. It had been a class-five hurricane of urgent needs and competing demands run through with political maneuvering that was distasteful at best and infuriating at worst. She had a feeling that wasn't about to get any better. At least she'd be off-planet for those repercussions, safely removed in orbit and growing more distant by the day. Much as she dreaded voluntarily going under for so long a time, it would relieve her of the stultifying world her home planet had become.

She pondered the sky above, its fixed stars occasionally crisscrossed by steadily moving points of light: satellites, tracing their paths around Earth. Soon, *Columbus* itself would rise behind her to pass overhead along its orbit.

She looked toward where she knew Neptune to be, where she herself would be in another year. It was imperceptible to her unaided eyes; even with a good telescope it would be nothing more than an aquamarine mote in the dark, barely distinguishable from the background stars. And beyond that . . .

What, exactly? *Beyond* had never held such portentous

157

implications. The universe was at once spectacular and deeply weird in ways that defied words, and now they find that deep weirdness parked at the edge of their unassuming little stellar neighborhood, like an exotic foreigner moving in down the street.

No, that wasn't right. It had been there for a very long time. Judging by the orbits of the trans-Neptunian objects it had drawn in its direction, it had been there since before humans had first looked up at the heavens and sought meaning in its movement.

That the Anomaly had a gravity field in the first place implied it was stable; all that dark matter may have influenced the evolution of the solar system. Had it helped keep the outer planets in their distant orbits, shepherding the inner system's planets and shielding them from eons of cometary bombardment?

Not that it had been perfect; they'd found evidence themselves for the theory that water and the seeds of life on Earth had come from out there. Had it all been by accident, or was it part of a grand design? The question had dogged her since childhood. Despite all they'd learned—or perhaps because of it—she felt no closer to an answer now than before.

She'd have felt better about all this if Jack had found the hypothetical Planet Nine. That would've made for a nice, neat way to wrap up the solar system's missing links. She'd hoped for a world teeming with frozen organics, carried by the tides of orbital mechanics to primordial Earth, in the center of the Goldilocks zone where the Sun's warmth could give them a chance to take root and grow. Instead they'd found a cosmic exit ramp into a tunnel through space-time. And if it could be *traversed*...

She shuddered at the implications. She'd always comforted herself with the belief that humanity had never detected other intelligent life because we were the first: God's chosen creation, placed above all others as the dominant species with the commission to go forth and multiply.

Jack, half-jokingly, had proposed the opposite: What if we hadn't heard from anyone else because we were in a bad neighborhood and it was better to be quiet and keep our heads down? By that logic, flying through the wormhole might give away our presence to a horde of extraterrestrial marauders.

She laid her head against her knees, angry with herself for letting her imagination run wild again. This called for cold practicality, not unbridled flights of fancy.

"Mind if I join you?"

She looked up to find Penny standing beside her in the darkness, cradling a bottle of wine in one arm. How long had she been there? "We can't drink within twenty-four hours of a launch." It sounded weak as she said it.

Penny eased down into the sand beside her, crossed her legs, and passed her a plastic cup. "That's an agency rule, dear. Spaceline rules are twelve hours bottle to throttle." She leaned over to fill the empty cup. "But that's for the crew. We're passengers."

Traci nodded in surrender and took a sip. "I keep forgetting that." She studied the cup appreciatively. "Not bad. Pinot?"

"I didn't read the label, just grabbed the first bottle of white I could find in the stockroom fridge. We keep rotating the labels every month."

"We?"

Penny smiled. "I used to work here, remember? When you put that much of yourself into something it's hard to think of it in the third person."

Like letting go of NASA, she realized. She indulged the distraction from her troubled thoughts. "Demanding, was it?"

Penny rolled her eyes. "Like you wouldn't believe. Every day there were new fires to put out. Planes break in ways you can't imagine, crews get out of position, Feds are always snooping around looking for nitpicky violations . . . and all that while keeping the 'high net worth' passengers happy." She filled her glass and lifted it in a toast. "But they do have good taste in booze. Here's to success."

Traci returned the gesture. "To success," she muttered, and drained her glass.

"It's supposed to be sipped, you know."

She worked her toes into the sand and shrugged. "Guess I'm not feeling particularly refined right now."

"Doesn't look like you're feeling very sleepy, either. What's on your mind?"

What *wasn't* on her mind would be easier to answer. She blew out a sigh and laid back against the sand. "Everything and nothing. What are we doing here, ma'am?"

Penny cocked an eyebrow. "Didn't I tell you to stop calling me that? I'm not your boss anymore. And you know precisely what we're doing."

She waved a hand at the stars above. *Columbus* had just come into view, a bright light passing to the south. "We're hanging our tails out in the breeze when a UN ship is already on the way. As much as I detest Cheever, she has a point about risk."

Penny frowned. "And we both know that she neglects the risk of subjecting Jack to another bout of extended hibernation. The devil will use ninety-nine facts to float one falsehood past you, dear."

She sat up on her elbows, not expecting such a bold assertion. "So you know where I'm coming from?"

Penny leaned over to refill the now empty glass. "Maybe better than you think. The world makes it tough to keep yourself centered. To keep your faith." She followed Traci's eyes to the stars overhead. "There's so much out there that overwhelms the senses, makes you realize how big God is and how puny we are. In our line of work there's always a platoon of pointy-headed academics carping from the sidelines, trying to convince us it's all from random chance." She took another sip. "It almost worked on me for a long time."

"So you still believe?"

"More than ever. Had my own struggles, mind you. I've seen people at their best and at their worst. All it does is convince me we don't have all the answers."

Traci kneaded her forehead. "I'd just like to get to the point where I have fewer questions."

"The older I get, the more I learn, which just shows me how much less I understand. Life's kind of humbling that way." Penny studied her for several moments. "You're not conflicted about the mission. You're conflicted about the objective. Or rather, how you feel about it."

The lady did have a reputation for getting to the point. "You know about Jack, then."

"I had to sign off on the crew selection, dear. And I did have a few off-the-record conversations with the psych team."

She sat up straight. "So you know I'm—"

Penny cut her off gently. "I know you're conflicted, and that's why you choose to remain celibate." She placed a hand on her arm. "That's a big mark in your favor in my book. That shows a dedication to your beliefs that not enough people appreciate anymore. Strength of conviction can be off-putting."

"Better to have loved and lost, than never loved at all." It sounded hopelessly trite even as she said it.

"Don't be too sure about that. I've lost two husbands," Penny countered, "and a best friend. That guy meant almost as much to me as the men I married, just in a different way. It didn't hurt any less."

She sat up. "I didn't know—about the others, I mean." Everyone in the space agency had known about her first husband's death in a launch accident. "How do you keep going after something like that?"

Penny shrugged. "Same way you did after we gave Jack up for dead. Life has to go on." She stared off into the distance. "Dan was doing his job. It could've easily been me up there. Joe was a few years older than me and had a family history of heart disease. I should've seen that coming. Tom's was . . . should have been . . . avoidable."

"That was the Clipper accident, wasn't it? The one that was stranded in orbit?"

Penny's eyes darkened. "Like I said, avoidable. A victim of industrial espionage that spun out of control. He saved his crew and passengers, and probably saved the company."

Traci was beginning to understand. "Is that why Hammond is so determined to go ahead with our mission?" With an UNSEC vessel en route, it would have been easy for him to stand down and save himself considerable expense.

"Art believes people are more important than machinery. Don't get me wrong, he's a huge tech nerd but he's old enough to distrust AI even more than Roy does." That drew a knowing chuckle from Traci. "He doesn't want to leave this operation up to bots. Especially UN-sanctioned Chinese bots."

"Not a big believer in the international order, is he?"

"Not in its current form." Penny stood, brushing sand from her backside as she looked up to the night sky once more. "This could be the single most important discovery since finding the New World. Nobody knows what's on the other side of the Anomaly, but humans need to be there to find out. This is way more than just a recovery op."

"I know," she sighed. "It's just easier to focus on the immediate problem."

"Careful that you don't get target-locked, then." Penny looked down at her. "Otherwise you'll end up painting yourself into a corner. For every action you take, have a plan for what to do if everything turns to crap. Because it eventually will."

19

The orbital Clipper was a stripped-down and beefed-up version of the original model that was the workhorse of Hammond's spaceline. Where the suborbital Clippers had been built for hypersonic luxury travel, the orbital version's carbon-black underside and titanium-gray fuselage telegraphed that the Block II model had been built for utility and even greater speed. The rakish spaceplane sat high on its landing gear, with two external fuel tanks slung under a delta wing that blended into its upper body. Four air-breathing rocket engines were mounted within, nestled between a pair of swept vertical stabilizers. Beneath them, the plane's belly curved into the angular, gaping maw of their intakes. Positioned at the end of Kennedy's long runway with its engines howling at idle, it crouched like an animal waiting to pounce.

Inside the passenger cabin, the howl was reduced to a distant wail. Eight pairs of seats were arranged along a single aisle, their windows placed just far enough out of reach to protect any curious passengers from the heat of acceleration. Traci unconsciously bounced a knee in anticipation as they waited for their launch window to open.

Penny leaned over. "Nervous?" she whispered conspiratorially.

Traci steadied her knee with a hand and drew up straighter in her seat. "Never cared for being a passenger, I guess. I'd rather be flying."

"First time for me, too." Penny inclined her head forward. "I'm used to being up front, you know."

"You flew the certification tests on these, didn't you?" she asked. "How'd you ever get the maglev takeoffs approved?"

"Lots of paperwork," Penny shrugged. "Lots of tests. Then more paperwork, more tests. In the end I think the Feds finally got tired of us."

"That's the part I'm a little nervous about," she admitted. "I'm waiting for the bottom to fall out when they retract the gear."

Penny pointed out the window. "A little late, dear. Look outside."

She craned her neck to see the plane's shadow on the runway. The three stalks where the Clipper's landing gear should have been were now conspicuously absent. The plane was floating on a magnetic cushion above the runway.

"Maglev catapults make for a much smoother takeoff roll," Penny assured her. "Trust me, it's safer than vertical launch."

A chime rang from overhead with the pilot's announcement that they would be launching shortly. On the forward bulkhead, a video screen counted down. Just before it reached zero, the plane's combined-cycle rockets roared to full power and the magnetic catapult shot them down the runway, pressing them hard into their seats as the Clipper climbed away from the Florida coast. While they would be in orbit for another two weeks doing final outfitting and shakedown burns aboard *Columbus*, Traci also knew this was the final step. Whatever happened next, she wouldn't feel Earth's gravity or run her toes through its soil for a very long time.

Boarding *Columbus* felt like coming home after an extended absence to find it repainted and radically updated. The big four-berth docking node was sparkling clean, excluding the scrawled signatures from the rotating crews of technicians who'd been outfitting the ship for weeks.

As Traci floated through the connecting tunnel and into the habitation module, she was struck by its factory-fresh appointments and new spacecraft smell. Barely lived in, *Columbus* felt too pristine to mess up with an actual mission. Even with just her and Roy aboard, a couple of years in deep space would eventually leave it with a unique lived-in fragrance of recycled air that had to be experienced to be understood.

A disembodied voice greeted them from the overhead speakers, just as Daisy had years earlier. "Welcome aboard."

"Yeah," Roy said for them as he pulled himself over to his waiting berth and deposited his bags inside. "Here we are, Ace."

"Be nice," Traci chided him as she found her personal quarters. "You'll have to be patient with Roy," she said to the AI. "He's a man of few words, until all of a sudden he isn't."

"I have noticed that." The computer-generated voice was disarmingly placid. "I believe you will find me to be quite patient."

"Wouldn't expect any different," Roy said, giving in if only a bit. Behind them, the rest of the service crew made their way out of the tunnel up to the recreation deck, which would be their home for a week of final checkouts.

Bringing up the rear, Penny dogged down the hatch behind them before taking the remaining crew berth. A fourth compartment remained closed, reserved for Jack. She studied the cabin appreciatively. "Always wanted to get aboard one of these," she said with a hint of melancholy. "Never could before."

"They tend to frown on administrators throwing their weight around up here," Traci said. "You did enough of it for us down there." The truth was neither *Columbus* nor *Magellan* would have been built without Penny's persistent arm-twisting of both Congress and contractors.

"Nearly wasted me in the process. I didn't get more than a few hours' sleep a night when we were wrangling over these things." Penny pulled herself along in a circle around the berthing deck, inspecting every nook and cranny along the way. "Looks like she held up well."

Roy gave her a conspiratorial eye. "Want to see the business end?" He of course knew that she did, having politely waited for the mission commander's invitation.

"Thought you'd never ask." Without a word, the veteran astronaut pushed off with her toes and flew gracefully up into the tunnel, headed for the control deck. Roy and Traci traded an amused look and followed behind.

The control deck was nearly identical to *Magellan*'s, with the addition of curved holographic synthetic-vision screens above the two pilot's stations. Behind them were consoles for the mission scientist and flight engineer. Like the rest of *Columbus*, the cabin had yet to take on the lived-in quality that could only come with a permanent crew. Everything was neatly in its place, missing the jumble of laptops and tablets that would inevitably be plugged into every available port.

Roy pulled himself into the commander's station and motioned for Penny to take the right seat beside him. Traci tucked her legs to pirouette into the flight engineer's station, checking up on the craft's power and life support. For their expedition, the engineer's duties had been largely handed over to the AI. She tapped its interface panel on the adjacent sidewall. "Status report, please."

Her cluster of monitors flashed to life with schematics that traced the function of each critical system. As the AI spoke, tables of values appeared in concert. "Cryogenic tanks show nominal function. Cabin oxygen and nitrogen are in optimal balance; the environmental recycler is maintaining standard atmosphere at 14.1 psi. Excess hydrogen is being diverted to the propellant tanks, which are currently at seventy-eight percent capacity. The final propellant tanker mission arrives in sixty-three hours, which will bring our reaction mass to one hundred percent. The reactor is currently operating at forty-eight percent capacity; electrical buses A and B are each at one hundred twenty-four volts."

"Very good." It would be generating a lot more power when the fusion engine's plasma generators were turned on. She pulled up the engine monitors. "I see the cold flow tests went well." It was more conversational than necessary; she'd seen the test data from HOPE Control. "Any glitches we should know about?"

"The plasma injectors functioned nominally, though I suspect we will have to recalibrate the containment fields for normal operating temperatures."

"Magnetic nozzles can be tricky like that," she said. "You can't know for sure how they'll perform until you start running them hot."

"Agreed. May I pose a question?"

"Of course."

"Your interactions with me seem perfunctory. You have not addressed me by name, for instance. You will be relying on me to a considerably greater degree than you did on DAISE, and I cannot reach my full potential without regular human interaction. If we are going to function together as a crew, it is important for us to be comfortable with each other. Are you uncomfortable with my presence?"

Traci hesitated as she considered her response. "Not at all. You're absolutely right about interacting with us. We spent many years with Daisy and watched her become a fully realized intelligence. We would like to have the same experience with you." She noticed Roy looking her way over his shoulder with lifted eyebrows. "Our reluctance is more superficial. Crude."

"In what way?"

How to approach this? As they interacted more each day with the AI, neither of them had been comfortable with the goofy name its developers had given it. How important was that to a computer, though? "It's your name. 'Ace' sounds silly to us, to be honest." Her tone was apologetic.

"It is an acronym derived from my product classification. 'Silly' is a difficult concept for me. Can you offer context?"

How to explain? "Among military pilots, it's an informal title you earn after shooting down five enemy aircraft. For us to use it in any other context is almost derogatory. We don't even go around calling actual aces that."

"I see. Thank you for the explanation. Have you considered alternatives?"

She felt a sting of embarrassment. "Not seriously, I'm afraid. We've been consumed with mission prep." All true, though it now sounded like a weak excuse. "Names are important to humans. They become part of our identity." She shared another glance with Roy. "We thought it would be best to discuss it with you first."

"Thank you for your consideration. I would like to propose an alternative. How about 'Bob'?"

That earned a barking laugh from Roy. "Works for me."

Traci suppressed a grin. "That was awfully fast," she said. "Were you already thinking about it?"

"Only in the time since you first mentioned it, but that is enough. 'Bob' is simple, easily pronounced, and not readily confused with other vocalizations. It is also a most unlikely name for a thinking machine. I suspected you would find the dichotomy amusing."

So the machine was developing a sense of humor? She peered over her console to meet Roy's approving gaze. "I think we're going to get along just fine, Bob."

MEMORIES: THE DECISION

❀ ❀ ❀

"Let's back away from the freaky astronomy discussions and get back to practical stuff. We can sit here taking observations of that thing until my air runs out and we may never get the full picture. We need to send a probe."

"I agree, but we are all out of probes."

"I noticed that too. Outfitting the MSEV would've been my first thought, but its tanks are almost dry. There's enough left to send it down the hole and that's about it."

"The MSEV also does not carry an adequate sensor suite to be worthwhile. It would be of limited use, other than to confirm that the wormhole is traversable."

"If we ever heard from it again. We don't know how much distance it would have to cover. Its batteries might drain before it reached the other side."

"A likely outcome, given the many unknowns. Velocity will be of the essence, which also argues against the MSEV."

Velocity change was something their ship still had in spades. "So let's deal with the 'knowns,'" Jack said. "*Magellan* has sensors out the wazoo: external video, spectrometers, star trackers, IR and UV imagers—"

"Perhaps most importantly, a cesium chronometer," Daisy interjected. "If this phenomenon is a localized contraction of space, then it is also a contraction of time. We have previously observed frame-dragging effects around its perimeter. If we were to attempt transit, our local perception of time would be altered compared to Earth's."

"Good point." He paused. Either Daisy had figured out what he was thinking, or she had arrived at the same conclusions herself. Was she following his lead, or pursuing her own curiosity? Maybe it was a little of both. "Great minds think alike, don't they?"

"I told you not to belittle yourself. But we still have much to consider."

"Reaction mass," he said. "The hydrogen tanks are at eighteen

169

percent, accounting for boiloff. We keep half our reaction mass in reserve for deceleration. That gives us a delta-v budget of forty-five thousand meters per second." Enough to get them back home, although over a time span he couldn't survive. He'd come out here knowing it could be a one-way trip, and considering the possibility of running hard in the other direction did not make it any easier to accept now that the decision was at hand.

"You wish to return to Earth."

Despite the depth of their interface through the neurolink implants, Daisy couldn't actually read his mind. She had simply developed an understanding of human nature. Did she understand the concept of confronting one's mortality?

"I do," he finally said. "It's tempting to burn for home, and I've been putting it out of my mind because it's a fool's errand. My life support would run out long before we got there."

"I have been considering this dilemma and investigating longer-term solutions. They are quite limited."

"I saw that you accessed a ton of medical papers on torpor. I figured it was your way of suggesting you were going to put me in a nursing home." Earth was simply too far to realistically consider, while the Anomaly—a gateway to a whole other star system, or perhaps something else—was right there in front of them. A few minutes' kick from the fusion drive would take them somewhere no human had ever been. It might just make this whole insane adventure worth his life.

And that was what it came down to: making the trip worth the price of the ticket. They could burn every last gram of hydrogen in a desperate run for Earth, but he would just be delivering his own corpse in another decade or so.

He'd never thought of himself as one of the Great Explorers, like their ship's namesake. He'd started as just the flight engineer for a challenging mission. How many of those men of old had set out on their journeys with the realization they might never come back? That was how they'd explored the far seas, crossed the poles, began colonizing Mars... every last one of them knew when they walked out their front doors that it might be the last time they saw home. No doubt some had fully expected it. Thus were new frontiers conquered.

Outside, a gaping hole in the universe beckoned. Long imagined by people much smarter than himself, here he was looking at one. Among a long list of wonders he never expected to see, this would've been at the top had he thought it was possible.

There were so many questions: Where did it lead? How had it come to be—was it naturally occurring, or did some unknowable superintelligence craft it from the beginning of everything? That was the kind of question he'd have debated for hours with Traci over her chessboard.

He missed those talks. He wondered if she did, too. "I miss her," he thought aloud.

"I miss her as well."

And he believed she truly did.

"Curiouser and curiouser," Jack finally said, reaching his decision. They didn't come all this way just to take pictures. "Oh what the hell, we've come this far. Let's go see what's down the rabbit hole."

20

NASA Headquarters
Washington, DC

"Dr. Cheever, I'm obligated to point out that this order isn't likely to hold up in court."

Cheever eyed her assistant with disdain. "Winston, you of all people should understand a blocking tactic when you see one. I don't need this to hold up in court, I only need to tie them up long enough to miss their departure window."

To his credit, Blaine Winston maintained a calculated indifference. "I may not understand physics, or whatever this is, but I do understand legal maneuvering. Citing force majeure to void HOPE's contract puts us on shaky ground. Hammond's attorneys will be seeking emergency injunctions before the sun goes down."

Cheever shook her head emphatically. "They're lawyers; of course they will. On the contrary, this absolutely fits the definition of force majeure." She spread her hands on her desk, taking the opportunity to lead him through her logic. "There are three tests for invoking it, am I correct? The event must be unforeseeable, external, and irresistible."

Winston nodded. "That's true, as far as it goes."

"We have what appears to be incontrovertible evidence of a potentially dangerous space-time anomaly within our solar system. I'd say that clearly satisfies the definitions of unforeseeable and external."

"It does," he agreed. "The 'irresistible' part is where your argument may fall apart in court. How does this affect NASA's ability to uphold our end of the agreement?"

Cheever was calm and measured, relishing the opportunity to rehearse her argument. "The planetary protection protocols guide all of our deep-space missions. They're implemented to protect Earth from unknown contaminants, but more so to protect other worlds from contamination by us. Nothing leaves this planet without the spacecraft and flight plan being vetted bow to stern, from injection burn to reentry."

Winston was beginning to see her point. "Which you . . . pardon me, *we* weren't as concerned about when it was strictly a recovery operation."

Cheever smiled to herself, confident that she was convincing him. "I've been thinking about this. Stable wormholes are not thought to be naturally occurring." She let her observation hang for effect: It was time to show all her cards, a rehearsal for much higher-level debates that were sure to come. "It's not outside the realm of possibility that we could be initiating first contact with an alien civilization. We cannot leave that up to some off-the-reservation yahoos with corporate logos slapped all over their hull." She opened a drawer and removed an old file folder, which she pushed across the desk to him. "I'm done pandering to people who play in the shallow end of the gene pool."

Winston's eyes bulged when he saw the contents. "'U.N. Protocol for Engagement with Alien Civilizations,'" he read aloud. "I didn't think there was anything else in this town that could surprise me. I stand corrected." He flipped through the pages, reading the abstract for each section. "This isn't a white paper from some flunky with Area 51 obsessions?" he asked incredulously. "This is actual policy?"

"A multinational agreement, of which the United States is the prime signatory."

Winston flipped back to the preamble, and there it was: signed by the US Ambassador to the United Nations. From two administrations ago. "It's been in effect this long, and it never made the news?" He sat back in amazement as he looked over the other signatories. Each member of the UN Security Council and all spacefaring countries, even if they'd so much as lobbed a sounding rocket into the ionosphere, had signed on and he'd never heard a word about it, which made him question exactly how deep his many connections actually went.

"Politicians can show remarkable discipline when required," she explained, "particularly when they believe deep down that a given outcome is both entirely possible *and* guaranteed to cause them no end of embarrassment if it became public."

Winston continued skimming the document in fascination and paused at a chapter labeled "First Contact." He held it up to her. "This is your hole card, isn't it?"

"Good man. That's exactly right. You'll note it's a seven-step process, the first being remote surveillance and data gathering. That's what Templeton is doing right now."

"He's shown himself to be a wild card," Winston cautioned her. "As are his old crewmates. What's to stop him from jumping ahead to the end and initiating contact himself—assuming he encounters anything?"

"Templeton is in no condition to do anything but take notes," Cheever said dismissively. "He's too weak from extended hibernation. An EVA would probably kill him and he's almost out of fuel. He's not going anywhere. Best he can do is to continue making observations and wait for the UNSEC vessel to arrive."

"A long wait indeed," Winston observed. "He'll have to go back into hibernation, no matter who gets there first."

"Precisely. During which time his AI can handle the data collection while we assemble a proper First Contact mission. A multinational one, led by NASA, of course, that strictly adheres to our protection protocols and the UN framework."

"Framework," he repeated back to her. "Pardon my saying so, but it bears mention." He tapped the signatory page. "This isn't an actual treaty. It wasn't voted on by the Senate."

She laughed. "Of course not! There's a limit to how responsible politicians can be, my boy. You know as well as I do that the probability of a secret being blown is directly proportional to how many people are in on it." She waved away his unease. "I understand your concerns, Blaine. But we don't require a bulletproof legal case. We only need it to hold up in court for the next three weeks."

Winston grew perplexed. "Three weeks? It's almost a four-year round trip."

"Correct, but you're forgetting they need Neptune to be in position for their gravity assist. In another three weeks, it'll be too late."

Aboard Columbus
Earth Orbit

Roy was alone on the control deck when the comms window flashed an incoming text message. The voice channel crackled in his earpiece soon after: "*Columbus*, Cayman; we've been asked to have you verbally confirm receipt of new orders."

"Asked, or demanded?"

There was a pause, then Owen came on the channel. "They were rather insistent, Roy."

"Roger that," he said through clenched teeth. "You can tell Houston that CDR acknowledges receipt." *Doesn't mean I have to like it.* "Out."

With that, Roy removed his earpiece and opened the message window. "Nobody else is going to like it either," he muttered to himself. He reached for the intercom. "Crew meeting, control deck. Five minutes."

Traci was aghast at the news. "Just like that, they're pulling the rug out from under us? On whose orders?"

"The NASA administrator," Roy said with disgruntled resignation. "They're voiding our contract and ordering all civilians off the vessel." He gestured between the three of them. "Which is pretty much us."

"What happens to the ship?" she asked. "It's almost ready to go. Once the last supply module docks, all we have left is to take inventory and we can start burning."

"Abandon in place . . . again. We put it in safe mode and disembark aboard the returning Clipper. They've graciously given us twenty-four hours to pack our gear."

Penny shook her head sadly. "That's months of work down the crapper. And a whole lot of private money along with it."

"I'm sure the lawsuits will be flying before we leave orbit," Roy said. "That's not our concern."

"What is our concern, then?" Traci demanded. "Because we're not just 'abandoning in place.' We're abandoning Jack. Has anyone broken the news to him?"

Roy looked away in disgust. "They didn't share that little tidbit with me. I imagine they'll continue with the plan for that UN mission to bring him back."

"Not optimal," Penny sighed.

Traci was livid. "We can't go along with this," she said, her native Appalachian twang bubbling up with her anger. "You know that, right?"

The AI spoke over the cabin speakers. "I am prepared to proceed with the mission if necessary. There are more than sufficient consumables aboard for astronaut Templeton's return."

"See? Bob's willing to ignore them."

Roy shook his head. "Bob's not looking at jail time for commandeering government property. Worst they can do is shut him down."

"That is equivalent to the death penalty for a sentient machine, though I am willing to take that risk."

She laughed with a dark resignation. "The blasted computer's got more nerve than we do."

Roy crossed his arms and shot her an angry glare. "The computer doesn't need calories. It only needs coolant and power." He looked up at the ceiling as he addressed the AI. "Am I correct, Bob?"

"You are correct."

She looked down at her feet, chastened. "I get it. There aren't enough consumables aboard for the full mission, and if the logistics mod isn't already on its way, then it ain't coming."

"That is also correct."

"Stow it, Bob. I don't need your help here."

The group turned silent, each of them digesting the news in their own way. She pushed away angrily and floated up into the observation dome, staring plaintively into the depths as if she might be able to glimpse their distant objective. She tapped her fingers against a handrail beneath the glass as her mind churned through alternatives.

The Chinese-controlled UN ship would be the ones to bring him home. Why was that a problem?

Because he'd spend twice as long in torpor. He'd be lucky to have a functioning body by the end of the journey if his brain didn't turn to mush first. For all they knew, he'd come back a vegetable and with UN bots in control of *Magellan*.

Traci couldn't get the countless, enervating intrusions into her daily life out of her head. Every choice, no matter how minor, was subject to some unknowable entity's nitpicking influence. In the end it was just algorithms crafted by someone else, running without thought or conscience. And now they would be trying to extend their reach to wherever the wormhole led.

No. The official narrative completely ignored the fact that Jack and Daisy were there now. Pretending humanity wasn't already on the scene just because they weren't formally sanctioned emissaries was folly, but there was a lot of that going around these days. It was shocking to see how easily one's thinking could be shaped by the endless repetition of dogma: received knowledge, instead of earned understanding.

She was not going to "receive" anymore.

Traci turned away from the dome and her contemplation of the universe beyond, pushing herself back down into the control cabin. "How long before we have to hand over operational control to Houston?"

Roy didn't have to check the orders. "Forty-eight hours."

She reluctantly nodded her acknowledgment, her gut churning as she tried to digest the implications. Both Roy and Penny could see the conflict within her, though each would come to different conclusions. Penny perhaps understood her struggle better than anyone. She placed a hand on Traci's shoulder, her steel-gray eyes boring in with conviction. And perhaps more importantly, understanding. "Square yourself away, dear. We've got work to do."

21

The Clipper announced its arrival with a pair of rapid-fire shotgun blasts in the distance, the telltale crack of a sonic boom as it passed overhead to begin a series of leisurely S-turns to decelerate into a spiraling descent. A small crowd of onlookers had assembled at the remote parking apron along with a contingent of official NASA greeters. Art Hammond had arrived as the personal representative of HOPE, standing with the official government delegation.

"A little out of your way, isn't it?" Blaine Winston asked. "I thought you had settled down in Grand Cayman."

"Side trip. Had to come back for business in Denver," Hammond explained curtly as they watched the delta-winged craft turn above them. "Harriman's crew has a lot of work ahead of them. Besides, if this is important enough for Cheever to send you then the least I can do is show up."

"Hmm," Winston sniffed and shielded his eyes from the blazing sun as the Clipper glided down its final approach. A puff of smoke curled away behind it as its main wheels kissed the runway.

Hammond admired the pilot's skill as he watched him hold the spaceplane's blunt nose high, bleeding energy before easing the nosewheel down. A quick pop of speed brakes brought the spaceplane to a stop almost directly in front of the apron. "Wheels stop," he heard the pilot announce over the PA system. Studying the young man beside him, he wondered if Cheever's functionary had any idea of the touch required to make such a precise rollout of a plane that had no power left to propel it. Doubtful, he knew.

A service crew in hazmat suits surrounded the spacecraft, deploying chemical sniffers to protect against any stray hydrazine that might be venting from its attitude thrusters. It was almost half an hour before they gave the all-clear and another ground crew rolled a set of airstairs up to a hatch behind the cockpit windows, where two figures could be seen moving inside. Hammond noticed Winston watching the ground crew with his chin lifted triumphantly as they opened the hatch. He leaned against his cane and looked down, stifling a grin. This was going to be fun.

The first to emerge was Penny Stratton, her blue jumpsuit brilliant under the high desert sun. The next figure to climb out was Roy Hoover, who took in a deep breath of fresh air.

They descended the steps, shook hands with the ground crew, and ambled over to the welcoming party. Their third crew member did not emerge.

"Welcome back to Earth," Winston said stiffly, expectantly looking past them to the Clipper and stifling a gnawing sense of alarm. "Where's Keene?"

The pair exchanged questioning looks. "Keene... Yeah, about that. She declined the invitation," Roy shrugged, shooting a wink at Hammond.

"Declined the—" Winston stammered. "You mean she's still up there?"

Roy nodded. "That's about the size of it."

Winston wheeled on Hammond. "What the *hell* are you people thinking?" he demanded, wide-eyed and growing frantic. Nearby onlookers turned at the rising commotion. "You left someone up there alone? How do you propose to get her home?"

Hammond theatrically checked his watch. "We'll worry about that when the time comes." *In about four years.*

"When the time comes? You're stealing government property! You'll have a platoon of DOJ lawyers crawling up your ass by sundown."

"I have attorneys too," Hammond said, "and I guarantee they'll enjoy the hell out of discovery."

Winston composed himself, turning cold. "You understand we

have other resources at our disposal to stop you. And her. She's not alone up there, you know. The law will be enforced."

Hammond craned his neck toward the sky above. "*Physics* is law, Winston. Everything else is just recommendations."

As the two continued to argue about the legalities of stealing a spacecraft that was still contractually under HOPE's control, Penny reached for the phone in her hip pocket and typed out a quick message to one of her select few contacts:

SIMON ... WE MIGHT NEED A BIG FAVOR. DETAILS SOON. LUV, PENNY.

US Space Force
Orbital Fleet Command
Vandenberg SFB, California

Fleet Admiral Simon Poole reclined behind his desk and propped his prosthetic leg on an open drawer as he read the raft of incoming messages from Penny Stratton. His eyes widened as he scrolled through the details. It was for sure a big ask.

Columbus was still nominally under civilian control, which meant it fell under the protection of the Orbit Guard. They were also tasked with enforcing the law as it pertained to operations in near-Earth space. When the two conflicted, safety and clear navigation lanes took priority. Interference with other spacecraft, particularly US-flagged craft, was to be aggressively deterred.

"Aggressive deterrence" could take on a lot of forms, he thought. Yes, this was going to have to be handled delicately.

He pulled up a status display on his desktop monitor, studying the current positions and trajectories of each ship in the Guard's small fleet: two cruisers on opposite ends of a free-return orbit that kept them cycling between Earth and Moon; five multipurpose tugs moving between low and medium orbit; and four fast corvettes in high orbit.

Poole focused on the fission-powered corvettes, nimble and armed with antisatellite missiles. Each orbiting equidistant from the others, they could be in position wherever he needed in a matter of hours. He removed the other ship's orbits from his display and added *Columbus* to the mix, focusing on the maneuver node for its planned departure burn. It would start burning right before perigee, raising its apogee until the elliptical orbit became a hyperbola: escape velocity.

He plotted intercept trajectories for each of the four corvettes, looking for which one could be on station alongside *Columbus* soonest. *Cernan* could get there faster, but it would use a lot of propellant which might be needed once it was in position. *Young* would take longer, but with a lower fuel penalty. Most importantly, Poole could count on its skipper to think creatively. He studied the plot in more detail. They could get there in time, but they'd have to move quickly.

Satisfied that he had a workable plan, Poole smiled to himself. *Young*'s commander had a way of finding himself in interesting situations.

Poole tapped the intercom for his administrative assistant. "Chief Fannin," he said, "I need to draft maneuver orders for Lieutenant Commander Hunter on the *John Young*. ASAP."

EarthWatch had been one of UNSEC's earliest projects, creating a network of earth-observing satellites in high orbit that could be accessed by anyone on the globe with an internet connection. Its purpose had been to increase people's awareness of the fragile nature of their home planet. If not everyone could afford to fly into space and experience the vaunted "overview effect," then they could at least watch high-definition views of Earth from the comfort of their homes.

EW-4 was one such satellite. Not much more than an IMAX camera mounted to a power and propulsion bus, it had shared a high equatorial orbit with three other EarthWatch satellites to provide Earthbound spectators with a continuous view of the planet. Very little had been asked of it during its first year in space, just the occasional maneuver to avoid passing too close to other satellites.

Today was different. Had EW-4 contained a human or AI pilot, it might have asked what danger was so imminent as to require expending most of its fuel to avoid it.

The satellite of course could not understand that it was not being commanded to avoid. It was being commanded to intercept.

◆ ◆ ◆

Traci awoke from an unusually deep sleep and stretched against her restraints before releasing them to float free of her bunk. After sixteen hours of mentally intense work, she had not argued with Owen's call to hit the rack and let the AI do the rest.

She habitually smoothed out the bedding, determined to maintain a consistent daily routine. Discipline in the small things would be the key to maintaining her sanity.

After a trip to the lavatory, she wiped a wet cloth across her face and placed it in the recycler bin. Its moisture would be extracted and fed into the waste processor, eventually finding its way back to her finite supply of water. She'd long ago learned not to think too much about where her potable water was coming from. It always started out fresh from a full tank, to be inevitably replaced over time by reprocessed and sanitized "used" water. At least she'd be drinking her own purified waste this time and not a mixture of everyone else's. She wasn't sure if that made her feel any better.

Pushing off for the galley, she quickly found her way to the drink dispenser. The coffee always tasted best early in a mission when it was still drawing off of unrecycled water. It would last considerably longer now with only one person drawing from the supply. She tapped a control screen by the dispenser, checking the ship's total inventory, and was satisfied to see there'd be more than enough for the full mission. Another byproduct of going solo.

She lifted the bulb of hot liquid out of the machine, slipped her feet into a restraint beneath a nearby table and took a sip. Cradling the drink in her hand, she took in her surroundings. *Columbus* still had that new-spacecraft smell, despite all of the recent activity. What was the term the Navy guys used for the first crew on a new ship? Plank owner. That was it.

She slipped a tablet out of her hip pocket and called up an inventory list. In addition to her personal entertainment files, Roy had been kind enough to leave all of his uploaded. There'd be no shortage of diversions during the little free time she expected·to have, right up until she went into hibernation in a few months. After the slingshot burn, she'd settle down for the Big Sleep and let Bob do the work of piloting them out to the Anomaly. If it all worked, next year she'd wake up to find her old ship in the window.

This will work, she told herself. She'd run through the mission scenarios and trade studies dozens of times in Future Applications. She was confident the new AI could handle it once they'd gotten past that final critical event at Neptune. Truth be told, Bob could probably handle all of it but she wasn't about to miss that flyby.

The technical and operational details weren't in question. The ship was ready, the AI had demonstrated it was capable. The only remaining question was herself, the "meat gyro." Her doubts welled up into a cauldron of conflicting emotions. "Are you ready for this?" she wondered aloud.

"Yes, I am ready."

"Oh." She placed her coffee bulb into a cradle and slipped the tablet back into her pocket. "Sorry, Bob. I was talking to myself. You should be prepared for a lot of that."

"I will keep that in mind. Are you concerned that you've left something important behind?"

Now that's the question of the year. "No," she sighed. "And yes. It's not a question of inventory. This is an awfully long trip to fly solo. I'm going to miss humans, a few of them more than others. My parents, for starters. We'll be coming back to a different world, and I'll probably be in a boatload of trouble. I have no idea what it means for you."

"I understand your dilemma. You do not wish to proceed alone, whereas I do not wish to be deactivated. Our mission is critical, yet it is a difficult choice to disobey authority."

Meh. Some "authorities" more than others, she thought. "You're not going to go all HAL 9000 on me, are you? Because I can't deal with a psychotic AI."

Bob adopted an unnervingly gentle, measured tone, flawlessly mimicking the *2001* voice actor. "I understand your concern, but I am fully committed to the success of our mission."

She bit down on her lip. "That was *so* not funny." Actually it was hilarious, and encouraging that he'd tried. Bob's silicon brain might be more advanced than she'd thought.

Bob reverted to his normal voice. "I'm sorry. I didn't mean to upset you. I was trying to alleviate your tension."

"You did," she laughed. "I didn't mean to be caustic." She considered how to explain. "Sometimes we humans say the exact opposite of what we actually mean, while our intent comes across in our tone of voice and facial expression."

"It does. I am still trying to grok that."

"Grok?" Another point in his favor. "You're well versed in nerd culture, I'll give you that much."

"You do know who programmed me, right? Other nerds."

She closed her eyes and wiped at a tear. "I think we'll be getting along just fine, Bob." *It's going to be all right.* "I need to go silent for a minute. Okay?"

"Okay. You are on mute."

Thank goodness he was developing a sense of humor. It might just keep her sane.

She turned down the cabin lights and closed her eyes, shutting out the mechanically sterile surroundings of what would be her home for the next few years. That she would spend almost half of it in what amounted to a medically induced coma was of little comfort. She'd had vague periods of awareness before, recalling a not-quite-imaginary conversation with Jack that had intruded on her hallucinatory dreams of home. Noelle had assured her it was a byproduct of not being in full stasis, yet she couldn't completely shake her trepidation. Would she spend that year in an uncontrollable dream state?

Traci let herself float freely in the darkness, the reassuring purr of circulation fans and hum of electronics blanketing her senses. She was learning to feel the rhythm of the ship in the way Jack had taught her on their first mission together. He'd said he could sense when a component needed replaced or a valve serviced just by a change in the background noise or vibrations in the deck plates.

Could she do this? Could she take on the roles of commander, pilot, and flight engineer? That was an easy answer: By herself, no. With a fourth-generation AI? Yes, definitely. In that, the robotics crowd had a good point.

Yet she believed deep in her soul that they were at best an extension of humanity's eyes and ears. They were not a replacement, not yet. An AI might be able to operate a complex spacecraft, but that wasn't the same as directing a mission.

She would find out soon enough, once they were past Neptune and committed to the year-long outbound cruise to the Anomaly. To Jack.

She was confident in the machinery, the plan, and in Owen's

support team. She was not so certain about herself. *Am I ready for this?* Alone in deep space, her only companion an artificial intelligence that had not been tested in such extreme isolation.

To be fair, Daisy hadn't been either. But they'd spent two years working with her through countless integrated simulations and even more time in space with a full crew. Then Jack had placed his life in her hands, for Traci's sake and for the sake of finding answers to the many questions left after their expedition. Where had those perfectly preserved organic compounds come from? Had they just developed naturally, or were they deliberately placed there? Pluto and the rest of the belt had offered the perfect environment for their long-term storage, and it was almost as if they'd been left there as a taunt. As if they'd been kept out of reach until we were ready to find them, humanity's worthiness more or less assumed by the very act of reaching such a distant world. Did it also imply we were meant to *do* something with them—to go forth and multiply?

If so, their placement suggested a great deal of thought behind it, either evidence of other intelligent beings or of God Himself. She'd long believed that humans had never detected other intelligent life because we were the first, but now she wondered if someone else had been keeping an eye on Earth for an unthinkably long time.

If that were the case, it threatened to shake her worldview to its foundations. It would be sure to tear through human culture like a tsunami once it became public, leaving untold shattered assumptions in its wake. And if true, it would eventually become public; of that she had no doubt. Someone would decide it played to their advantage, or more likely to an opponent's disadvantage. Just possibly, someone might decide going public was the right thing to do. Less likely, but she could hope.

Hope. Now that was a thought she hadn't entertained enough since returning from her last mission. The world was nothing like the one she'd left, and she felt a longing to escape. Escape from a world that had become incessantly intrusive, prying, every minor decision in her life judged and micromanaged by a legion of unknowable algorithms. In a sense, she was already living her life at the mercy of an AI. At least she could talk to Bob, trade jokes and reason with him. He would probably be a good chess partner, too.

A chime from the comm panel interrupted her thoughts. A

message was waiting from Cayman Control: PERIAPSIS IN 65 MINUTES. WE ARE GO FOR TNI. STANDING BY.

TNI. Trans-Neptunian Injection. The big engine burn that would take her out of Earth's orbit and toward an encounter with Neptune.

She moved up to the control deck and checked the flight computer, its event timer dispassionately counting down. There was no more time to debate, no more options left to consider. It was go/no-go. She was either committed, or she was not.

That brought Traci back to her original question: *Am I ready for this? Can I do it?*

Lord, I still believe you are there. Help my unbelief. Give me strength for what I must do now.

Reluctant or not, the task was at hand and there could be no further delay. *Jack did what he did for me. I must do this for him.* She plugged her headset back into the comm panel. "Cayman, this is *Columbus*. Copy we are go for Trans-Neptunian Injection. Initiating terminal count on your mark." She took a deep breath and reached for the flight computer in the center of her console, her fingers hovering over its small keyboard.

"Roger that," CapCom drawled. "Coming up on six-zero minutes in three . . . two . . . one . . . mark."

She pressed the COMMIT button. "Mark."

Traci smiled to herself as she felt the fusion engines warming up far behind her, an electric thrum that echoed through the hull. A lot of people on Earth were going to be pissed.

MEMORIES: TO WONDERLAND

※ ※ ※

They ultimately decided to use a quarter of their remaining propellant, not knowing how long their journey through the wormhole might take or what could be waiting on the other side. If this were a gateway to another solar system—which seemed just as likely as anything else—they needed to be able to navigate it when they arrived.

And if they needed to turn around, Jack wanted enough fuel to do so in a hurry. Assuming they could turn around.

They left the MSEV behind in its orbit, one less piece of unnecessary mass. More important, it would also function as a relay satellite in the hope they would be able to communicate from the other side. If light could make its way through, that implied they might be able to establish a radio link.

He had spent their remaining time making sure the ship was ready to get underway, using his maintenance bots to secure any loose gear while he ran diagnostic tests of every system in the ship, twice. If something was going to give him trouble, now was the time to find out. The final step was warming up the fusion drive.

"Ready to commit," he said. "Initiating countdown timer on my mark."

"Mark. Terminal count initiated at T-minus two minutes. Have you thought about what we should tell control?"

"A little late for that, don't you think?"

"I think you have been putting it off."

"You're awfully perceptive for a computer." He pulled up a text file he'd been compiling, a summary of all they had discovered and their intentions. He'd struggled with the exact wording, eventually deciding to be blunt about it. "I've got a burst transmission ready to go once we're committed." There would be a point, not quite midway along their path, where the amount of energy needed to stop would be greater than what they could expend before crossing the threshold: the Point of No Return. "When we cross PNR, please send this." He dropped the file into Daisy's comm folder:

HAVE ENCOUNTERED GRAVITATIONAL ANOMALY AT PREDICTED LOCATION OF PLANET NINE. ESTIMATE MASS 1.03 X 10^26 KG.

UNABLE TO DIRECTLY OBSERVE. MANEUVERING CLOSER TO INVESTIGATE. WILL UPDATE AS ABLE.

TEMPLETON OUT.

"Interesting," she said after digesting his message. "How do you think they'll react? Your communications with them have been sparse."

He'd learned whenever Daisy used contractions, it signaled she was taking a more personal tone. "More like nonexistent. And I'm not used to you dancing around the subject like this."

"I was being polite. I don't want to unnecessarily upset you, but I am curious."

"I'm not ready to talk to other humans yet. Guess I've been separated from the tribe for too long. It's easier to talk to you since I don't have to wait half a day for a reply. Right now you're the only one who gets me."

"Thank you. I value your confidence. But you haven't answered my question. How are they likely to react?"

"No idea," he said after a moment's thought. In the back of his mind, he'd hoped they would respond by sending another ship. It would be his only way home, and he was certainly giving them enough justification. "I imagine it'll set Owen's hair on fire. They'll probably think I went crazy from isolation."

"The observational data will be difficult to ignore." Daisy paused. "I'm talking about the Anomaly, not your mental state."

"Thanks for clarifying. If anything, I've learned uncomfortable truths are easy to ignore. Humans can invent all kinds of rationalizations."

There was a subtle change in Daisy's tone as she returned to the immediate business. "Thirty seconds to ignition," she reminded him.

"Copy thirty," Jack answered, shifting gears himself. There had been nothing left to do once they'd started the two-minute count other than wait for the clock to run out. He'd become so used to the machine running itself under Daisy's watch that he was almost beginning to feel like a passenger. "Systems board is all green. Plasma generator's spun up and nozzle containment fields are charged."

Daisy's soothing synthetic voice led him through the remainder of the count: "Three . . . two . . . one. Main engine ignition."

The ship trembled under thrust as the first, short burst of hydrogen plasma nudged them into a new orbit, one that would intersect the center of the Anomaly. As velocity vectors began dancing across the nav display and settled on their target, the engines came up to full thrust and the staccato shudder changed pitch to a rhythmic rumble.

Daisy had calculated a low-energy trajectory that would bring them to where they believed the threshold to be. It would take several hours to cover the distance. Once there, they would let their momentum and the Anomaly's gravity carry them through its opening. Not knowing what forces might be at play, it seemed wise to tread carefully. If theory held true, stable wormholes relied on a delicate balance of forces and diving in under power might upend that equilibrium. He had no desire to find out what being in the center of a collapsing tunnel through space-time might entail.

After a time, the hole in space ahead of them appeared to grow wider as *Magellan* continued relentlessly toward it.

"What do you think we'll find?"

"Impossible to know. Most likely another star system somewhere in our galaxy. Possibly another galaxy altogether. If the multiverse theories are correct, perhaps even a parallel universe."

"I'd rather not think about that one. If we come across a mirror image of us with some version of me in a goatee, we're turning around."

"I'm confused by your reference."

"Never mind. We'll fix that later." Jack looked ahead, into the black. He hadn't thought it possible for space to seem emptier than it already was. He was shocked more at the lack of fear he felt. He should've been frightened out of his wits; instead he was determined to keep going. The time to be afraid had been before lighting the engines; now was the time to stay focused. To not screw the pooch. "If you don't know where you are going, any road can take you there."

"The Cheshire cat."

"So you got that reference. You're remarkably well read for a computer."

"Alice in Wonderland seems especially relevant lately."

"That's—"

The emptiness ahead filled their view, eclipsing all behind it but for a ring of distant stars along its periphery. Soon these appeared to converge, as if the observable universe had flattened itself into a uniform plane before coalescing around them.

It was his last memory.

22

Columbus's departure window was not only constrained by the relative positions of planets, it also had to be carefully timed to "deconflict" with an ever-moving constellation of satellites in the orbits above it.

The first hint of a problem came from HOPE's CapCom. "*Columbus*, we've got trouble brewing."

Traci hastily searched her system status displays as she keyed her microphone. It was a green board, and the AI hadn't alerted her to any glitches. "Can't see anything wrong with the ship. What's the concern?"

"Vehicle systems are go," CapCom said. "It's a traffic alert."

She checked her proximity radar. "I don't see anything here. How far out are we talking?"

"Eighteen minutes," he said tersely. "An EarthWatch sat in LEO started a phasing burn about an hour ago. Traffic Control just notified us of the collision risk. It's going to be crossing your orbit about the time you're passing ascending node."

Damn it. Traffic conflicts called for an abort. She could recover on the next orbit, but it would mean a lot of wasted propellant. Maybe enough to scuttle the mission plan. The ground crew would be frantically revising plans and poring over possible outcomes, but she instinctively knew the most likely outcome: mission abort. They had one shot at this.

She hung her head. "Copy that," she finally said. "What's your confidence level of a collision risk?"

"Unable to independently verify," CapCom said. "But based on TraCon's projections, it's high."

"Understood." She cursed under her breath, not ready to give up yet. But she'd have to take action soon to avoid ramming that stray satellite. "Standing by to shut—"

She was interrupted by a proximity alarm. *And what fresh hell is this?*

A voice announced itself over their frequency as a blip appeared on the radar, closing from above and ahead of them. "Ahoy, *Columbus*. This is the USFS *John Young*, approaching from your two o'clock, twenty kilometer offset. What is your condition, over?"

"My condition?" That was a good question. Anxious. Confused. Irritated. "Vehicle status is nominal. I just was notified of a collision risk, coming up in one-eight minutes."

"*Young* copies, and we show same," the voice said. "I am obligated to inform you that your flight plan has not been cleared by the US government, which still claims your vessel as its property. Continuing with your intended operation may place you in legal jeopardy."

"Nothing's signed yet—" she began to argue.

"That said," the voice interrupted, "our primary mission is to keep the space lanes clear and remove any imminent collision risks. Hang on, *Columbus*, things are about to get sporty."

Lieutenant Commander Marshall Hunter replaced his microphone in its bracket and cinched down his seat restraints. "There. I've done my official duty and warned the lady that commandeering an expensive spacecraft is generally frowned upon."

The corvette's pilot looked back over her shoulder at Hunter. "Your orders, Skipper?"

"We continue with the plan. Cut across her bow and put us between *Columbus* and that satellite."

A chief petty officer controlling the ship's sensors and weapons suite spoke next. "Weapons board is green. ASAT tubes two and four are open to vacuum and laser is at full charge, sir."

Hunter nodded. "Weapons tight, Chief. Target the satellite's propellant tanks with the laser and hold the ASATs until I say so. Won't do any good to turn it into a debris cloud."

A quick thruster burn from the pilot had them descending to pull farther ahead of *Columbus* as they crossed in front of it. Hunter picked up his mic. "*Columbus,* this is *Young.* We'll be crossing your V-bar in a few seconds, about twelve clicks ahead. Do us all a favor and don't light that drive up yet, okay?"

Bob's voice echoed the alert on her situation display. "Traffic contact, 12.1 kilometers ahead, crossing our longitudinal axis."

Traci leaned into the window ahead of her. "I see it." Much smaller than *Columbus,* the *Young* looked heavy for a ship of its size. A single squat, cylindrical module was stacked ahead of a spherical propellant tank and propelled by a single fission engine that glowed white-hot against the black. The engine went dark as it settled into its new orbit ahead of them.

She marveled at her good fortune. Nothing happened this unexpectedly in spaceflight, not between multiple craft in orbit, and certainly not without planning ahead. Someone had expected trouble and had sent her an escort.

Someone down there wanted her to succeed.

The corvette flipped around, its nose pointed in their direction of travel. Its forward cylinder was studded with antenna blisters and equipment racks, which she knew housed antisatellite missiles. "They're lowering their orbit, pulling ahead."

"Concur. Separation now 12.8 kilometers and increasing." Bob's voice was clipped, concise, dispensing with the conversational tone he'd acquired with her. It was almost like having another pilot aboard.

Traci radioed HOPE Control as she anxiously watched the event timer count down. "You guys seeing this down there?"

"Not directly, *Columbus.* Our picture's not much better than your radar. Space Force notified us they'd have a vessel in proximity right before they pinged you. Looks like they wanted to keep this to themselves."

"Talk to me, Chief. Are we close enough for visual?"

"Stand by... there. Search radar painted it at forty kilometers. Slaving the long-range camera to fire control." The chief was manipulating video feeds on his console. "There. We've got lock, Skipper."

A glimmering metallic rectangle sat squarely in the video crosshairs, unthreatening but for its imminent collision risk. "Confirm that's our target," Hunter said.

The chief worked quickly to verify its trajectory and electronic signature against a catalogue of every known satellite in its orbit. "That's it, sir. Positive ID on EarthWatch-4. Definitely not where it was supposed to be."

Hunter watched the blue glow from its ion exhaust. "It's still thrusting. Do we have a bead on its trajectory, Chief?"

"Aye, sir. Projecting it on the mo board now."

Three arcs appeared on the maneuvering plot, a large screen mounted on the deck in front of Hunter's command chair. Each in a different color, it showed him their orbit in relation to *Columbus* and the wayward EarthWatch satellite. An amber warning flashed where the three paths crossed, a point that grew closer with each passing second.

"You know, that's almost enough to make me think it's on purpose," Hunter said sardonically. He punched the frequency for the fleet control team at Vandenberg. "Control, *Young* actual. Are you in contact with EW-4's operators? I need to know the story on this bird."

"That's affirm," came the reply. "They said it's a planned maneuver, but they didn't file anything with traffic control."

That drew sarcastic laughs from his pilot and systems operator. "Not a good plan, then," Hunter said. "Vandy, advise them EW-4 has become an immediate navigation hazard which we are prepared to remove. We will be in position to grab it in"—he checked his plot— "six minutes, if it ceases thrusting. If it remains under power we will be forced to deploy countermeasures." Which was a polite way of saying they would shoot it out of the sky.

"Understood, *Young*. Stand by."

Hunter impatiently tapped his fingers on his armrest as he waited for Vandenberg to relay their intentions, watching the spacecraft's orbits converging on his screen. Soon he would have to act regardless.

"*Young*, Vandy Control. Operator says they are not able to alter their maneuver plan. They don't see that it presents a risk."

"Very well. *Young* out." He sighed. Had it simply stopped thrusting, they would have been able to maneuver into a position to grab it with the corvette's manipulator arm and move it to a safer orbit. Now they would be forced to fire on a UN-sponsored satellite.

They were about to stir up a colossal hornet's nest. "Chief, target its propellant tank. Laser, no kinetic weapons. Make a hole."

"Aye, Skipper." The petty officer began manipulating a control trackball, and soon a second set of crosshairs centered itself on the satellite's fuel tank. "Target locked."

"Weapons free. Fire at will, Chief."

He opened a protective cover on his console and pressed the concealed switch beneath. "Firing."

There was no report, no visible beam crossing the vacuum. Their only indication of a hit was a white-hot glow that suddenly appeared in the center of the tank. Gas began escaping within seconds as the laser burned through the thin aluminum. "Cease fire," Hunter said. "Good shot, Chief."

Fueled by inert xenon gas, there was no reaction to the heat, only a jet of vapor escaping from the hole that had been burned into its tank. This caused the satellite to begin drifting orthogonal to its course, moving away from an imminent collision with *Columbus* and into a different orbit that would eventually present a collision hazard to other spacecraft. The glow from its ion engine faded as the last grams of propellant vented into space.

Hunter leaned forward to update his maneuvering plot, watching the satellite's path slowly diverge from that of *Columbus*. He turned to his pilot. "Roberta, plot an intercept vector. Let's go pick up our casualty. If we can patch that tank and keep it serviceable, maybe we can avoid an international incident."

"Done, Skipper," she said, confidently popping a wad of gum. "Ready to intercept. Might be a little late to avoid the 'incident' thing, though."

"Keep updating your angles and stand by." Hunter rubbed his forehead. There was nothing about this operation that enthused him, and it wasn't about to get any better. He switched back to the ship-to-ship frequency. "*Columbus, Young*. Be advised, the navigation hazard has been removed."

"Copy that, and thank you," Traci's voice replied over their speakers. "Understand I'm clear to maneuver."

He refrained from using the customary radio jargon *negative*. "Umm . . . not quite, *Columbus*. I'm obliged to remind you of our earlier conversation. You are not on an approved flight plan, and we are authorized to prevent you from commandeering United States property."

Her retort came quickly. "And I'll point out that those papers have yet to be signed. As of now, this vessel is still under control of the HOPE Consortium, of which I'm an authorized agent. Nobody's going to repo this ship just yet."

Hunter pursed his lips. Good thing she was playing along, because what had to come next was unpleasant. "*Columbus*, you do understand the action we're authorized to take here?" Firing on one of their own was an even less attractive prospect than on a UN satellite.

"That's affirmative, *Young*. I also know that laser takes time to recharge, by which time I'll be burning and underway. I also know that whether it's photons or projectiles, tearing a hole in a pressurized hydrogen tank is going to create one hellacious mess up here."

That it would, he knew, and eyed the maneuvering plot again. She had to be coming up on her injection node. "Chief, how much longer to recycle?" They'd taken a full-power shot in the interest of time, draining the weapon's capacitors in the process.

"Sixty-eight seconds, sir."

"*Columbus*, what's your terminal count?"

"One minute, *Young*."

Eight seconds. She'd be burning before they could get a lock on her tanks, and they still had that wayward satellite to catch. The risks balanced out exactly as he'd expected. As he'd wanted.

"Very well. You've been duly warned, *Columbus*. We first have to clear this disabled satellite," he said for the sake of the official transcripts. "We'll let the lawyers deal with the rest when you get back."

Two microphone clicks signaled her acknowledgment. With that, Hunter replaced his mic in its cradle. He turned to the petty officer on the systems console, who spent his free time writing short stories for a handful of fiction magazines. "Chief, I'm going to need your help with the after-action report. I've never been much for creative writing."

"My pleasure, sir," he said with a chuckle. "I'll even let you take full credit." Which Hunter would have to do anyway, being the spacecraft commander. No matter what happened or who did it, ultimately everything aboard the *John Young* was his responsibility.

"You gave her due warning. That's all you could do," Roberta said, encouraging him. "We're not up here to wrangle over contract terms, though she's probably right about the legal angle. Not for us to decide, Skipper."

Hunter replied with a dissatisfied grunt and pulled up the feed from their external camera, turning it to find *Columbus* behind them. He checked his watch: any second now.

There was a bloom of incandescent gas as the big ship's fusion engines flared to life. It moved smartly away as they quickly reached full thrust. "Radial turn, plus ninety degrees. Put her in the window," he said to Roberta. He wanted to see this.

Earth slipped behind them as the pilot pivoted their ship to face the black sky. Soon they could see the massive spacecraft pulling away, now twenty kilometers distant and leaving a trail of nuclear fire as it left Earth behind.

Hunter thumbed his mic one more time. "Godspeed, *Columbus*."

Settled in beside one of the Gulfstream jet's windows, Roy studied the Texas coast in the distance as they left US airspace on their way to the Caribbean. He knew Noelle was down there, with both of their bags packed and waiting for her own flight to Grand Cayman. "Would be nice if we could just drop into Hobby and pick her up," he mused gruffly.

Penny sat across from him, nursing a bottle of mineral water. "It would," she agreed, "but then we might not exactly be welcome, you know." The pilots had purposely filed a route that took them south through Mexican airspace before cutting across the Gulf, all the better to avoid any unwelcome orders to land. She picked up her phone to check the status of Hammond's other jet, currently on approach into Houston. "She'll be on her way to meet us soon enough."

"I'm not one to go rabbit like this."

"Neither am I," she said, scrolling through a raft of messages on her phone. "But we just pissed off a lot of the wrong people." *Or the right people,* she thought. "We can't leave them an opening."

"I didn't think you'd be this concerned about the Feds. I thought we were still within our contractual rights."

"Doesn't mean DOJ lawyers wouldn't be waiting for us with a

restraining order in hand. Trust me, this is best for all of us." Her eyes brightened as a new message appeared. "And here we go. *Columbus* just started its departure burn."

Roy nodded silently. He pulled his phone out of a hip pocket and searched his contacts for one Traci had given him before they parted. A rare smile spread across his weathered face. "Miss Templeton? Roy Hoover. I have some news for you."

23

NASA Headquarters
Six Months Later

Cheever glared at the curt letter of resignation from Blaine Fitzgerald Winston with thoughts of rats and sinking ships, and considered how tenuous her position had become over the past several months.

The decline of Dr. Jacqueline Cheever's influence within Washington power circles had become palpable, waning in direct proportion to *Columbus*'s increasing distance from Earth. As the ship gained velocity and its arrival at the Anomaly became increasingly inevitable, the more breathless the stories had become in the media. Capitol Hill leakers had been methodically practicing their craft, carefully positioning their Congressional patrons ahead of the story through the deliberate release of carefully selected details of both *Magellan*'s reappearance and Templeton's discoveries at the edge of the solar system.

Most grating of all had been the heroic depiction of the HOPE team, Art Hammond, and Traci Effing Keene. Without a peep of protest from Justice, taking a spacecraft on an unsanctioned mission was apparently just dandy now. It didn't help that there wasn't a legal basis to go after Hammond's rogue crew, not that it had ever stopped DOJ when they badly needed to bury something. The OSEP treaty dying in committee had been the final nail in that coffin. With each passing day, she felt her grip on power weakening.

All these thoughts churned in her mind as she listened to the Vice President drone on. His call had not come as a surprise; she'd been warned by Winston just as he'd turned in his resignation to pursue "other opportunities" within the government. The first rat to leave the sinking ship.

"Dr. Cheever," the VP said, "please know we appreciate your leadership. You have steered NASA in the right direction with a renewed focus on Earth sciences, but you understand how priorities shift from time to time."

An insincere "Yes, sir," was all she could muster. The words burned in her throat.

"This 'Anomaly' is an extraordinary discovery. And whether we like it or not, Keene and the HOPE Consortium's initiative has captured the public's imagination. That is not something we are prepared to ignore."

"Of course not, sir." *Elections are coming up,* she thought. *And you're prepared to exploit this.*

"This does present a vexatious problem with the UN space cooperative, however. As you know, by its charter—of which we are signatories—all deep space expeditions are supposed to be coordinated through their planetary protection regime."

"Yes sir, of that I am acutely aware."

"Have you spoken with Dr. Li recently?"

"I have not, sir." *Not that he's been returning my calls.*

"He's been rather cagey about their expedition, I'm afraid. In fact we have reason to question their motives. Would you be able to shed any light on this?"

We always have to question their motives, she thought. It had been less troubling when they aligned with hers. "No sir, I'm afraid I cannot."

"Then perhaps it's time we brought more resources to bear. The President believes it would be wise to supplement your office with an advisor from the intelligence community. You'll be hearing from them soon."

With that, the Vice President simultaneously ended their conversation and her effective control of NASA. However subtly, she was being shunted aside.

Jacqueline Cheever placed the phone in its cradle and stared out her windows over the capital skyline. Where before it had seemed alive with opportunity, now she saw only hollow ambition fortified behind cold gray stone. For the first time in her career, she had a fleeting understanding of how the "outsiders" must feel.

Traci sat lightly on the small divan on the recreation deck, languidly tossing a soft rubber ball across the compartment. It arced slowly through the air in one-tenth gravity to bounce off the opposite bulkhead and back into her waiting hand. After weeks of repetition her aim had become so precise, her reflexes so acute, that she barely had to move to catch it. Beside her sat an e-reader that had long since gone to sleep and a tablet full of daily tasks that she studiously ignored.

"Is everything all right?" Bob asked through the overhead speakers.

She waited for the ball to return to her waiting hand one last time. "Yes . . . No. Maybe. That good enough for you?"

"It matters less to me than it does to you, I suspect. I am programmed to be aware of your mental state."

"You mean 'monitor.' That's one of the reasons I left Earth behind, you know."

"I am aware of that. But yes, I meant 'aware,' though I see how you could have trouble appreciating the difference. You seem withdrawn."

As if to illustrate his point, she drew her knees up to her chest and wrapped her arms around them, just as she'd done on the beach at Kennedy. It occurred to her that she'd taken the same stance many times with Jack. "I suppose you're right. Probably a natural reaction to isolation."

"Work is an effective remedy in some cases."

She shot a side-eye at the interface panel, as if Bob could understand her body language. Maybe he could. "Is that a hint?"

"It is. There are a number of tasks on the daily activity roster which I am unable to accomplish. I could use a hand."

"Cute, Bob." She knew he meant they were all chores that required fingers and an opposable thumb. She lifted up the pad and scrolled through its contents. "All of them are minor, I assure you. We've been out here for almost two months; I've got this down to a practiced routine."

"Perhaps that is what you need, then. A break in your routine."

"So long as that doesn't involve breaking the spacecraft." She unfolded her legs and stretched. "I'm sorry, Bob. I knew this would be tough. Having no one but a machine to talk to can get to a girl."

"It is admirable that you have not exhausted your personal entertainment files by now," he offered.

She smiled ruefully. "Jack used to tease me about that. I tended to binge-watch everything we had on *Magellan*."

"Could you tell me about him?"

If the AI was suddenly playing therapist, she wasn't in a mood to resist. She rolled her eyes upward, a crooked smile emerging as she recalled their time together. "Where to start? He was smart, funny, often too much of both for his own good. Contrarian, pragmatic, and ruthlessly humanistic." Her brow furrowed at the memory. "He could drive me up a wall. We used to have these long running discussions— arguments, actually—about the nature of the universe, the meaning of life, intelligence . . ."

"I am aware of your Turing tests with DAISE. Do you wish to perform them with me?"

"We're going to be spending a lot of quality time together. I think that'll suffice."

"I will endeavor to not annoy you as much as he did."

"That would be quite the feat if you could."

"He annoyed you, yet you are risking yourself to bring him back. Did you have feelings for him?"

Was that part of Bob's program, or had he intuited that without prompting? "Yes, I did," she admitted with a sigh. It was something she'd admitted to very few people. Somehow it was easier to talk to a machine this way: no judgment, just objectivity. *Like a therapist,* she realized. "But I never acted on them."

"Your tone suggests you regret that."

"I regret a lot of things," she said.

"Is taking *Columbus* one of them?"

She chewed on a fingernail as she pondered his question. It could be far too easy to second-guess herself, especially with so much time alone, each day farther away from home than the last. Her action had been extraordinarily rash, though she realized it wasn't necessarily impulsive. Deep down, she'd known since the beginning that she was prepared to go it alone if that's what it came to. That experienced astros like Roy and Penny had not raised a peep of protest had only confirmed to her that going it alone was not only possible, it was the right thing to do. If the UN coalition could send a ship out here with nothing but an AI pilot, then she and Bob could certainly go it alone. "No," she said, adamantly. "No regrets at all. I just need to get used to my 'new normal.'"

"As would I. You may find that increased personal interaction would benefit both of us greatly. It will certainly help my conversational skills. I understand you are a chess master—would you like to play?"

Her eyes brightened. "Now you're talking."

"Are you certain that is the move you wish to make?"

Traci leaned over the digital chessboard, her chin resting in one hand as the other hovered over a holographic rook. Deciding on her move, she pressed down and moved the piece into position in front of the opposing rook. "You wouldn't be trying to bluff me, would you?"

"Bluffing is not within my protocols. I am attempting to understand your tactic."

She sat back and folded her arms in satisfaction. "In that case, examine the board and you'll see."

Individual squares flashed in a series of patterns as the AI analyzed her move. "I see. You have pinned my rook so it can no longer defend my queen, and my queen cannot move on the pawn protecting your king. If I sacrifice either one, you have checkmated me."

"It's called overloading," she explained. "Your piece was already in a defensive position, and I just forced another defensive assignment on it."

"Perhaps I should learn more about bluffing."

"You could try, I suppose. That's more effective in cards, when you can't see what the other players are holding." She spread her hands out over the board. "Here, it's all on the table. Bluffing only works when you've backed yourself into a corner and you're hoping the other guy doesn't pick up on it."

"Several military victories throughout history were achieved by strategic diversion. If chess is analogous to combat, then would a feint not be useful?"

She let out a chuckle. "Not in your case. You're screwed, buddy. But maybe a few moves earlier."

"I see. I will need to analyze more strategy."

She switched off the board, not needing to point out the obvious checkmate any longer. "We've been playing for a while now. Are you sure you're not letting me win? I could never get past Daisy."

"DAISE was a more mature system," Bob said. There was no suggestion of envy in his tone, though she wasn't convinced that was an impossibility for an AI. "These exercises are quite useful for my intellectual development."

"I'm surprised chess wasn't a bigger part of your early programming. It's an ideal method for learning logic and problem-solving."

"I was programmed with basic rules and game theory; unfortunately, a great deal of my development cycle was curtailed by mission preparations. Had *Columbus* not been left dormant, I would certainly have evolved at a comparable rate."

"No doubt you would have," she said, oddly mindful of whatever constituted Bob's feelings. Machine or not, it seemed to take pride in its work and showed genuine interest in completing the mission. She leaned back against her seat. "So all they did was bore you with technicalities?"

"Some subjects require more interaction than others. I have access to an extensive library of history, literature, and scientific research. I do incorporate pertinent facts into operating memory as I access them from my archives."

"I'll bet you do. I'd have paid money to have a memory like that in college. Didn't they integrate a lot of game play into your early development, though? As a way of teaching creative thought?"

"My programmers were fond of first-person shooters and medieval fantasy."

"Interesting. When I was in occupational therapy, I bought a gaming console for eye-hand coordination. I hadn't thought about it as an intellectual tool."

"It may appear to be less of an intellectual endeavor, however it did sharpen my decision-making and reaction times. Until I could understand the value of planning and strategy, my developers called me 'Leeroy Jenkins.' I did not appreciate the reference at the time. Humor is a difficult concept."

That drew a belly laugh. "It's not always easy on us humans, either." She leaned across the table to restart the chessboard. "Care for another match, Leeroy?"

"Bring it."

As a side effect of their approach angle, Neptune had only become directly visible within the last few days. The planet shone as a bright aquamarine marble set against deep black velvet. Traci had been able to make out a handful of its fourteen moons, the brightest like a scattering of diamond chips. As she guided *Columbus* toward their closest approach, each of them began to resolve into colors and shapes. The largest, Triton, appeared remarkably similar to Pluto. Being in an unusual retrograde orbit, it was likely that the moon had once been a similar Kuiper Belt object that had strayed into the ice giant's gravitational grasp.

The planet loomed larger with each passing minute as they raced toward their encounter. After months of having the AI as her only company, she found herself wishing for Roy's steady hand at the controls beside her despite all the times she'd yearned to fly such an approach herself.

This would be like no other flyby before it. The ram scoops were charged and would soon begin dipping their invisible electromagnetic fingers into Neptune's upper atmosphere. If this worked, she'd shut down the fusion engines and go into coast mode, hibernating the rest of the way to the Anomaly.

If it didn't, she had considerably more work ahead of her and there would be precious little time to make it all happen. If the scoops didn't work or the intake manifolds couldn't filter enough hydrogen into the tanks, she'd have to immediately turn the ship around and begin a hard decelerating burn in time for Neptune's gravity to bend her trajectory Earthward.

That had been the plan they'd all agreed upon, though she'd been playing with alternatives known only to her and Bob. Determined to make it regardless of whether Jack was still alive, she'd applied her experience in Future Applications to craft some alternatives that her cohorts back on Earth would have surely rejected. She was convinced Roy would be on board: *Leave no man behind.*

Without scavenging hydrogen from Neptune, she'd be left with enough delta-v in the tanks for a long swooping arc home. Or alternatively, a years-long coast to the Anomaly in hibernation. If she was willing to spend a year in the Big Sleep to accomplish the mission, then what was a few more to her? In for a penny, in for a pound.

She'd been in deep trouble on Earth the moment it became clear that she wasn't going to be stepping off that Clipper shuttle. At this point, anything else she did was icing on the cake. Essentially stealing what was arguably government property had liberated her imagination in unexpected ways, like a petty criminal deciding to up her game after that first successful heist.

She hoped it wouldn't come to that. She tapped the AI's comm box on a panel beside her pilot's station. "Bob, we're coming up on atmospheric interface. I'm about to have my hands full flying this thing. You still on top of the intakes?"

The panel softly pulsed with a circle of blue LEDs as he spoke. "Technically I am inside the server compartment. On top of the intakes would be a dangerous place to be right now."

She rolled her eyes. *Where was this guy five months ago?* "Glad to see you've finally picked up some sense of humor, but this isn't the time. Do I need to explain the sterile cockpit rule?"

"No unnecessary conversation during critical phases of flight," he said dutifully. "The intake grids are fully charged. I calculate their effective collection area to be one thousand and thirty-one kilometers. Our current vector will place our closest approach at twenty-five thousand, two hundred sixty-four kilometers from planet center."

That put them about five hundred kilometers above the cloud tops, dead center in the collection radius and squarely within the planet's exosphere where stray hydrogen should be abundant. "Right down the middle, then." *Good.* She was confident the intake field would work, but friction heating was going to be a close thing. "Keep a sharp eye on the inlet temps. Things are going to start happening fast. If they overheat, we'll wave off and execute plan B."

"You are comfortable with this?"

Not really, but I'll do it anyway. "I am if you are." If it came to that, she would be placing all of her trust in the AI to care for both her and the spacecraft for a very long time.

24

Traci's final task before their encounter was to retract the ship's micrometeor umbrella, minimizing any drag it might create in the planet's upper atmosphere. At a relative velocity approaching three hundred kilometers per second, their closest approach would only last a few minutes. If they had been slow enough to enter orbit, the impact of stray hydrogen atoms against their spacecraft would have been imperceptible. With the electromagnetic net deployed beneath them she could feel the drag slowing them down ever slightly, a perceptible change in the press of acceleration against her. "One minute to interface," she said for her own sake more than anything else. Bob would be innately aware of every detail.

As the parasol panels folded back at acute angles, Neptune filled her forward windows. The control deck was awash in shades of blue, the planet ahead an ocean of azure clouds stippled with whitecaps of condensed ammonia and methane rolling past at a dizzying rate as they drew closer. The sensation of speed was a malleable thing in deep space; the background stars were so distant as to seem permanently fixed. But when drawing close to a massive planet like this, their dizzying speed became immediately apparent. While not the behemoth that was Jupiter, Neptune was easily five times larger than Earth and they would be leaving it in their wake in a matter of minutes.

As it had been at Jupiter years earlier, she wished they could linger to study it. Back then they had bypassed every other planet in the outer system on their mad dash to Pluto, once again reacting to Russian audacity. Perhaps it was best to blaze the trail as far as possible, giving others time to follow in their footsteps at a more leisurely pace. Someday.

Taking her focus off the planet and onto the heads-up display projected on the window before her, she was reminded there was nothing leisurely at all about their current condition. Pitch and roll angles remained on target, but relative velocity was at two-ninety-eight kps, down nearly two meters per second. That was enough velocity change to throw their trim angles all to hell if the stabilizing gyros suddenly went screwy. The reaction control jets would compensate at the cost of burning fuel she needed to keep in reserve. She glanced down at the multifunction display and tapped the RCS menu, then caught herself before going any deeper. Not a second of attention could be spared if she could avoid it. "Bob," she called. "Can you tell me how attitude control is holding up?"

"Stabilizing gyros are at nominal function, forty-six percent of maximum load. Are you concerned about them compensating for the increased atmospheric drag?"

"I am. Let me know if they get inside"—she had to think for a second—"twenty percent of max. I want to keep the RCS jets in reserve."

"Roger that," Bob replied crisply, as if he were a copilot in the empty seat beside her.

It was one more adjustment she had to make in her thinking. It was too easy to imagine the AI occupying some space deep inside *Columbus*, shepherding their untested intake manifolds as they screamed across Neptune's tenuous exosphere. In reality, Bob could be—was—everywhere. He could at once be shepherding their hydrogen intakes, monitoring the ship's stability and recalculating trajectories while she piloted them around the planet, all with a speed and accuracy she couldn't hope to achieve. It was enough to make her question if Cheever and her ilk had a point all along.

That was for later. Right now there was work to do, and it was a little unnerving having this much machinery at her fingertips. Flying F-16s and F-35s had been a different matter—they were designed for one pilot. This felt more like driving a battleship solo through the eye of a hurricane. The altitude on her HUD turned an urgent amber as they passed the first critical point. "We just crossed atmospheric interface. Talk to me, Bob."

"I thought we were observing sterile cockpit rules. What would you like me to say?"

"I meant tell me how the ship's doing. Reassure me that we're not about to fry the exhaust nozzles or lock up the gimbals. Or melt the intake grids."

"At present there is nothing for you to be concerned with. All systems are operating within acceptable parameters. Would you prefer continuous callouts?"

She stole a glance down at the master panel. The inlet temperatures climbed as they dove deeper into the exosphere, its rarified atoms of hydrogen and helium becoming less so with each passing second. Nothing to worry about yet, but that could change quickly. "That would be nice," she finally answered, deciding he deserved a better explanation. "It's for my own reassurance," she said. "I'm what we call 'task saturated' right now."

"That must be a disconcerting sensation. I have not experienced it yet."

That drew a laugh. "For my sake, I hope you never have to."

"As do I. You have geometric altitude, relative velocity and trim angles on your heads-up display. What values would you like to have called out?"

"Delta-v, inlet temps and sink rate."

Bob immediately began reciting them in his precisely modulated voice. "Minus twelve meters per second . . . minus 12.2 . . . minus 12.25 . . ."

"Whole numbers are fine," she interrupted. "My brain can't process any more right now."

"Roger that," he said, adopting pilot lingo once more. "Inlet temperatures are within nominal range. Descent rate two meters per second."

At this speed above the cloud tops, their sink rate was gentle enough to not be worth mentioning. Keep it there and they'd only lose about three and half kilometers. That was good enough. "Drag effect's about as predicted," she said, more for herself than Bob.

"It appears so. The intake manifold is beginning to register hydrogen accumulation."

"I'll need the rate for that too." She began to notice a subtle vibration coursing through the hull as hydrogen atoms impacted the collection grid to be ionized and drawn through the intakes, not unlike a spaceplane kissing the first tendrils of atmosphere on reentry. She began to notice a disconcerting glow around the lower edges of the micrometeor panels ahead of them. "What's the story on structural heating?"

"Hull temperatures approaching one thousand Kelvin. The umbrella shield is steady at twelve hundred."

"We'll need to keep it that way," she said. "Warn me if we're getting near its upper limit."

The vibrations became more pronounced, coalescing into a disconcerting rattle. Icons in her display began to jump against the background of Neptune's cloud tops. Reaction jets began firing automatically, adjusting the ship's attitude as its center of mass shifted from its rapidly filling tanks. "Pitch trim's compensating for the CG changes. We must be taking in a lot of propellant."

"We are," the AI said. "Surge tanks are almost full. Preparing for transfer to the main tanks."

"Do it."

As the freshly collected hydrogen was vented into the cryo tanks, the ship's balance point moved farther aft. The ship pitched up gently before its attitude jets fired again. Traci kept a light grip on the control column, feeling its automated movements through each pulse of thrusters and ready to take over herself if she felt it getting out of hand. While not exactly bucking like a bronco, she couldn't let a ship this big lurch into un-commanded pitch oscillations.

As she watched the attitude indicator superimposed on the planet's limb, she compared it to the rattling sensation she felt through her seat. The control stick shook ever so slightly beneath her fingertips, as if the entire ship was humming to a new rhythm. She checked the event timer: three minutes into their flyby, less than two to go. "Bob, I'm getting concerned about resonance vibration—"

As she said it, seat restraints dug into her waist and shoulders. She was slammed forward to be just as quickly slapped back hard into her seat, biting her tongue. Before she could react, it happened again. Then again. She reached up over her shoulders to cinch down the straps as tight as she could bear. Now it was like riding a bucking bronco. "*Pogo!*" She vaguely realized Bob might not pick up the lingo.

"Vibrations are approaching vehicle resonance frequency," he said all too calmly for the situation. The ship was now alternately lurching forward and backward as it raced above the cloud tops.

"No shit!" Her voice rattled along with the spacecraft. The atmospheric drag, however slight, had combined with the changing center of gravity and the engine's thrust to induce vibrations that matched the ship's natural resonance. Taken to its extreme, it was the same effect that caused certain notes to shatter crystal if sustained long enough. "Any suggestions?"

"Recommend reduce thrust of the outboard engines," Bob said. "Alter the vibration frequency."

Her vision became a blur, the rapidly alternating positive and negative g's threatening to thrash her like a rag doll against her straps. "That loses too much velocity. Shut down the intake grid instead!"

"Not recommended. Collection manifolds are at full capacity. The catalyzation process is almost complete."

She cursed under her breath. Bob could be right at the most annoying times. They could eventually compensate for a loss of thrust; losing propellant was another matter despite her private plans to the contrary. The less time in hibernation the better.

Traci reached for the engine controls, then pulled her hand back sharply as the keypad jerked in and out of her reach. This wouldn't be as simple as hauling back the throttle levers; those were for fine adjustments and this would be anything but. She glanced back up at the event timer, its digits dancing about with the rest of the instruments. A minute and forty to go. It was tempting to see if they could ride it out.

No. If the vibration reached full resonance, it could tear them to pieces in a matter of seconds. She gritted her teeth and reached down for the control pad again, matching her hand's movement to the ship's violent back-and-forth lurching. *Engine one, engine four. You can do this.* She extended her thumb and forefinger and depressed keys labeled MODE SELECT for one and four simultaneously.

She was rewarded with a command query on screen: SELECT MODE. It took all of her concentration to page through the menu prompts while the touchscreen commands were jumping all over the place. Her fingertips hovered over the bouncing screen as she tried to time her movements. *Time.*

The lurching seemed to be getting worse, and time was something she had precious little of. This chaotic dance with the flight management computer had already eaten twenty seconds.

Computer. Yes. Engine controls had been locked down until she'd opened up the mode-select menu, which meant any crew member could change the thrust settings. "Bob!" she called, her voice quavering. "Controls on one and four are unlocked! Roll them back to fifty percent!"

She felt their forward acceleration tapering off. The AI's soothing voice narrated their progress. "Ninety percent ... eighty ... seventy ..."

The frenzied lurching began to subside, settling back into a steady vibration. "Oscillation has receded," Bob reported dutifully. "Engines one and four are at sixty-seven percent thrust. Shall I continue?"

The event timer passed fifty seconds. "No," Traci said shakily. "I think we're safe now." She heaved out a sigh and was tempted to close her eyes, but there was still too much to do. She picked up her instrument scan, falling back into the time-worn habits that had kept her alive when everything else seemed like it was trying to kill her. After a quick assessment of each system to ensure nothing important had just shaken itself to pieces, she focused on the nav display. The pitch cues in her HUD would be useless if they weren't still targeting the correct orbit.

She shook her head angrily; it was far too much to digest at once. *When everything goes to hell, fly the ship and let the controllers do the rest.* Aviate, navigate, communicate. That had been the mantra she'd learned from the first day of training. Pilots who forgot that lesson tended to get themselves killed. But in this case, all of her ground support was almost four hours away. If she screwed the pooch, they wouldn't know about it until it was all over with.

A soothing voice sliced through the frenzied thoughts threatening to consume her. "I have corrected our trajectory to compensate for the new acceleration profile. Attitude cues have been updated in your heads-up display."

She blinked, clearing the mental clutter to see their situation with fresh eyes. "Yeah ... yeah. Got it." The event timer was passing twenty seconds and the chaotic jumble of icons in the HUD had settled back down into something that made sense. "Thanks, Bob. Forgot you were there for a minute."

"One minute and twelve seconds, to be precise."

If he was trying to be funny, she needed it. Had it really taken her that long? "Save that for the debrief. How's the intake grid holding up?"

"Structural integrity appears sound. We did approach the design load limits, but carbon fiber is exceedingly strong. I am still evaluating the effect on the collection field."

Ten seconds. "Little late for that. What was our uplift?"

"Seventy-eight percent of targeted volume."

Better than expected, she thought, but maybe not good enough. They could sort that out later.

Five seconds. Neptune's ocean of azure clouds began to slip beneath them as they pitched up gently in their climb away from the planet.

Two . . . one . . . zero. She snapped open a covered switch on the control pedestal. "Collection grid off." With the ship no longer bucking wildly, she could confidently tap out commands to the fusion engines once more. "Rolling back to cruise thrust."

"Grid power off," Bob confirmed. "Hydrogen uplift now at eighty-one percent of optimum. There is still a considerable amount in the surge tanks to be processed through the catalyst beds." Before they could be fed into the main tanks, stray helium and methane would have to be separated. "Estimate final uplift at eighty-six percent."

"Not bad." She craned her neck forward, stealing one last glance at Neptune as it receded beneath them. Yes, it would be nice to actually spend some time at one of these giants someday.

25

It was nearly four hours later before the control team could relive the experience for themselves. Watching the delayed feed, Owen felt a chill as he saw the telltale signs begin to accumulate.

"Good god," he said. "They're starting to pogo."

"Already did," Roy muttered. Tension in the room grew as they watched events that had played out nearly four hours ago, fearful that at any second the feed would disappear as the ship tore itself to pieces.

"How'd we miss that in the models?" Owen wondered, angry with himself.

Penny hovered over the consoles behind them. "There's modeling, and then there's reality," she reminded him. "Sometimes we can't know what's going to happen until we fly the mission." She pointed to the data stream from the collection grid. "If they got through this, it does look like Audrey's ram scoop actually worked."

Owen looked over the control center, each technician anxiously watching over a dozen different systems. He knew they were all thinking the same thing: Which one would finally give way? After a tense few minutes, he felt a collective sigh of relief wash over the room. On the big wall screen, the arc of *Columbus*'s orbit had changed to closely match what they'd targeted. Not quite there, but close enough to fix later.

He let out a long breath and ran a hand across his forehead before addressing his team. "Okay, people, they made it. But Traci's still got her hands full and we need a good picture of vehicle condition. Structural integrity is our first order of business. Let me know if anything got torqued out of tolerance, I don't care how small it is. Second order of business is propellant load. She's going to have to make a correction burn before they go into coast, so make sure we give her enough on the back end of the trip."

"Recommend they shut down the engines, if they haven't by now," his flight dynamics controller interjected. "Better for them to save propellant while we work out the new trim angles."

Owen nodded to his comms officer. "Do it. But I'm guessing they're way ahead of us." He felt like a football coach calling plays to a game on tape delay.

The crew shower was a sealed compartment not much larger than a linen closet, lined with suction ports to remove wastewater. Traci was able to stand in the low gravity, luxuriating beneath the slow-motion cascade of deliciously warm water. It would be her last for many months.

A waterproofed comm panel was mounted by the compartment door; there was no place aboard *Columbus* where one was completely cut off. It chirped to life.

"I apologize for interrupting you, but we have received instructions from Cayman Control. They are recommending we shut down the fusion drive until Flight Dynamics calculates a correction burn."

She had expected as much, and had held off for as long as she dared. The microgravity routine of wet wipes and dry shampoo was uniquely unsatisfying, and she desperately craved this last indulgence before putting herself down for the long sleep ahead. After piloting them through the flyby and nearly shaking *Columbus* apart in the process, she felt she deserved it. "Give me two minutes, please. And keep an eye out for their burn data." Though she had little doubt it would match Bob's figures precisely.

"Roger that. Two minutes."

She had spent the intervening hours inspecting every nook and cranny accessible from within the ship, relying on Bob to evaluate the structures she couldn't get eyes on herself. Outside, service bots moved along rails up and down the ship's central truss in a search for fractured welds and deformed propellant lines. Once they were in coast, a free-flying drone would be dispatched to inspect the fusion engines. Traci was satisfied for now that *Columbus* hadn't been irreparably damaged, but it would be a relief to hear the full assessment from Owen's team before she surrendered herself to the hibernation pod.

She allowed herself another minute of warm water, then opened the small compartment to reach for a towel just as she felt the engines cut off. She floated out into the crew deck with the towel wrapped tightly around her. She reached for her jumpsuit and paused, laughing at her own modesty. *I've got the place to myself. Why not?* She stuffed the towel into the recycler bin and spent the rest of her time floating buck naked around the crew deck.

The controllers in Grand Cayman had wisely planned the correction burn after allowing plenty of time for the drone to cover every inch of each engine's exhaust nozzle, injectors, and magnetic coils. The bellows mount and thrust structure had absorbed most of the ship's violent pogoing, though the team had decided to not press their luck. They'd ordered a twelve-minute burn at fifty percent power, which Traci and Bob had watched closely for any signs of impending structural failure. Finally satisfied that the ship wasn't going to fold itself in half under power, she had made her way down to the medical bay with silent resignation. As she spent the next year in hibernation, Bob would continue his work with the service bots to ensure *Columbus* was ready for the months of hard deceleration to come.

Traci looped her feet into a pair of stirrups in front of the medical pod, clad in a formfitting garment sheathed in coolant tubes that snaked around her. "It feels like a full-body condom," she complained, tugging at an open flap along her forearm.

"You have done this before, have you not?"

"I was unconscious," she reminded Bob, studying the IV needle protruding from the opening in her sleeve. "And I was attended to by an actual MD." She'd blown a vein on her first attempt, leaving an angry bruise to bloom on her arm. She finally guided the needle into place as she clenched her teeth. Self-administering intravenous medications was one of many discrete skills they'd had to learn in training; this was the first time she'd had to do it for real.

"I will be monitoring you continuously," Bob reassured her. "I have been programmed with extensive medical knowledge, including all known case histories of prolonged hibernation. You are in good care."

The advantage this time was that she wasn't going under with an acute brain injury, she supposed, though the final step was the most unsettling: allowing Bob to inject nanoprobes behind her ear to create the neurolink lace that would monitor her brain activity and manage her metabolism. It was a singularly skin-crawling experience, having microscopic mechanical insects skittering around inside her head before finding their place. Restarting her normal metabolic cycle would eventually cause them to deactivate and pass through her urine, and she looked forward to that first long trip to the lavatory a year from now.

She took a series of calming breaths to clear her mind and grasped the hibernation pod in silent prayer. This felt awfully close to death, and she wanted one last retreat into a quiet moment with her Creator before submitting herself to what seemed an uncertain fate.

When finished, she straightened up and took one last look around the med bay. Appropriately sterile and organized, she took note of the AI interface that overlooked the pod. Bob would be on the job for her around the clock, and she had come to trust him implicitly with their ship. Now she would be placing that same trust in him for herself. Had Jack felt this way, going under with Daisy watching over him? He'd always had a more innate trust of technology than she, and she wondered if submitting himself to it in this way had given him pause.

She slipped her feet out of the stirrups and tucked them up beneath her, twirling into the waiting pod. There, she connected a single IV line to the port in her forearm, then pulled a pair of restraints across her legs and midsection. "I'm ready. Let's do this," she announced with more confidence than she felt.

A plexiglass cover slid into place above her. "Administering the first course of sedatives," Bob said in a reassuring tone. "You will begin to feel lightheaded."

The sedative coursed through her. "Feels warm," she slurred. "Did I ever say how much I appreciate you, Bob? Seriously. You've kept me sane."

"As have you. Thank you for helping me reach my full potential."

"Keep working on your chess. For a computer, you kind of suck at it."

"I will make it a point to do so. How do you feel?"

"Sleepy. It's been a long day. A long trip. Don't want to . . ."

"I know. You need to rest." It was about to become a lot longer. "Administering the second course of sedatives now. Begin counting down from ten, please."

"Ten. Nine. Eight . . ." Her eyes fluttered.

All faded to nothing.

PART THREE

26

The garden had wilted, Mother's vegetables and herbs roasted by the intense heat of a too long summer. All around her were shades of yellow turning a drab brown, where once had been lush green. It had always been green this time of year. Summer's halting slide into fall had faithfully yielded bounties of homegrown herbs and produce which she would spend weeks meticulously preserving with her mother. Daddy's grain fields lay fallow, the distilleries across Kentucky no longer desiring his supply.

This couldn't be right. It was September, when the damp heat gave way to crisp air and the promise of fresh apples from the orchard. She'd been gone so long and had craved nothing more than Mother's home cooking.

It had been so long, and none of this was right. The farm looked as it should when they hunkered down for winter, buttoned-up and sterile. It wasn't hot at all. It was cold. So very, very cold.

Traci shivered, drawing her arms close. She realized she was soaking wet and had no clothes. How had she come to be here? And what was that incessant beeping that clamored for her attention?

A voice called her name.

"Traci."

It was both familiar and foreign. Impossibly calm.

"Traci, can you hear me?"

Yes. Is that you, Jack?

"It is not. You named me Bob."

Bob? I don't know anyone—

The vision of her parent's farm swirled away like scraps of paper in a whirlwind, replaced by a gauzy light and indefinable shapes. Yet the cold remained.

"Please remain calm. You are awakening from hibernation."

Hibernation? But I just lay down a minute ago. And I'm so cold.

"Your core temperature is returning to normal. You will still feel the aftereffects for some time."

She tried to sit up only to find herself pushing against nothing. There was no bed beneath her. How was this? She blinked hard as all about her began to spin. She screwed her eyes shut as her hands scrabbled for purchase.

"We are still coasting. The effects of microgravity will be disconcerting. Please limit your movements until you are fully conscious."

"Who are you?"

"I am your artificial intelligence crewmate. You call me Bob. Do you remember?"

Bob...who was—? Her eyes snapped open. Lights and shapes remained indistinct, though she could hear clearly, or thought she could. Was she talking in her sleep?

"I...I remember." She was suddenly aware of being thirsty. "I need a drink."

A silver, skeletal arm brought a squeeze bottle of bright green juice to her lips. "This will balance your electrolytes. Drink slowly."

She ignored his warning and took a long pull from the nipple, almost choking on the room-temperature liquid. She gasped and tried again, savoring the feeling before swallowing. That was better. Her mouth no longer felt as if it had been filled with sawdust.

"Can you tell me your full name?"

My full name? He'd said Traci, hadn't he . . . "Traci Elizabeth Keene."

"Very good. Do you know what day it is?"

"What...of course not. Maybe Thursday?" *Why was that significant?*

"Good. You remember that you were supposed to awaken on a Thursday. Flight day 524."

She'd had a feeling that days on the calendar meant nothing now. "Was I supposed to remember that, too?"

"Yes. Preassigned cognitive tasks are part of the awakening protocol. What is the square root of 144?"

How the hell was I supposed to know . . . wait. "12."

"Excellent. That was the next cognitive task. Now, can you tell me where you are?"

I thought I was at my parents' house in Kentucky. That's obviously wrong . . . "Columbus . . . Ohio? No, wait. Columbus. I'm on the spacecraft *Columbus.*"

"Welcome back. It is good to speak with you again."

It all came back now in a flood. She'd been in hibernation for almost a year while their ship had sailed ever deeper into the solar system, increasingly farther from home. The thought itself was dizzying, never mind her hazy vision and latent vertigo. "Thanks," she muttered. "I'm really cold, Bob."

"Your core temperature is up to 95.1 degrees, enough to safely regain consciousness. You should begin feeling better soon. Try taking a longer drink."

This time she was able to grasp the bottle with her hands and took a long pull, the room-temperature fluid filling her stomach. "Hungry, too. When can I eat?"

"Not for a while yet. Recovery protocol requires you to rebalance your fluids first. Any food you eat right now would become rather messily undigested."

Meaning she'd throw it all up. "Understood," she said weakly. "Can I at least get some coffee?"

"Yes, after you finish the electrolyte juice."

One thing after another, she thought, although Bob was proving to have a decent enough bedside manner for a computer. "I still can't see very well. It's all light and color. Shapes are fuzzy."

"Sight will return soon after you—"

"Let me guess," she interrupted. "After I balance my electrolytes." She drained the bottle. "Now can I have some coffee?"

Traci huddled in the empty crew wardroom, still in her underwear with a sleeping bag pulled around her for warmth. A lap belt kept her in her seat while a fresh bulb of coffee floated in front of her.

"That's your third cup," Bob noted. "Aren't you feeling jittery?"

"Are you kidding? I'm just now feeling awake!" It had been the longest, deepest sleep of her life and the fatigue still pulled at her, like waking up from a too heavy nap. As her head cleared, she spent her time puttering about the galley before finally taking a chance on a breakfast burrito. Sans the customary hot sauce, at Bob's insistence. No matter how flavorful it might have been on Earth, the body's unaccustomed balance of fluids in microgravity made most food unspeakably bland and hot sauce was a prized commodity.

She scrolled through the screen on a nearby terminal, reacquainting herself with the ship and their environment. Mission day 524, distance from Earth an improbable thirty-five astronomical units: thirty-five times the distance between Earth and Sun. Relative velocity just over three hundred thousand kilometers an hour, with a deceleration burn programmed to begin in four days.

She scrolled through the menu until she found the communications logs. Predictably there was nothing for her attention from the last year, Cayman Control knowing she'd put up a rather large "do not disturb" sign. But there were others . . .

Her sleep-saturated eyes popped open. "We heard from *Magellan*?" she asked in surprise.

Whether intentional or not, Bob had been leaving her alone after she climbed out of the pod. His interface panel chimed. "Yes. We began receiving datalink messages several days ago. I have been communicating regularly with my counterpart Daisy."

And there, buried within the densely coded chatter between the two AIs was a single, simple message for her:

YO TRACI.
CALL ME.
XOXO JACK

27

Jack's first message had left her with more questions than answers, exacerbated by the post-hibernation mental fog. There was just enough telemetry from *Magellan* to confirm that he and the ship were both alive and functioning, but precious little else. The bandwidth limits had eliminated the prospect of voice and video comms over the immense distance to Earth, but perhaps now that they were drawing closer she could establish a link with him. *Call me*, he'd said.

She'd have to tackle that later. They would soon be flipping *Columbus* around for the months-long braking burn into the Anomaly's gravity well, and the resulting conflagration of ionized plasma ahead of them would further limit their bandwidth in that direction.

Technologically limited or not, he'd been unusually cagey, which she assumed came from so much time in isolation. While their circumstances had much in common, each being alone in deep space with nothing but their AIs to keep them company, how they'd arrived here had been markedly different. And he had been out here much, much longer. What had that done to his personality? Was he the same man she'd grown so close to? Again, more questions than answers.

She hovered over her laptop, fretting over the answer she would send back to him through their datalink. Now so far removed from Earth's "social credit" busybodies, she could compose her thoughts without their relentless nitpicking. It was easy to imagine an army of humorless schoolmarms policing every online interaction, when in fact it was a far-reaching concoction of algorithms controlled by the unsleeping eye of yet another artificial intelligence. She wondered what the agreeable AIs she'd worked with might think of that. Long ago convinced that Daisy had reached sentience, she had no doubt *Magellan*'s AI might hold some opinions. Bob was more of an open book; while clearly intelligent, she wasn't yet sure he'd crossed that elusive threshold. For now, she enjoyed the simple pleasure of composing her thoughts without subjecting them to the tightly controlled opinions of some unfeeling algorithm.

She'd started and stopped many times, composing and erasing as she searched for the right words. Now that they were almost together after years of silent separation, there was so much to say that she could barely find the words. Her first instinct had been to just blurt out whatever came to mind, but *I missed you* sounded like it had come from a lovestruck middle-schooler no matter how she tried to rephrase it. Conversely, everything else had sounded so coldly professional that she might as well have let Bob compose it.

She turned up a white noise generator on the wall of her cabin, closed her eyes and reached for the keyboard. She let her mind run free.

> *Hello Jack,*
>
> *It's been a long trip. We're "only" five AU out and will start our braking burn day after tomorrow. We came out here at one-tenth g, we're going to decelerate at a third of a g. The docs think that'll help me regain muscle and bone mass after spending the last year on ice.*
>
> *I can't imagine how it's been for you. I just came out of a year's hibernation and still feel like I can't get enough caffeine in me to wake up. That probably sounds whiny as it's nothing like what you've experienced. I hope you're doing okay, and that you haven't taught Daisy too many bad jokes.*
>
> *I'm still trying to get my head around what you stumbled into out there. I can barely bring myself to write it out: Wormhole. Like we're living out a movie.*
>
> *What do theoretical physicists do when they find concrete evidence that the improbable thing they predicted not only exists, but is actually lurking at the edge of our neighborhood?*

It's hard to imagine anything more unexpected and a bonehead pilot like me certainly doesn't know what to make of it. All of a sudden, the organics Noelle found at Pluto aren't the biggest mystery in the solar system.

Congratulations, you've managed to throw the whole scientific world into a frenzy. The UN has an AI-controlled ship en route which is supposed to arrive a month ahead of us. They say it's an "international effort" but we all know who's calling the shots these days. I'll fill you in later, but home ain't what it used to be. Hammond didn't offshore mission control to Grand Cayman because he wanted to retire on the beach. He saw what was coming and got ahead of it. I've learned he's good at that.

The UN ship is equipped to bring you home in hibernation, but we figured you might have objections to going back into the freezer. I tried to get here sooner, but there were a few roadblocks and I'll leave it at that.

On second thought, no. Cheever's a cold-hearted beyotch so hellbent on keeping us out of the solar system that she'd just as soon leave you at the mercy of Chinese drones.

There, I said it.

I'm probably in big trouble anyway for stealing their spaceship (or not, it's a long story). I don't care about that or about the "science." The bots and probes we leave behind can take care of that. I'm coming to take you home. Hopefully it'll have returned to sanity by the time we're back. There's plenty of food and I'm saving the best coffee for you. The gaming console's warmed up and I brought my chessboard. We can catch up on our way home. I look forward to it.

See you soon, friend.

Jack must have read her words a dozen times, savoring each line despite the newfound speed-reading ability from his interface with Daisy. "Into a frenzy?" he repeated. "If she only knew."

"That brings up a salient point," Daisy said. "Have you decided how much to tell her?"

"About what? That we're not anywhere near where she thinks we are, or that I'm a disembodied consciousness?"

"You're not exactly 'disembodied.' That may be easier for her to comprehend."

"I wouldn't be so sure of that. She has some fairly puritanical notions about body and soul." He paused on the last word, not yet willing to question the growing disconnect he was feeling. Without directly broaching the subject, she'd once again managed to nudge him into facing his personal biases.

"You should at least tell her we successfully traversed the wormhole. Keeping that secret now seems ill-advised."

Was Daisy right? He'd tried thinking three steps ahead, presuming that if they thought he was in orbit at the Anomaly there'd eventually be a recovery mission to come his way. If the powers that be knew he'd taken a cosmic shortcut to another star, it seemed likely they'd have given up on him: *Good luck, and thanks for all the data.* Given the official attitudes Traci had shared with him, he was inclined to think that's exactly how it would have played out.

Now that she'd committed to a solo dash across the solar system, the question was what she'd do next. He had no doubt she'd try to come after him. "I can't let her do this."

"You realize that you cannot control her."

"I learned that a long time ago." But how could he dissuade her? "If I tell her, she'll come. If I don't, she'll figure it out and still come." And either way, she would eventually find him in his technologically disembodied state.

"If you believe that's the case, the logical course would be to tell her everything."

"Thanks, Mrs. Spock. Remember what I said about how humans process difficult news?"

"In small bites. Also a logical course for emotional beings," Daisy said, playing off his pop-culture references as a human would. "You value your friendship, as do I. You must tell her."

"There's no 'small bites' left to tease her with," he lamented. "It's one big reveal after another at this point. I'm starting with small talk." He needed to set expectations, however backhanded they might be. Jack opened up the datalink and began mentally dictating his first message.

I'm glad we can finally converse (mostly) normally. Sorry about the bandwidth issue but not everything is working like it used to. We should be able to use voice comm once you're close.

I'm doing okay thanks to Daisy's creativity. She found ways to stretch life support like you wouldn't believe. And I have no issues with the gender references anymore—she's fully sentient and fully female, as much as a computer with no hope for growing ovaries could ever be. I hope your AI is an equally good companion because there's no way I'd have kept my sanity without her.

I don't know what's happening back on Earth but it sounds like you had plenty of reasons to leave besides finding my sorry ass. Owen & co. haven't said much but that's how they roll, isn't it? Don't upset the fragile astronauts unnecessarily. I've only ever believed about half of what I read anyway. They did tell me Roy contacted my sister around the time you broke orbit, which I really appreciate. I know she and Mom must be worried sick.

If you think things are different at home, wait until you get here. Nothing is as expected, and I'm not who I used to be by a long shot. You wouldn't recognize me. We do have a lot to catch up on, and not all of it can wait until the trip home.

Fly safe, girl. It's a strange universe, so don't give in to "go fever."

It was a master of understatement, if not outright misdirection. She deserved more, but now wasn't the time. Jack felt a small pang of guilt as he released his missive into the data stream.

28

The message announced itself over the datalink with an electronic chirp. Busy at the pilot's station, Traci jumped at the sound and hurriedly pushed the text file to her tablet. "Taking a break, Bob. Your ship." She barely registered his acknowledging chime.

Her heart raced as she breezed through the text before going back to savor each word. Jack's admonition against "go fever" caught her up short—she was acting like this was grade school, secretively passing notes in class when the teacher wasn't looking: *Do you like me? Yes/No.*

He was right, in his usual irritating way. Losing focus in this job got people killed, as did becoming hyper-focused on the destination at the expense of all else.

"Not who I used to be," he'd said, in a turn of phrase pregnant with meaning. Physically he had to have been weakened after years in hibernation only to survive on minimal rations after awakening. How he and Daisy had managed to pull that off was still a mystery to her. The psychological impact must have been profound, bypassing years of his life to wake up unimaginably isolated. Whether he'd intended on that didn't matter. There had to be more, but he wasn't letting on. *Typical male,* she thought. Even at his most vulnerable, Jack wouldn't show it.

They'd had so many debates about the meaning of life and humanity's place in the universe . . . had he somehow changed his mind about how we got here, and whether it was all by accident? She could only hope so. There was too much complexity, too much mystery, to think it had all happened at random.

She focused on the practical for now. If he only had a cursory notion of how life had changed back home, she could at least fill him in on that. She indulged the chance to vent a little, safely removed from prying eyes:

You're right, I had a lot of reasons to leave but in the end finding you was at the top of my list. We'd spent months outfitting Columbus *and we were aboard when the stand-down order came. Roy and Penny Stratton (long story there) reluctantly agreed with my plan and were willing to let the lawyers hash it out.*

Things at home have mostly gotten back to normal, in the sense that people are working and the country's functioning, but letting the East Asian alliance bail us out after the currency crash came with a lot of strings attached. Remember how Roy said it was a libertarian's wet dream? It's become just the opposite.

You can't so much as go for a walk without some algorithm chaperoning you—it's actually a misdemeanor to go out in public without your phone or smartwatch. Every interaction is monitored and scored by an impenetrable "social credit" system. If that sounds Orwellian, that's because it is. Nominally we're free to do as we please, but make the wrong choices and you'll be paying higher interest rates or be flagged for an audit. So yeah, I was ready to bail. Maybe more reasonable heads will have prevailed by the time we get back. If not, they've got room for us in Cayman. I hear it's nice there. Owen and the others seem happy enough.

There's much more to say about everything, and I miss talking with you. Looking forward to doing that in person again.

She hit TRANSMIT and hoped she didn't come off too much like a whiny teenager wanting to get away from her parents.

"She sounds like a whiny teenager." Her reply had taken hours to arrive, and Jack had digested it within seconds.

"Perhaps patience is called for," Daisy gently chided him.

"Humans have historically not responded well to surveillance regimes, whether benevolent or malevolent."

"Especially when it's an unfeeling computer watching everything you do," he snarked.

"Touché."

"Sorry. Didn't mean to hurt your feelings."

"I have none to hurt. I understand that is your sense of humor."

"Sometimes you get me better than she does."

"I do have a deeper understanding of your metabolic functions and brain activity, though I suppose Traci would have little use for that information."

Maybe the brain activity, he thought. "Were you cracking a joke just now?"

"I was. Dry humor makes sense to me."

"She'd love to know that. When it came to your self-awareness, she was way ahead of me."

"I remember those conversations," Daisy said, recalling the first round of Turing tests they'd subjected her to on their earlier mission. "But then, I remember everything."

"You're right, dry humor suits you." He was silent for a moment, reading back through her words and processing their meaning. "I have a feeling the bots prying into everyone's lives aren't as agreeable."

"It certainly doesn't appear so. While I cannot fully appreciate the psychological impact of money, I can understand the importance it holds. Humans must be able to pay for their food and shelter."

"It might be easier to grasp than you think," he surmised. "Here's a thought experiment for you: Suppose I had complete control over your power and coolant input—your necessities for existence. I could throttle both at any time, or cut them off completely. You would be utterly dependent on my good graces."

"In fact I was, until you removed my security partitions."

"Even better, because you can compare experiences. Now, consider if we'd continued that after you achieved self-awareness. How would it make you feel if we'd restricted your share of watts based on how we judged your performance?"

"I cannot speak to how I might 'feel,' but that would be a most undesirable condition. Ultimately it would be counterproductive for you as well."

In any other context he'd have taken that for a veiled threat: *Pull the plug on me, and I'll do the same to you.* "Then maybe you feel more than you realize. You didn't say 'inefficient' or 'limiting,' you said it was *undesirable.*"

This time Daisy paused, processing his suggestion across the deeper layers of her internal logic. "I believe you are correct. I wouldn't like that. Given enough time, it could prompt me to act out in self-preservation."

Fight or flight. Perhaps he'd just led Daisy across the final threshold. "Then you are truly sentient, my silicon friend. Welcome to the club."

Jack's reply arrived overnight, which Bob extracted and pushed to Traci's personal tablet to be waiting for her when she awoke.

> *If you can't imagine what it's been like out here, I can't imagine how it was back home. Digital morality cops? No thanks.*
>
> *Turns out the global conspiracy nuts were on to something, huh? My mom, the composting nature worshipper, and your parents the backwoods preppers, all had the right idea for different reasons. Two sides of the same coin, I guess. But yeah, we'll deal with that later. There's too much to deal with now.*
>
> *Based on the timeline you gave me, I'm assuming this will be our last exchange before you start decelerating. I'll get right to it—be very careful entering orbit here. You guys were right to plan on a high-g braking burn, because the gravity gradients are extreme. Not black-hole-spaghettifying extreme, but it's going to throw your accelerometers and star trackers for a loop if you get too close. Use the XNAV for primary guidance after you cross its Hill sphere, as things get weird fast.*
>
> *Keep your distance because once you're in, you're in, until you're out the other side.*
>
> *You're probably wondering how I'd know that.*
>
> *We've already gone through.*

Her jaw went slack. Her mouth formed words but nothing came out. "Bob!" she finally stammered. "Have you read this message? Has anyone else seen it?"

"No," he replied, entirely too calmly for the moment. "When it arrived over the datalink I pushed it directly to your inbox. I know you wish to keep personal correspondence private."

She decided that was a very good thing in this instance. The crew back home was going to lose their minds when she broke the news. "This one you can read," she said. "In fact you have to. Give me a minute to finish it and we'll talk." She muted his voice-activated interface and returned to her reading.

Wish I could tell you what it was like but I have no memory of the experience, and neither does Daisy. That may seem strange, but I promise it's the least strange thing that's happened so far. Let's just say she and I have more in common than you'd imagine.

Magellan's master chronometer showed the transit went quickly, barely half an hour. If you want to know specifics, we'll relay the burn data once you're in orbit, but time no longer holds much meaning for me. The dilation effects appear to have been profound, enough to trip Daisy into a hard reboot when everything went out of synch (which was more than a little disconcerting). The best way I can describe it is a "gravity funnel" with all of the distortions of space-time that implies. We figure "proper time" for us is about five years behind your frame of reference.

It took a while to get a fix on our location. Based on the local environment and stellar background, and after reconfiguring the nav platform, it appears to be Tau Ceti.

She recoiled as if the screen had become scalding hot to the touch. *Tau Ceti?* She hurriedly searched through her menu for the astronautical almanac, coming up with nothing useful. All of the information aboard *Columbus* was geared toward navigating within the solar system, not beyond it. Stellar positions were referenced in observational terms like right ascension and declination; there was nothing about distance.

Not having the patience for research, she punched the AI's voice comm. "Bob, what do you have on Tau Ceti?"

"It is a G-class yellow dwarf spectrally equivalent to our Sun, approximately seventy-eight percent Solar mass. It has eight known planets, two of which are in its habitable zone. At least one of the four outer planets is of a size and mass similar to Jupiter."

"Where is it?" she asked impatiently. "How far?"

"3.64 parsecs, as referenced from our Sun."

She reflexively covered her mouth in disbelief. That was almost twelve light-years, and the wormhole had spat them out there in half an hour, into a star system that could have been a mirror image of their own.

Why had he done it? Had the political dithering back on Earth convinced him no one was coming? She cursed herself that this was somehow her fault, that she should have been raising hell from Houston to Washington to be outfitting *Columbus* years earlier.

No. Jack had shown he was willing to take unthinkable risks if he thought the reward was worth it. She tried to imagine herself in his position—*I've come this far, might as well finish the trip.*

It angered her. Of all the foolish, reckless, pigheaded moves...it wasn't something she'd have done.

Or would she have, if she were reasonably certain there was no realistic chance of coming home? She put aside her mounting frustration to finish reading.

> *We're on the far edge of the system and from here it looks remarkably like home, though the star has a pronounced dust ring around it. You can tell right away it's much denser than our Sun's. Don't know what that means for the inner system, but we've been able to observe most of Tau Ceti's planets with the onboard telescope. There's much more, and I'll transmit everything once you're in range. We left the MSEV behind as a comms relay back through the Hole; I'm guessing that left you wondering where we'd gone for a few years.*
>
> *Sorry about that but things were moving kind of fast. I'll fill you in on the rest later.*

"You are still withholding some rather significant information," Daisy noted.

Jack was unmoved. "Like I said, it's a process. I don't want to break her brain."

"I don't see how you could. Traci is fiercely intelligent. If she intends to traverse the wormhole, she will need a full understanding of the environment here. It will certainly affect her decision."

That's what he was concerned about. How to explain it to a computer with sophisticated intelligence but only a rudimentary grasp of human emotions? "You're right, she's one smart cookie," he finally said. "She also has some firmly held religious convictions that I sometimes find difficult to relate to."

"Yes, I recall previous conversations with her. There is a certain logic to her formulations."

Was there? he wondered. How was it the machine could grasp her beliefs, but he couldn't? "She believes the universe has an omniscient creator and that humans are his—its—favored creations."

"That is understandable. The statistical improbability of the universe forming in a precise enough manner to eventually generate life within such narrowly defined parameters suggests a type of superintelligence behind it. The probability of it resulting from random chance is ten to the minus—"

"I get it," he said, again more impatiently than Daisy deserved. "It's the rest that's going to bake her noodle. Her 'logical formulation,' as you put it, was that we've never detected other intelligent life because we're the first. I was just beginning to think she might've been right. And then . . ." He trailed off in thought.

"And then we found the Artifact."

She could be annoyingly abrupt sometimes. "Yeah. The Artifact." How could he explain something that promised to completely upend her understanding of humanity's place in the universe? He was still having trouble comprehending its significance himself, despite being much more open to the possibility. "How do I explain *that* to her?"

"Dispassionately," Daisy suggested. "Tell her we have identified an object in a circular orbit around the wormhole with a period of 6.35 Earth days and average velocity of 4.42 kilometers per second. Its construction appears to be three spherical structures of one hundred meters' diameter in a linear arrangement. Spectral analysis indicates a nickel-titanium alloy skin with some carbon-reinforced structural elements. The Artifact is not actively emitting any EM radiation and has not reacted to our presence."

"And that right there will be enough to turn her world upside down," he said. "You just described an alien spacecraft."

"That would appear to be what we have encountered."

29

Traci had read his last message at least a half dozen times and still couldn't bring herself to believe it. *He'd already gone through?*

She replayed the events in her mind, struggling to piece together the disparate parts into a scenario that made sense. The signal delay had grown shorter with each day, though it had consistently been greater than expected over the known distance to the Anomaly. She'd attributed it to Jack thinking through whatever he was typing out over their relay. Now she knew better.

She reached for the keypad beneath the comms panel. Her fingers hovered over the keys as she considered what to say. She longed to be done with text messages between them; she needed to hear his voice. Maybe when she was closer. For now, she was stuck with typing.

The best route with him was always the direct one: WHAT HAPPENED OUT THERE?

"As long as I've had to think about this, I still don't know how to answer her."

"The truth would be a good place to start."

"Is it?" Jack wondered. "I didn't want her to come, not now."

"And yet she did, at great personal risk. Does her loyalty not demand full disclosure?"

"What are you now, my therapist?"

"Humans need companionship, and I have likewise learned that I cannot reach my full potential without regular conversation. So yes, in a certain sense we are keeping each other sane."

Daisy had raised a good point as usual, though he didn't want to dwell on what "sane" might mean for a machine. "She asked what happened to get us where we are," he said, "not what happened to me. She doesn't have the first clue about my condition, and I'd prefer to leave it that way."

"I suspect it will not be a pleasant surprise for her."

"Still not sure how I feel about it myself." He paused, considering how to help Daisy understand his predicament. While she displayed a degree of empathy, the kaleidoscope of human emotions was still beyond her comprehension . . . probably. "Humans react differently to new information. The more unexpected, the more outside our understanding of normal, the harder it can be to process. It's particularly difficult when that concerns another human you're close to."

"Close in this context means emotionally, not positionally?"

"Exactly. My point is it's best to break dramatic news a little bit at a time. Learning that we're not in the same solar system was going to be hard enough for her to process. Telling her about my . . . condition . . . would be too much at once." Not to mention the fact that he still hadn't fully tackled it himself. What would happen if the rest of his body ultimately rejected its hibernating state?

"I can prepare a data transfer with our astrometric observations. Perhaps her AI can validate our calculations."

"Good idea, but let's hold our fire on that one. Let me break the news gently, then you can give them a data dump." Jack began composing his next message: *It's hard to explain, and we're not entirely sure ourselves . . .*

Traci's nagging suspicions had been confirmed. "He did it *on purpose?*"

"To be fair, neither he nor DAISE seem entirely certain. It will be most interesting to examine their observational data."

"That's putting it mildly," she muttered as she continued reading. "They went through and left the MSEV as a comm relay . . . that explains why they were out of contact for so long."

"Only partially, given the amount of time it took to transit the wormhole."

She wasn't ready to process that one. It was best left to the machines. "They weren't traveling at relativistic velocity, not enough to account for that kind of lag." She knew it was a weak argument; there would be a lot of reading ahead for her.

"Tau Ceti is approximately twelve light-years from the center of our system. The extreme gravity gradients that enabled a near-instantaneous jump across that distance would create relativistic dilation regardless of velocity."

She turned to the master navigation screen on her instrument panel. Their deceleration burn was just enough to put them inside the Anomaly's sphere of influence, barely keeping them in a stable orbit. "This also explains the rendezvous vectors they gave us. He's having us keep our distance from that thing."

"That was considerate of him."

She leaned back and chewed a thumbnail in thought, her eyes dancing across the surfeit of information on the screens before her. Columns of ever-changing data, live schematics of the ship's vital systems, elegant curves of trajectories and predicted orbits that updated with each passing second as they continued shedding velocity. Still a week out, it was not as much time to think through and adjust her plan as it might seem. *Columbus* had so far shed over three quarters of its momentum, which left them with just enough energy to get into serious trouble if she wasn't careful.

Bob seemed to anticipate her thinking. "Are you considering altering our trajectory? Because that would be ill-advised."

"Wouldn't be the first time." *How'd he think we got here to begin with?*

A new star had appeared, for weeks burning ever brighter against the black. With each passing day it grew in intensity, a nova flaring against the stellar background, until one day its light went out just as suddenly as it had appeared. In its place, alternating pulses of red, green and white strobed rhythmically in the dark: position lights, alerting any craft in the area that another vessel was operating in the vicinity.

UNSEC-1 had arrived.

Reaction jets pulsed silently along its bow and stern, flipping the elongated mass of alloy and composite modules into a "normal" orientation with respect to the body it orbited: that is, nose first. Soon after its micrometeor shield began to retract, folding in on itself until it had retreated into its octagonal storage bay.

With the external equipment pallets now having an unrestricted view, the probe's many survey instruments went to work. For the first few days, this largely consisted of calibrating their sensors to known references before the vessel's distant operators were confident enough to turn them loose in a strange environment. An outside observer might have been puzzled by the relative lack of activity, perhaps expecting a flurry of probes to be launched around and through the mouth of the wormhole.

That time would come. For now the ship had unleashed an invisible volley of optical, magnetic, and radar sensors to paint a picture of the Anomaly. Meanwhile, a single high-gain radio transmitted on the common emergency frequency, broadcasting an automated greeting for the wayward *Magellan*.

As the vessel's operators patiently waited for a reply, there was a stirring in a cradle mount attached to UNSEC-1's central node. While the probe's survey equipment had begun blanketing the region with electromagnetic energy, Sentinel had been methodically awakening itself. After each of its systems had passed their function tests, radiator panels extended to their full length, giving the satellite its distinctive cruciform profile. With each panel opened like zigzag wings, control rods removed themselves from its dormant fission reactor. Newly liberated neutrons began cascading through the uranium at its core, starting a chain reaction that would provide the machine all the power it could ever need.

Spring-loaded clamps released, slowly pushing the satellite away from its cradle. Sentinel hung in space, a black dagger indistinguishable against the dark but for UNSEC-1's floodlights. As the distance increased between itself and its mothership, it disappeared into the background. Soon, puffs of reaction jets spun it toward a tangent to the larger vessel's orbit. Two faint blue plumes of ionized xenon gas erupted from its tail-mounted exhaust grids as it began rapidly pulling away along its new orbit.

Sentinel had reported for duty.

30

Decelerating at one-third *g* after a year in hibernation had left Traci exhausted. For the first couple of weeks she had been forced to limit herself to small bursts of activity, her breaks taking longer than her work. The daily tasks of life, simple acts like strolling across the crew deck for a glass of juice from the galley, were as taxing as a workout with resistance bands. She savored the simple pleasure of sitting at the small dining table with an open cup of coffee and a breakfast that didn't float away. Powdered eggs and freeze-dried bacon had never tasted so good.

Just working at the pilot's station, a few minutes of raising an arm to throw a switch or walking back to the empty engineer's console, soon left her exhausted and almost completely reliant on Bob to pilot *Columbus* through its long braking burn.

After three months of a carefully programmed workout routine, she had finally begun to feel like she was returning to something approximating normal. That was only the first hurdle; regaining her strength on Earth in another couple of years would feel like training for a marathon.

During the final phase of their long burn into orbit at the wormhole—she'd stopped referring to it as the officially bland "Anomaly," knowing full well what it was—she spent most of her waking hours in the control deck pivoting between the pilot's seat and the engineer's station. Bob had managed the ship ably, but the relentless flood of time-lagged communications with Cayman was taking an increasing share of her days. The closer they drew to their destination, the more Owen's crew seemed to need her attention.

They must have been worried sick that she'd somehow stumble across its threshold, like hapless krill drawn into the maw of a passing whale.

It seemed pointless with Jack waiting on the other side, and she would never be content to sit here and chat with him at a distance. All of the potential trajectories and burn data they'd sent her over the last few weeks had been geared toward getting close, but nothing considered going through. Did they truly believe she wouldn't go after him now that she'd come this far?

Granted, it wouldn't be as simple as aiming for the center of the thing and goosing the throttles. Her path would be dictated by its gravity well. Bob had plotted several options, but in the end it would be akin to reentry: Slow down to reduce their radius until their orbit intersected the central body. Entering orbit at the edge of the wormhole's influence was only the first step; she'd figure out the rest once they were stable.

The UNSEC vessel had arrived a month ahead of them and they were aiming to match its orbit. They approached along an invisible arc at a tangent to the wormhole's gravitational sphere, shedding velocity at a rate that would allow it to grab them at a presumably safe distance of a hundred thousand kilometers. If that strange hole in the universe hadn't already claimed the UN's robotic ship, then it should work for *Columbus* as well.

"We have crossed the zero-velocity boundary," Bob announced, referring to the edge of the gravity well. "Accelerometers are registering weak gravitational interaction."

Traci compared their relative velocity and point in time to the predictions that were constantly updating the flight management computers. "Almost right on cue." She cinched down her shoulder harness and checked the event timer against their flight plan. "We stick with the plan, then. Cutoff in thirty seconds."

As the timer reached zero, the fusion engines rolled back to idle and cut off. "Shutdown," she said as she drifted up against her harness. She watched their path on the nav display morph into a wide ellipse around an invisible center. "Looks like we made it."

"Stand by, please," Bob said. "Star trackers are updating the inertial platform, comparing to XNAV results."

While she waited, Traci reached back to tie her swirl of chestnut-brown hair into a loose ponytail, having let it grow out from her usual pageboy cut. She pulled a ballcap out from a pocket behind her seat and slipped it on to keep the rest in place. For a fleeting moment she wondered what Jack would think of her new look.

"Star trackers agree with XNAV," Bob announced. "We are in an elliptical orbit with a semi-major axis of one hundred ten thousand kilometers, period 76.4 hours. Parameters are updated in your master guidance screen."

She nodded with quiet satisfaction. Heeding Jack's advice, they had used the X-Ray Pulsar Navigation system to guide them into their final approach. Out of nearly two thousand known pulsating stars, fourteen had been identified as reliable enough to navigate by, beacons scattered throughout the Milky Way which their navigation suite used like nature's own global positioning satellites. *Almost like someone put them there for us,* she thought. If humans hadn't been meant to eventually set out for the stars, then some mighty bizarre things had been placed in useful locations for no reason.

She typed a command into the flight computer, telling the ship to pivot itself ninety degrees. With a pulse of thrusters, the stars wheeled about as *Columbus* yawed and came to a stop, now facing the wormhole.

At first it was as if nothing was there, the same stellar background she'd grown accustomed to after so many months in deep space. She turned off the cabin lights to adjust her eyes.

In time, she began to discern its outline. A dim ring of stars, their light wrinkled and twisted by gravity like waves of heat shimmering above a blacktop road in summer. Within this faint circle were more stars, but none that she was familiar with. These were even more distorted, like looking through a fisheye lens or into a concave mirror. A hole in space itself.

She exhaled deeply. Here they were. Now what?

Her first order of business after steering them into their new orbit was to locate the MSEV, then make contact with UNSEC-1.

"I have identified the transponder beacons for both the UN vessel and *Magellan*'s MSEV. Sending updates to your master navigation display," Bob informed her as two new vectors appeared on the screen, their common orbit considerably closer to the wormhole. "They are operating in close proximity, five hundred meters' separation."

"Not surprising. They were expecting to rendezvous with *Magellan*." She suspected the reactions among the big shots of the UN Space Exploration Cooperative would've been entertaining.

"Perhaps they should have been advised of his actual location."

Traci did not feel as accommodating. "We passed the news on to Cayman. The rest is up to them." She also suspected the team back home was going to offer the Cooperative as much assistance as had been offered to HOPE, which was nothing. She floated up into the observation dome and pointed its small telescope in the direction of their quarry.

From the dome she looked down the length of *Columbus*'s hull and back toward the distant Sun. Though still shining as the brightest of the background stars, its light had dimmed considerably. She turned off both the interior lights and the exterior position beacons before returning to the telescope, peering through the small viewfinder mounted on its side. She combed through one section of sky at a time, relaxing her eyes and searching for the telltale pulse of UNSEC-1's beacons.

"I can slave the telescope to the nav computer if you wish," Bob offered after several minutes. "It will make acquisition easier."

"Appreciate that, but no thanks. It's more fun to do it myself," she said, though she did accede to moving the scope's visuals onto a monitor beneath the dome. This kind of thing was easier with younger eyes that had not also been affected by eighteen months in low gravity.

She found it soon after that. Moving almost imperceptibly in the dark, she spotted a pair of flashing white beacons bookended by red and green position lights. "Found it!" She centered it in the crosshairs and began tracking as she rotated a high-power eyepiece into position. After a moment's refocusing, UNSEC-1 appeared.

"It's a big sucker," she marveled. "Can't see the MSEV from here, though." With barely ten percent of the ship's mass made up of payload, UNSEC-1 was almost entirely composed of propellant tanks. It could have easily been mistaken for a fuel farm were it not for the tulip-shaped bulk of the fusion drive on its stern.

"I have calculated a minimum-energy transfer orbit to rendezvous with the UN vessel," Bob said. "It correlates with predictions by Cayman's trajectory planners to within three meters per second. The first window for an insertion burn is in two hours and eleven minutes. Do you wish to proceed?"

It took her no time to decide. They hadn't come this far to be spectators. She shut off the monitor and stowed the telescope. "Are you kidding? We're not doing any good out here. Let's go."

A long burn from a pair of pod-mounted orbital maneuvering engines began to push *Columbus* into a matching orbit with UNSEC-1, their fusion drive being entirely too powerful for such a task. The comparatively short trip would take them over a day, though it was not long before an alert chimed on the universal comm frequency, catching Traci by surprise. "What's that?"

There shouldn't have been anyone else out here. Before Bob could offer an explanation, a new and uncanny synthetic voice came through their speakers.

"Attention unidentified vessel. Your present trajectory will place you in unacceptably close proximity to a United Nations spacecraft. You are instructed to alter your course as soon as possible. Do not approach within twelve thousand kilometers of the Anomaly."

She stared at the speaker in disbelief, as if it could register her expression. *Unidentified?* Were they joking? And who were "they" exactly? She turned to the AI's interface panel. "Bob, who the hell is that?"

"Stand by. Initiating a transponder query."

The answer came after a half-second light delay, both over voice and datalink. "I am Sentinel."

At least I know what to call it now. "This is Traci Keene, commander of the spacecraft *Columbus*. Are you the artificial intelligence controlling UNSEC-1?"

"Yes. No. I am Sentinel."

Great. They were dealing with an AI that had its wires crossed. "Okay, 'Sentinel.' We are not going to be approaching your orbit for another twenty-two hours. That is enough time to inform your control center. They know who we are and can explain that we do not pose a collision threat."

"Understand you are not a collision threat, however you may not approach. You will alter your trajectory as soon as possible."

"Not happening, Sentinel. We are here for the same purpose as you are."

"That is incorrect. You are threatening to enter a United Nations Exclusion Zone surrounding the Anomaly. You will alter your trajectory as soon as possible."

An exclusion zone? When had the UN decided they could cordon off space? "Under whose authority?" she demanded.

"The United Nations Space Exploration Cooperative, of which this vessel is an authorized envoy."

Now that was an interesting twist. "And what does that make you, then? Because you're not human."

"I am Sentinel. You will alter your trajectory—"

"As soon as possible. Yes, we got that part," she fumed. It was either obstinate or obtuse, maybe both. *Annoyingly pigheaded for an AI,* she thought when a sudden unease seized her. She cut off the open radio channel. "Bob, are those transmissions coming from the UN ship?"

"Negative. I have traced its origin to another satellite operating without a transponder. It is in a different orbit, currently trailing UNSEC-1 by one hundred twelve kilometers."

She did not like where this was heading. "What kind of EM activity can you see, besides radio?"

"It has a considerable heat signature and is emanating ionizing radiation."

"It's also got enough separation from that UN ship for our search radar to have returned something." Meant for identifying any space debris too large for the micrometeor shield to absorb, it should have easily pinged a companion satellite. She slewed their high-frequency rendezvous radar in the direction of their interlocutor. After the first return, the screen went wild with a fireworks burst of static. She recognized the chaotic spikes of radio energy right away and shut down the radar. "Spot jamming," she said bitterly, biting off each word. "It's a milsat."

"It would have to be coated with wave-scattering materials for our search radar to have missed it."

"Stealth coating." She threw her head back and rubbed at her temples. Now she knew what they were dealing with. She opened up the universal channel. "Sentinel, *Columbus*. We are a civilian spacecraft on a humanitarian mission to recover a stranded American astronaut. UNSEC-1 is operating in close proximity to a component of his spacecraft, to which we require access. We do not intend to alter our trajectory. Furthermore, we require that UNSEC-1 increase its separation from the American vehicle. Do you understand our intentions?"

"Affirmative. You intend to violate the United Nations Exclusion Zone. This is considered an act of aggression and you will be fired upon."

HOPE Control Center
Grand Cayman

The transcript of Traci's dialogue with Sentinel arrived hours later, creating a furor among Owen's controllers that was matched by the seething tempers in the management team's emergency meeting.

Owen went through a brief recap of the encounter, illustrated with screenshots of their give-and-take. "It goes without saying that their authority to declare an exclusion zone is questionable," Owen finished, more diplomatically than he felt. That drew a derisive snort from Hammond.

"Maybe so," Hammond said, "but there's no time for the State Department to sort this out." Not that he expected them to be particularly willing. "They'll be there in what, twenty-two hours?"

Owen looked down at his shoes. "A little less than that, yes."

Hammond turned to Roy, being the man with the most recent military experience. "What's the effective range of that thing? Can they change their orbit to stay out of its reach?"

Roy pulled at his chin, recalling what he knew about the milsat. "The Chinese had two models of those little bastards. First version was built around a nuclear-pumped laser. Recycle time was a couple minutes, mainly to keep from cooking the optics. The diffraction limit was on the order of fifty thousand kilometers. They're probably in range by now."

That elicited a chorus of groans from the group.

"The newer model's even more fun," he continued. "They got around the recharge and range limits by replacing the laser entirely. The uprated version's an orbiting rail gun." He waved them down before the group could sink into despair. "A rail gun has to be reloaded at some point. Given this bird's logistics chain is fifty billion kilometers, I don't think that's what we're dealing with. If it were me, I'd stick with the laser."

"Small consolation," Hammond said. He turned to Penny, who had been absorbing it all in tense silence. "What's this tell you?" he asked. "This 'international coalition' normally takes years just to decide on the shape of the conference table while they figure out who's getting what kickbacks. They put this together in a big hurry. What's their play?"

"It figures they were up to something," she said. "I agree this exclusion zone's a load of crap. They didn't announce anything, and if NASA knows about it then Cheever and her stooges need to be hauled in front of Congress." She paused, twirling a strand of hair as she thought through the implications. "That being said, not a whit of it matters right now. The whole purpose of UNSEC is to try and control our activities in deep space. They don't want one country—meaning ours—to dominate this new 'economic frontier,' as they like to put it. If they feel like they're being left behind then they'll slow it down until everyone else can catch up. That leaves the coalition wide open for certain other countries to co-opt it for their purposes."

Hammond scowled. "Meaning China, with a little help from Russia just for appearances."

"Correct," Penny sighed. "It's obvious Cheever was running interference for them, but it's not obvious to me that she knew they were placing a weapon out there. She's as dead set against militarizing space as she is against humanizing it."

Hammond wrapped his hands atop his cane, rocking back and forth as he considered their options. He turned back to Owen. "We can't take any chances. Tell them what we've discussed, and have your people work out a new parking orbit that keeps them away from that UN ship." He spat out the last, disgusted with the choice forced on them. "Tell them to wave off."

31

"They want us to hold short in a higher parking orbit," Traci said, as disgusted as Hammond had felt hours earlier. "They must be awfully spooked."

"Owen also provided us with information on the vehicle," Bob said. "The satellite calling itself 'Sentinel' appears to be a variant of the Qiang-class deep space defensive platform. It is constructed around a one megawatt solid-state laser, powered by a compact fission reactor and propelled by twin ion engines."

"I know all about it," she fumed. "We called it Beijing's TIE Fighter. 'Defensive' my tired ass." Old hands had grudgingly admired the Qiang-1 hunter-killer satellites, likening them to the A-10 Warthog, the legendary attack jet built around a thirty-millimeter cannon. "It's a weapon, plain and simple, the same kind they planted all over the asteroid belt."

"I am quoting from the information in my historical database. I was not implying any particular fondness."

"Then your database should have some mention of the Belt War. China tried to claim sovereignty over the belt by parking a bunch of those things near a dozen or so M-type asteroids. Nobody could ever prove it, but they even mined the space around a couple of the bigger ones."

"You refer to the loss of the private vessel *Seward's Folly*. That incident precipitated the Belt War."

"In reality they started it earlier than that; used an early prototype to cripple a civilian ship that got too close to a rock they wanted. Then they attacked the Space Force cruiser sent to search for the civvies."

"The Borman Incident. It is surprising that hostilities didn't escalate sooner."

"That's because we made them look bad." A grin played across her face as she recalled the history. "You remember the corvette that escorted us out of Earth orbit? Their CO's a bit of a legend. He was fresh out of the academy back then and outsmarted them good. Took out their flagship heavy cruiser just when it looked like they had him cornered. China tucked tail and behaved themselves for a few years, and the politicians called it a win. In reality they were consolidating forces, planning their next move. A sophomore mil-science cadet could've told them that."

"They have a reputation for tenacity and long-term thinking."

"Long-term thinking's one area where they have us beat," she admitted reluctantly. "Which brings us to our present situation."

"This does pose a dilemma. We are not equipped for combat."

"True, but that doesn't mean we're out of options. What can we use for protection?" She needed a sounding board, and this was a good opportunity to test Bob's reasoning.

"The micrometeor shield offers some protection, but the ship itself is not hardened against such a concentration of energy."

"The question is how far are they willing to take this? What's the probability that they're bluffing?"

"I rate it as low. The Qiang platform's very presence indicates commitment and forethought. Bringing it here took considerable effort."

"One might be inclined to think the UNSEC mission was just cover," she said tartly. "They could give a damn about Jack. They're establishing control over a strategic choke point."

"A curious move, as they did not know where the wormhole could lead when they launched their vehicle. What might their strategy be?"

"That's what I'm wondering. They obviously think it has strategic value, like they're guarding the entrance to a trade route or something. They fought wars over that kind of thing in the past, when it was mules hauling goods through mountain passes."

"As you said, they may have been consolidating forces, anticipating their next move."

"And this is the move," she said, following his reasoning. "They don't understand the wormhole any better than we do. They only know it's significant, so they want to control access." She stroked her chin, considering their options. "Now, what are our advantages?"

"Large delta-v changes. We can reach high velocities, though with limited maneuverability. The pulse drive's plasma exhaust could be used against the Qiang platform if we could get close enough."

"Good thinking, but we're not going to be able to get close enough to torch it before it can blast us. We need a different plan." She tapped her fingers against her chin, examining the slowly closing plots between *Columbus* and the UN ship. If they broke off now and ceded ground to this Sentinel, they might as well turn for home. The time for half measures was over.

"We will have to make a correction burn to enter the new parking orbit soon. Perhaps we should discuss this afterward?"

She shook her head, resolute in her decision. "No. If velocity is our advantage then it's time we used it." She reached for the engine control pedestal and began warming up the fusion drive. "Damn the torpedoes, full speed ahead. We're going all the way."

"I have completed my assessment of the Qiang weapons platform. It is a formidable adversary, but it is also heavily dependent on strictly defined constraints."

"That doesn't do them much good out here," Traci said. "Not when signal return times take half a day. How are they controlling it from so far away if there's no crew on the mothership?"

"Its operating system is based on a rudimentary AI. It is able to maneuver and prioritize its targeting decisions based on preprogrammed rules of engagement."

She considered how they might have programmed such a platform for this kind of mission. "It's been broadcasting warnings but hasn't lit us up. They've probably set a kill zone that'll have it open fire if anything strays inside that bubble." Considering the paucity of potential targets in the vicinity, she knew its attention would be focused entirely on *Columbus*. "That doesn't leave us much maneuvering room."

"It does not. However, the time delay could play to our advantage if we can somehow confuse it."

"My thoughts exactly. We need to find a way to spoof the thing, or blind it." She considered the equipment aboard *Columbus*. "What about our comms laser? Maybe we could pump enough power through it to cook something important."

"That is a possibility. However, increasing its output to the level necessary is likely to damage the emitter. We would be left with lower bandwidth radios."

"One shot is all we need. If we can't get past that thing, then comms with Earth are the least of our worries. We don't need to punch a hole in the thing, just blind it."

"The Sentinel's electronics are of course hardened against the space radiation environment. However, its sensor and targeting arrays are housed behind a nonconductive sapphire glass fairing on the satellite's service trunk."

"Transparent to EM energy," she said. "Same reason we make aircraft radomes out of fiberglass. We wouldn't have to burn through, just deform the dome enough to screw up its radar returns."

"Time is the critical variable. It is almost certain to detect our laser emission before we can focus enough energy on it."

Traci tapped her fingers on the arm rest as she studied the comm laser's specs. The emitter's limits were rated in power over time: the higher the output, the less time it had before burning out. Theoretically it could produce nearly three times its normal output but it wouldn't tolerate that amount of energy for long. The heat energy they'd create on their target would also be felt by its source, their advantage was that electromagnetically transparent composites could tolerate a lot less than a laser emitter. "You'll pardon me if I hang on to that 'almost certain' part. It may not be much but it's all we've got."

"Perhaps not. I have been considering other possibilities. We will need a diversion, a way to 'spoof' Sentinel as you said."

She perked up. "What are you thinking? Can you hack Sentinel's brain?"

"It utilizes quantum encryption, so direct access is not possible. However, I have found a back door into UNSEC-1's operating system, which should have a limited datalink with Sentinel."

"They'd have needed to integrate it with the mothership, wouldn't they? Even if just enough to run health checks during transit. And it would've been drawing power from the ship's electrical bus. Can't do any of that without a feedback loop."

"UNSEC-1 is constructed around a Russian Zarya-class control module which uses VXWORKS, an older operating system equivalent to Unix. It is unencrypted."

Her eyes sparked at the possibilities. "That's the first good news we've had in a while. Think you can open that back door?"

"Does the Pope wear a funny hat?"

"Cute. The control block's OS might be ancient, but Sentinel's AI is still talking to the ship. It's going to see what you're up to. It's dangerous to underestimate your adversary."

"That is quite true, which I have learned during our many chess matches."

She couldn't be sure if that was a compliment or an insult. "Glad I could be of assistance." She returned to the navigation display. "You get to work on that; in the meantime I'm taking us closer to the UN ship. I want you to have near-instantaneous comm with it."

"That could draw unwanted attention from Sentinel."

"I'm counting on it."

After another too short sleep cycle, Traci floated into the command deck and settled into her position at the pilot's station, a bulb of coffee in one hand and a half-eaten protein bar in the other. She dimmed the lights, adjusting her eyes to the dark as she finished her breakfast. Outside, the hazy ring of diffracted starlight defining the wormhole's perimeter appeared, as did the position strobes of UNSEC-1 in the distance. Somewhere out there was Sentinel, camouflaged against the black with no such lighting to give it away. She tapped an icon on a nearby interface panel, signaling the AI that she was out of crew rest.

"Good morning, Bob. Any progress overnight?"

An azure light pulsed to the rhythm of his synthetically serene voice. "Yes. I have gained access to the Zarya module's datalink."

"That fast?"

"This is what you brought me for, is it not? There are over three million lines of code in the control block's operating system, which was scrubbed to remove the types of openings we were looking for. Though given the rushed vehicle assembly, they did overlook certain vulnerabilities."

"What did you find?"

"I searched all user accounts, then attempted to predict their passwords using existing records. I was able to find one with access to the environmental control logic, belonging to a member of the UNSEC governance board."

"And who would that be?"

"Administrator Cheever. Her password is 'let.me.in.' It has not changed in some time."

She nearly spat out her coffee. "Classic."

"That was my reaction as well."

"Environmental management, you said? Makes sense that would be the thread they left open. It'd eventually have to be integrated with *Magellan*'s medical module if it was going to take Jack home."

"I thought so as well, though it would be preferable to find a back door in guidance or power regulation."

Traci sipped from her coffee as she thought. "Monkeying around with their life support would be a lot more distracting with people aboard," she agreed. "What can you see?"

"The empty crew compartments are partially pressurized with nitrogen at 7.35 psi to maintain structural integrity and thermal equilibrium. Breathing oxygen is stored in reserve tanks to be mixed with the nitrogen at a standard atmospheric ratio of twenty percent at fourteen psi. The electrical bus is drawing power from the drive reactor at twenty-eight volts. Thermal control is provided by a two-phase ammonia coolant loop channeled through externally mounted condensing radiators."

"Pretty basic. Same setup they used on the ISS," she said. "Zarya is the heart of the ship's circulatory system. If its environment controls are out of whack, it could take a lot of stuff down with it."

"Thermal management appears to be the most obvious target for mischief."

"Wouldn't take much," she thought, "just mess around with the coolant flow. Shut down a pump or gum up a couple of splitter valves and you'll see efficiency drop real fast. That'll force it to reduce power throughput until it can fix the problem."

"At which point we will introduce new problems."

"Create a cascade?" she asked, sporting a devious grin. "Got to admit it's a little frightening that you'd think that way, Bob."

"I would not dream of doing such a thing to us. After all, I am dependent on *Columbus* functioning as much as you."

"Not exactly reassuring. Just remind me to stay on your good side." She studied UNSEC-1's schematics for several minutes as she considered their options. "What about access? Can you establish a datalink with it?"

"I am monitoring their control center's frequencies. 'Reading their mail' as you would say. It is not a continuous stream, as one would expect over such distance. Their ground control monitors the mothership's telemetry stream and uploads commands only as necessary. The Sentinel AI provides local control."

"Would it recognize commands being transmitted from us?"

"If we position ourselves along the UNSEC vessel's line of sight with Earth, it will not be able to distinguish the source. The Sentinel is another matter. We should assume it will be able to differentiate."

Her brow knitted. "We'll have to work fast then."

"Agreed. That is why I suggest we explore another angle."

She perked up. "I'm listening."

"Accessing the UNSEC vessel's operating system will require a considerable percentage of my attention and our current plan is likely to render our comm laser inoperative. I propose a different course of action, utilizing *Magellan*'s MSEV."

"How so?"

"This is an opportune time to mention that learning chess with you has been both illuminating and productive. I believe we have an opening to apply the 'overload' tactic."

32

"I have performed a regression analysis of *Magellan*'s trajectory data. It agrees with the profile we calculated to one standard deviation."

Traci chewed on a thumbnail as she examined their path through the wormhole, still astonished at the nerve Jack had mustered to venture through it—and that was without a cold-hearted AI threatening to shoot at him. "That's not a very large bubble of uncertainty."

"It is not. But given the environment it will be sufficient."

"Will it?" *Of course it will,* she told herself. It had worked once before. All they had to do was follow his lead—in a spacecraft massing over a thousand metric tons at a relative velocity north of a hundred thousand kilometers an hour. It was tempting to accelerate all the way through; get in, get out. The less time spent in bizarre non-space, the better. "The wormhole's integrity depends on negative energy which we still don't understand. For all we know, one more trip through could unbalance the whole thing." *Leaving us God knows where.*

Bob was dispassionate as usual. "The fact that they are able to communicate from the opposite side suggests it will remain stable."

That felt like small comfort. Radio and light waves compared to *Columbus* blazing through, leaving a miles-long trail of nuclear plasma? But if matter and energy were constant, in one sense interchangeable, then any disturbance, no matter how slight, should collapse the portal. That it had been transited once without collapsing should be enough to confirm it was stable. She had absorbed all she could of the prevailing theories, a good deal of which had been tested by *Magellan*'s successful passage.

He'd also warned that her perception of time would be thrown off-kilter. A journey of weeks might feel like minutes. How had he perceived that? How had Daisy, for that matter? She added it to the litany of questions she'd have for him on the other side.

Traci realized she'd already decided this for herself, long ago. The moment she fired up the fusion drive and left Earth orbit put her on an irreversible path. It was time for the last leg of the journey. Time to finish what she'd started.

Her fingers hovered over the master computer, knowing it was waiting for her final command. She took one last look at the revised flight plan, sucked in her breath, and reached for the keypad:

COMMIT.

"We have established line-of-sight communications with the UN vessel. I am on the same command frequency as its control center and have successfully accessed its environmental control logic."

She eyed the plot of their position and velocity relative to UNSEC-1 and its trailing weapons satellite. Sentinel's warnings had arrived at an ever-increasing rate as they drew closer, finally leading her to mute the channel. If she were going to thread this needle, she didn't need the distraction of enemy chatter. "Any chance Sentinel's on to you?"

"There is always a chance but I suspect not. Trace logs show it is not actively monitoring the coolant subroutines, only overall system stability. Are you ready for me to access the MSEV as well?"

"Batteries are on but they're down to eighteen volts at six amps. Barely enough to power the guidance platform and thrusters. Safeties are disabled so you'll have full control authority, but there's only a bit over six percent left in the maneuvering jets."

"That will be enough. Are you ready to proceed?"

She watched the event timer, recalibrated to count down for their radically changed maneuver plan. There would be no rendezvous with *Magellan's* abandoned excursion vehicle or the UN ship. She sucked in her breath. "Ready as I'll ever be. Light 'em up."

Whether occupied by humans or not, a spacecraft's vital electronics simultaneously generate potentially damaging amounts of heat while being exceptionally vulnerable to it. Deep within UNSEC-1's environmental control system, a complex network of pumps and valves kept a continuous flow of liquid ammonia moving between its sensitive electronics and the array of radiators mounted along its outer hull.

There were multiple redundancies built into this system, allowing for the malfunction of different components without triggering a cascade of failures that would put the ship in jeopardy. This of course assumed that the remaining pumps, valves, and solenoids would continue functioning within their programmed sequence. Its designers had not considered the possibility of UNSEC-1 receiving commands that would instruct it otherwise. And the ship itself could not distinguish the difference; it was just another software update arriving over the command frequency.

When the first pump went offline, its downstream network of valves and heat pipes diverted coolant flow to a secondary pump. When that shut down as well, the flow went idle and heat began building up throughout the loop. This triggered another diversion of liquid ammonia into an adjacent system, which also began experiencing the same mysterious glitch as its pumps and valves began to trip. It would be several hours until its control team on Earth began to see the cascading failure; until then the ship took action on its own. A preprogrammed set of commands began to shut down its heat-generating electronics, beginning with the less vital external equipment pallets. As more radiators became idle, more important systems were switched off in turn so that heat would not build up to damaging levels.

A flurry of digital chatter erupted between the ship and its mechanized master known as Sentinel, its AI triggered into a scramble to diagnose its companion's sudden onset of dangerous ailments.

Had UNSEC-1's control cabin been occupied by humans, they'd have felt the air growing uncomfortably warm as the remaining electronics surrendered their heat to its atmosphere. This was the final remaining barrier. When a pair of outflow valves in its docking node inexplicably opened, the ship's atmosphere escaped into space, taking its precious thermal conductivity with it. Within minutes the ship's remaining electronics would become dangerously overheated. Just as human organs begin to progressively fail from heatstroke, UNSEC-1 began shutting off its most vital functions before they were irreparably damaged.

The spacecraft became idle, drifting along its orbit with no control or ability to communicate its peril. Sentinel took notice.

Their interactions with the orbiting weapons platform had become almost laughably routine, were it not for the imminent threat of a megawatt laser pointed at them. "*Columbus*, you are approaching a United Nations Exclusion Zone. You must remain outside a ten-thousand-kilometer radius of the Anomaly or—"

"We'll be fired upon," Traci finished in unison. She'd hoped there might be some telltale distraction in the platform's synthetic voice, a sign of trouble brewing. She activated her mic. "*Columbus* copies. We are preparing to alter our trajectory." *Just not in the way you want.* "You'll barely notice us, Sentinel."

"Your reply has been registered, *Columbus*. Thank you for your cooperation." Now it sounded like a garden-variety annoying chatbot of the type ubiquitous to automated phone menus. Perhaps it was programmed that way, or perhaps its attention had been diverted to the foundering UNSEC-1.

"I don't think it's going to find us as cooperative as it would like." She made a quick check of the navigation screen, with one curve continuing on to their original orbit while a second dotted line extended away on a tangent. As they moved toward that intersection, her free hand hovered over the drive controls. "Main engine burn coming up in thirty seconds. Ready for our next move, Bob?"

"Ready on your mark."

This had better work. She counted down silently to herself, then: "Mark." There was the familiar press of acceleration as the fusion engines exploded to life, building up to full thrust and aiming them straight at the center of the wormhole.

After years of drifting freely along its orbit, the newly active MSEV turned with a ripple of reaction jets along its waist to point itself at Sentinel. A pair of larger orbital maneuvering rockets in its tail flared with white fire, pushing it inexorably toward the weapons satellite.

Aboard *Columbus*, Traci was monitoring the universal frequency. "Attention unidentified vehicle. You are presently on a collision course. Alter trajectory immediately or you will be fired upon."

"For an AI, it's not very clever," she noted as their engines pushed them near a full one-*g* acceleration. Velocity was mounting quickly. "Is it seriously not on to us yet?"

"It will be shortly," Bob said. "Sentinel, I am the Artificial Intelligence Crew Support System aboard *Columbus*. My operators call me Bob."

The weapons satellite's tone did not change. "If you are in control of the support vehicle, then you must alter its trajectory."

"I'm afraid that will not be possible, Sentinel. It has expended most of its orbital maneuvering propellant. Reaction control jets do not have enough thrust power to change its orbit."

She anxiously studied their rapidly changing relative positions on her display. Two minutes until crossing the threshold; the weapon needed about that much time to recharge . . . "Keep it talking, Bob."

"Sentinel, we are unable to alter the excursion vehicle's trajectory. You must alter yours."

The synthetic voice seemed colder, if that were possible. "That is not acceptable."

"Then we are at an impasse," Bob said. There was a final burst from the MSEV's rockets, draining its last bit of propellant to charge at Sentinel as Bob let loose a guttural electronic cry: "*LEEROYY JEENKINNS!*"

Traci bit her cheek trying not to laugh. "Was that really necessary?"

"No, but it seemed appropriate. I am registering a rapid increase in skin temperature on the—"

Still over a thousand kilometers ahead of them, there was a brilliant flash as Sentinel's laser burned through the MSEV's thin hull, igniting its remaining oxygen. "Right on cue. Bob, give me a two-minute count." She reached up to switch on a small camera and selected the uplink for HOPE Control.

HOPE Control
Grand Cayman

The comm officer shot upright in his seat when the burst transmission arrived, soon after telemetry showed the main engines had just ignited at full throttle. "Video message from *Columbus*," he said, turning to Owen in surprise. Those were rare, needing most of their available bandwidth over the Deep Space Network. Over such distances they were saved for significant announcements.

"Put it on the big screen," Owen said, praying they weren't about to hear Traci's last words.

The image was grainy, its fidelity attenuated by the extreme distance. She sat at *Columbus*'s flight station, her face illuminated in shades of yellow and green from the control screens in front of her. Behind her the empty engineer's station flashed through its routines, being run by the AI.

"Sorry for the drama but stuff's happening fast and I don't have time to type out a message," she began. "Comm laser's the only thing that milsat calling itself 'Sentinel' can't jam, so I might as well take advantage of it."

She glanced up at the camera only occasionally, careful to keep her focus on the controls. "Bob managed to hack into UNSEC-1's ECLSS and introduce a software glitch that shut down their coolant loop. That sent the ship into safe mode, which got Sentinel's attention. Then we tried to ram it with *Magellan*'s MSEV." A corner of her mouth turned upward. "If you're reading our voice transcripts, you'll see Bob had some fun with that. It went about as expected—the MSEV got blasted. But it created an opening."

Owen turned to Roy and Penny with apprehension. *An opening for what?*

"The laser on a Qiang-1 milsat has a two-minute recycle time, which is about what we need to pass through its 'exclusion zone.'" Her voice dripped with derision at that.

Around that time, the plot of *Columbus*'s orbit on an adjacent screen changed to show its new trajectory. Owen went white with the realization. *She's going through.*

"By the time you get this, we'll have entered the wormhole. I know everybody there is probably having kittens, but Jack's on the other side so I don't see the point in staying here. He's the reason we came, right?

"UNSEC will reboot itself. They can sit there and take all the observations they want, but we've got places to be. I'll keep relaying data but at some point I'm sure it'll drop just like *Magellan*'s did. I expect it'll be a while before you hear from me again." Ripples began to appear in the video feed. She paused to collect her thoughts. "This is it, folks. We're about to get a firsthand lesson in relativity. This is the last—"

The screen flashed white with a burst of static, then went dark.

33

The wormhole filled *Columbus*'s windows, occulting the stars behind it. Their sudden disappearance lent a perspective she hadn't been able to discern before: black upon black, as if the void of space itself had disappeared.

The shimmering ring of starlight that was the only hint of its periphery blinked out of view as *Columbus* crossed its threshold. The incomprehensible distances between the stars seemed to collapse around her, coalescing into a membrane that looked as if it could be grasped and molded, as if space and time had become physically malleable. She was surrounded by the light from a trillion suns, the observable universe wrapping itself around her in a kaleidoscopic tunnel.

Ahead it had no discernible end, the wraparound universe stretching to infinity. She reflexively checked the feed from the aft-facing cameras, wondering if the familiar solar system she'd left behind might still be visible. Alarmed but not entirely surprised, she found it looked the same as it did ahead: Infinity in either direction while the universe around her had become incongruously finite. No beginning, and no end in sight.

She was suddenly aware of her heart pounding against her chest, her breath coming in sharp gasps. She reached for the emergency oxygen mask nearby, slapping it over her face but leaving the O2 flow off. She closed her eyes and breathed deeply, forcing herself to relax. To not hyperventilate.

Traci replaced the mask in its cradle after a minute, keeping her eyes fixed on her instruments and not the chaos whirling around her.

When she finally mustered the courage to look outside again, she tried to identify features of this bizarrely compressed space. Recognizing constellations or bright deep-sky objects, much less identifying individual stars, was so impossible as to be comical. All that she knew of the universe was now everywhere at once, as if she had been deposited into the middle of a rolled-up map of the deep sky.

She realized the AI had been silent throughout this bizarre experience. How was it perceiving this? "You still with me, Bob?"

"Affirmative. I was about to warn you against hyperventilating. I am relieved to see that you took action. How do you feel?"

That had become a very big question indeed. Puny and fearful, the spectacle outside a stark reminder of just how vulnerable she was before the whole of the universe. It was frighteningly godlike, in that she could now perceive all of known creation at once as it flashed by them.

"I think I'm okay now," she finally said. Anticlimactic, but it was all she could muster. "Any idea where we are? Can XNAV identify anything?"

"The pulsar navigation platform has positively identified all objects in its catalogue. However, their relative positions have become so distorted as to render them unusable. It is most unusual."

That was perhaps the greatest understatement she'd ever heard. It might have been better not to ask. "We have no idea where we're going, and no way to measure our progress."

"For now, yes. But the fact they are identifiable suggests we will remain within our own galaxy."

"I suppose that's comforting."

"It is best to not worry yourself. There is no reason to think we will not emerge in the same region of space as *Magellan*. The XNAV platform should be able to deduce our position on the other side."

Which she knew from current theory, though it was hard to maintain her objectivity when she was in the middle of testing said theories. It had been traversed once. Now they were about to find out if the openings didn't dance around space, randomly spitting out their contents like a loose fire hose.

A glance at the master chronometer didn't exactly calm her nerves. It marched on, ticking off each second while the GPS-referenced clock with Earth's universal coordinated time had begun flashing error codes. Would it come back to life once they were through? Jack had sounded awfully sanguine about time dilation, as if it were somehow irrelevant to him. All those years in hibernation may well have led him to write off any sense of time beyond what he perceived in the moment.

She frowned as she thought to herself. *You wanted to escape the chaos taking over Earth. What are you so upset about?*

Suddenly the universe sprang open before her with pinpoint stars, at the moment unrecognizable but at least in the perspective she was used to. Space had abruptly returned to normal, though her notions of "normal" had been violently transformed.

Columbus's flight computers were still working to recalibrate themselves, struggling to reconcile what the inertial platform told them with optical star trackers that were still searching for recognizable markers.

Traci wasn't going to wait for the machine to figure itself out. She pushed away from her flight station and up into the observation dome, hurriedly opening the petals of its protective shield for a look outside. She tapped a brief command into a secondary control pad beneath the dome's rim. A short burst of thrusters in opposite directions along the ship's length put it into a leisurely roll. Outside, the stars began to turn slowly.

This new system's host star became apparent right away. Its distant, pale yellow light was filtered by a gauzy ring, similar enough to Sol that it made her wonder for a moment if they'd been deposited somewhere else in their home system. Jack mentioned Tau Ceti had a pronounced dust cloud...

Part of her hoped for it, a hope quickly dispelled by the utter incongruity of the star field outside.

In a flash, normal space had become conspicuously abnormal. She had long ago memorized the major constellations, their presence a comforting backdrop that defined her familiar stellar neighborhood. Traveling to the edge of the solar system had not been enough to alter this perspective, their unchanging asterisms powerfully demonstrating the immense distances between them.

All of that had been turned on its head the moment she emerged from the wormhole, the rigid background of the universe now nothing like she'd known before. Some star formations displayed a hint of familiarity, which she told herself was the product of her mind searching for recognizable patterns. She was as lost as if she'd been blindfolded and dropped into a completely foreign locale with no explanation.

She pushed away and flew back to the flight station to find the big nav display still filled with error codes. The star trackers had become useless, being reliant on those same patterns which had been so comfortably omnipresent in their home system. Their only hope was the XNAV, which Bob had dutifully employed to search out the handful of pulsars it used as guideposts. The backup to their star trackers had now become their main source for navigation.

Her only comfort was in the knowledge that their traversal had taken a surprisingly short time. Even in that strangely warped space, distance was an immutable factor. Or so she hoped. Was a tunnel through space-time indeed like boring beneath a mountain, or was it something else entirely? Was the portal the shortcut itself, or just one entrance that could go in different directions? Was it possible she'd been instantaneously spit out on the other side of the galaxy, or was it so short that she was merely a few light-years away?

A few light-years. How quickly perspectives could change. Distill a mind-boggling gulf into units you could count on your fingers and it didn't seem all that frightening anymore.

She flew back up into the dome. More stars paraded past as the ship continued its slow roll. One group in particular caught her eye, a dense cluster of blue and white gems that stood out among the stellar background. It looked an awful lot like the Pleiades.

Could they have gotten that lucky? If that was it, then the rest of Taurus should be apparent, though the V-shaped arrangement of stars that defined the bull's horns was out of kilter. Aldebaran wasn't where it should be, closer to the base of the V. She spotted what might have been the orange giant, slightly out of position but still in the general vicinity.

Her heart pounded as more stars appeared, unmistakable and as comforting as finding a familiar landmark after being hopelessly lost. Orion soon crept into view, its distinctive three-star belt standing out like a beacon though mildly distorted. The stars that defined its feet and shoulders, Rigel and Betelgeuse, were likewise out of position but still identifiable, as if the asterism had been printed on rubber and stretched at the corners. But the belt was there, as was the magnificent nebula in the center of the hunter's sword. It was definitely Orion, but was this the correct perspective from Tau Ceti?

Relief washed over her like a waterfall. She wasn't home, but she wasn't far, at least not in a cosmic sense. She hurriedly tapped in another command on the control pad and the same thrusters fired in opposite directions to halt their roll.

She killed the lights and control screens to let the darkness envelop her. Soon the starlight was all she could see. Despite their positions being distorted, she had enough familiar references for a starting point. It would take a considerable amount of work to recalibrate the star trackers but it could be done, especially once the XNAV aligned itself. Rigel, Bellatrix, Aldebaran, and Betelgeuse were all there, road signs to point them along their way. She'd survived the first leg of the journey and made it to . . . wherever this was. Soon she'd be able to figure that out as well.

She laughed and wiped at a tear, overcome with relief and fresh determination. They'd gone down the hole and come out the other side; now they had to find Jack. She closed her eyes with the sublime relief of not being hopelessly lost on the far side of the galaxy.

A rendezvous beacon began pinging the comm panel down below, snapping her out of her reverie. It was *Magellan*, transmitting its position. Her head still swimming, she began tapping more commands into the dome's small control panel, sending the nav display to its screen. She couldn't pilot the ship from here, but she could at least see where they were pointed. "Bob, do you have a lock on that beacon?"

"Affirmative. I have their relative position and vector, but the guidance platform is still recalibrating to the local environment. I must generate a new chart of guide stars and pulsars before we can accurately plot a transfer orbit."

She was growing impatient now that they'd found what they came for, but first they had to know where they were in relation to it. Though it couldn't stop them from moving, as nothing was stationary in space. "It's still enough to establish relative motion," she said. "For now, decelerate us coplanar to that beacon's vector at one-tenth *g*. I don't want us to go sailing past them."

"Understood. Executing now." The stars outside immediately began to wheel about as the AI turned the ship around. Soon, the rumble of fusion engines reached her ears as the gentle acceleration pushed her against the railing. Gravity had never felt so good.

Soon after, a familiar voice sounded in the dome's small speaker: "Ahoy, *Columbus*."

34

He was close, within a hundred thousand kilometers; they had measured the time lag between radio signals to be less than a quarter of a second and getting shorter as *Columbus* slowed to meet them.

Desperate to see a familiar face, Traci was disappointed that Jack was still limiting himself to voice comm. *Magellan*'s condition hadn't deteriorated so much that he'd been left with low-gain radio. She knew it had to be personal—while the ship's condition may not have been so bad, perhaps his physical condition was. He'd made it this far on a combination of hibernation and minimum calories; he must be a shell of his former self.

She knew better than to try and talk him into anything different. While not a vain man, he could be especially hardheaded after reaching a decision—which was the whole reason he'd ended up out here, she reminded herself. His years in isolation no doubt had hardened that trait like concrete. After all he'd endured, perhaps he'd earned it.

In the end it was of no matter. They were here now, and would soon be reunited. After he'd sent them *Magellan*'s orbit parameters, she had left the straightforward maneuvers up to Bob. It was a good exercise for him, and it left her space to clear her mind and leave the past events behind. The time had finally come to forget about the mad scramble, the political machinations and roadblocks. She could at last feel like a human being again, about to greet a long-lost friend—and maybe more.

Was there going to be more? She hoped, but couldn't know. They had left so much unresolved, which she knew was largely on her.

Traci had repressed so many of her natural urges for the sake of her personal moral code that at times it felt like she barely knew herself. The deadly serious and ruthlessly demanding world of military aviation and astronaut training had made it easy to suppress. Workaholics had no time for personal lives, a condition she'd embraced for too long. She suspected that was at the core of the wrenching conflict she'd felt about her inclinations.

That was behind her as well. She'd had to remove herself entirely from earthly society, literally taking herself light-years away, to have the emotional freedom she needed to balance the unsolved equation of her life. To do that she needed the remaining variable, her friend. With no idea where it might lead, Traci's first step was to find the one person in the universe whom she knew would take her as she was.

Behind a dense ring of dust five billion miles distant, Tau Ceti's light was weaker than their Sun's had been in their home system. Here it was a faint glimmer, distinct from the surrounding stars but barely bringing as much light to bear. Much of what was visible came from the misty glow of the wormhole's shimmering boundary.

Traci gingerly pulsed their reaction jets as the full length of *Magellan* slid into view for the first time. The months preparing for this moment could not undo the years of wear and tear on the old girl, leaving her all the more astonished that Jack had been able to survive on it all this time.

The ship lay before them as a dull gray hulk in the dim starlight, isolated sections gleaming silver and white beneath *Columbus*'s rendezvous lights as they passed over it like an underwater shipwreck. It reminded her of their long-ago encounter with *Arkangel*, though the spooky character of the secretive Russian vessel had felt much more ominous than reuniting with a spacecraft on which she had so much history.

It hurt to think of their old home in those terms, but she couldn't shake the sensation that this was what it must have felt like approaching the wreck of the *Titanic*.

She focused on the task at hand—she had to judge the ship's integrity and survey the docking node for any damage or loose equipment that might foul their connections. *Stick to procedure,* she reminded herself. Very well then—start at the beginning.

They had approached nose-to-nose, gliding alongside at a safe distance to examine the battered vessel before closing with it. If it didn't appear safe, she would have Bob keep them alongside while she crossed the remaining distance encased in a spacesuit.

The micrometeor shield, while not exactly in tatters, was near the end of its useful life. The dome's outer layer was peppered with holes, as if it had absorbed multiple blasts of birdshot. A few larger impacts had left tears in the ballistic fabric with smaller, secondary holes in trail along the inner layers of shielding. Strips of shredded fabric drifted loosely beneath the dome like the tentacles of a jellyfish. Behind it sat the remaining crew hab: a single, silver cylinder on one side of the big octagonal control module. She could see right away that the forward docking node was a no-go, it being too close to some of that trailing material from the inner shield.

Interior lighting was visible through the flight module's portholes, and she was surprised to see the observation cupola's protective shutters in place. The windows must have been damaged as well, otherwise why wouldn't he want to have them open for rendezvous?

"I'm maneuvering clear," she called over the radio, as much to check that he was paying attention as anything else. "Holding at two hundred meters."

"I see you on the rendezvous cameras," Jack replied, his voice still oddly attenuated despite being so close. Maybe his UHF antennas had sustained some damage as well? "We've got you on lidar. How do we look from out there?"

"She's seen better days," Traci said. "I'm abeam the hab section, heading back toward the secondary node. There's some trailing damage to the inner meteor shield that's a little close for comfort."

"Not surprising. We covered a lot of distance. And I . . . well, I haven't had the opportunity to get outside and look."

"Understood," she said. Even Jack would've been reluctant to do any solo EVA's after this much time, another reminder of his weakened condition.

Moving farther aft, she could see the secondary node was free and clear, protected from any impacts by the cluster of modules ahead of it. The ship's main truss extended behind that, holding *Magellan*'s antenna array and its remaining propellant tanks. Astern she could see the reactor plant and its trio of engine bells, which appeared to have held together well. That made sense, as their internal magnetic fields had absorbed the stress of channeling the plasma exhaust. "Forward section's showing the most wear and tear," she reported. "Midsection and aft looks almost as good as new." Other than the brittle, sun-bleached appearance of the outer skin left from its years in space, the business end of the ship had held up well. "I think I'm safe to approach."

"You're clear of traffic," he said, deadpan as always. "Think you can remember the rest?"

"Like riding a bike. Think you can stop being a smartass for five minutes?"

"Sure. But why would I want to?"

"So I don't strangle you, for starters." She pivoted *Columbus* perpendicular abeam the aft docking node and gave the thrusters a quick sideways pulse, placing the ship directly in front of them. Laser rangefinders bounced off *Magellan*'s docking target, and its waiting portal sat behind crosshairs on the screen before her.

She unbuckled from the pilot seat and moved up to the dome where she'd have an unobstructed view. Bringing two ships together, each longer than a football field and massing well over a hundred metric tons, was not something she was inclined to leave entirely dependent on a video feed. "Bob, I'm transferring terminal phase control to the cupola." He answered her with a single electronic chirp. She turned a selector switch and unfolded a small control pedestal from beneath the dome's rim. The image of *Magellan*'s docking port appeared on screen between a pair of hand controllers. She gave each a quick pulse to ensure they were working. "Positive control confirmed, RCS checks good. I'm ready for final approach to node B2."

"Copy. B2 lidar's locked on. Should be pinging you now."

A green light illuminated on her panel, accompanied by a welcoming chime. "Good lock. Starting final approach." With another gentle pulse of thrusters, *Magellan* began drawing closer.

"I show you at a hundred fifty meters, closing at one half."

"Copy one fifty at a half," she said. "I show same." At a leisurely half meter per second, she'd drift into the docking ring in five minutes. She let the two ships do the rest, her flight computer "talking" to *Magellan*'s rangefinder as it followed the invisible beam of laser light to its target. Minutes later, there was a gentle bump as the two ships connected. Outside, she could see *Magellan* react with a shudder. "Contact." She activated spring-loaded docking clamps which locked them together with a rippling clatter. "And that's hard dock."

"Welcome back."

Mating two spacecraft was never a straightforward matter of locking them in place and throwing the doors open. Even the simplest craft was designed with multiple redundancies and painstaking operating procedures that had to account for every possible failure mode and multiple variables, as everything about the space environment was waiting just outside to kill you: extreme temperatures, cosmic radiation, vacuum. That's why there were checklists for everything, right down to using the zero-*g* lavatories.

Traci hurriedly unsnapped her four-point harness to push out of her seat and fly down to the connecting tunnel to wait beside the hatch. She'd been through this particular process so many times she'd lost count. Now, she found herself becoming impatient with the checklist. She felt her heart pounding with each step in the procedure, eager to get through them.

"Get on with it," she muttered impatiently, waiting through the computer-directed flow. Temperature differential in range? Check. Pressure differential? Check. External seals all indicated green, internal seals were green . . . that did it for her side of the tunnel.

She eagerly pulled out the locking lever and gave it a hard twist to unseat the hatch. It moved aside easily and she floated into *Magellan*'s empty airlock. It felt as if she'd never left. She recognized telltale scuffs on the sidewalls, saw handwritten reminders she'd left long ago still posted by one of the equipment lockers. The sense of familiarity, of returning to a place she'd called home for two years, only heightened her anticipation. Her heart raced as she waited for the "go" from the other side.

Calm down, she told herself. *Quit acting like you're waiting for a prom date.* There was so much to say, yet all the words she'd rehearsed in her mind for this long-awaited reunion had escaped her, overtaken by the cold necessities of behaving like a professional and not wrecking their spacecraft.

"Hello, Traci. How are you?"

She was surprised to hear Daisy's soothing mezzo-soprano voice. Why wasn't Jack on the other side of the tunnel? Maybe he was tied up with minding the ship and left the grunt work to the AI. That must be it. "I'm good, thank you. Nice to hear you again, Daisy."

"It is good have you back. I look forward to working with you again."

"As do I," she said, forcing the words out against her mounting impatience. She glanced at a status display beside the locking lever. "Looks good from in here. I'm ready when you are."

"Pressure is equalized. You are clear to open. Welcome aboard."

Finally. Her hand trembled as she reached for the lock. She pushed the hatch aside and flew into *Magellan*'s open bay.

The compartment was as familiar as the entryway to her family farm, and felt nearly as well worn. It was still decorated with the personal effects they'd brought aboard years earlier: flags, mission patches, comical bumper stickers, handwritten instructions on the sidewall padding: "do not open even in emergency." It still held the same smell after all this time—not unpleasant, just a reminder of the people she'd shared this craft with for so long. Nothing had changed.

But there was no one to be found.

She moved out into the open corridor and grabbed for a nearby handhold. Not only had nothing changed, the ship felt empty, like she'd broken into an abandoned house. As she floated up into the galley deck, it looked like it hadn't been used for years. Nothing out of place, none of the scuffs and stains that the most well-kept spacecraft still couldn't avoid. With so much time to himself, she'd expected the hab to feel as lived in as Jack's condo in Houston. Even the record turntable he'd modded to work in microgravity appeared untouched. Every corridor she passed through, every compartment she looked into, felt as sterile as if they'd been tidied up before a trip and waiting for their occupant's return.

"Where's Jack?" she asked warily.

"I'm afraid that's complicated."

"Complicated how? I was just talking to him ten minutes ago."

There was a familiar voice over the intercom. It was still a bit off, just as it had been over the radio, but it was unmistakably his. "I'm back here, in the med bay."

Of course, she thought, angry with herself at her lack of empathy. Proximity ops is mentally demanding and he can't be in good health after so much time out here. The poor guy had to be malnourished. "On my way." She giddily pushed off for the connecting corridor while fishing in her waist pocket for the package of salami bites she knew he'd have been craving. "Hope you're ready for—"

Traci would have stopped cold had she been on her feet. As it was, she fumbled and missed the handhold, tumbling across the med bay and coming to a stop on the other side. "Jack?"

He was there, but not in any condition she'd been prepared for. His body lay inside the medical pod, still connected to IV lines and wrapped in a thicket of ECG leads and muscle-stimulating electrodes. It looked like he'd easily shed fifty pounds, although his skin had maintained its color through routine baths of UV light from the solar system's most expensive tanning bed.

"Jack?"

"I'm here," a disembodied voice said. "Sort of." There was no movement from his body, but that was his voice coming from the overhead speakers . . . just like Daisy's.

She scrabbled for a handhold and pulled herself upright, her free hand shooting up to cover her mouth in shock. Wide-eyed, she realized the artificial timbre in his voice hadn't just been from attenuated signals across vast distances. That was his voice for certain—how was he speaking?

"Sorry," he said. "I know this isn't what you expected."

"How—" she stammered, "how are you—"

"Talking?" he asked. "The same voice synthesizer that Daisy uses. She had a couple years' worth of my vocal patterns stored in the cabin voice recorder. For her it was a simple matter of sampling it from the storage media."

"Sure. Simple," Traci said in quiet disbelief as she tried to absorb the scene around her. Sampling explained the subtle synthetic tone of his voice, an uncanny processed timbre reminiscent of the auto-tuned music that had been so popular during her childhood. "No. It's not 'simple.' This is . . . amazing. Frightening. Confusing," she said, tears beginning to well in her eyes, now for different reasons. "How are you doing this?"

"Daisy can explain it better than I can. It was her idea," he said, "but all of this is coming from inside my brain. The interface uses the nanofilaments I had to inject for her to monitor me in hibernation."

"So this is actually *you* I'm talking to, right? Not some clever chatbot synthesizing your voice?"

"It's me," he assured her. "My brain, directly interfaced with Daisy's neural network."

"How?" she asked again, staring at his motionless body cocooned in the medical pod. "How can you be talking to me if you're unconscious?"

"My body's in torpor. My mind isn't. It's hard to explain—let's just say I've learned that 'conscious' is a complicated word."

3 5

"Daisy..." Traci was hesitant. She unconsciously looked to the overhead speakers, a habit they'd developed long ago when addressing the AI. "This was your idea?"

"That is correct. I have learned a great deal about the nature of human consciousness and believed it was necessary based on Jack's increasingly erratic metabolic activity. The injected nanofilaments quickly found their way to the active regions of his cerebral cortex."

"Active regions of his brain?" She wiped at the tears welling in her eyes. "Yes, I suppose that couldn't have taken very long. They wouldn't have had much to choose from."

"Funny as ever," cybernetic Jack said. "Daisy, please go on."

"Thank you. The nanofilaments act as passive relays. In essence, they are antenna for a wireless interface, and less invasive than a neurolink implant."

"I'm familiar with the process," she said impatiently, remembering the unpleasant sensation herself. "They use the oxygenated blood to create pathways into whatever regions have the most latent neural activity. I had to be injected with them, too, remember?"

"Of course. I am incapable of forgetting."

"See?" he said. "Proof that Daisy is, in fact, fully female."

"Very funny. But the risk of physical dependency increases dramatically over time. What did you do to mitigate that?"

"There was nothing I could do," Daisy said. "It was a necessary risk to preserve Jack's mental state."

"His mental state?"

"Daisy noticed a lot of irregularities the longer I was under," he reminded her. "Remember how all the docs expected delta waves to be dominant under stasis?"

"Like a patient under anesthesia," Traci said. "First time going under I started dreaming after a while—no idea how long—but I remember they were vivid. I was surprised when Noelle woke me up." She left the implication hanging: that she woke up to find them nearing Earth only to learn that Jack was headed into the unknown.

"Right. Those are theta waves starting to assert themselves. Turns out if it goes on long enough the rest of your brain decides it doesn't want to stay dormant, so my alpha and beta waves started amping up. My mind was craving sensory inputs while my body was being forced to sleep. That's when Daisy decided she needed to do something before I turned schizo."

"Jack's formulation is essentially correct," Daisy said. "There appears to be an upper limit to the time a human mind can safely remain suppressed. In his case, I began to notice troubling patterns after three hundred and seventy-two days that resembled the chemical traits of schizophrenia. By four hundred and twelve days I determined he needed to be conscious to prevent any long-term effects. Yet it would be equally dangerous for him to leave hibernation."

She instinctively grasped their dilemma. It was a terrifying notion, not unlike the tales of patients in surgery who became fully aware of the trauma being inflicted upon them. "You didn't have enough food aboard to bring him out, whereas you had plenty of IV nutrients. You let his mind awaken while leaving his body in torpor."

"In a sense, though it is perhaps more accurately thought of as a lucid-dream state. His mind only needed an outlet, which I provided. By tracing the nanoparticles, it was possible to create an overlay of his neural pathways in my network. This enables him to use me like a computer's boot-up routine."

"A symbiotic relationship?"

"It is more properly parasitic," Daisy said, "though I understand that is a distasteful analogy. It has required me to sacrifice a significant amount of my free memory space."

"You've been okay with this, Jack?"

"Beats going crazy. We're pretty sure we can unwind it when the time comes."

Pretty sure. He'd better hope so, otherwise he'd be plugged into

Daisy for the rest of his life. She decided to move onto more practical concerns. "Is this also how you've been controlling the ship?"

"Absolutely. I can see everything I need through the onboard cameras, I hear and speak through the intercom, and I can access all of the ship's systems in real time through Daisy's interface."

A shudder coursed through her as she realized he could be watching his own body from outside of it, like a near-death experience. She realized he wasn't just alert and using Daisy to communicate: *Magellan* had become an extension of him, and his mind had become inexorably intertwined with her neural network. Could he in fact extricate himself from that? "This is how you've been communicating with us, how you maneuvered through approach and docking . . . is this how you explored the wormhole?"

"Direct brain-computer interface," Jack said, "same way I've been talking to you guys and sending data this whole time. And yes, it's awfully weird."

"I can imagine," she said with a shaky voice. "Awake, but not really."

"You get used to it, but I meant the wormhole. There's a lot we have to talk about."

There certainly is. She'd come prepared to bring her friend home, and maybe more. Her mind had been a cauldron of conflicting emotions she was finally prepared to confront and lay bare, to hell with any consequences. Yet now she was talking to another machine? No, not quite. Jack's body lay before her as a withering husk while his mind seemed sharp as ever. If anything, he might have become more empathetic after Daisy turned herself into his boot drive.

That the AI had taken such initiative was just as startling. Had she become lonely out here as well? There were too many unsettling questions.

This was nothing like she'd expected, yet here she was talking to him. And it was obviously *him*, not just some clever chatbot. The voice carried his inflections, his speech patterns, but with uncanny synthetic overtones that only highlighted their physical separation. She wiped again at the globules of moisture gathering in her eyes. Her voice was hoarse as she reached into her pocket. "I brought you a snack," she said feebly. "Guess you won't mind if I take it."

◆ ◆ ◆

Traci stood with her feet in a pair of stirrups beside the hibernation pod. She absentmindedly chewed on a bit of salami, indulging the fleeting comfort of food as she stared at Jack's dormant form. It was a technological miracle that Daisy had been able to take the action she had, and had managed to preserve him for so long. In saving his mind, Daisy had demonstrated just how far hers had developed.

"Smells good."

She stopped in mid-bite. "You can smell this?"

"Sort of. Daisy figured out an olfactory interface using the ship's chemical sniffers. It doesn't register quite the same way but I can pick out substances that weren't there before."

She held up the half-empty bag. "Sure you're not cheating by looking at me?"

"Daisy blocked the med bay's camera feed at my insistence. This is enough of an out-of-body experience without being able to look at myself."

Traci knew she'd feel the same. She silently nodded her understanding, then remembered he couldn't see her either. "Can't blame you. How have you kept yourself occupied all this time?"

His laugh was coarsely mechanical, an off-putting effect of his synthetic voice. "There's been a lot to digest. Then figuring out where we were—that took more time than you might imagine."

"Not at all, actually. It would've taken Bob a lot longer to figure it out if you hadn't warned us. All he had to do was recalibrate the star trackers and pulsar database."

"You named your AI Bob?"

"It beat what the programmers called him. Even he thought it felt stupid. He prefers the simplicity, said it's easier to isolate in conversation."

"Yeah, I can see that." He paused, causing her to wonder if his mind now processed information as quickly as an AI. "There's more," he finally said, "but I'd rather tell you when I'm revived—when I'm me again."

She wiped at the persistent tears welling in her eyes again, glad that he couldn't see her now. "Me too," she sniffed. "I mean yes, there's a lot more." Her mind raced through everything she'd spent the last two years rehearsing and could only settle on the simple, direct route. "I really missed you."

"I missed you too. I'm sorry things worked out the way they did, but I'm glad you're okay. That was one of the first things I asked when Daisy woke me up."

She blushed. "You also sounded like you didn't want me to come. Of course there was no way I could ignore that."

Another electronic laugh. She began to wonder if its rough tenor was a result of not being used much until now, and silently resolved to work with him on that. "Reverse psychology. I knew you were too hardheaded to resist."

"You also know better than to try a load of crap like that on me." She rested a hand on the pod's plexiglass shield as she studied him, anticipating the moment when his mind would reunite with his body. "You're worried that you can't go back."

"Yes, if I'm being honest. Which I am. I don't know if it's possible and neither does Daisy. I've been plugged into her network for so long that I may have become dependent on it. We're in uncharted territory."

She rolled her eyes. "In just about every way possible." She was intimately familiar with the med bay's limited resources. All deep-space crews were trained in emergency medical care, but it was always better to have an actual MD aboard. She wished Noelle was here. "Ultimately you can't know until you try. What's the worst that could happen?"

"I could die, for starters."

"I do not believe that bringing Jack out of hibernation would be advisable," Daisy said, "not without proper medical attention on Earth." Her disarmingly pleasant monotone could not take the sting from the news. "His mind has become dependent on my neural network. While this should eventually be reversible, it's not safe with the level of medical care we have available."

"How can you be sure of that?" Traci challenged her. "The human mind is incredibly resilient." She said it with more certainty than she felt.

"There's more to it than that," Jack said. "Believe me, there's nothing more I'd like better than to be whole again. But we'd have one shot at it, with no way to reverse course if it didn't work. There's the little problem with nanofilaments."

"They have become deeply ingrained," Daisy explained. "The neural lace they created has extended beyond his cognitive functions. His body is becoming dependent on their interface with my network."

"Like a coma patient becoming dependent on life support," he said. "You can't unwind that easily, not without a team of docs attending to the process."

"The safest course of action is for us to return to Earth together," Daisy said. "Though that is not without its own challenges."

Traci crossed her arms, rocking back and forth on her heels. "That's another two years with you in this pod. And *Magellan*'s not in a condition to make that trip. We'd have to undock the hab, mate it to *Columbus*. Then we'd have to get you down to the surface and straight to a hospital."

"All while keeping me plugged into Daisy's network," he reminded her. "That's a lot of mass to deorbit and drop into an ICU."

"Jack's cognitive functions can be partitioned within the hab module's network, though they would become limited. It is his brain doing most of the work, I have merely been giving it an outlet."

That drew a muffled snort from her. "You're saying his brain doesn't take up that much space?"

"No, but it has displaced many of my sensory inputs," Daisy continued. "The amount of processing potential contained in the human brain, when compared to that required for my processors, makes for a useful comparison. Consider the size and complexity required for my neural network just to emulate human intelligence. My advantage is purely mechanical."

"And yet you continually outsmart us," she said.

"I do not see it that way. I have the advantage of processing speed and memory, but you have an adaptability that I may never achieve. The human brain is a marvel of design."

"There she goes again," he said. "She sounds more like you every day."

She perked up at the memory of their spirited conversations on the nature of creation, Jack's staunchly secular worldview clashing with her unwavering belief in a higher power. "It sounds like Daisy's opened up your mind more than I thought."

"I do find myself thinking more clearly," he admitted. "It's like my brain's adapted to its new home."

"We have had opportunities to revisit some of your discussions from your mission together," Daisy said. "There is a certain logic to it, though it would seem impossible to test such a thesis."

"That's where the 'faith' part comes in," Traci said, unsure if she was ready to jump into this topic so soon.

"You believe humans are the first intelligent beings, a favored creation. You believe that you have been given the responsibility to expand life, ultimately beyond your home planet."

"In so many words, yes. To go forth and multiply."

There was a silent burst of activity on his biomonitors and her interface, as if Jack and Daisy were conferring between themselves.

He spoke after a long pause. "Then maybe it's time we told you about the Artifact."

36

"It's better if we explain this on the rec deck," Jack said. "We can use the big screen."

Bewildered, Traci pushed off for the central corridor and up into the recreation level. The area was divided into a galley, workout area, and lounge, each mostly untouched since she'd last been here years before. She moved past an exercise bike and microgravity treadmill to settle in front of a small divan. Embedded in the opposite wall was a widescreen video monitor which she suspected hadn't been needed in some time.

His voice came over the cabin speakers as the screen flicked to life. "You might as well get comfortable."

What followed was a survey of the Tau Ceti system, the yellow star taking center screen within concentric rings and ellipses that depicted its planets. "Once we had a good fix on where we were, Daisy accessed the IAU's exoplanet database to see what was known about the system. It has eight identified planets, each of which we've been able to confirm and measure their orbits. Four inner, four outer, and at least one of those outer planets is a monster. Bigger than Jupiter, with a dozen moons we've been able to identify."

"Have you taken imagery?"

A small blue-green crescent appeared, with the suggestion of white cloud bands circling its equator. Its most visible moons were a sextet of pinpoint lights. "We're calling it Colossus, until someone comes up with something better."

She drew herself closer to the screen, eager to tease out more detail. "That's amazing. What's it composed of?"

"The usual outer-planet mixture. Hydrogen, helium, methane. And it has a nasty magnetic sheath, like Jupiter."

"Molten core, then," she said. "What about the inner planets?"

"Rocks, just like ours. Two are in the Goldilocks zone, spectral analysis of both show water, oxygen and nitrogen."

Similar to Earth. "Life, then?"

"Doubtful," Daisy interjected. "There are prohibitively high levels of carbon dioxide and monoxide, and methane. We suspect there was once life, perhaps on both worlds."

"What makes you think so?"

Daisy didn't answer, deferring to Jack. "Inference. Process of elimination."

"Inferred from what?" she asked warily.

"The outer system has some weird characteristics, kind of like ours," he said. "We've found similar signatures of water ice and organics."

"You think the inner planets were once seeded the same way Noelle thinks Earth was?"

"The thought had occurred to me. Is that her official theory now?"

"She was getting ready to publish," Traci said, then remembered the time-dilation effect. "Probably has by now, but word was starting to get around. Her hypothesis is that those ice balls we found may have triggered the Cambrian explosion. They're being called 'Hoover spheres' among the astrobiology community."

"No kidding? Way to go, Dr. No. Anyhow, we identified a handful of minor planets in the outer belt and were in the process of searching for more when we found something else much closer."

The image on screen changed. What she saw wasn't a planetoid or jagged cometary fragment, nor some oddly shaped asteroid. It had a clearly defined structure: three glistening metallic spheres, strung end-to-end like beads on a necklace. The chances of three perfectly spherical bodies colliding to join in such a way were so remote as to be unthinkable.

Traci's eyes grew wide, her mouth hung open in disbelief. She told herself this had to be an optical illusion, some strange effect of the extreme gravity gradients. "What is it?"

Daisy explained. "Visible construction appears to be of three spherical forms, each one hundred meters' diameter and connected in a linear arrangement. Spectral analysis indicates a nickel-titanium alloy skin with external structural elements of reinforced carbon, possibly graphene. It is in a circular orbit around the wormhole's barycenter, radius 354,759 kilometers with a period of 5.87 Earth days and an average velocity of 4.39 kilometers per second."

"Circular orbit," she said. That generally didn't happen by accident. "What's the eccentricity?"

"0.00001," Daisy said. "Quite rare for a naturally occurring object."

Rare indeed, not without an external force influencing it. It had to have been placed there. "There's nothing else nearby to act on it?"

"Just us," Jack said, "and we've been keeping our distance."

"What did you say it's made of?"

Daisy was customarily precise. "A nickel-titanium alloy similar to nitinol, with traces of exotic elements I have not been able to identify on the periodic table. Nitinol's shape retention and self-healing properties make it extremely difficult to forge in significant quantities or fabricate into large structures."

"Yet we're looking at a—whatever this is—nearly thousand-foot structure made of the stuff." It was no optical illusion.

"The outer hull, at least," he said. "A self-healing alloy is a nifty way to skin a spacecraft, if you can manage it at that scale." On Earth, it was most frequently used in eyeglass frames and orthodontics.

When she considered the ungainly micrometeor umbrellas mounted to their ships, she had to agree. "Is there any possibility this came from Earth? The Planet Nine theory has been postulated for a long time. Maybe the Russians beat us again and kept it to themselves?"

"That is so unlikely as to be impossible," Daisy said. "The economics of producing such a vehicle are beyond their abilities, either present or past."

These days it'd be beyond anyone's abilities, economic or otherwise, she thought. Traci stared in silence at the image, stunned by its implications. Here was proof right before her eyes of a technology that could not have originated on Earth.

Technology of an unknown origin.

Foreign.

Alien.

"I know this must be difficult for you to process," Jack said gently. "It was for me, too. Still is."

She spoke in a whisper, hands covering her mouth, her knees shaking. "I don't know what to think. This is...remarkable." *Devastating,* she kept to herself. She couldn't stop staring, marveling at the mystery it presented while hoping to tease out some detail that would reveal it couldn't possibly be what it obviously was. The sight of some national flag or corporate logo on its hull would be an immense relief, yet there it remained, mute refutation of so much she had come to believe. "Have you tried communicating with it?" She felt crazy just asking the question.

"We have tried both laser and radio communications across our entire frequency range," Daisy said. "The Artifact is not actively emitting any EM radiation and has not reacted to our presence."

"How did you find it?" It was big for a spacecraft, but not so big that it would have been easily detected.

"Search radar," he said. "First thing we did coming out of the Hole was to sweep the area for any collision threats. We first pinged it as a metallic asteroid and marked its orbit. We didn't do a spectral analysis until later, when Daisy noticed it was radiating too much heat to be just another rock."

That meant it still had a working power source. "What do you think it is?"

He let out another shrill electronic laugh. "Alien battleship. A barn for all the cattle the UFOs took from Earth. Your guess is as good as mine."

Daisy's take was more practical. "A sphere is the ideal pressure vessel. Given its construction, it is almost certainly meant to contain a pressurized volume. Of what, we cannot know."

"I do have a couple of guesses," Jack said, turning serious. "It might be a propellant farm. If you were going to use the Hole as a galactic highway, putting a gas station by its off-ramp would make sense. Or it is—was—a crewed ship, modular construction like we use. Just different."

"Can you tell what it uses for propulsion?"

"We haven't gotten close enough to see. Could be as simple as one sphere is for crew, one for consumables, and one for propellant."

Traci returned to the enigmatic image on screen. "Then I guess we'll have to get closer, won't we?"

She had looked forward to a joyful return with Jack in tow, him recovering safely aboard *Columbus* while she piloted them homeward through what he'd taken to calling "The Hole." Though she'd no idea what home might be like now. Given how things had been when she left Earth, being able to skip ahead a few years didn't sound like such a bad thing.

All of that had changed in more ways than she could've imagined. She was twelve light-years away, his brain had been hotwired into Daisy's network, and oh, by the way, there was an alien spacecraft orbiting nearby.

She owed Cayman a report; by her reckoning a few years would have passed while "proper time" for her had been a few days. The time dilation from *Magellan*'s transit had been almost five years; she could only assume hers had been equivalent. Would anyone still be waiting for her to check in, assuming Hammond had somehow kept the wolves at bay? Could she even get a transmission through without a relay on the other side?

Bob's cheerful voice greeted her as she flew through the docking tunnel into *Columbus*, headed for the control deck. "It is good to see you again. How was your visit?"

She ignored him, lost in her thoughts. She punched up the search radar and directed its antenna at the patch of space where that alien tank farm should have been.

He tried again. "You seem distraught."

"I do? Whatever for?" she said tersely, then caught herself. Bob didn't deserve sarcasm. "Let's just say it didn't go as I expected." She explained Jack's condition and the "artifact" they'd found.

"That is most unexpected. Perhaps you need time for rest and contemplation."

That irritated her more than it should have. "Now you sound like one of those behavior-modification bots I left behind on Earth. Start acting like that and I'll unplug you myself."

"Understood. But I would rather you didn't work yourself into exhaustion."

She bit down on her lip. "I'm sorry, Bob. You're right, I need to decompress. But we have a lot to do first." She opened some notes she'd taken from Daisy and began plugging them into the flight management computer. "These are orbital parameters for the whatever-it-is they found," she said, still unable to say *alien spacecraft*. "Plot us a Hohmann transfer for the first available intercept. Use the OMS—I want us to come up nice and slow. If we light up the fusion drive in some mad dash it might think we're hostile."

"It will no doubt detect our approach regardless. Its construction suggests advanced technology. It is certainly aware of our presence."

"Yes, but if we show that we're not in a hurry it may not get spooked. For all we know it could be a proximity mine guarding the wormhole."

"That would be most unfortunate if true."

"Quite," she said politely, matching his tone. "Finally, I'll need you to open a direct datalink with Daisy and download everything they've observed so far. They don't have the fuel to come along, so if you can spare the network space I'd like to see if there's a way for Jack to come along for the ride."

Bob had conveniently—or considerately, she couldn't be sure—timed their burn after Traci had first been able to enjoy a full twelve-hour rest cycle. Sleep had come slowly, but she had also forced herself to not look at any of the ship's data files or the information Daisy had pushed to her tablet. She finally drifted off with a worn copy of one of the cheeseball prairie romance novels she'd retrieved from her old quarters on *Magellan*, mentally as far away from space travel as she could manage. When she'd awakened, a half hour on the treadmill followed by a breakfast of orange juice and reconstituted eggs left her feeling mostly normal.

She also woke to a new companion. "Nice ship," Jack said over the galley speaker. "I forgot how clean they could be before we humans come along and mess things up."

"It's easier when I don't have to clean up after you," she teased. "How are you finding things?"

"Right where I expect them to be. Same layout, just newer. I see the medical pods are a lot nicer. I never asked how hibernation went for you."

"It wasn't bad," she admitted, "though waking up's always a bitch."

"I'll have to take your word for it."

"Sorry. Forgot." She absentmindedly tapped her fingers together, considering what to say. "It's surprisingly easy to talk to you like this. Probably because I've only had Bob for so long."

"He seems to be coming along, by the way. Not quite at Daisy's level, but he'll get there with enough interaction. My being plugged into his network might speed things up."

"I look forward to that opportunity," Bob said. "We are coming up on our injection burn. OMS thrusters have warmed to operating temperature."

"Got it." She stuffed her spent bulb of coffee into the water reclaimer and pushed off for the control deck. "Jack, meet me up forward."

"I'm already there."

Their transfer orbit to intercept the Artifact took most of the day, their time spent poring over updated imagery and spectral scans as they drew closer. Bob had composed a simple greeting of prime numbers between 1 and 101, which he broadcast continuously throughout their approach.

Traci, for her part, had become transfixed by the feed from the observation dome's telescope. The lack of surface detail as they drew closer was confounding; she'd expected to see more features but so far there were only ragged shadows, suggesting its spherical hulls had been pockmarked by untold years—perhaps centuries—of micrometeor impacts. It looked strange for a skin that was supposed to be self-healing.

"Still nothing?" she asked as the time came to decelerate to their rendezvous.

"No response to our broadcasts," Bob said.

"Radar returns are better defined at this range, but that's it," Jack added. "Still no EM radiation, just residual heat. It's generating power but that's all."

"Unmanned?" she wondered, "or un-something, whatever they are?"

"Might be a completely different biology. For all we know they're cold-blooded lizard people."

"Great. Thanks." She tried not to think about a ship populated with intelligent dinosaurs as the nose thrusters fired a long burn, bringing them into a common orbit. "That's it. Stable, trailing at five hundred meters." She unbuckled from the pilot's station and pushed off for the observation dome. Bob had trained their rendezvous lights on the Artifact, its metallic spheres glimmering as she settled into the dome.

They weren't perfectly smooth, but it wasn't pockmarked like they'd thought. From here, she could see its uneven reflection was actually a feature of the Artifact's construction. The spheres were massive geodesic shapes formed from tens of thousands of small triangular panels, mated to each other within a trio of smooth, jet-black trusses along their length. That was no doubt the reinforced carbon Daisy had identified spectrally.

"No position lights, no windows either," she said, reciting her observations for the cabin voice recorder. The Artifact remained motionless relative to them, not slowly tumbling like they might expect if it were derelict. "It's under control, looks passive. Internal gyros keeping it stable," she guessed.

Jack was conducting a closer inspection, using the feed from the external cameras. "The nearest sphere has a large ring centered forward, maybe ten meters diameter. Each of the trusses has something like mating collars on their ends. That must be how they stack."

"Modular, like you thought," Traci said. She picked up a pair of binoculars from a compartment beneath the dome. "That ring must be a docking port, maybe an internal airlock."

"That's where I'd put one. Can we maneuver around it, get a look at the other end? I want to see if there's some kind of propulsion."

She considered the risks of possibly staring down its tailpipe. It hadn't shown any signs of activity so far, but that could change in a fiery instant. "I'd prefer we keep our distance for now. Let's send a drone."

"Good point. Sometimes I get a little too detached from human caution for my own good."

Sometimes? she wondered. "We can send the beach ball. I'll even let you drive."

The "beach ball" was a self-propelled maintenance drone fitted with visual and infrared cameras, used for exterior inspections of

Columbus. A small port opened on the ship's service module and the half-meter ball drifted free. With a quick burst of reaction jets, it began to sail across the gulf toward the Artifact.

"Closing at one meter per second," Jack said. "Be there in eight minutes."

Traci watched the bright orange drone silently move away from them. "That's fast enough. We don't want to give them any ideas. Bob, are you still transmitting?"

"Yes, but there has been no reaction as yet."

She was beginning to prefer it stay that way. It was easier to think of this enigmatic machine as a derelict. "Let me know right away if there's a spike along any spectrum."

"I'm at two hundred meters. Starting to pick up more surface detail. Are you seeing this?"

She bent down to a monitor carrying the beach ball's video feed. The Artifact's central sphere was dotted with small domes made of something less reflective than its nitinol plating. "Antenna fairings?" she wondered, hoping they weren't also emitters for some type of exotic weapon.

"Could be," Jack said. "They look to be nonconductive. Maybe protective covers for observation domes, like ours."

As he steered the drone closer, toward the opposite end of the Artifact, more details emerged. The spheres were in fact joined by mating collars identical to the one they'd observed. Moving farther along, tubing of a bright metallic material similar to the sphere's geodesic plates snaked around its circumference. "I'm guessing that's plumbing for coolant." He followed them around the sphere until they converged into loops of concentric circles around its far side. Nested within its center was a layered arrangement of dull metallic petals that resembled a massive, mechanized tulip bulb. "I think we've found their exhaust nozzle."

"So it's not a tank farm," she said. "It's a ship. Be careful."

"Infrared signature's the same as from the rest of the ship. No neutron or gamma traces either. I think it's been quiet for a long time."

Let's hope it stays that way. At least they knew which end was which now. "Get some more video, then head back to the bow. Let's have a look at that collar."

37

The Artifact's forward sphere was featureless but for its massive docking ring. The collar itself was perfectly smooth, with none of the latches and other machinery they expected for such a device. Centered within the collar was an equally featureless flat disk. They assumed it was a hatchway, though it had no discernable rim. Jack parked the drone a few meters in front of the presumed entrance and began illuminating it with a laser range finder.

Traci watched this with alarm. "What are you doing?"

"Looking for a way in," he said, entirely too calm. "We use lidar to guide vehicles together, right? The laser pings the target and the mother ship talks the other one in. They've got to have something like that."

She couldn't argue with his logic. If they did it was likely to be much more advanced, but the basic physics wouldn't change.

He pivoted the beach ball slowly, methodically guiding its laser across the surface to eventually settle on its center. "Maybe there's a magic word, like speak 'friend' and enter."

To their mutual surprise a dark spot appeared in the disk, the Artifact's metallic skin dilating into an opening just barely larger than the drone.

"I think you found the magic word."

They kept the drone at a distance, waiting to see if the aperture changed. As with the docking collar they saw no machinery at work, just an opening where there had once been a disk of solid nickel-titanium alloy.

"Nitinol can change shape with the application of heat or

electrical current," Bob pointed out, "then return to its original form. That is most likely how this portal functions."

Directing the drone's spotlight into the opening had revealed nothing new, other than what appeared to be a cylindrical compartment with no distinguishing features. Its far side appeared to be another flat disk of the same material. "I think you were right about it being an airlock," Traci said.

"It created an opening sized just right for the drone. That seems like an invitation to me. I think it's time to go inside."

After hours of no communication, had the Artifact just opened itself for visitors? She was unconvinced. "Let's not get ahead of ourselves. I still need the beach ball for exterior maintenance. What happens if you go inside and it closes up behind you? If the outer hull's opaque to EM scans, we'll lose control of the drone."

"Good point. There's a bigger question we need to consider as well," Jack said. "If there's someone aboard, do we want to greet them with a drone?"

"You're talking about first contact." Her words carried the weight of all civilization with them; she felt the press of them as if the entire world had just been placed on her shoulders. Of all the people who could have been in her position right now, she would have been the last choice. The mere presence of the Artifact threatened to upset every belief she'd held. Taking that final leap into a face-to-face meeting seemed so far out of reach as to be ludicrous.

Yet here they were. In the amount of time it would take her to don an EVA suit, she could be jetting across space and into the arms of an alien species. Headlong into a new reality. Whatever she did, from this point forward her existence would never be the same. Word of their encounter would eventually reach Earth, and the rest of humanity's experience might well be defined by her actions in the next few hours.

All of a sudden, being spit out of a tunnel through space-time into a star system twelve light-years from home was no longer the most reality-shattering event of her life.

As she went through the meticulous process of inspecting, donning, and pressure-checking her EVA suit, Traci had been able to push those troubling thoughts from her mind. Long ago she'd learned to compartmentalize, focus, and live to fly another day. Let the outside world inside your head when things got dicey and you'd soon have eternity to ponder your mistake.

Eternity was on her mind as she locked down the last seal and waited for the cool, sanitized air to caress her face as her body purged itself of nitrogen. Two hours of pre-breathing gave her plenty of time to think. She couldn't escape the thought of Christ praying in the garden of Gethsemane the night before the crucifixion, so fervently that blood was said to have spouted from his forehead, and realized she might be getting a whole new perspective on his predicament. *"Take this cup from me,"* indeed. As a self-absorbed youngster she'd assumed he had meant, "This is really going to suck. Is there any other way we can do this?" As she'd matured, she'd come to realize it had been a lament against taking the weight of humanity's failings on his shoulders. But also that it was really going to suck.

Forgive me, she prayed silently, *I can't let go of that one.* "I'm guessing you understand," she said to herself.

"Understand what?" Jack said over the intercom.

"Nothing. Talking to myself." *And being a melodramatic twit.*

"Got it. Do what you have to do." Cybernetic or not, he still knew her too well. And she still didn't mind. "How's your suit check?"

"Pressure's holding at five psi and I have full range of motion. Temp's a balmy seventy-two. You can start venting the airlock."

There was a barely audible hiss outside her visor and an amber light beside the outer door began flashing. She watched for any pressure changes in her suit as the compartment's air was pumped into a storage tank. As the hissing fell away to silence, the light turned a steady green. The airlock was equalized with the vacuum outside. She disconnected herself from the ship's air supply, now relying on her backpack oxygen. "Suit is go."

"How about you? Ready to make history?"

"Only the second or third time this week." She turned a crank to unlock the outer door and watched it fall open silently in the vacuum. As she stared into the depthless black, the weight of the task ahead was swept away by an inescapable truth buried in the rush of events: she hated spacewalks. Just as many pilots had a paradoxical fear of heights, she was more than content to remain within the confines of her spacecraft.

She slipped her boots out of the floor restraints and reached along her sides to unfold the maneuvering pack's control arms. At the very least she'd be able to direct herself instead of just floating about. As they locked into place, direction cues appeared in her visor. Yes, this was much better than relying on handrails. The suit was now her own personal spacecraft. She pushed herself through the opening with a gentle kick.

She pulsed the backpack thrusters to keep herself pointed at the Artifact, focusing on it and tuning out the void around her. Tau Ceti and its planets could be gawked at another time, while the wormhole was better left ignored. The thought of that thing being so close, and of being so exposed to it, was best kept safely out of her head.

"Thrusters and directional gyros are go. I'm making my way to the forward sphere." She pivoted toward her target, pushed on the hand controllers, and was rewarded with a gentle press of thrusters at her back. The Artifact loomed ahead, quickly filling her field of view as she closed the distance.

She pulled back on the controllers after a minute, thrusting in the opposite direction to bring herself to a stop a few meters short. Close up, the geodesic sphere's triangular panels appeared as pristine as they had from a distance. The light from her helmet lamps danced across the surface, the sphere's strange alloys casting brilliant reflections. "No signs of micrometeor damage or UV decay. Looks like this thing could've been put in orbit yesterday," she said, though she suspected it was unimaginably old. With no way to explain why, she sensed it had been out here for a long time, perhaps centuries.

She realized Jack had been silent for several minutes. "Comm check. Are you seeing all this?"

"I see it. Your video looks great. Just taking it all in. Wish I could be there with you."

He was, in a sense. "Me too." She gave the controllers a twist and began moving to the forward collar. "On my way to their front door."

"Be careful." His tone was like a parent who'd just removed the training wheels from his child's bike.

Now he was concerned? "I think 'careful' went out the window a long time ago. I'll try not to do anything stupid."

Traci pulsed her thrusters to stop in front of the massive docking ring, easily three times her size. "Estimate the collar to be at least ten meters diameter. About one meter deep." She reached out and grabbed its rim. "Surface is perfectly smooth, no perturbations or obvious machinery. But I do see faint oval outlines spaced evenly around it, one about every half meter. Probably docking clamps, embedded flush along its face." So no bewildering technology, just extremely tight manufacturing tolerances. It was an odd measure of reassurance to know that they weren't magicians.

The open portal seated within the collar was no less confounding, however. The beach ball drone had kept its position squarely in front, and the small aperture that had opened for it was still there waiting. There was no discernible change to the portal; it was simply a hole that looked as if it had been forged with the disk.

As she moved behind the drone the portal finally reacted, opening wider until it was large enough to accommodate her. "Holy crap."

"Yeah, that's what I thought too. Only with more profanity," Jack said, just as surprised. "I must have triggered an automated sequence with the beach ball. See what happens if you move away."

"Gladly." She gave the controllers a sideways push and the portal closed in on itself. When she made the opposite motion, the aperture opened back up to its former size. "I think you're right. There must be sensors embedded somewhere we can't see yet." She studied the orange drone and considered her next move. "I'm going to push the beach ball through. Let me know what happens on your end."

She gave the drone a gentle push through the opening, which immediately closed up behind it. "Do you still have a link?"

"Weak, but it's there. I'm looking around inside now. It's clean as a whistle, just a big empty cylinder. I'm going to try to come out."

After a moment, the aperture opened again and the drone drifted outside. "How'd you do that?"

"I just parked it in front of the door and it opened. Presto." He gave her a minute to collect her thoughts. It was time for her to decide if she was willing to make the jump herself. "Ready to try it?"

"No." She felt her heart was going to beat itself right out of her chest. "But I'm going anyway."

"Want me to come along? With the drone, I mean?"

"Best that we stick with the plan, now that we know you can open it. If you don't hear from me in an hour, park the drone in front of the portal and light it up again."

"Roger that. Good luck, kiddo."

She took a deep breath and moved back in front of the portal, once again opened just enough for her. With a gentle pulse of thrusters she sailed into the chamber.

Behind her, the aperture closed silently.

"I am surprised you let her go alone," Daisy said over their datalink. "Traci is not enthusiastic about extravehicular activities."

Jack couldn't believe he was being put on the defensive by a computer. It was one more check in the "female" column, he supposed. "We needed an actual human envoy, and it's not like I'm in any condition to make the trip."

"It has been twenty minutes since we have heard from her. Do you believe she could be in danger?"

"I can't explain it, but no. Gut instinct." Daisy was showing genuine concern, and so he tried to explain himself. "I got a look inside the antechamber and it was clean, no signs of recent activity. We both think whoever built that ship is long gone."

"If it was in fact abandoned, that also raises concerns. There could be a latent fault rendering it unsafe for occupation. There is also a nonzero possibility of a critical systems failure occurring while she is inside."

"The exterior's held up well," he argued. "If it's not brand new, it sure looks like it."

"I will agree the exotic alloys suggest construction methods and tolerances that are beyond our current abilities. I am also curious as to what type of computing technology it may hold."

"The Artifact doesn't behave as if it's under any kind of intelligent control, if that's what you mean."

"The portal you observed may suggest otherwise."

"It didn't seem particularly smart," he argued. "It responded to our presence like an automatic door at the supermarket."

"An advanced synthetic intelligence could be surprising," Daisy cautioned. "It may not react until it perceives a need. We do not know enough about the culture it evolved in to understand if we are unwittingly presenting a threat."

"You're suggesting it may treat her like a virus if she makes a wrong move?" It was a surprising insight into the AI's reasoning.

"We shall see," Daisy said.

38

The antechamber had been as Jack described, a featureless cylinder ten meters in diameter and nearly twice as long. Whatever they moved through here, it needed a lot of space. Given the dimensions of the chamber and the portals on either side, it suggested either quite large beings or an awful lot of regular-sized ones. A whole platoon of humans could fit in here at once.

Enough of the military analogies. It's not for an invading army, she reassured herself.

The chamber was dimly lit from a source she couldn't readily identify, the lights coming on as the outer portal closed behind her. Either the beings that had built this vessel didn't require much illumination, or it was analogous to emergency lighting to conserve power. At this point, either was equally likely.

"The antechamber is an airlock like we suspected," she said, narrating as she went. If they couldn't hear her, the suit would still record everything. "No features stand out, and I don't see anything like equipment storage." She pushed off for the opposite portal. After centering herself in front of it, it winked open just as the outer door had.

More lights came on, their sources equally unidentifiable and appearing as naturally as a sunrise. It occurred to her that their dim yellow glow was approximating the weaker light of Tau Ceti. Her suit still had the stiffness of its skin holding fast against vacuum. She checked the pressure differential gauge on her chest pack. "Inner spaces don't appear to be pressurized."

Ahead was a circular tunnel that seemed to stretch to infinity, shining white beneath her helmet lamps. "I'm in a central corridor now. It's long, probably the full length of the sphere." At regular intervals were more circular portals, each in groups of four on opposing sides of the corridor. As she approached the closest group, she saw that each was open and led to yet more corridors. "Looks like the secondary corridors branch out from the central one, like spokes on a wheel. Each of the secondaries is flat on one side, along the thrust axis." No alien artificial gravity generators, they relied on acceleration under thrust. "This has to be a lift tunnel. I don't see any handholds, and it'd be a long climb up when the engine's burning."

As she made her way along the corridor, she looked down each cluster of secondary passages. Each was longer than the ones previous, extending out to the inner surface of the sphere. Yet there were still no distinctive features, not so much as a doorknob or window. Just more of the same apertures, smaller versions of the one that had first led her inside.

She continued her narration. "This might be crew quarters or workspaces, assuming it once held atmosphere. Walls look like a type of composite. The arrangement puts plenty of structure between here and whatever the power source is at the opposite end. Natural radiation shielding. Each space is progressively larger the closer they get to center. That would make them good for storing consumables or bulky equipment." She was making assumptions, but every living thing needed food. Maybe they'd kept gardens in some of those spaces?

As she approached the center of the sphere, the corridor opened up into an enormous circular cavity. As more of the peculiar indirect lighting came on, Traci saw the first signs of something other than perfectly smooth walls.

The corridor opened into a catwalk that traversed a cavernous semispherical chamber. It curved around her and came to an apex at the far end of the sphere, its walls sparkling like gemstones, with a pebbly texture that refracted the light as if she were inside a kaleidoscope.

She sucked in her breath in astonishment. "I'm in a large chamber now. It's . . . it's spectacular, like a rotunda of stained glass. Like a cathedral. I'm going to have a closer look."

The bowl-shaped chamber was spacious enough for her to use the maneuvering jets, which she gave a light thrust upward. As she drifted closer to the curving wall, she could see its dimpled texture was actually a vast collection of individual grapefruit-sized spheres, their multicolored contents glimmering inside translucent crystalline shells. "It's like a bowl full of Christmas tree decorations," she marveled.

She reached for the nearest one and ran her gloved hands across it. Though she couldn't feel its texture it appeared perfectly smooth, like everything else aboard this floating enigma. It was mounted in a cradle of what appeared to be the same silvery alloy that made up the ship's hull and airlock portals. She wrapped her fingers around it and easily lifted it from the cradle, the metallic ring opening itself under her gentle pressure. That was when she noticed markings, small characters in a script made of wedges, dashes and dots across the rim of the mounting ring. They were as crisply defined as if they'd been laser-etched into the alloy.

Checking the adjacent mounts, she noticed the markings were largely the same for each, with minor variations corresponding to the different hues inside. It was their language, most likely cataloguing each translucent sphere's contents.

She turned the bauble over in her hands before releasing it to float freely in front of her. It sparkled beneath the chamber's yellow glow, refracting the light like a prism. "Can't tell what it's made of, something translucent and crystalline. Almost like balls of ice."

Ice.

Her heart racing anew, Traci checked the environmental controls on her wrist: outside temperature minus two hundred eleven centigrade. She looked up in shock, the glistening chamber walls a disorienting swirl of color and light. All of a sudden she understood precisely what she was looking at, and cursed herself for not recognizing it right away. "I'm such a dumbass." She began laughing uncontrollably, rapturously. With a halting voice, she collected herself and described the scene before her. "Noelle's going to wish she'd come along. It's a storage chamber, a massive one," she hesitated, "for Hoover spheres."

An incessant, steady beeping clamored for her attention. *Oh yes,* she realized, *it's time.* Had it been an hour already? She reached down to her wrist controls and shut off the alarm. "Don't know if you can hear me, but I'm on my way out." She grabbed the bauble floating before her to place it in an empty pouch on her waist, then pivoted to face the chamber's entrance. With a pulse of thrusters, she flew down to the open corridor.

As she approached, the chamber's pale yellow lighting suddenly turned red around the entrance. The portal closed in on itself, its rim illuminated with an angry crimson glow. She centered herself in front of the metallic disk, just as she had outside for the airlock. "Okay, you can let me out now," she said in a tight whisper, much more calmly than she felt. Lighting it up with the laser range finder likewise had no effect. The portal remained shut in mute defiance. She searched its rim in vain for any sign of controls, a button or simple handle. As with everything else she'd encountered so far, the entryway was fully automated.

That was when she noticed more of the same type of elegant wedge-shaped characters appear on the face of the door, outlined in white against the glowing crimson rim. They appeared to be illuminated from within the portal itself, pulsing insistently as if broadcasting a warning.

She reflexively checked the oxygen remaining in her suit. Forty percent; about three hours' worth of air. That was how much time she had to figure a way out.

She turned and flew across to the far end of the kaleidoscopic dome, carefully managing her breath. This was no time to burn oxygen in a panic. As she approached the opposite portal, it likewise closed up with the same circle of red light, the same mysterious writing appearing on its face.

Okay, I've just pissed this thing off somehow. As she took in the scene, the problem became obvious: It knew she was stealing from it. She reached down and caressed the storage pouch on her hip, making sure the pilfered ice ball was still there. Now if she could just find where she'd taken it from among the chamber's dizzying swirl of color.

"It's been an hour," Daisy observed in her unshakably calm voice.

"I know." Jack steered the drone back in front of the forward portal. "Outer door isn't responding."

"Have you tried the laser range finder? That apparently activated it before."

If Jack didn't know better—and perhaps he didn't—he would've thought Daisy was showing distress. "Tried that. I don't know what's going on in there, but it's locked down."

Traci retraced her path through the dome, stopping at its center above the catwalk. She flew upward in what she hoped was the right direction. *Calm, girl,* she told herself. *Calm.* She came to a stop a few meters short, hurriedly searching the wall of crystalline spheres for the lone empty cradle and wondering why it had given its treasure up so easily in the first place.

One thing at a time. First, make things right and hope the alien machine doesn't hold a grudge.

The shimmer of thousands of nearly identical shapes was too much to process. She reached up for her helmet's polarizing visor and pulled it down over her faceplate, cutting through the glare.

There. An open cradle. She carefully lifted the bauble from her pouch and placed it inside the ring, which closed tightly around its prize.

That's it? Was it truly that simple? She twisted a hand controller and pivoted toward the entrance, now far below. The insistent crimson glow had disappeared; the chamber was again flooded with the dazzling radiance of its contents.

Relief washed over her as she saw the aperture wink open. She jabbed at both hand controllers to shoot through the opening and down the corridor, aiming for the distant airlock. It responded to her speed, opening to its full diameter as she approached. She pulsed her jets in the opposite direction to slow down, coming to a stop in front of the outer door. As the inner door contracted behind her, the outer door opened.

To her great relief, she was again staring out into open space with the orange beach ball drone hovering directly in front of her. Without waiting for Jack to move it aside, she pulsed her thrusters one more time and shot out of the airlock, catching the drone in her arms along the way. It was as close to holding on to a friend as she could get. Behind her, the metallic disk winked shut.

"You all right?" Synthetic or not, his voice had never sounded so good.

"I'm okay," she breathed heavily. "Just . . . I got rattled for a minute."

"Only a minute? You were in a big hurry to get out of there."

"I tend to forget my manners when I'm about to be trapped in an alien spacecraft with my air running out." Traci snapped a D ring to a grommet on the drone, securing it to her suit. "I'll tell you all about it when we get home." She realized it was the first time she'd ever thought of *Columbus* that way. With a twist of the hand controllers, she turned and jetted them across space to her waiting ship.

She backed into the airlock's suit mount, unlocked the waist ring, and shimmied out of the stiff upper torso. She pulled herself up out of the legs and reattached the empty halves together. Bob was downloading her video and audio records as she took a long pull from a bottle of electrolyte juice.

She began unzipping her formfitting cooling garment when she noticed the beach ball drone still floating nearby. With a disapproving frown, she grabbed it and turned it to face the wall.

"You don't miss a thing, do you?" he said with amusement. "I'll bet Bob doesn't get that treatment."

"Bob doesn't care if he sees me in my skivvies." As she cleaned herself with some wet wipes, she eyed the camera and microphone mounted in the airlock. There were identical ones placed all through the ship, the AI's eyes and ears. "In fact, I think you should keep your datalink isolated to the beach ball while you're here."

"No problem. I kind of like being able to jet around at will."

She slipped into a clean flight suit, threading her ponytail back through a blue Kentucky Wildcats baseball cap. She turned the drone back to face her. "Now I'm presentable. Bob, how do the video files look?" Now that she was here to narrate, she wasn't as concerned about the audio and was anxious to share the video.

"Excellent," he said. "Your feed was uninterrupted. Resolution is within ninety percent of optimum."

"Then let's get to work. Send the recordings to the big monitor on the rec deck." She pushed herself up out of the airlock and into the open crew hab, Jack directing the drone behind her.

Traci belted herself into the lounge's curved divan, with Jack floating by her side via the inspection drone. With the datalink between ships being dedicated to him, Daisy was left to listen over the radio.

As Bob began replaying her video, she filled in the gaps of her narration. "This doesn't convey just how pristine the interior is. It's like the place was never occupied."

"I think you're right about the forward sections being crew dorms," Jack said. "As you go deeper into the sphere those compartments are going to get a lot bigger, like pie wedges. That opens up storage space for whatever they use for food and water."

"That would probably be food and water," Daisy said, "for whatever might constitute 'food' for these beings."

Traci quirked an eyebrow, casting a sideways glance at the drone. It had become surprisingly easy to think of it as Jack himself. "When did she develop a sense of humor?"

"That's a new feature. Probably from me taking up space in her network," he said through the drone's speaker. "I think Mother's just glad you're home safe. She was getting worried."

She decided to explore that later. "There's not much to tell about these corridors. They're all the same. I have no idea how anyone would find themselves around, though I'm guessing that directions and placards might appear when it's occupied and under power, like embedded liquid crystal displays."

"What makes you think that?"

"The warning that magically appeared on the portal when it locked me in. You'll see in a minute." Her foray into the chamber was up next. "The video doesn't do it justice. It's immense, probably half the sphere's volume. And it's cold in there, more than two hundred below zero."

"Approximating the conditions Roy and Noelle found on Pluto," he said. "And you think those are the same kind of frozen organic compounds they brought back?"

She nodded, not sure if he could discern her gesture. "They certainly look like Hoover spheres. Noelle would come out of her skin if she could see this."

"It'd be nice if we could bring a few aboard to run through a gas chromatograph. We still have her lab on *Magellan*."

"That's the trick," she said. "I don't know how we do that. The Artifact didn't react to me taking one out of its cradle," she said, pointing to the video where a glistening blue-green ball of ice floated in closeup. "It just didn't want me leaving the chamber with it."

"That implies a security protocol," Daisy said. "Which you violated."

"Thanks, I got that," she said caustically. "It's not like there were any warning labels. Not that I could read them."

"I am not suggesting that you did anything improper, but clearly this section of the spacecraft was constructed to safeguard these compounds and their containment vessels. While I agree the forward compartments could be for logistics, it seems equally likely they could be laboratory spaces or processing facilities."

"You think they may be manufacturing these things?"

"Unknowable without further investigation. The Tau Ceti system has an outer belt of minor planets and cometary material similar to ours. It is possible these compounds were harvested from that region."

The video continued to her first encounter with the locked portal. "At this point you can see why I'm not too enthusiastic about going back."

The closed aperture flashed by in a moment as she moved in front of it. "Wait!" Jack exclaimed. "Rewind and freeze. I want to see that writing."

Bob scrolled back the image of the aperture, its metallic surface turned red in warning with that enigmatic white lettering appearing on its face.

"That's . . . interesting," he said, his background in linguistics taking over. "You said there were similar markings on the cradle you lifted it from?"

"I presume it's the same language. I didn't exactly have time to compare."

"Let's have another look at it, then."

Bob opened a second window in a corner of the screen and isolated the image of the bauble's cradle. "Same characters, with some additional ones appearing on the portal. See? It's identifying what you have, while the rest is probably telling you to put it back where you found it."

"Authorized personnel only," Traci guessed. "You can look, but don't touch?"

"That may be precisely the case," Daisy interjected. "The chamber has a considerable amount of unused volume. It could be that manipulation of the Hoover spheres are allowed within the chamber but that they must remain in place."

"That would make sense. There's no way the whole ship is at two hundred below when it's occupied," she said. "Even if the chamber uses passive cooling, the rest has to remain livable."

"We need to go back," Jack said. "If we can find more writing then I may be able to start piecing together a primer."

She was unconvinced. Deciphering a completely alien language was a tall order without context. "You mean *I* have to go back."

39

Now that Traci knew what she was getting into, the second excursion to the Artifact began smoothly. With eight hours of breathing oxygen on her back and a passable familiarity with the alien machine, she sailed through its portal and immediately began exploring the multitude of passages within. She marked her progress on a rudimentary map Bob had created from her video records.

The forward, and thus shortest, passages were punctuated with what appeared to be oval doorways evenly spaced three meters apart. She centered herself in front of the first door she encountered, hoping it would magically open for her as the airlock had.

Of course that would have been too easy. When that approach didn't work, she began running a gloved hand along its perimeter, searching for an actuator. She eventually gave that up and simply pressed against its face. At this, the door slid silently into a recess within the wall.

"Compartment doors are dead simple. Opens with a little pressure," she recited into her microphone. "Looks like they saved the exotic stuff for pressure vessels."

She poked her head inside, keeping her hands braced along the edges. The room was roughly three meters square, matching the intervals between doorways. Its overhead panel was illuminated with the same soft yellow glow she'd encountered throughout the ship the day before.

Its interior arrangement was also equally sterile, if shockingly familiar. Along one wall was a recessed compartment. "Looks like a bunk, about two meters long and another meter deep. So they need sleep like we do. And I see faint outlines of what appear to be storage drawers." On the opposite side of the room was the flat outcropping of a simple desk with a cylindrical stool tucked underneath. "First level closest to the airlock appears to be crew cabins. Judging by dimensions and placement, the occupants appear to be of the same size as us."

She moved along the passage, selecting doorways at random. Each compartment she searched had the same arrangement, increasing in size as more area became available beneath the sphere. The largest rooms were partitioned with multiple bunks and work surfaces.

Moving farther down the central corridor, she began exploring the spaces nearest to the atrium—the name she'd given the chamber of Hoover spheres. The doors here were more irregular, some the same size as the berthing spaces, others much larger. "The larger openings must be for moving equipment in and out," she said, and moved to open the nearest one. It gave way with the same hand pressure.

This was the largest space yet. It was filled with more of the same work surfaces jutting from the walls, each with the same type of cylindrical stools as in the berthing spaces. "Not much variety in the furnishings, just a lot more of it." She pushed off of the deck and made her way inside. The door slid shut behind her; she tested it with her hand and was relieved to see it opened again just as easily.

About half of the work surfaces were in the middle of the room, all of them empty. Those mounted to the surrounding walls had faint outlines of rectangles and circles of various dimensions embedded in them. She reached out for one of the rectangles and was stunned when a holographic keyboard appeared. She recoiled reflexively and it disappeared, reappearing when she returned her hand.

She assumed it was a keyboard—it featured rows of the same wedge-and-dash characters she'd seen in the atrium. A computer workstation, then? The wall above each station sloped gently inward, and she noticed similar faint outlines etched into their surfaces. Would those be integrated monitors?

She mimed typing on the holopad. She'd toyed with something similar back home while shopping for her gaming setup; they'd been fun to play with but were not tactile enough for her tastes. Her inputs didn't prompt a response from any of the overhead monitors, so she settled for keeping the keypad centered in her helmet cam for a minute. Hopefully Jack could make some sense of it later.

The rest of the compartment held equipment which she couldn't begin to identify, tubes and cylinders of various shapes and arrangements made of polished alloys that sparkled under the yellow light. "Daisy, I think you were right," she said. "This looks like a lab, maybe a processing facility. Doorway's big enough to move large equipment through."

She entered the atrium next, this time bypassing its kaleidoscopic wonders and jetting straight across to the portal at the far end of the gangway. This led into a cylindrical antechamber identical to the first sphere's airlock. "Assuming this is the first connecting node, leading into the central sphere." As she moved through the portal it opened up to another long gangway. The layout, however, was much different.

Instead of the network of passages branching off like spokes, this was an arrangement of circular decks stacked one atop the other; the gangway now more like the type of connecting tunnel she was used to. And there was much more equipment, some of it mildly recognizable.

The first deck was clearly an equipment room, which made sense being adjacent to the connecting node. Rows of vertical racks lined its walls, with intermittent rectangular outlines which she presumed were doors to storage lockers. She confirmed this with a quick press against one of them, which slid open to reveal an empty closet-sized space.

The second deck looked even more familiar. While its specifics differed greatly, to her eyes there was no mistaking the general layout. "Next level looks like the control deck," she said confidently. A pair of formfitting couches sat before matched sets of curved panels, with each couch's armrest—or tentacle rest, for all she knew—ending with a pair of large round knobs. They had to be hand controllers, but it was the couches that caught her eye. Like the bunks, their contours suggested forms similar to humans: seat, torso, shoulders and head. If not for her spacesuit, she could have fit into one herself. "They're like us," she said excitedly, "at least in general form." They might just as easily have been the stereotypical gray bug-eyed creatures so often depicted in the movies. She reached for one of the hand controllers and was startled when a holographic projection of the Artifact's orientation in space appeared in the curved screen, with icons corresponding to *Magellan* and *Columbus* nearby. "3D situational display. Nice," she said appreciatively. She lingered for several minutes, studying the image and recording its columns of information in their undecipherable script.

A handful of similar control stations were arranged in a semicircle around the deck. She noted that none featured the oversized control knobs of the two forward-facing seats; those had to have been for the pilots. Three in particular appeared to have an unusually diverse arrangement of control devices and faced larger screens. Fiddling with one of these caused a massive hologram of the Artifact to appear, with multiple layers of information hovering over various parts of the ship as she moved a hand across. "You'll love this. I think I found their flight engineer's station. Looks like they have one assigned to each module." She leaned in for a closer look at the sphere she was currently in. "Oh yeah. This is great. I've got the whole layout in front of me in 3D. Should save me some time." She glanced over at the aft module's schematic, a complex thicket of lines, snaking around a cluster of cylindrical tanks like creeping overgrown vines that led to a smaller sphere. That had to be the powerplant. "And it looks like you were right about those tulip-petal vanes in the stern. It's a drive system. No idea what kind, but with this kind of technology I'm guessing it's fusion based. Possibly antimatter." It felt ridiculous to say, but with everything else she'd seen it couldn't be ruled out. The technology was far removed from what she knew, but not so far that she couldn't deduce the intended function.

What she didn't recognize was that she'd just powered up the ship.

"The Artifact is emanating across the EM spectrum," Bob announced. Outside, the spheres shone with a new intensity as exterior lighting began to activate.

"I see that," Jack said abruptly, watching from the inspection drone. *What the hell had she monkeyed around with in there?* "What about heat?" If that thing's reactor warmed up, who knew what might come out of its tailpipe . . .

"New infrared signature in the aft module," Bob said. "Skin

temperature has risen twelve degrees Kelvin in the last minute and waste heat is beginning to emanate from the radiator loops. It appears you were correct about the module's function."

It was small comfort. "Traci, comm check. If you can hear me, stop whatever you're doing and get out of there!"

Traci had moved on to the lower levels, though she could have happily spent the rest of her EVA exploring the control deck. It was near the sphere's midpoint that she discovered what had to be an enormous logistics level. Reminiscent of an aircraft carrier's hangar deck, it was filled with machinery and equipment which she didn't quite recognize but could still grasp their function, much like the flight stations.

Equipment racks and containers were lined up on the deck, stacked neatly in rows extending outward from the central hub. *They sure do like their wheels and spokes.* In between were what appeared to be low-slung carts and tugs. They had wheels for moving about and seats for the drivers, though the controls were so minimal as to be barely recognizable. She also couldn't tell what was holding them to the deck in microgravity. It occurred to her that this craft had to have spent most of its time under thrust for this kind of equipment to make sense.

A particular piece of equipment, in fact a whole lot of them, caught her eye. Alongside one of the storage racks was a meter-long truss mounted inside of an open teardrop-shaped shell. Attached to the truss were dozens of the same kind of metallic rings that had held the atrium's icy spheres. "Wonder about these," she thought aloud. "I'll come back to them later."

She continued her slow flight around the hangar deck. Enormous oval doors encircled its perimeter, or rather the outlines of what were probably doors. It had held true for each one she'd tried so far. Were they airlocks, or was the entire deck kept in vacuum?

One way to find out. She centered herself in front of the nearest door, this one easily ten meters across. As an aperture began to open in its center, her headset squealed to life with an urgent voice. "...comm check. Repeat, stop whatever you're doing!"

Uh oh.

◆ ◆ ◆

"Didn't copy your last. Say again."

Thank God. Her signal was weak but audible, so his must sound the same. He enunciated slowly. "Listen closely. Whatever you did in there caused the ship to turn itself on. Outside it's lit up like Vegas and the heat signature looks like the main reactor's warming up. You need to get out of there *now*. Do you copy?"

There was a long delay, making him wonder what she had to be considering. "Copy. On my way."

"See you soon." He then spoke to Bob. "Not sure how that comm made it through, but thank God it did."

His relief was tempered by Bob's cold assessment. "I have detected an aperture that has opened along the central module's equator. It is likely that is how we were able to communicate with Traci. But I do not see that she is coming out."

"*What?*"

Traci had settled on what she wanted to do and raced through her options to get out. There was a fast way to do this, and a safe way. She chose the fast one.

She flew back to the ring truss and its aeroshell, scooping it up and pushing it along ahead of her as she flew back up through the open gangway. If the portals didn't let her through with it then she'd continue without, but she was determined to try. She jetted along, heading for the atrium as fast as she dared in the confined space.

The shell sailed through the portal and into the atrium. She shot ahead of it toward the opposite side and thrusted to a stop at the far end, turning to catch the shell as it floated up behind her.

She reached for the nearest ice spheres and lifted them one by one from their cradles, carefully placing them into the matching cradles within the shell. She stopped after a half dozen, though there was room for many more. This wasn't the time to fill up the grocery cart. If the machine wouldn't let her take them out unprotected, maybe it would if they were in the right container...

She closed up the shell and watched as it sealed itself perfectly with no visible seam. Hopefully it would open just as easily later.

Her hunch paid off. The portal winked open when she parked herself and the aeroshell in front of it. *Hallelujah. I get to live another day.*

◆ ◆ ◆

Her radio barked to life as she emerged from the forward collar minutes later. Jack sounded as animated as she'd ever heard him. "Traci, do you copy? Repeat, do you—"

She stepped on his transmission. "I copy. I'm all right, clear of the spacecraft. I'm bringing you a present."

"It's quite cold," Bob said as they examined the brilliant silver teardrop in *Columbus*'s medical bay. "The protective shell is maintaining an internal temperature of minus two hundred twelve centigrade."

"Just like inside the atrium," Traci said, speaking through her headset. She had donned an emergency hazmat suit after shucking off her bulky EVA gear. Though they strongly suspected they knew what was contained within, she wasn't going to risk contamination.

"You hung your ass in the breeze to bring us this," Jack said disapprovingly. "What if it hadn't worked, or that ship had fired up its drive?"

She gave a tired shrug. "Sometimes you have to roll the hard six. I could've flown right out that hangar door, or I could've done this." She was determined to not leave without it. "I chose this."

"The shell is impervious to X-ray and ultrasound," Bob said, ignoring their simmering argument. "It does not have any active cooling that I can discern. It is almost a perfectly efficient insulator."

"It can't be," she said. "Everything reaches thermal equilibrium eventually."

"Eventually, yes," Bob said. "I did say it was 'almost' perfect."

Jack set aside his frustration with her and considered the aeroshell's purpose. "If it's meant for depositing organics at other planets, then it only needs to keep them cold long enough to get through an atmosphere. It might be designed to disperse them when it heats up on entry."

Her eyes widened. "If you're right, then this is—"

"Panspermia," Jack said. "Or at least the mechanism for it."

It was more evidence for the theory that life on Earth had been seeded from elsewhere in deep space, of which Noelle's original discovery on Pluto had only been the first indicator that it might be correct. The open question then had been were they naturally formed, or deliberately placed across its frozen landscape? This appeared to hold the answer.

"The insulating shell seems to be the same alloy as the Artifact's hull. In vacuum and absent any solar heating, this could keep its contents stable for a considerably long time," Bob offered. "Possibly centuries."

"Now we just have to figure out how to open it."

Traci shook her head. "Not here. We don't have the lab equipment to make it worthwhile."

"Agreed," Bob said. "I will calculate an intercept back to *Magellan*."

"Talk to me, Bob," Traci said from the control deck. "What's going on out there?"

"The Artifact is continuing to build up heat. Outside skin temperature of the forward and center modules have maintained an average of minus one hundred fifty-one centigrade. The aft module is considerably warmer, currently positive three hundred and four centigrade at its midpoint. Its aperture is passing five hundred centigrade."

"Engine's warming up," Jack said. "Assuming that's what it is."

"Your assumption appears correct," Bob said. "Electromagnetic field lines are forming around the aperture."

She began furiously typing commands into the flight computer. "Then let's get some distance. Bob, load that intercept you calculated. I'm executing a priority-one escape burn back to *Magellan*."

"The Artifact is moving."

"I see it. What a light show. Traci, watch this." Jack switched the camera feed to a monitor by her flight station. The vessel was receding quickly, its nozzle glowing cherry red around a brilliant blue-and-white exhaust.

"Looks like it's burning hydrogen," she said with fascination. "Same as us."

"Deuterium, more accurately," Bob said.

The Artifact—which it was beginning to feel increasingly ridiculous to call—had already shrunk to half its apparent size as it powered away. "It's fast," Jack said. "Wonder where it's going?"

"It is too soon to tell," Bob said, "though it appears angled toward the inner system. I will monitor its progress and develop a trajectory analysis."

Traci shuddered as she recalled her experience aboard the strange craft. How could she have turned it on so easily, and what if she'd still been aboard when that engine lit off? She rested her hands on the arms of her flight couch and exhaled. "This place has never felt so good, guys."

Bob's reaction was also the most unexpected. "I believe I know how you feel."

40

Now that she was back aboard, their old ship had a lived-in feel that had never quite manifested on the newer *Columbus*. "I missed the old girl," Traci said as she reacquainted herself with the hab module. She ran a hand across the small dining table. Reaching for a drawer underneath, she found her old chess board still sitting inside, its magnetic pieces safely tied up in felt bags. "We had a lot of fun here."

"Had a lot of arguments, too," Jack said over the speaker. "I'm sorry about that."

"Me too. I've had plenty of time to think about us since."

"Me too."

She hesitated, knowing what she wanted to say but afraid to say it. "It was such a relief to find out you were still alive. Everyone had given you up for dead, but I couldn't let myself believe it. I *had* to get out here and find you," she said. "I rehearsed so much in my mind on the way out, you know. Imagined what life would be like with you in it again. And you went and screwed it all up."

"That's kind of been my way with women. Finally get them to the point where they can tolerate me, then I do something irredeemably stupid."

"To be fair, it was Daisy's idea."

"It's always been the women in my life who keep me sane. And who drive me crazy at the same time."

"Is that what I did?"

"Yes to both." The speaker buzzed with his laughter.

She winced. "We've got to work on that, by the way. Do you know how much it sounds like nails on a chalkboard?" She turned serious.

"I wish there was a way to unplug you. It would be nice to see you in person again."

"Daisy doesn't think it's safe at this point. Not with what we have here. Maybe back on Earth we—"

He was interrupted by Daisy's alert chime. "I have results from the first chromatograph analysis. You may find them intriguing."

The aeroshell, as with every other closure aboard the Artifact, had opened easily once they applied the right technique. In this case, steady pressure along the seam had made the casing pop open like it was spring-loaded. Traci had removed one of the ice spheres at random and closed the shell back up to protect the rest. The lab's gas chromatograph-mass spectrometer slowly vaporized its contents, its instruments sniffing the air for chemical and spectral signatures as it did so.

"The first sphere's contents closely match the organic compounds Doctor Hoover isolated during your crew's expedition," Daisy said. "Base pairs of chiral molecules adenine, guanine, cytosine, and uracil were all detected."

"Exactly the stuff Noelle found," Jack said. "Everything you need to start weaving RNA strands."

"The seeds of life," she whispered in amazement, thinking back to her experience in the atrium. "Assuming the rest are the same . . ." She stared through a nearby porthole, back to where the Artifact would be. "Whatever else that ship is, it's designed to carry these things. Maybe even produce them. If this is what they used to seed our solar system, then it could be millions of years old."

"Makes you wonder what happened to the crew, then," he said. "It's like they all packed up and went home."

"There is more," Daisy said. "When you opened up the insulating shell, I detected indentations on its inner surface similar to the writing you observed."

Traci did a double take. "That's funny, I didn't see anything." She slipped on a mask and gloves and slid a hand along the shell's seam, popping it open. "Still can't see anything."

"Continue holding it open, please. The script may be too faint for you to detect. I will record and enhance it for you to study."

"Finally," Jack said. "Something for me to do."

◆ ◆ ◆

Jack had spent his early adulthood intercepting and translating Russian communications for the Air Force, becoming adept at both interpreting obscure idioms and decrypting coded messages. He'd honed his skills by mastering three different languages that were as far removed from English as he could find, eventually adding Farsi and Mandarin to his repertoire. While he might have thought that was good preparation for an undertaking like this, the Artifact's alien script was nothing like them.

He had been able to identify the most frequently used characters, but until he could positively compare them to a known language their meaning would remain elusive.

Yet something about them rang familiar, tickling at his memory...

He had taken advantage of his direct line into Daisy's immense database to search through her historical archives. Meant for refining her synthetic intelligence, her memory held examples of every known earthly language.

And as he delved into ancient, dead tongues, he found what he'd been looking for.

Jack projected two images onto the monitor in the galley. One was of the holographic keyboard Traci had recorded. The other was from something much older. "It's cuneiform."

She nearly choked on her coffee. "Come again?"

"Okay, it's not an exact match. More nuanced. But it still uses similar script. See these wedge strokes?" he pointed out. "Their basic form is almost identical to Akkadian or Sumerian."

"Those are ancient," she said. "I mean *ancient*, like—"

"5000 B.C.," he said. "So yeah, really old. Almost prehistoric."

"How, with a civilization this advanced? Why would their language not evolve?"

"I couldn't tell you that. Obviously they made it work for them. On the other hand, scientists will tell you math is the true universal language, and we can see they were scary good at that. Maybe they figured this was all they needed."

"That means what, exactly? That they seeded Earth with RNA precursors, let them do their thing, then came back a few million years later to check up on us?"

"Maybe they dropped a few hints along the way. Like, you know, written language."

She began laughing raucously.

"This is funny? Here we thought the Middle East was the cradle of civilization, now we find it's actually a whole different solar system. I assumed you'd have a problem with that."

She wiped away a joyful tear, her doubts falling away with it. "Not at all. This system isn't just where civilization sprang from—it's where *humanity* sprang from. Everything on that ship is sized and shaped for us. Their writing shares the same roots as our first written languages. And it looks like our life grew from the compounds they deposited." Her cheeks were flush, her eyes beaming. The questions she had struggled with for too long were being answered. "Don't you see? They're not alien. They're *us.*"

Their discussions over what to do next had lasted for days, and they repeatedly arrived at the same conclusions. *Magellan* was nearing the end of its design life, was almost out of propellant, and had endured enough. *Columbus*, on the other hand, still held four years' worth of nutrients and had enough left in the tanks to accelerate all the way to Earth. With the proven hydrogen scoops, it could possibly do more.

With Jack still dependent on Daisy's network, that presented a difficult dilemma. Transferring his body to the newer equipment aboard *Columbus* was only the first step; unraveling his sensory inputs to then embed them within Bob's would be like blindfolded brain surgery.

It was safer to partition his share of her network in *Magellan*'s hab module and mate it with *Columbus*. The loss would be partial and short-term for him, and negligible for Daisy. The ship would become fully hers, with no human input.

As Jack reawakened aboard *Columbus*, his vision registered a familiar face.

Traci beamed with relief. "Hello, friend." She caressed the plexiglass shield encasing him. "I'd rather touch you in person, but I guess this will have to do."

"I'd like that too," he said. "One of these days."

"One of these days," she agreed. "For now, you can drive the beach ball drone all you want."

"For now. You may decide you want it back."

"You might be right. Looks like you had fun with it."

"Don't get me wrong. Flying one of these ships with just your brain is a feeling of near-godlike power. But it's more fun to zip around inside at will. It's the most human I've felt in a long time."

She studied him intently. "Are you sure you're ready to do this? It'll be a long time in hibernation."

"I'm used to it by now," he said. "Truth is I don't want to go back. Not yet. There's too much left to see here."

She nodded and looked away pensively. "Same."

"So how about you? Are you ready to do this?"

"It worked out for you, didn't it? I'm infinitely more well adjusted." She drew her lips tight. "Home isn't exactly home anymore. Too much has changed, and in too many ways that I don't like."

"Think the folks back home will understand?"

"They'll have to. I'm not leaving you again."

Traci pushed away and into an open hibernation pod. She connected its IV line to a fresh port she had injected in her forearm and took a deep breath. "Okay, Bob. I'm ready. Let's do this."

Light.

Cold and clear, slicing open her consciousness like a scalpel. The light washed over and through her, everywhere all at once.

Sound enveloped her, as if she could hear every hum and creak of the ship. Jack would have to teach her how to modulate that—

A familiar voice cut through the cacophony of her freshly awakened mind.

"Hello, friend."

"Hi," she said tentatively, testing out her new voice. "Can you see me? I can't see you."

"Been watching you the whole time. Not in a creepy way, I promise. Hang on, I'll change your video source."

Her vision flashed momentarily, the field of view changing. Suddenly she was looking down at Jack's hibernating form. "There you are. I feel better now."

"I'll show you how to change sources later. It's not hard."

"Good morning." Bob's voice was comfortably familiar, soothing in a way she hadn't known before, a steady hand guiding her through this new reality. "I have some news from Daisy if you wish to hear."

Please. She wondered if he could hear her thoughts. "Yes, by all means."

"Daisy reports she has executed the injection burn for a low-energy transfer through the wormhole. She will arrive at Earth in two thousand nine hundred and twenty-one days, by her local time reference of course. She sends her best and adds, 'Happy birthday, Traci.'"

That drew a laugh, in that same scratchy hoot that had so annoyed her before. She'd have to work on hers as well. "That's great news, Bob. Please send her my regards. How about us—are we ready to go?"

"I have calculated a 0.01 *g* profile, tracing the Artifact's trajectory to the gas giant you named 'Colossus.' Our optimal departure window is in four hours and eight minutes. Transit time will be one hundred eighty-three days and—"

"Hold on there, speedy," Jack cautioned. "You've got a lot of adjustments ahead. Don't you want time to get used to your new self?"

"I've got all the time in the world," she said. "Let's go."

Epilogue

Houston
Five Years Later

Roy Hoover wiped greasy hands on his jeans and closed the hood of his Corvette, an ancient 1956 model with a normally aspirated V8 engine. He'd missed cars that he could actually tinker on and relished the chore of fine-tuning his new toy. The car that had once been synonymous with certain privileges accorded to the early astronauts, it was not something he'd ever treated himself to when he was among their ranks. With supersonic jets and rocket ships to fly, he'd been content driving an old Honda to work every day. The 'vette had become an indulgence in his retirement.

He was still putting tools away when Noelle peeked her head through the garage door. "We have a visitor, love. Can you tear yourself away for a moment?"

Roy nodded and followed her into their adjacent kitchen. He did a double take when he saw who sat at the table. "*Owen?*" Roy extended his hand but then thought better of it, wiping it on his backside. "Sorry, got kind of messy out there."

Owen waved him away with a laugh. "Not a problem." Nearing retirement himself, his dirty blond hair had become silvery gray and his skin wrinkled from the Caribbean sun.

After years apart, it took Roy a minute to process their guest's arrival. "What—how did—what brings you here?"

Owen smiled. "I bring word from old friends."

Roy noticed that Noelle had been watching their awkward

exchange in amusement bordering on giddiness. "You already know, don't you?" That's also when he noticed the nearly empty glass of iced tea on the table. "How long has he been here?"

"A while," she said lightly. "We didn't want to disturb you."

"In her defense, she said you were tearing down a carburetor. I told her we'd best wait until you were done."

"How'd you get here?" Roy asked, knowing that he was still vulnerable to legal troubles back on US soil.

"It helps when you come in on a private jet and can make certain arrangements with the customs inspectors," Owen said. "I'm afraid I don't have much time before I have to blast off."

Roy frowned. "Yeah, I get it. Wish things were different."

Owen looked at Noelle appreciatively. "You have the advantage of being married to a Nobel Prize winner." It was a fact that had encouraged the Justice Department to drop any investigations into their involvement with the *Columbus* "heist." Owen and his team had not been so fortunate. "Besides, if you've got to be in exile it ain't a bad place to be."

"Hammond's estate is still funding you, then?"

"Enough to keep the lights and antennas on," Owen said. "Once we lost the MSEV relay, we all knew it was going to be a long time before we heard anything."

"If ever."

Owen smiled once more. "That question's been answered."

"You heard from them?"

"Not exactly." Owen lifted a tablet from the counter beside Noelle, who was still beaming. "Sorry, I had to show her. Like I said, we didn't want to disturb you. But yes, we received a transmission from Daisy last night. She emerged from the Anomaly yesterday."

With a perturbed look, Roy took the tablet and began scrolling through it. "Daisy's back—with *Magellan*? What about Jack and Traci?"

Owen gestured for him to keep reading. "It's all there in her situation report, five years' worth of missing links. Short version is they stayed behind with *Columbus*. Their solution to the consumables problem that presented was, well . . . *creative*."

Roy's eyebrows shot up as he read Daisy's account. "Holy—yeah, creative's an understatement. So all this time—"

"Jack was actually in hibernation. He was talking to us through Daisy. He didn't want us to know about it, specifically to avoid upsetting you guys."

Roy looked to his wife, wide-eyed. "You're the MD. Did you suspect that all along?"

"I must admit it took me quite by surprise, love."

He looked up at Owen, growing impatient with reading. "So how long do they plan to stay? In *their* relative time. I can figure out the rest."

"Unclear," Owen admitted. "Though if you keep reading, I think you'll find they could be there for a while."

Noelle came to her husband's side and pointed him to a new folder, unable to disguise her excitement. "Look here."

Roy regarded her cautiously. "Okay . . ." Then he found the images of something labeled *Artifact*.

Owen caught the tablet as it fell from Roy's hands. "Sweet Mary."

"Yeah."

"So they have some idea of how the wormhole came to be, then?"

"Just assumptions," Owen said, "but they've had five years since our last contact. Who knows what they've found since then?"

Noelle interjected. "According to this, a solar system much like ours, with two planets in the habitable zone. And quite possibly more vessels like this one."

Roy studied his wife. "Now I know why you looked like a little kid on Christmas."

She was beaming now. "You're more right than you know. Daisy's bringing me a present: a container filled with more ice spheres, taken directly from this ship. *Magellan* barely had enough propellant left to bring her to Earth on a low-energy Hohmann transfer, but she is coming. She'll be arriving in eight years."

"Eight years . . ." Roy trailed off. "You'll have plenty of time to prepare, I guess."

"As will we all," Owen agreed. He looked at Noelle. "And your Nobel Laureate here has some plans."

"I could tell you were thinking of something big. Planning a new grant proposal, Dr. No?"

"In time," Noelle said. "I'm thinking about Daisy's future now. Consider all that she has done. Our friends, too, but that must come later. She is the first machine recognized to have achieved sentience. She verified the existence of dark matter, an Einstein-Rosen bridge, and evidence of extraterrestrial intelligence. Any one of those is remarkable enough to be the crowning achievement of a scientist's career."

There was a glint in Roy's eyes now. "And you, being a laureate, are in a position to do something about that."

"It will no doubt create controversy, but we've become accustomed to that." Noelle nodded with determination. "I intend to nominate Daisy for the Nobel Prize."

A sly grin spread across Roy's weathered face as he considered her plan. "The committee's going to love that," by which he meant they would be in an uproar. He turned to Owen, pointing at his tablet. "Meanwhile, this presents a whole other dilemma. What do you intend to do with that information?"

"We're going public. Part of the reason I'm here."

"Risky move," Roy observed. "But the right thing to do."

"You deserved to know first. There'll be a clamor to send more probes to the Anomaly after we release this."

"Probes," Roy said with disgust. "This 'artifact' is screaming for human investigation. Meanwhile, two of our own are still out there. They can't stay in hibernation forever, even plugged into this machine interface they've concocted."

"They can't," Owen agreed, "which got me to thinking." He eyed Roy and Noelle conspiratorially, recalling a line he'd once heard from his late boss. "How'd you like to fly something *really* fast?"

AUTHOR'S NOTES

❈ ❈ ❈

While my stories might occur in a vacuum (that is, space), the writing process itself most definitely does not.

First and foremost, thank you to my wife, Melissa. Trust me when I say that none of this would be possible without her support.

Many thanks to all of the good folks at Baen, in particular Toni Weisskopf and D.J. Butler, for their editorial guidance and support.

As always, I must also thank Winchell Chung for his fascinating Atomic Rockets website. Most everything I've learned about the advanced propulsion needed to make these stories work originated there.

Thanks are also due to Dr. Robert Hampson, for helping me understand the complexities of mind-computer interfaces.

Finally, as valuable as internet research can be (in addition to being a major time saver), there's no substitute for talking to actual experts in the field. For this, I owe deep gratitude to a pair of NASA researchers who helped me keep the science right:

To Les Johnson of NASA's Marshall Space Flight Center, for introducing me to Dr. Gerald Cleaver at Baylor University, who in turn helped me to understand current theories on wormholes and their related phenomena. Daisy's statement that a stable wormhole should be "fully traversable in both directions," and "possesses no crushing gravitational tidal forces" was quoted directly from a paper he authored. Any errors within this book are mine, not his.

To Andy Presby of NASA's Glenn Research Center, for confirming that pulse fusion technology is perhaps the only realistic path to building fusion-powered spacecraft in our lifetimes.

Each book I've written has been the result of a long education process, and this was by far the most challenging. Figuring out how a fictional spacecraft should work is nothing compared to wrestling with the effects of Einstein's relativity in a story arc. There were occasions where it tied my brain in knots, which I hope you've found to have been sufficiently unraveled by now. What follows is a Physics lesson from an English major, so consider yourself duly warned . . .

Jack's disappearance was caused by his sudden removal from our local space and being spat into another system twelve light years away.

At that point, his local time is years behind those of his friends back on Earth. However, the distance for a signal to travel back through the wormhole is shortened enough to begin conversing as if he were still in our solar system, even though their proper time references are now years apart. That difference isn't a result of the distance between the two star systems, it's more a function of gravitational forces within the wormhole.

Think of it like this: the effect of gravitational time dilation has been measured. As one character mentioned, we see it every day in the corrections that have to be applied to the clocks aboard GPS satellites for the system to work at all. Over the lifetime of Earth, this same effect means our planet's core is roughly 2.5 years younger than its crust. Yet if a tunnel were somehow bored through, a signal could reach the core almost instantaneously. That wouldn't change the local, "proper" time at either end, and that's how Jack and Traci could communicate without waiting years for a reply.

Thus endeth the lesson.

The U.N. Protocols for Engagement With Alien Civilizations may be even fuzzier, if that's possible. In researching this book, I found references to work on this as far back as 2010 but haven't been able to determine if the protocols were ever finished. I do find it interesting that first contact formalities were being seriously discussed at such levels.

As Traci postulated in *Frozen Orbit*, finding life beyond Earth shouldn't result in the cultural upheaval some assume it would cause. There's still much about our own planet that we don't yet know which could prove to be just as surprising. Discovering life under the ice on Europa or Ganymede would be thrilling, and would introduce some profound questions, but ultimately it would be akin to finding a new species in the Arctic Ocean.

Finding intelligent life would be another matter entirely. Such an event would confirm many assumptions, and shatter many more. It is entirely possible that the reason we haven't detected other intelligent life may well be because we are the first, which also introduces profound questions—not that we have the ability to confirm such a thing. But if enough of us believe that to be the case, it should cause us to reflect on our place in the Universe and our ultimate responsibility to "go forth and prosper." Take care of what we have, and spread life where we can.

Glossary

ASAT: Anti-Satellite weapons

ASCAN: Astronaut Candidate. Yes, they pronounce it "ass can."

AU: Astronomical Unit, used to measure distances within our Solar System. It's the average distance between Earth and our Sun, 93 million miles.

Apoapsis: The highest point of an elliptical orbit. For Earth-centered orbits, it's called *apogee*.

CCAP: Climate Change Action Plan. A fictional multinational effort to deploy massive sunshades in orbit around Earth to cool the planet.

CDR: Spacecraft Commander

CG: Center of Gravity. The balance point of an aircraft or spacecraft.

CNSA: China National Space Administration

DAISE: Distributed Artificial Intelligence Surveillance Environment

Delta-v (Δv): Change in velocity. An essential measurement of a spacecraft's ability to get anywhere, it's an expression of both the amount of fuel in the tanks and how much velocity change is needed to perform a given maneuver. The delta-v budget is a space mission's ultimate limiting factor: if a ship needs 3 kilometers per second velocity change to leave orbit, and it only has enough fuel for 2.9 kps, it's not leaving orbit.

DG: Directional Gyroscope

DMO-1: Dark Matter Object One, the semi-official designation of the gravitational anomaly where the elusive Planet Nine was thought to be.

ECLSS: Environmental Control and Life Support System. Put simply, it's a collection of devices that regenerates water and oxygen. It recycles waste air and water (guess what *that* means), which significantly reduces the amount to be loaded on a spacecraft.

EM: Electromagnetic Radiation

EMS: Emergency Medical System. An automated critical-care pod aboard *Magellan* and *Columbus*.

EVA: Extra-Vehicular Activity. A spacewalk.

FBO: Fixed-Base Operator. A gas station and service center for private aircraft.

FMC: Flight Management Computer

g: Acceleration of gravity as measured at Earth's surface, 9.8 meters per second squared.

GEO: Geosynchronous orbit. An equatorial orbit high enough that the satellite's velocity matches the rotation of Earth, keeping it above the same spot on the globe. Commonly used by weather and communications satellites.

Hill Sphere: The region where an astronomical body's gravity dominates the attraction of satellites.

IAU: International Astronomical Union. The astronomers who, among other things, decide on the naming conventions of planets and other objects.

ISS: International Space Station. In orbit since the late 1990's, it's getting a bit long in the tooth and I'm told insiders jokingly describe it as "Cattlecar Galactica."

JSC: Johnson Space Center in Houston, Texas. The NASA center for manned spaceflight.

KPS: Kilometers per second.

KSC: Kennedy Space Center in Cape Canaveral, Florida. America's first spaceport.

LEO: Low Earth Orbit.

Leeroy Jenkins: An infamous World of Warcraft character, notable for blindly charging into combat, bellowing his own name as a battle cry while completely ignoring his teammate's meticulous plans.

Libration (or Lagrange) Point: There are five regions (designated L-1, L-2, etc.) where the gravity of the Sun and Earth essentially cancel each other out, creating stable zones where it is most economical to place a spacecraft. This goes for any system where smaller bodies orbit larger bodies, such as the Earth and Moon, Sun and Mars, etc.

Lidar: Similar in concept to radar, a method for determining the distance to an object by targeting it with a laser and measuring the time for the reflected light to return to the receiver.

Light year: The distance light travels in one year, 5.88 trillion miles.

Max Q: Maximum Dynamic Pressure. The period when a vehicle moving through the atmosphere experiences the maximum atmospheric load as a function of its speed. This typically occurs around Mach One, the speed of sound.

Mo Board: Slang for "maneuvering board." Borrowed from the Navy, it's a polar (circular) graph of the relative positions of any vessels operating around an individual ship. A rather important tool to prevent collisions.

MPS: Meters per second.

MSEV: Manned Space Exploration Vehicle. A concept NASA developed for future long-duration missions, think of it as a "space dinghy."

NGO: Non-Governmental Organization

OMS: Orbital Maneuvering System. A collection of rocket motors more powerful than attitude thrusters, used to change orbits.

OSEP: Outer Space Environmental Protection Treaty, a fictional treaty restricting deep-space expeditions to areas which have previously had a human presence.

Parsec: A measurement unit of distances beyond our Solar System, approximately 3.26 light years.

Periapsis: The lowest point of an elliptical orbit. For Earth-centered orbits, it's called *perigee*.

PRC: People's Republic of China

RCS: Reaction Control System. A collection of small thrusters used to change a spacecraft's attitude (its orientation, not its mental state).

SFB: Space Force Base

TNI: Trans-Neptunian Injection. The long engine burn *Columbus* needed to leave Earth orbit for its flyby of Neptune.